LAURA TAYLOR...
SHE CHANGED THE LIVES
OF ALL WHO KNEW HER

Clarry Taylor—The sister who was always envious of Laura—and used her own striking blonde beauty to get revenge.

Garrick Eastman—He would always want Laura, but he married her sister out of spite.

Ross Kenyon—He was there when Laura needed him most, and his devotion would cost him his life.

Julia Kenyon—The daughter who bitterly resented growing up in Laura's shadow and became her most implacable rival.

Brad Northrup—The architect who wanted Laura—but was tenaciously pursued by her daughter.

Jack Galloway—The syndicate money-man who used his charm and looks to try to destroy Laura.

Other Avon Books by
Jude Deveraux

THE BLACK LYON
THE ENCHANTED LAND

CASA GRANDE

JUDE DEVERAUX

AVON
PUBLISHERS OF BARD, CAMELOT, DISCUS AND FLARE BOOKS

CASA GRANDE is an original publication of Avon Books.
This work has never before appeared in book form.

AVON BOOKS
A division of
The Hearst Corporation
959 Eighth Avenue
New York, New York 10019

First Avon Printing, August, 1982

AVON TRADEMARK REG. U. S. PAT. OFF. AND IN
OTHER COUNTRIES, MARCA REGISTRADA, HECHO EN
U. S. A.

Printed in the U. S. A.

WFH 10 9 8 7 6 5 4 3 2 1

CASA GRANDE

Part I

1935

Chapter 1

Laura stepped back from the paintings and squinted her eyes, studying each one in turn. There were ten, all portraits, painted in a unique style that was Laura's alone. The colors glowed, rich deep velvet earth tones that reflected the New Mexico land that surrounded the people in the paintings. Unconsciously, she ran her hand through the neat finger waves of her short dark hair. "I don't know. I just don't know," she said under her breath.

"And what could there possibly be that my talented daughter doesn't know?"

Laura turned to her father, her concentration broken, and smiled. They were the same height, Laura tall for a woman, her shoulders too wide. There was an unfinished quality about Laura's face, a rawness that was striking.

"I want to know," J.W. Taylor repeated when Laura didn't answer.

She sat down on the bed, took the tie of the old chenille robe and began to chew on it as she frowned at the paintings against the white plaster of the adobe walls. "Do you think they're good enough, Dad? I mean, for...?"

J.W. sat down beside her and slipped his arm around her shoulders. "For New York?"

Laura sighed and leaned against her father's strength. She did not look at him. There was no need. They understood each other.

"Laura," he said quietly. "Tell me what you feel about them."

"What I...?" She was startled. "You know what I feel about them. It's not me I have to worry about. It's them—in New York. Oh, Dad! New York! The capital of the world. Do you realize how many people will see them? Even write criticisms of them?"

J.W. tightened his arm. "Yes, I know all that," he said patiently. "I want to know about you, how you see them."

3

Laura tried to clear her mind. How could she explain what her painting meant to her? It was like asking what her own heart meant to her. Painting was a part of her, as necessary to her life as a part of her body. She never thought about it or stopped to consider it. It was sunlight and darkness to her, food and sleep. "They're me," she finally whispered. "All ten of them are part of what's inside me."

J.W. moved and put his hands on his daughter's shoulders. He could see she was fighting tears. "Yes, Laura, and that's all you have to worry about. Even in New York they couldn't ask for more on canvas than a person's soul."

Laura blinked at him, then began to smile. "But do you think New Yorkers consider New Mexico souls worthwhile?"

J.W. hugged his daughter to him. "Why, even our jack-rabbits have more of a soul than any New Yorker. All those people on that little island! Souls don't have room to grow there."

He could feel her laughter against him and knew that for the moment she was all right. He looked over her head toward the far end of the room at the old carved pine chest of drawers. It, like nearly everything else in the house, had been made by local craftsmen. The mirror over the cabinet was framed by an ornate piece of pierced tin work, and taped down one side of the glass were several excellent reviews of Laura's work—*Art Digest, Art News, The New York Times*. On the wall was a framed document, last year's John C. Gatenby Award for the most promising new artist, selected from the juniors and seniors of twenty-three American colleges and art schools. And propped up on the dresser was that most important letter of all, now a little worn from two months of constant handling. The Jules M. Grey Gallery at 49 East Fifty-seventh Street, New York, requested the pleasure of an exhibition sale of fifteen of Miss Laura Taylor's paintings, to be hung from June 2 through June 16, 1935. Only five students had been chosen from throughout the United States for a two-week one-man show, and Laura had been one of them.

He knew that, as happy as she was, she also feared both success and failure. He held her closer, as if he could take some of the fear from her. He understood this oldest daughter so well, as he knew no one else did. Laura didn't allow other people to see her vulnerability. To the rest of the world she seemed a most sensible young woman, sure of herself and her goals. Her art was her life and she appeared firm in her pursuit of what she wanted. But J.W. knew the pain inside her, her need for more than just art. He knew because they were alike. And because they were alike, he could not tell her his own fears, the fears that ate at him each day. He closed his eyes for a moment and made a silent vow that at all costs Laura's art would not be taken away from her.

As the first notes of the radio concert of the Casa Loma Orchestra floated into the room, they broke apart and looked at each other.

"We're in for it now," Laura said, her eyes sparkling into her father's.

"Hurry," J.W. said, "you get a comb and I'll—"

"Laura!"

The exclamation from the doorway stopped him. He gave Laura a shrug of helplessness as he rose and turned toward his other daughter. Even after eighteen years, Clarry was an amazement to her father. Laura he could understand, even at times identify with, but Clarry was completely another matter. Even now as she stood scowling at Laura in justifiable anger, Clarry was beautiful.

There were times when he stared at her in wonder. Clarry resembled no one from his or her mother's family. It was as if she had been switched by fairies while still in her cradle. Even as a five-year-old, Clarry had been lovely, a tiny pink and white angel of a child, quiet, eager to please, so desperate for affection. And she received it, too, more than anyone else he had ever seen. No one could resist hugging the child, touching her soft blonde hair.

"Don't, Clarry," Laura said. "I know just what you're going to say and there's no use wasting your breath."

Clarry walked slowly into the room. None of her movements were ever fast or without grace. "I left you two hours ago and you promised you'd be ready. Look at you, even your hair! Laura, how could you, after it took me so long to arrange it?"

J.W. chuckled and winked at Laura over Clarry's head. "I think I'll retreat from this battle. Clarry," he said as he looked down at her, "you look lovely, as always." He bent

5

forward and kissed her forehead. No desperate, clinging hugs for Clarry.

As he left the bedroom Laura smiled. "You do, you know. Is that a new dress? I haven't seen it before, have I?"

Clarry smoothed the champagne-colored satin that molded to her lushly curved body. "No, it was Marian's. She let me have it and I cut it down."

Laura frowned. "Surely Dad could have afforded a new dress for you so you wouldn't have to take Marian's left-overs."

"It's not—" Clarry said defiantly, then stopped. "Oh, Laura, you look awful. How are we going to get you ready in time for the dance?"

Laura looked in the mirror and could see her own reflection as well as her younger sister's. She had long ago given up comparing her own looks to Clarry's. There wasn't one woman in a thousand who could come close to Clarry. "I do, don't I?" Laura said without concern as she again ran a hand through her hair and put out the other one to touch the letter from the Jules M. Grey Gallery. She needed constant reassurance that it was real.

"Oh, no, you don't," Clarry said as she grabbed the letter and hurriedly tossed it in a drawer on top of Laura's jumbled underclothes. "I've heard all I'm going to hear about art and art galleries and yellow number one versus yellow number two. Tonight, for once, you're going to smell like something besides paint thinner and you're going to wear something other than denim and corduroy."

Laura gave a look of disgust at the drawer containing the letter and then sat down on the corner of the bed. "Clarry," she began, "I know I promised to go to this dance with you, but really, I have so much work to do. Five more paintings to do in less than a month! And you're probably right, I could never get dressed in time to go."

"Bend your head forward a little," Clarry said as she ran a comb through Laura's dark hair, carefully read-justing the waves she had set that afternoon.

"Clarry? Did you hear me?"

"I heard you. I just choose to ignore such a silly state-ment."

"And what's silly about it? Ow!" Laura cried as her

head came up but the comb Clarry had entangled in her hair didn't.

"Laura, please," Clarry said softly as she pushed her sister's head back down. "You haven't been home one whole day and you can't spare one evening for anything but your art. Everyone's been asking when Laura's coming home from that fancy art school of hers. Dad shows everyone all the clippings about you and they're beginning to say you're too stuck-up to visit your family anymore."

"You don't believe that, do you, Clarry?" Laura looked at her sister with concern.

Clarry turned away, pulling loose hairs from the comb as she replaced it on the dresser. "I don't know, Laura. You're gone so much and when you're home..."

"And when I'm home, what?"

Clarry looked back at her sister. "I don't know. Everything seems to run so much more smoothly when you're home, and Dad's always so much happier with you here."

Laura couldn't help feeling pleased by the compliment, but she was troubled also. She knew Clarry was constantly hurt by their father's lack of physical affection toward his youngest daughter. He often kissed her forehead or cheek but never with the enthusiasm that he gave to Laura.

She wanted to lighten the mood. "Cut down that dress, did you?" Laura stood and studied the dress critically. "Haven't I seen that particular dress somewhere else— Jean?" A glance at Clarry's heightened color told her she was correct and she couldn't resist teasing. "Didn't I see you on Wally Beery's arm? Or maybe on Hollywood Boulevard with your Afghan hounds? Or maybe—"

"Laura, stop it!" Clarry laughed. "I get enough of it from everyone else and I don't need it at home. Come on and let's get your dress on. We're going to be late as it is."

Laura watched as Clarry went to the closet and removed the blue silk dress. Clarry protested, but Laura knew she was pleased. It was a common joke around the little town of Montero, New Mexico, that the people had their own Jean Harlow. Laura wondered how much Clarry's resemblance to the actress was natural and how much rehearsed. Every time Laura came home, she could swear Clarry looked a little more like the legendary Harlow. Her blonde hair seemed to get blonder, her eyebrows thinner, and every article of clothing seemed to be taken from the star's own closet. Clarry's bedroom had several framed photographs of Miss Harlow.

"Tell me about the band." Laura could see Clarry's eyes lighten.

"They're from New York originally."

"Aren't they all?" Laura mumbled as the silk floated over her head.

"The saxophone player traveled with Tommy Dorsey for two years and the trombone player used to be with Duke Ellington. And Marian says—" Clarry broke off as she stole a glance at Laura. She knew Laura didn't care for Marian, that she considered the girl shallow.

"Marian said what?" Laura asked noncommittally. She was determined not to upset Clarry with her criticism.

Clarry was silent.

"Come on," Laura urged. "What did Marian say? Is she in love with the band leader or the singer this time?"

Clarry gave a shy smile, her eyes dancing. "The singer."

The two sisters looked at each other and Laura tried to keep from laughing out loud. Clarry began to fasten the back buttons of Laura's dress.

"Clarry, you wouldn't think of doing something like that, would you?"

Clarry stopped and stared at Laura in the mirror. "You never have to worry that I'd fall in love with the singer of a traveling band."

Laura was startled by the firmness in Clarry's voice and for a moment she was aware of how little she knew of her sister. After all, she hadn't been home much in the last four years, not more than ten days at one time since Clarry was fourteen. "Who would you fall in love with, Clarry?"

"A rich man," Clarry said without hesitation.

Laura thought she was making a joke and laughed. "Every woman's dream, a rich husband to support her in the style to which she could become accustomed. I hope you don't expect to find him in Montero."

Clarry's face was serious. "I'll go where I have to, to find him."

Laura looked at Clarry in surprise and began to see that she was completely serious. "Clarry, you can't expect—"

"Are my two beautiful daughters ready?" J.W.'s voice

8

cut off Laura's words. As her father entered the bedroom, she shrugged. Clarry was young. She had a lot to learn yet. Her words were perfectly ordinary. What girl hadn't dreamed of meeting and marrying a millionaire? It was just Clarry's expression that was startling.

The three of them walked to the front door. "Wait, I have to get our wraps," Clarry called as she disappeared down the hall.

J.W. and Laura stepped out onto the portal, *vigas* overhead supported by posts and corbels on a low adobe wall. Laura closed her eyes a moment and breathed deeply of the cool, crisp mountain air. "This is what I came home for. There's no other place like it on earth. Look at that sky!" She leaned forward, her hands prickled by the rough plaster over the adobe. The sky was black, solid and deep with the stars sparkling pinpoints of light. "It's hard to believe it's the same sky I see in Ohio. I'll be glad to graduate. One more year and I can come home."

"Will you be glad, Laura? I mean to leave your school and the other artists? Do you think you'll be content in a little nowhere place like Montero?"

"Dad, have you really looked at my paintings? I mean *really* looked at them?" She didn't expect an answer as she looked back at the sky. "There's something about this land—I'm not sure how to describe it, but it affects me inside. No matter where I go, this is my home. In the summers in Cincinnati it's so hot and humid, sometimes I can't breathe and I think I'd give up art forever for one breath of clean, pure air. That's why all my paintings are taken from here, from the people and the land, the sun, the mountains."

Suddenly she stopped and looked back at her father. "Listen to me go on. Next we'll be hearing violins in the background. Clarry wants me to forget about art for one evening and I plan to try."

J.W. was serious. "I hope you never have to forget your art for one moment."

Laura stared at him in the dim light and shivered. "What is that old saying? Someone just walked over my grave. You sound too serious, Dad. This is a night for dancing and laughter."

"I agree with that," Clarry said as she handed Laura a dark blue capelet and gloves.

9

J.W. inspected them. "Beautiful. Absolutely beautiful."

"Well, one of us is anyway," Laura laughed. "I'm not trying for beauty, just to get the paint off my face."

"I checked carefully," Clarry said, without a trace of humor.

Laura tried to hide her smile. "All right, then, I think we're ready to go. Your golden carriage awaits, fair damsel," she said as she swung the door to the Ford pickup open.

Clarry carefully arranged her satin skirt about her. Laura gave one last wave to her father, then took the driver's seat.

The short drive to the center of the little town was at once familiar and unfamiliar to Laura. Now, in May 1935, the town had changed little since she was a child. It was a town of just over two thousand people, set at 7200 feet altitude in the San Juan Mountains. Montero was surrounded on three sides by the Carson National Forest, which drastically limited its size. To the south was Santa Fe, across the forest to the east was Taos, the Colorado border to the north and Indian land to the west.

"Clarry, where are those new houses Dad's building?"

"New houses? What new houses?"

"That's what I'm asking you. Dad wrote that the lumber yard had a new contract to supply the lumber for six new houses. That was months ago. I thought they'd have been started by now."

Clarry gazed intently at her sister's profile for a moment before turning back to look out the window of the old truck. "I don't know anything about it."

Laura frowned at the intensity of Clarry's statement and suddenly she felt like an outsider. There were too many things Clarry "didn't know" and too many unanswered questions. She reminded herself that she had a month before her New York showing and she'd find out all the gossip of the town.

As they pulled into the parking lot of the Masonic Lodge the first person to greet them was Marian Stromberg. She ran to open the door for Clarry.

The sight of the two richly clad young women next to the battered old Ford made Laura laugh.

"Like two butterflies around a cesspool, huh?"

Laura turned. "Emmett!" she said as she held out her

hands. "It's been years since I've seen you." She stared for a moment. "You've changed."

"For the better, I hope," he said as he eyed her silk dress, clinging to her body, a long ruffle around the neckline. "How did Clarry get you into that?"

"Emmett Romero! How do you know I don't dress like this every evening in Ohio? They're civilized east of the Mississippi."

"I believe there's a saying that goes—you can take the girl out of the country but you can't take the country out of the girl."

She laughed. "I think you're right—about everything. Clarry had this dress ready for me as soon as I got home." She took his arm and they began to walk toward the hall. Music drifted toward them. "You really have changed, Emmett. I remember you as a shy little boy and now suddenly you're a . . ."

"Man?" He smiled down at her.

To Laura that, too, was startling, that Emmett could smile *down* at her. Four years ago he had been shorter than she was, although they were both the same age, now twenty-two. The dark skin and hair of his Spanish ancestors was in startling contrast to his even, white teeth. He had a farmer's strong shoulders and calloused hands.

"Do I pass?" he asked as she looked at him.

"I imagine you know the answer to that as well as I do. I've always liked dark men."

"And I've always liked women, so we're matched. Now, if we don't hurry we'll miss the entire dance."

"Oh, Clarry, you're beautiful! I can't believe that was my dress. I wish I looked half as good in it."

Clarry instinctively soothed her friend. "Marian, the pink dress really heightens the color in your cheeks. It looks very good on you."

"Do you think so?" she asked as she held the skirt away from her and twirled around once. "Mother helped me pick it out. We had to drive all the way to Albuquerque. I just couldn't find a thing I liked in Santa Fe. What do you think of the bunny fur cape?"

Clarry touched the soft white fur with a gloved hand. Marian didn't notice the longing in Clarry's eyes, but then Marian rarely noticed anything aside from her own basic needs. Laura had often said that Marian's problem was

11

her father's money. Marian only had to have an idea of something she wanted pass through her mind and Mr. Stromberg would rush to buy it. Laura said it kept Marian from thinking.

"Did you see him?" Marian whispered in conspiracy.

"Who?"

"The singer, silly. The one I told you about." Mr. Stromberg had personally driven Marian to the lodge earlier in the day so she could see the band members arrive in their bus. "He is...Oh, Clarry, I don't know how to tell you. He's the most handsome man ever created."

"Even better than Vaughn Monroe?"

Marian waved her hand in dismissal. "Wait till you see him. He is really dreamy."

Clarry wasn't interested. "We're going to miss the whole dance if we stand out here."

They lifted their long skirts and started up the stairs.

"Oh, Clarry, did I tell you my cousin Scott was coming to spend the summer with us?"

Marian had Clarry's full attention now but was not aware of it. "No, you didn't tell me," Clarry said quietly. "How old is he?"

"Not too old." Marian was concentrating on the dresses of the guests ahead of them. There were very few young people in Montero who weren't at the dance. "About nineteen or twenty, I'd say."

Clarry put her hand firmly on Marian's arm. "I want to know about him."

Marian sighed. She knew there was no stopping Clarry when she looked like that. "He lives in New York, not the city, but somewhere in the state and—" Marian stopped to laugh. "He's being sent to New Mexico as a punishment. Of course, neither Father or Mother will tell me the whole story, but it seems he got into some trouble at his father's business and...," she leaned forward, "I think there was a woman involved. Not a girl but a woman. I think she was in her forties, at least. Oh, look! There's Estelle. We have to—"

"What's his father's business?"

Marian gave a startled look at Clarry's fingers digging into her bare arm. "Clarry! You're hurting. I don't know what his father does. I've only seen him once. Father said that his brother, that's Scott's father, owns things, build-

12

ings and things like that. How would I know? Now can we go inside? Oh, Clarry, look! How awful! The band's taking a break. It will be a long time before you get to see him."

But Clarry's mind was far from concern about seeing the singer of a traveling band.

"Hey, Toby! Look what just walked in. This may not be a worthless trip after all."

Toby walked to the curtain that Freddy held open and looked at the newly arrived guests. He was prepared for another one of Freddy's dogs. Freddy liked anything female—streetwalkers and society heiresses were all the same to him.

The first girl Toby saw was an overweight brunette in a baby pink dress, nothing at all remarkable or interesting in her quick jerky movements. Then she stepped to one side and Toby gave a low whistle. He looked at Freddy in surprise—and appreciation. The girl was a blonde, her hair shoulder length. She wore a long, slinky satin dress that looked as if it were part of her skin. As Toby watched she glided across the empty dance floor. His eyebrows raised in appreciation. Her walk was slow and rather sedate, but she gave the impression that a lot of things were moving under the thin satin.

"What did I tell you?" Freddy said. "Think you'd find a dish like that in this dump?"

"Never," Toby agreed. "I would have bet my saxophone on there not being anything like that anywhere in the world. Hey, Eastman," he called to another band member walking behind them. "Come over here and look at what we found."

Garrick Eastman paused for a moment. His head hurt, he was tired, and he desperately wanted to slip outside for another drink before he had to go on stage and sing again. But he also realized the need to get along with the other players.

He saw the girl the men meant right away. She was beautiful and her every gesture, every look, screamed that she was well aware of it. He saw her look up through her lashes at some fat old man, probably a judge or county official, Garrick thought.

"What d'you think?" Freddy asked. "A looker, huh?"

Garrick let the curtain fall shut. "Yeah, a real beauty,"

13

he said with a big smile and a wink. "Thanks for showing me." He turned away and headed for the backstage door. He still had enough time for a few swallows.

The cool night air felt good as he leaned against the rough plaster wall and took a deep slug of whiskey. As it burned its way to his stomach he put his head back with a sigh of relief. He thought of Toby and Freddy. "Probably still drooling over little Miss Lovely," he muttered and gave a half laugh, half snort.

A girl like that, he thought, could go far with her looks, if she had any brains and could get what she wanted before her looks went. Who knew better where good looks could get you than Garrick Eastman? He took another drink. Didn't he have women from east to west coasts pining for him? And what good did it do him? A two-bit singer in a two-bit band, traveling all over the country doing one-nighters. Hell! Singers weren't even paid as much as the musicians.

Freddy and Toby were fools. Someday they'd get their wish and marry some beautiful, brainless lovely and spend the rest of their lives regretting it. But Garrick had more sense than that. The woman he wanted would be able to take care of him.

The noise of the band returning to the stage brought him back to reality. One last slug before he hid the flask away inside his coat. The last time he was found drinking, the band leader had threatened him. The last thing Garrick wanted was to find himself stranded in a nothing town in New Mexico. He had too many plans for his life.

"Having a good time?" Emmett asked Laura as he led her in a fox-trot.

"Surprising as much as anything."

"How's that?"

"I was looking forward to telling everyone about my showing in New York—"

"At the Grey Gallery?" Emmett interrupted.

Laura smiled and shook her head. "That's just what I mean. Everyone seems to know as much about me as I do."

"Didn't you know you were the town celebrity? Hardly a week goes by that the *Montero Bulletin* doesn't run an item on Miss Laura Taylor's progress at her art school."

"Oh, Emmett! Not really! Please tell me it's not true."

"I wouldn't want to if I could. Montero's worked hard for its celebrity."

She stopped dancing and frowned at him. "Montero? What are you talking about? Dad and Clarry have been saying the oddest things ever since I arrived this morning."

Emmett forcefully swung her back into the dance. "Montero's very proud of you, that's all," he said quickly, looking over her head. "What in the world is Marian up to? Whose attention is she trying to get?"

Laura stopped frowning long enough to look at Marian twisting and turning her dance partner constantly so she'd be in view of the band. She started to laugh and tell Emmett about Marian's new love for the singer when Laura saw him for herself. She was used to people's reactions to Clarry's beauty and rarely paid any attention to it, but now she experienced a similar response. The singer was more than handsome. He had high cheekbones that made his face look as if it were carved from granite. Odd, serious, sad dark eyes looked out over the dance floor.

"Laura!" Emmett's voice made her look back at him. "Don't tell me you're going to fall for him, too?"

She looked at Emmett in surprise, then smiled. "I'm an artist, remember? I look at people in terms of chiaroscuro. He'd make a wonderful subject for a portrait."

"Mmm," Emmett said noncommittally as the dance ended and they broke apart and applauded the band.

"Thank you, Emmett. I think I'll see what Clarry's doing now." She started to walk toward the buffet set against one wall. "Enjoying the dance?" Laura asked Clarry as she picked up a plate and chose two small cakes from the abundance that had been brought by the townspeople who acted as chaperones.

"Yes, all right, I guess. The band could be better."

"You weren't expecting Eddy Duchin, were you? How's Marian doing with her singer?" Laura looked across Clarry's head at the dark man. His voice was excellent, smooth. As she watched he turned his head and looked at her. Laura could feel herself blushing, the blood seeming to rise from her toes.

"Laura?" Clarry asked and Laura hastily looked down at her plate. "Is something wrong?" Clarry looked at her sister in amazement. Clarry was always aware of men's glances and she had seen the look the singer gave Laura. It hadn't surprised her, after all, it was the man's job to entertain. But what Clarry couldn't understand was Laura's reaction. Clarry wasn't sure she'd ever seen Laura blush. Laura always knew where she stood, always said and did the right thing. Even as a child, Laura had been an adult. After their mother's death, Laura had been Clarry's mother, a firm disciplinarian even at the age of fourteen. With new eyes, Clarry tried to see Laura as a man would. She was too tall, too unfeminine to interest men.

Clarry gave a backward glance to the singer and saw that he was still staring at Laura's downcast face. "Why is that man staring at you?" Clarry asked absently.

"I'm sure it's you and not me. Why should he look at me with you so near?" she said quickly with absolutely no hostility in her voice.

"Laura!" Marian walked up behind them. "Do you know him?"

"Who?" Laura lied.

"Why, him," Marian said as if there was only one "him" on the earth. "It looks as if he was singing for you. He hasn't looked at anyone else for five minutes."

"Look, I don't know what either of you are talking about," Laura said almost angrily as she set the full plate down and walked away.

"What did I say?" Marian asked Clarry as they watched Laura leave the building.

"I don't know. She's worried about her painting, that's all. It has nothing to do with you."

Marian was glad to believe Clarry. She smiled up at a young man as he asked her to dance.

Clarry stood watching the door Laura had gone through when something made her turn and she saw the singer say something to the band leader, then walk off stage. Without hesitation, Clarry set her punch cup down and left the building. It took her a moment to adjust to the darkness. She saw the glow of the cigarette tip only when she was very close to it.

"Looking for me?" he said quietly.

Clarry stepped back to look at him. He was very tall. "In a way."

"In a way," he mocked. "That's a good one." He reached inside his coat pocket, withdrew the flask and held it out

16

to her. When Clarry shook her head, he took a deep drink. "I've had women following me *in a way* all over this country."

"Have you always had such a high opinion of yourself?"

"About as long as you have," he said as he took another drink. "Who was the girl with you?"

"Marian," Clarry said firmly.

"The tall one in the blue dress."

"She's no one you need to know," Clarry retorted and started to walk past him to return inside.

He grabbed her arm and she could smell the whiskey on his breath. "I asked you a question."

"And what makes you think I have to answer? Who are you?"

He looked for a moment, then put his head back and laughed. He released her arm. "Lord, honey, but you're right. Who am I? You know it and I know it but who else does? Look, you sure you don't want a drink?"

"I'm sure I want nothing from you."

He looked her up and down, the satin of her dress gleaming. "And I want nothing from you either, baby. You know, I think we understand each other. It may be too soon to tell but I think we're two of a kind."

She looked at him coldly. "Yes, I think it is too soon and I hope we never have the time to find out."

"You're not going to get mad, are you? It's not your style. Why don't you stay here and talk to me a minute?"

Clarry was silent for a moment, then asked him, "Why were you watching her?"

"You mean our mystery lady in blue? Oh, I don't know. She reminds me of someone, I guess, someone I've never met but would like to know. For two years now I've been traveling from one hick town to the next, and while I'm up there singing, I watch people and I guess what they're like. Most people are the same, you can divide them into a few groups, but now and then you see one that stands out—like that girl in blue. It's good to watch her, the way people talk to her. They like her, you know what I mean?"

"Yes, I do," Clarry said quietly.

"Now, you take people like you and me. We never know whether people like us or not. You ever talk to a man and not have his eyes slip downward?"

Clarry didn't answer; she couldn't.

"Oh, well, the problems of the rich and the problems of the beautiful. My name's Garrick Eastman."

"Clarry Taylor," she responded quietly.

"And the girl in blue?"

"My sister Laura." Clarry didn't know why she felt like a traitor. The singer would leave in the morning and that would be the last they'd see of him. And Laura, especially Laura of all the people in the world, could take care of herself.

"Thanks," Garrick said and smiled at her. "I've got to get back now or I'll find myself out of work. Thanks again," he said over his shoulder as he went inside.

Clarry stood alone in the dark for a moment, then suddenly looked around. She did not like the darkness, nor being alone. She went inside.

"Hello."

Laura turned, a smile on her face, toward the man's voice behind her. She stopped, frozen, as the band singer smiled at her.

"I know I'm being forward," he said, "but I'd like to introduce myself. I'm Garrick Eastman from Westover, New Hampshire."

Laura continued to gaze, fascinated.

"Maybe I am too forward. It's just difficult to make acquaintances in a strange city. Perhaps I shouldn't have bothered you." He half turned as if to walk away.

Laura began to regain consciousness. "Oh, no! Please, Mr.—" She stopped because she couldn't remember the name he had told her.

"Garrick Eastman," he said, his eyes dancing, his hand outstretched.

Laura took it, unable to control staring at him.

He didn't seem to notice anything unusual. "And you're Laura Taylor?"

"How did you know?" She was startled, caught off guard.

"I make it a point to find out about interesting women."

She recovered her composure and dropped her hand. "Interesting, is it?" she laughed. "At least you didn't say beautiful and make yourself a liar."

Garrick's smile broadened. "I only lie when necessary and at this moment I find no need for anything but the

18

truth. This is the band's supper break, would you care to join me? I hate to eat alone."

"Why, yes, of course." Laura was still surprised but very pleased.

"Laura!" Marian appeared from nowhere. "I meant to tell you how lovely you look tonight. Oh, dear!" she acted as if she had only now spotted Garrick standing beside Laura. "I didn't know you were busy," Marian remarked but made no attempt to leave.

"Mr. Eastman, this is Marian Stromberg and this, Marian, is Mr. Garrick Eastman. You may have noticed that he is the singer with the band."

"Why, of course I noticed. How could anyone not notice a...voice like yours? Mr. Eastman, tomorrow night I'm having a party and—"

Garrick cut her off. "I'm sorry but I have to leave for Arizona tomorrow. Now if you will excuse us, Miss Taylor has consented to be my dinner partner." Firmly grasping Laura's arm, he led her away from the stunned Marian. "I hope I wasn't too rude to your friend," he said when they were alone by the buffet table. "But in my business you soon learn to separate reality from fantasy."

Laura looked puzzled for a moment, then laughed. "I assume I am reality."

"Oh, no...Laura, you are fantasy." He handed her a plate. "Now fill it up and let's find a place where we can talk. I'd like to know a great deal more about you."

As Laura and Garrick walked to a quiet corner of the Masonic Hall several people looked at them in curiosity, but Laura didn't notice.

"You seem to know everyone here."

Laura took a seat on a wooden folding chair. "I grew up here and it's a small town. Everyone knows everyone else."

"How naive you are, Laura," he said as he sat beside her. "Knowing everyone is not all that's necessary. I've watched you all evening and I see how people seek you out."

She ate a forkful of potato salad. "I've been away, at school and—"

"What school?"

"The Art Academy of Cincinnati."

"Then you are an artist." It was a statement.

19

"I try to be, or maybe I should say, I hope to be."

His expression was serious for a moment. "I think you'll make it. I think that Miss Laura Taylor can be anything she wants to be."

Laura couldn't help laughing. "How can you say such things when we've only just met?"

"The one thing I've learned over the years is that I am an excellent judge of character."

Laura felt herself blushing again. "And what about you, Mr. Eastman? You said you were from New Hampshire?"

He waved his hand in dismissal. "Not an interesting life. I sing. I have always sung."

"And you plan to keep on singing?"

"Actually, no. For all that I've done for years, it isn't very important to me. Is your art important to you?"

"Yes. Very!" Laura said passionately, then smiled in embarrassment.

"That's the way an artist should feel."

"You wouldn't say that if you were around me very long. My sister says that my blood is probably oil paint. I'm afraid it's all I talk about."

He watched her. "It must be nice to feel so dedicated to something."

"Surely there must be something in your life you care about deeply."

"Only myself."

Laura smiled. "Well, we all do that, but there must be something else or someone in your life."

Garrick's eyes sparkled. "You are just as I imagined you would be."

Before she could answer, she saw the sheriff walking toward her, his face grim, and through some primitive instinct, Laura knew what he had to say. She stood. The plate of food in her lap crashed to the floor.

J.W. Taylor was leaning over the books again. Either his eyes were getting worse or the light was. The tiny penciled numbers seemed to vibrate on the page. He ran his hand over his eyes and tried once more to add up the figures. He had already balanced them once but he was hoping he was wrong. Laura's school, he thought. Laura's school. Just one more year. One more and she'd be through. Then she could come home and...and what?

20

He stood up and the sudden movement made his breath come short. He rubbed the left side of his chest, thought of dinner eaten too quickly, and went to the cabinet to get some baking soda. At the second pain, he dropped the soda in the sink, its contents spilling, the cardboard of the box soaking up water. He stood and stared at it, one hand clutching his chest, the other holding onto the rim of the sink. The soda spilling into the sink seemed like the most important thing on earth to him. He felt he had to get the box out of the water. Everything depended on getting the box onto the counter top.

The next pain brought him to his knees, and as he gazed at the cabinet doors he knew what was happening. The pain in his chest was building and for a second his mind was clear. He thought first of Laura—so many people would depend on Laura. He knew her better than anyone else did. Clarry was a survivor, a cat that would always land on its feet, but could Laura survive?

He used his dwindling strength to put his hand up to the edge of the kitchen table, but more pain came and blinded him. His fingers clutched at the edge of the ledgers on the table. When the next—and last—pain overcame him, he pulled them down on top of himself. He lay there silently, his back against the cabinet door, three cloth-bound ledgers upside down and twisted on his long, still legs.

Sheriff Moya didn't know when he had ever hated his job more. J.W. Taylor meant a lot to Montero.

"It's Dad, isn't it?" Laura said firmly as she met the sheriff's compassionate eyes.

"Yes. Heart attack."

"He's been taken to the hospital?" Laura was unaware of Garrick's arm as it slipped about her shoulders, or of the people beginning to gather around them. "I'll go there," she said as she stepped blindly forward, slipping slightly on the spilled food. She walked ahead and the crowd parted for her. Clarry followed silently.

"Is there any chance he'll recover?" Garrick asked the sheriff.

"He was dead when I found him. There was a radio show we were going to listen to together, but he was dead."

Garrick listened to the man and looked at the silent

21

people watching Laura and Clarry. Some were beginning to move forward to offer help, but as yet the sisters' grief was their own. Garrick pushed forward and began to follow them.

"Where you goin', Eastman?"

Garrick looked up to see the band leader frowning at him. He had a choice and now was the time to make it. "With them," he said quietly.

"You walk out of here and you don't come back. You understand that?"

He understood all too well. He jerked his arm away and hurried out the door.

Chapter 2

Laura wasn't sure who drove them to the hospital. She was aware of little. The only thing that occurred to her was prayer. She prayed to herself, to God, to anyone or anything that would listen, pleading, begging, that her father would be all right. She felt as if the world needed him to continue.

"Laura," Clarry whispered.

She turned to her younger sister and saw something other than fog.

"I'm scared, Laura," Clarry said and her face showed it. No studied gracefulness now. Clarry was very scared and she turned to her older sister, as she had always done.

For a moment Laura wanted to withdraw. No one could be more frightened than she was. How could she be expected to give comfort to someone else? Laura's reluctance, her hesitation, increased Clarry's fear, but Laura pulled her sister into her arms.

Laura's first thought was to go home, that when she got home her father would be there. Then she would be safe again. But her father wasn't there, he was in the hospital. Her head began to hurt, pressure building behind her eyes and spreading. The car stopped before the big glass doors of the hospital. Actually, it wasn't really a hospital, but more of a clinic. These things went through Laura's mind. She thought of traveling with her dad to the Albuquerque hospital. He'd have better care there, more thorough. Yes, definitely they'd take him to Albuquerque.

The door opened and Clarry sat up. Her eyes were dry and there was less fear showing in her face.

A hand reached in to help Laura from the car. It was Dr. Thomas.

"I'm sorry, Laura. We all are. J.W. was a friend to us all."

She blinked at him.

The doctor continued. "I don't think there was much pain. It seems to have been over very quickly. When it happens that fast, the patient doesn't usually have time to experience much pain."

"Pain?" she asked. She was beginning to understand and she wanted to push it out of her mind.

Clarry stepped forward. "Do you mean he's dead?"

The doctor looked surprised for a moment, then reached out to take Laura's hand. "Laura, I'm very sorry. I thought you knew, that you'd been told."

She was trying to swallow the lump in her throat. Dead? How could her father be dead? He was alive, laughing, smiling. She would go home and he'd hug her and tell her how pretty she was. He'd listen to her about her painting and he'd make pancakes on Sunday morning.

"Laura!" Dr. Thomas's hands dug into her shoulders. "Listen to me and understand me. Your father is dead."

"No," she whispered. "No."

The next moment she heard someone screaming. The screaming went on and on and sounded as if it would never stop. Laura wondered why they didn't do something to stop the screaming. Something sharp stuck her arm but it didn't really hurt. She was glad when the screaming stopped.

"Laura?"

She didn't want to wake up. There was a reason why she didn't want to wake up but she couldn't remember it.

"Laura?" the voice said again, a man's voice.

Reluctantly, she opened her eyes. Emmett Romero stood over her, a single red rose clutched in his hand.

"For you. I know how you like flowers."

She glanced from him to the rose. Why did he have such a look on his face? She started to sit up, and the ache in her back made her look about her. She was in bed, a white bed, a hospital bed. Sun was streaming in through the window.

She remembered.

"How long have I been here?"

"Dr. Thomas said you needed sleep more than anything, that you were run-down as it was. You've been asleep for about thirty some hours."

24

She lay back on the pillow and turned her head away. "And Dad?"

Emmett put his hand over hers. "Everything's been taken care of. The funeral is tomorrow. You don't need to do anything but rest."

Laura looked back at him. "And Clarry? Is she all right?"

"Yes," he said solemnly. "Clarry's fine. She's staying with Marian."

"Would you call the nurse, please? I'd like to get dressed. I have to go home."

"My car is outside. Take your time and I'll drive you when you're ready."

Laura realized as soon as she entered the house that it was not the same. She had been prepared for it to be empty, to feel the loneliness, but it was as if it were a different house.

"Would you like me to stay with you?" Emmett asked.

"No...I...I think it would be better if I were alone."

"All right, but only for a while. I'll be back in a couple of hours."

She didn't answer and was hardly aware of the door closing behind him. An hour later she looked up to see Clarry standing over her.

"I thought you'd be here," Clarry said as she sat down beside Laura on their father's bed. "You all right now? The doctor wouldn't let me see you."

"Yes," Laura nodded. "And you? Emmett said you'd been staying with Marian."

"Yes." Clarry's voice was quiet, as if her mind were somewhere else. There was a bond between the two sisters, one that Clarry was more aware of than Laura. Clarry had been only ten years old when their mother had died. For years before that, Jane Harlan Taylor had been an invalid, as much in hospitals and sanitariums as at home. Early on, Clarry had turned to her big sister for many of the things she needed. Laura had always seemed like an adult. Laura never giggled or fell in love with movie stars like other girls. No, Laura was perfect. She studied hard in school, and after school she helped her father with the bookkeeping at the lumberyard. For a while Clarry had tried to help at the lumberyard, but after several accidents had been caused by the young men watching the adolescent Clarry walk across the yard, her father suggested she stay at home. She tried cooking but it wasn't long before Laura and her father took that over, too. It was only when Laura was gone that things began to fall apart.

"What do we do now?" Clarry asked.

Laura stood up, nervous. She walked to the window, tried to control her tears as she thought how her father would never look out any window again. By instinct, she protected Clarry from the sight of her tears. She still remembered Clarry's fear on the night—the night of the dance. "I don't know. I guess we'll go on as before." She turned around and tried to smile. "Only not quite as before." Tears were still trying to form.

Clarry's look was dry and level. "No, I mean about the house, the lumberyard."

"What?" Laura was frowning. "The lumberyard? What do I care about the lumberyard?" It was too easy to go from one emotion to the next. She tried to control the anger that threatened to take over. "Clarry, how can you even think of such a thing while Dad is . . . is . . . Oh, Clarry, are you so selfish that that's all you can think of?"

Laura couldn't remember being angry with Clarry before. She was her little sister, to be protected and sheltered, loved always. Laura could see Clarry crumbling beneath the onslaught and she was immediately repentant. "Oh, Clarry, I'm sorry." She ran to her little sister and hugged her.

Clarry clung desperately, frightened at what she had seen in Laura.

"I'm very sorry. I didn't mean to get angry." Laura drew back and gave her sister a smile. "Look, don't worry about the lumberyard. Mr. Martinez can run it, he's been doing it for years. As soon as I finish school, I'll come back and maybe we'll sell it. We'll do something else then. I'll paint and you—maybe we'll buy you a dress shop or something. How does that sound?"

Clarry didn't answer but continued to gaze at her sister.

"Clarry, what's wrong? Why are you looking like that? It won't be easy now, I know, but we'll make it."

"I . . . I'm scared."

Laura pulled Clarry to her again. She was also frightened. She didn't know how she was going to live without her father's constant support and understanding. And now she felt so selfish. Clarry had also loved him and Laura hadn't realized until right now how much.

"Do you promise, Laura?"

"Promise?" Clarry sounded like a child again. Whenever she had hurt herself, she had always made Laura promise her that in a day it would quit hurting.

"What can I promise you?" Laura easily stepped back into the role of mother.

"That it will be all right. That we can, I don't know, I guess...live."

Laura tried to hide her disgust. She had often had to overlook Clarry's habit of thinking of herself first. "Yes, I can promise that. We'll hire someone to keep house while I'm at school next year, and then when I return, we'll see what happens." She held Clarry away from her. She couldn't be angry with her. Clarry was a product of her father's and her own indulgence.

A knock at the door startled them. Questioningly, Laura looked at Clarry.

"People have been bringing food all day," Clarry said as she stood, straightening her skirt and sweater before leaving the room.

Laura was reluctant to leave the bedroom. She knew that her father was dead, but she didn't want to see concrete evidence of it yet. In her life she had cooked several casseroles and taken them to bereaved families, but now she would be on the receiving end. Memories of her mother's death flooded her consciousness. But the death of a mother she had hardly known was not the same as the loss of her father.

She stood, smoothed her seersucker dress, and took a deep breath. She walked to the doorway of the kitchen where Clarry was talking to Mrs. Martinez.

"And if there's anything we can do," Mrs. Martinez was saying, "anything at all, please let us know. And don't worry about the lumberyard. My Manny will take care of everything until, well, you know what I mean."

Clarry studied her hands on the table and gave a brief nod.

Mrs. Martinez fumbled in her purse, withdrew an envelope and held it out to Clarry. "I wish we could do more."

Clarry took the envelope but didn't look at Mrs. Martinez.

27

The woman patted Clarry's hand. "I must go now, but please let me help in any way I can."

Clarry followed her to the front door. Her hands were empty when she returned to the kitchen and saw Laura standing there.

"What was in the envelope?"

"Nothing," Clarry said quickly as she picked up the casserole from the table and put it in the oven. "Emmett just pulled into the driveway. He should be here any minute."

"Clarry, what was in the envelope?"

"What envelope?" Emmett asked. "I let myself in."

Clarry, her back to Laura, gave him a pleading look.

Emmett went to Laura and put his arm around her shoulders. "You have enough to worry about now. There are a lot of people at the funeral home and maybe you should be there."

Laura pushed away from him. "No, I don't want to go. I don't want to be there." She backed away, stopping against the sink. "I'm not going."

The three of them stood there, Clarry and Emmett watching Laura, frightened by her out-of-character behavior.

"Excuse me."

They turned to look at Garrick Eastman standing in the doorway, his body dark against the sunlight.

"I knocked but I guess no one heard." He looked at each of them, took in Laura's wild-eyedness. He put his hat on the kitchen table, walked in front of Emmett and drew Laura into his arms.

At first she didn't respond. He was a stranger to her, someone she had spent less than an hour with. But gradually, the comfort he offered her began to sink in. She had given comfort to Clarry. Emmett had said the right words, the nurses had said the right words, but no one seemed to think she needed someone to protect her. Montero, New Mexico, had known Laura Taylor for twenty-two years and they knew that she was a giver. Laura had only leaned on her father. Now, arms were around her, strong, comforting arms.

"Cry, Laura," Garrick said quietly. "Cry."

She shook her head, her face buried in his shoulder. She had worked hard for the last few hours at not letting go. She had done well so far and she couldn't break down now.

"He's gone. Do you realize that? He's gone and he'll never come back."

The tears began to come before she was aware of them. He held her close as she cried. Several minutes later he offered her a handkerchief. She wiped her eyes and blew her nose.

"Better?"

"No," she said honestly. "I feel so selfish."

"How?"

"Because I'm crying for me, not him. Dad's at peace now, but I'm not. I need him. I need him for *me*."

"And wouldn't he have liked that? To be needed, I mean. Didn't he need you, too?"

Her head hurt too much to think. "I don't know." In spite of her head hurting and her swollen sinuses, she did feel better. She knew that she did have to go to the funeral home.

Garrick lifted her chin in his hand. The unfamiliarity of him, his extraordinary beauty, was a shock to her. Tall, awkward career women did not have handsome young men's shoulders to cry on.

"Now, go wash your face and put on a hat. We have to go to the funeral home."

She nodded silently and left the room.

Garrick went outside, leaned against the wall, and lit a cigarette.

"Some show."

He turned slightly to see Clarry sitting at the end of the porch. He didn't bother to turn all the way. "What happened to the boyfriend?"

"Emmett had to go home."

"Is he?"

"Is he what?" Clarry asked obstinately.

"Laura's boyfriend."

Clarry waited a while before answering, looking out at the brilliant sun. "No. Emmett's engaged to someone else. Why didn't you leave with the others?"

Garrick drew deeply on the cigarette. "Let's just say I heard opportunity knocking and decided to open the door."

"We're not rich if that's what you mean."

29

He gave her a glance and then looked at a large crack in the plaster wall. "I wasn't led to believe you were."

Clarry stood and faced him. "Then why? Why are you here? Why do you come in here like something out of a third-rate movie begging my sister to cry on your shoulder?"

He tossed the cigarette down and ground it out. "When I want you to know my business, I'll tell you."

She glared at him, then angrily started for the door.

He grabbed her arm. "What do you care anyway? Since when have you ever cared about anybody but yourself?"

She stepped away from him, astonished. "Laura's my sister. I love her."

He smiled at her. "That's good of you to say but I have my doubts. Look, you just take care of yourself and let me worry about what concerns me. Now why don't you be a good girl and go get dressed?"

If anyone noticed anything unusual about Laura arriving at the funeral home on the arm of the good-looking stranger, nothing was said. Once she was there, she felt better. The waxen man in the coffin was far removed from being her father.

"Now that Laura's home, everything will be all right."

She heard this over and over. The people seemed to think that because she was silent she heard nothing. How could anything be all right when her father was gone? By evening, the voices around her became incessant and she took more notice of them. Clarry stood in one corner, away from Laura, almost as if she was hiding. People went to Clarry, whispered to her, and again and again Laura saw envelopes pressed into Clarry's hands. Twice she saw Emmett and Clarry huddled together, as if sharing secrets.

At nine o'clock, Garrick drove her home. She had hardly noticed him all day, yet his presence had helped her. She told him good-night and then sat down in the dark house and waited. Emmett had taken Clarry to Marian's earlier in the day, but he'd promised to bring her home before it was too late.

It was ten-thirty when she heard the car pull into the driveway. She walked slowly to the door and waited.

"Laura's probably asleep," Emmett said, "so I won't come in. I'll pick you both up tomorrow morning at ten."

With one deft movement, Laura grabbed Clarry's purse from under her arm and turned on the overhead hall light.

"Laura! What are you doing?" Quicker to react than Clarry, Emmett made a grab for the purse Laura had already opened.

She didn't know what she had expected, but it certainly wasn't what she found. Clarry's purse was filled with money, one dollar bills, fives, a few tens. There was well over a hundred dollars in the purse, enough to support the two of them for more than a month. She looked up in astonishment at Clarry and Emmett, both of whose faces had a look of defiance.

"I think we need to talk," Laura said as she led the way into the living room and switched on a light. "Sit down, both of you." When they were seated, she said, "I want some answers. Clarry, why is there so much money in your purse? Is that what's been in the envelopes?"

Clarry looked down at her skirt. When she looked back at Laura, she had the same look of fear Laura had noticed twice before in the last two days.

"Clarry, I want an answer now."

The fear in Clarry's face increased.

"All right," Emmett spoke up, taking Laura's eyes off Clarry. "I don't guess we could have kept it from you for much longer anyway. The lumberyard is bankrupt and has been for some time. Your father has been acting as a general handyman about town for the last year. He traded the stock in the yard for whatever people could spare, either in garden produce or cash if anybody had any."

Laura stared at him. "But what about his contract for the six new houses?"

Emmett and Clarry exchanged looks. "There were no houses," he said. "There's been no building in Montero for two years, not since the Depression hit New Mexico. Everybody's afraid to part with any money and the banks aren't loaning any. They've had to make too many foreclosures."

Laura's head was whirling. She couldn't yet believe what Emmett said. "If the yard was bankrupt, how has my tuition at school been paid?"

Emmett's eyes met hers, then he nodded to the full purse in her lap. "That money is for you."

"Me?" She looked down at it as if it were poison. "Do

you mean that the people of Montero have been paying my tuition?"

"For the last two years."

She put the purse on the table and stood up. She walked to the bookcase at one end of the room. "Then that's why everyone knew about my paintings and what I did in school? Tell me, are there other town charity cases or am I the only one?"

"Laura, please," Emmett said and went to stand beside her. He put one hand on her shoulder, but she angrily shrugged it off. "We knew you'd take it like this and that's why we tried to keep it a secret."

She turned on him. "We! Do you mean you and Clarry or the whole town? Oh, I can see you mean the town. Poor little Miss Laura! She must be sheltered from the truth. Surely there must be other people more needy than me! Lord, if this weren't so serious, it would be laughable. Do you know what the Depression is like in the East? We have it easy here. I guess the mountains keep us safe from bread lines and twelve-year-old girls who become prostitutes in order to survive. And all this time I've felt so secure while I was in art school. *Art* school! People are starving and yet my tuition is being paid so I can paint pictures."

"Laura, you're tired and upset now. Things will look better in the morning."

"You're damn right I'm upset. And tell me, while I'm across the mountains indulging myself and spending my charity allowance, what happens to Clarry? Clarry! Where did you get that dress?"

Clarry looked at her skirt again. "Marian."

"And the shoes?"

"Mrs. Martinez."

"And the—"

"Stop it, Laura!" Emmett commanded. "It wasn't as if the town had no choice. You belong to us. You're one of us and we believe in you. J.W. showed us your paintings, your reviews, and let us decide."

Laura paused, then took a deep breath. Her voice was deceptively calm. "Do you mean that my father tucked one of my paintings under his arm and went around begging? Alms," she mocked in a falsetto voice, "alms for my poor daughter." She glared at Emmett. "Do you know what a

32

proud man my father was? He raised two daughters practically alone and he worked in that lumberyard sometimes seven days a week in order to pay for Mother's doctor bills, and he never asked help from anyone. How could it have happened? How could the business have failed?"

"Come back and sit down, Laura, and we'll discuss this rationally."

"Don't patronize me. I want to discuss it and how I do it is my own concern. What caused the business to fail?"

"I told you. There was no building in Montero."

"Then why didn't Dad build something, a house, a hotel or something and sell it? He's done that before."

"He tried but the banks wouldn't loan him any money. And besides, who would buy the building? The Strombergs are the only ones here with any money, and when they spend, they go to California. They don't want a second house in Montero."

Laura began to pace the floor. "So he started begging."

"Not really begging. These are hard times."

"Tell me, have any other family businesses in Montero failed?"

"Of course," he answered. "All the contractors have either moved or taken other jobs. The hardware store is in trouble, too."

"Did Montero get behind any other of their daughters, or sons?"

"Laura, why are you getting so angry? You should feel honored that the town cares so much about you and wants to see you succeed." He tried to smile. "I told you you're the town celebrity."

"Emmett," she said in a deadly voice, her eyes narrowed. "I am not some child you can soothe with a piece of candy. Do you know how Sheriff Moya found my father? With the ledgers from the lumberyard spread across his legs. My father wasn't even fifty years old. He was much too young to die of a heart attack. What must have gone through his mind before he died? He'd been looking at those books for two years, each day seeing the debts increase. Dad could never stand to owe anyone money. He was always proud of the fact that he never owed anyone. Now how much does he owe? One thousand? Two? And what about the men who'd worked for him for twenty-five years? What's become of the Martinez family? Louise Mar-

33

tinez's grandfather worked with my grandfather. Now what do they do for a living?"

"Laura, this isn't the sixteenth century where your father was *patrón*."

"Bull! Don't give me that. I'm not talking about a Spanish concept, I'm talking about decency. My father chose me over them. Maybe he could have made the lumberyard work if he hadn't had me to support. And again, what about Clarry? Why do my needs come before hers?"

Some things suddenly became clear to her. She went to Clarry and knelt before her, took her cold hands. "This is why you've been so frightened, isn't it?" she said quietly. "This explains all those things you've said, like wanting me to promise we would survive."

Clarry could only nod.

"Has it been awful for you since the yard failed?"

Clarry's eyes looked like an animal's—desperate and hungry.

Laura pulled Clarry to her. Her look to Emmett over Clarry's shoulder was hard. "How could the people have done this to us?"

"*Done* to you? We've been proud of you. Can't you see that?"

Laura pulled away from her sister. "Clarry, go to bed," she commanded. Clarry didn't hesitate. When they were alone, Laura turned back to Emmett. "My father is dead, killed I'm sure, by worry over how to support his family; Clarry is reduced to a frightened child and you say I should be grateful?"

"You're being melodramatic. You have no way of knowing that your father wouldn't have died at this age no matter what, and Clarry's always been a child, more of a beautiful doll. It's you we wanted to help."

"Oh, so now Montero plays God and decides who is worth saving and who is not."

"You don't make sense. You act as if we did something wrong."

"Wrong!" She threw up her hands in disgust. "You say my father gave the people a choice." The idea of her proud, strong father virtually begging from door to door made her stomach cramp. "Well, someone should have given me a choice."

"Sure, and you would have come home and helped your
34

father and baby-sat Clarry like you've always done. Don't you understand our own selfishness? We saw a chance of putting Montero on the map."

"My father's dead and my sister is nearly scared out of her mind, but Montero just might be on the map."

Emmett grabbed his hat. "Look, I'm sorry I had to tell you. You're too stubborn to understand."

"You're wrong. I understand all too well. It's just that I don't like it. What did you expect me to do, take that money and happily return to school in the fall, just walk off and forget about everyone except myself?"

Emmett was incredulous. "Laura, you can't mean you aren't going to return."

She shook her head at him. "How could I?"

He tossed his hat in a chair. "This is serious. You can't make a decision like this right away. Think about it. Think about what your art means to you. Think of all those reviews. You have a chance, Laura. You have to take it."

"You have no idea what you're saying, do you?" she said softly. "It's a decision long overdue, one that should have been made a long time ago."

"Think, Laura! What are you going to do if you remain here? The lumberyard won't suddenly spring to life because Miss Laura Taylor decides it should. You could keep on painting but there are ten artists to every tourist now. No one is buying out here."

"I don't know what I'm going to do. Thanks to you, I've only just heard that it was so vital to do anything."

"Well, then, go back to school or at least consider it."

"I have some thinking to do now. I'd appreciate being alone." She picked up Clarry's purse, pulled the money from it. "Here, take this."

As Emmett glanced from her to the money, she pulled her hand back. "No, I'll need this. As much as I hate it, I'll need it. But one thing is for sure, next month I won't need it."

"Laura, you're being childish. Let us—"

"I'd like you to leave now."

When Laura looked at him, it wasn't as one friend to another. She felt a change beginning.

35

Chapter 3

When Emmett left, the first thing Laura did was to check on Clarry. It was a habit based on years of practice. Clarry was asleep, exhausted by two days of grief and worry. Laura smoothed the white-blonde hair from the sleeping girl's face. Clarry looked especially young and vulnerable and Laura tried to imagine what her sister's life had been like for the past two years. Quietly, she left the room and closed the door behind her.

She went first to the kitchen. The little adobe house had been built the year before Laura was born, when J.W. Taylor had only recently married the quiet, coughing Jane Harlan. It was a small house, three bedrooms, living room, bath, kitchen and dining room, with a central hallway at the entrance. A long portal ran across the front of the house. The exterior adobe walls were the thickness of two adobe blocks. The two feet of dried mud and straw made the house cool in summer and warm in winter. Adobe, a single thickness, was also used for the interior walls and it made the house virtually soundproof. The ceiling was done in traditional style. Long, thick, skinned aspen logs were placed on top of the adobe walls. These were the *vigas*. On top of the *vigas*, placed in a lattice-work design, were *latillas*, cleaned sticks hardly bigger than a man's thumb. On top of the *vigas* and *latillas* were piled six inches of dirt.

It was a house made from the soil, part of the earth. Adobe houses rose out of the earth slowly and gently. There were no awkward contrasts of sharp angles opposing the soft slopes of the land, or artificial masses of glass and steel. Even new adobe houses looked as if they had been set in their places for generations.

The kitchen cabinets were pine, roughly cut, crudely made. The latches were wrought iron of the same crudeness. New Mexico was not a place where one worried much about craftsmanship, and the ill-fitting doors and drawers had a charm all their own.

For the first time since she had begun studying art, Laura became aware of her surroundings. She opened pantries, cupboards, and at each empty space, her self-centeredness screamed at her. She had never been home long enough or cared enough to worry about her father and Clarry. On her holidays she had risen at dawn, made herself a sandwich, taken her easel, canvas and paints, and left. She usually returned only after dark. Then her father would be waiting with a bag of groceries, and the two of them would cook a huge supper of meat and green chili, *sopapillas* and honey. Now, as Laura looked at the empty spaces that should have been filled with cans and boxes, she wondered how much those wonderful meals had cost her father—in pride.

She put her hands on the sink and tightened her arms as she stared through the window at the black sky. It suddenly came to her how much of an indulgence grief was. Only the rich, the ones who didn't have to worry about their next meal, could afford to give themselves over to grief. The funeral was tomorrow and now she had too many other things to think of besides the dead. As crude as the idea was, the living must be thought of first. The idea of putting food on the table had to take precedence over the memory of her father.

She closed the window curtains, walked through the little dining room and into the living room. Anything built out of mud could never satisfy a carpenter's level. The room felt the gentle undulations, the soft curves of the plastered walls. It felt warm and soft, a place where people lived and loved. The couch had been made in Montero, with a wooden back and sides, long cushions over the pine, hand-woven Mexican cotton covers. The fireplace, in front of the couch, was the traditional beehive shape, a *nicho* cut into the adobe by the chimney. Several of the objects in the room were from Mexico, such as the pre-Columbian man who grinned from the *nicho*. There were two baskets made by the White Mountain Apaches on a shelf above the window.

A fire had been laid by Laura's father, meant to remain unused for the summer. She lit it now, blew on it for a moment before it took hold. The piñon wood had a lot of

37

pitch and was a little too green. She would have to constantly readjust the wood before a good fire would start. She sat down on the Navajo rug before the low hearth and watched the fire, the flames beginning to devour the soft wood.

All the time that she had been walking around the house or checking on Clarry, Emmett's words had echoed in her mind. He was right about something: this was a time for an important decision, one that couldn't be made lightly. She had exploded when first confronted with the truth, but now was the time for rational thought, without hysterics.

Of course, she really had no right to be angry with the people of Montero. Her father had asked for their help and they had loved him enough to give it, even though at times it must have been a hardship to them. They loved her enough to want to see her succeed. She couldn't overlook that fact. Her father hadn't been the only person to have received their love. Emmett was right, she should feel honored and proud.

But their love had killed her father.

This awareness was as tangible to her as the flagstone of the floors. To the outside world, J.W. Taylor had seemed like a rock of a man, but Laura knew what a worrier he was. He took the burdens of life and carried them silently. Some men could laugh at everyday problems, but not J.W. There had been hundreds of times when Laura, as a little girl, sleepy and thirsty, had stumbled along to the kitchen and found her father huddled over the ledgers. Later, in high school, she had kept the books for the lumberyard and she had been able to hide the times when business was doing poorly. People paid their bills whenever they could or whenever it occurred to them, but J.W. paid his promptly. Sometimes their accounts receivable total was high but their cash on hand was low. Laura was an optimist. She knew that things would get better—and they did. But early on, she learned not to tell her father when they had less than enough in the bank on Thursday to pay the men's wages on Friday. J.W. would have paced the floor all night worrying about it, but Laura didn't worry, she did something. First thing Friday morning, she would drive to the houses or places of business of the people who owed them money. She always smiled and was very polite but she got her money; she didn't leave until she did. Her father would have been appalled if he had known. The people of Montero teased her constantly, saying how they might as well get their checkbooks out when they saw Laura coming because no excuse in the world was going to keep her from collecting the debt once she'd made up her mind to get it.

But it was odd how the people seemed to know that J.W. knew nothing of his daughter's collection methods. No one ever mentioned it when he was near.

Now, as Laura stared at the fire, she wondered if maybe the people of Montero had known how much pride her father had had. They would have been able to see how much it hurt him to ask for help to support his own family, yet Laura and her art had meant so much to him that no sacrifice was too much. Yet if Montero hadn't helped, Laura wouldn't have gone to school and...

She pulled her knees up to her chest, put her arms around her legs, her head down. Her father had given so much to her, and the people of Montero had, too. The idea of the love that had caused them to open their wallets overwhelmed her. It was a wonderful concept but it was a responsibility, too. How could she repay them? What in the world could she ever do for them? If by some chance she did return to school, how would that help them? Emmett said she could put Montero on the map. That was a nice sentiment, but it was little else. She owed them more.

Laura lifted her head, then moved to put another split log on the fire. Clarry couldn't be forgotten, either. She had as much right to get what she wanted as Laura did. It was not fair to whirl off to New York and leave Clarry alone to fend for herself in a dying New Mexico town. Every year several families left Montero for California or the southern part of the state. Her father once said that at the rate it was going, in twenty years Montero would no longer even qualify for a post office.

The coldness of the flagstone was coming through the rug. She stood and stretched. She had identified the problem—she owed the people of Montero something. She had a responsibility to Clarry, and most of all, she had to live up to her father's belief in her. She had told Emmett that she would use the money given to Clarry for one month, then she'd make her own way. She had said that in anger but now it seemed like a good goal. Tomorrow was the funeral and tomorrow she would begin to act. She didn't know where she was going but she knew she wasn't going to sit still and wait for someone to offer a living to her.

Clarry's purse still lay on the table by the couch, the money tossed on top of it. She picked up one dollar and looked at it.

"A remembrance," she whispered in the quiet, still room. Folding it very carefully into a tiny little square, she put it into the open clay headdress of the pre-Columbian man in the hollow in the wall by the fireplace.

The early morning light found Laura still awake in her bed. After several hours' thought, she realized that it was easy to vow to change the world but much more difficult to come up with a partial solution.

"Laura."

Clarry was standing in the dimly lit doorway. The rumpled, bewildered-looking Clarry made her smile. It couldn't possibly be the Clarry whose most innocent walk turned men, young and old, into quivering fools. She smiled, pulled the cover back, and Clarry snuggled in beside her.

"You're not mad?" Clarry asked after a while. She was so much smaller than Laura, every bone plumply covered, whereas Laura's tall, big-boned figure was composed of angles and planes. The two young women were so different that there was no competition between them. Clarry's life revolved around men's glances while Laura's was only concerned with art.

"Why should I be angry? Oh! You mean about what Emmett said."

Clarry nodded. "You were mad last night."

"Yes, I was, but I thought about it and—" She pulled back from Clarry. They lay close together, Laura's arm protectively around Clarry's shoulders. "Why didn't you tell me what was going on? Emmett said the lumberyard failed two years ago. You could have said something in that time."

"Dad made me promise. He said you were our hope of

success, that if we helped you now then you'd help us later."

Laura lay back against the pillow and the pine headboard. Her father hadn't been fair to Clarry. "How did you live?" she asked quietly.

Clarry suddenly began to fidget. It was as if the question made her nervous. "We . . . we were all right," she finally said. "What are we going to do now?" She seemed to be trying to block out the bad memories by pretending they didn't exist. "Are you going back to school?" She looked at Laura anxiously.

"No, I don't really see how I can."

"But what about the New York gallery? Will they like it if you leave school? I thought the showing was only for students."

All the buoyancy Laura had worked up in the last few hours suddenly left her. She hadn't thought of the Grey Gallery since she had talked to Emmett. Her mind raced. Maybe she could take the town's money, finish the five paintings needed, crate them, travel to New York—she quickly realized that Clarry would be left out. Clarry was her responsibility. "I guess I'll have to turn them down." She tried to make her voice nonchalant, to sound as if her decision were of no consequence.

Clarry let out the breath she was holding so tightly. "Then you'll stay here? You won't go away?"

"I guess not. I can't see how I can."

Clarry hugged her sister. "Oh, Laura, everything will be all right if you stay here. I knew you would. I knew you wouldn't leave me."

"Clarry, just because I stay in Montero doesn't mean everything will be all right. We have no money and no way to make any. You do know that it takes money to live, don't you? Not just a big sister who stays home from art school." Laura didn't want to be angry with Clarry but she wished she would show a little more sympathy for what Laura was giving up.

Clarry didn't usually notice subtle emotions. "It will be. You'll see. Now that you're home you'll fix everything and Marian's cousin is coming—Oh, Laura! I'm hungry, starving!" She jumped out of bed and headed for the kitchen, leaving Laura to her thoughts, glad that at least one of them was optimistic.

41

At the funeral, the two sisters stood side by side, Clarry
with her head down, unwilling to look at the black-draped
coffin.

Laura felt as if she had wakened from a pleasant dream
that she very much wanted to slide back into. She looked
with new understanding at the several hundred people
who crowded quietly around them. She had spent all morning buried in her father's ledgers. He had kept a careful
record of every penny anyone had given him for Laura's
education. The numbers had almost made her ill. It was
astonishing how little J.W. had kept for Clarry and himself. Laura wondered again how they had survived.

"Laura," someone was saying, "I don't guess anyone
can tell you how sorry we are. We'll miss him."

She looked at Mr. Gomez, his little wife beside him,
seven of their eight children lined up behind them. Mr.
Gomez had given J.W. and Clarry a bushel of green chili
and two bushels of apples from his orchard. Mr. and Mrs.
Woodman came next. They had given two dollars a month
for Laura's tuition. On and on the people came and it was
as if each one had numbers branded on his forehead. She
remembered every item in the ledgers, every penny, every
piece of fruit. They made her feel small, unworthy.

She shook her head. She couldn't keep on flogging herself. "Mr. Ortiz," she said to the man in front of her. "Could
I borrow Lady this afternoon? I think I'd like to take a
ride."

"She's yours any time you need her."

Two hours later, Laura rode out on the Old Mission
Road. Even as a child she had gone to the Old Mission
when she needed to be alone. She saw the ruins from some
distance away and they gave her the same calm feeling.
The Mission, with its huge chapel and the quarters for the
friars, had been built in 1720. The roof had fallen in, in
1898, and the whole Mission had been abandoned for
newer quarters south of Albuquerque. The Mission was
the reason Montero had been settled, and the town had
been dying gradually in the thirty-six years since the friars
had moved. The adobe and sandstone ruins were impressive to the people of Montero, but compared to Abo in the
middle of the state and Gran Quivara in the south, they
were nothing. The chapel itself was too small and too

young. In New Mexico, any ruin built after the seventeenth century was hardly worth the notice of either the scholars or the tourists.

"Laura!"

She became aware of someone calling her and turned to see an old Ford struggling along the steep dirt road. She didn't recognize the car or the voice until it stopped beside her. She bent forward in the saddle, steadying the horse. "Mr. Eastman! I had no idea you were still here. I would have thought the band had left by now."

He opened the car door and stood on the running board, watching her with speculation. "The band did; I didn't." He turned toward the horizon and the tall adobe ruins. "What is that place? Besides a pile of mud?"

Laura liked his eastern cynicism. She smiled, for the first time in days. "It's the Old Mission. Are you out for a drive or do you have to be somewhere?"

"I have a job but it doesn't start until seven, so my afternoon is free. Care to show me the sights of Montero?"

"Gladly. Just follow me and not too closely. Lady doesn't like your ... car." The wreck barely qualified.

He grinned, his dark eyes wrinkling. "I'll have you know your own sheriff sold me this."

Laura laughed. "I'm so glad he finally got rid of it. He's been trying for years."

Garrick watched her a moment before climbing back into the torn seat. "There's something else Montero has that I want, Laura honey," he said over the backfires of the engine.

Ten minutes later they were standing outside the old, weather-grayed doors of the chapel.

"I take it this was a church."

"More than a church. It was a mission, halfway between a monastery and a church travel court, I guess. The missions were self-contained towns. Come on and I'll show you the rest of it."

The ruins covered a half acre. Laura showed him the roofless church, open to two stories where the ornate corbels that had once held the *vigas* still stood, now open to the brilliant blue sky.

"Why doesn't this place just dissolve?" Garrick asked.

"It does eventually, only in New Mexico we don't have

43

constant rain like in the East, so it takes longer. We measure things here in centuries, not years."

There were two enclosed courtyards attached to the church, each square surrounded by large, empty rooms, the quarters of the friars. At the second courtyard Garrick stopped. Four big old cottonwoods hung on tenaciously in spite of years of neglect. He listened to Laura's explanations carefully. "I can't believe there are more of these ruins," he said, sitting down on a stone bench and pulling out a pack of Chesterfields. He offered Laura one, then when she refused, lit it himself. "It seems like the state would keep these things from falling apart. Doesn't Roosevelt have one of his programs for this kind of thing?"

Laura leaned against the tree. She loved the Mission, always had. "Yes. The WPA. But the Mission at Montero isn't considered worth saving. You should see the ones in the south. Some of them are made out of handhewn stone and they're old—very old. This place isn't."

"It looks old to me."

"It would be in the East, but some of the New Mexico missions were already abandoned in the 1620s, long before the American Revolution. Our mission wasn't even built until 1720. From an archaeological point of view it's too young to consider."

He stood up, tossed the cigarette on the ground and crushed it. "Listen, I brought some sandwiches. I thought maybe you'd be hungry after this morning. I don't think you ate before you got on that horse."

"How did you know that?"

He walked toward her so that he was standing very close. "I made it my business to find out."

She frowned. Some of her awe at his good looks was wearing off. "Why are you here? Why didn't you leave with the band?"

"If I told you the truth, you wouldn't believe me. Something's happened since the last time I saw you, hasn't it? From what I hear about you and your paints, I thought you'd spend the afternoon with them. Don't you have more to do before your New York exhibit?"

She didn't know whether to be pleased or annoyed at his knowledge. "I guess you could have found that out from anyone in town since they have a share in me." She turned and started back through the labyrinth to the church.

Garrick caught up with her. "So, you found out."

She stopped. "Don't tell me you know that, too?"

"What are you worried about? It doesn't matter if I know about your finances or not."

She started walking again. "No, it doesn't matter but I don't like to think of myself as being discussed over dinner."

"You weren't—aren't. It's just that I can usually find out what I want."

They were at the car. "And you wanted to find out about me?"

"Come on and let's get some food. And quit being so hostile. How about that hill up there? Then you can look down over your dear mud pile. No smile?"

She did smile a little.

When they were seated on the pine needles coating the hillside, Garrick began to question her. "What are you going to do this summer before you go back to school?"

"I'm not returning to school." She kept her eyes straight ahead, ignoring his astonishment.

"Why not? It seems like everybody in town is chipping in for your tuition."

"That's just the reason. I don't want to be an object of charity any more."

"Good Lord!" he said in disgust. "This is no time to be a martyr. You should be grateful they're willing to help you."

"You sound like Emmett. And what am I supposed to do with Clarry? Who's going to take care of her?"

"Did it ever occur to you that Clarry could take care of herself? Maybe you should worry about who's going to take care of Laura."

She put her half-finished sandwich on her lap. "I don't understand why you're getting involved in this. I never saw you before two days ago and now you're trying to tell me how to run my life. And what could you know about Clarry? I've lived with her eighteen years and I do believe I know her better than you do."

"I'm not so sure."

"I think I've had enough of this conversation."

She started to rise but Garrick held her arm. "You're right. I was out of line. If you'll forgive me, I promise not to give any more opinions. I just want to be your friend.

45

You've got problems and I'm a great listener. Now sit down and talk to me." Garrick knew how to use his looks to advantage. He made a very appealing black angel.

"All right, but I don't want to hear any more about Clarry. She's my concern, and besides, you don't know her."

"So tell me what you think Clarry's like."

She chose to ignore the hint that her opinion of Clarry could be wrong. "She's a sweet girl, very innocent, and she needs someone to take care of her."

"So you're going to quit art school and do that?"

Laura nodded. "I can't see what else to do."

"Did you tell Clarry of your plans?"

"Yes, this morning."

"And what did she say?"

She looked at him in surprise.

"No protests?"

Laura glared at him. "I don't think I like what you're saying."

"Nothing bad, I assure you. You know, Laura, I think you may be one of the most amazing women I've ever met."

The sun was just dropping down behind the western wall of the church, and as Laura sat quietly on the grassy hillside Garrick casually put his arm around her shoulders. She was startled. As he began to pull her closer to him, Laura stiffened.

"There's nothing to be afraid of. Just relax."

The idea that a man would want to kiss her, especially a man who looked like Garrick Eastman, took her by surprise.

When Garrick's lips first touched hers, his first thought was that it was like kissing a board. He didn't like having to be a teacher. He preferred women who could teach him. He pulled away from her. "Not so bad, was it?" he said quietly as he smoothed her hair back. She hadn't bothered to renew Clarry's finger waves and it now clung softly to her head, pretty but not fashionable.

Laura stiffened even more. She put her hand against his shoulder and pushed away from him. "Please, I have to go." She moved clumsily away from him.

"Laura, what's wrong?" Garrick was truthfully puzzled. His good looks had distorted his view of women. More than once he had been offered—and taken—money for what he now offered Laura. "You seem angry."

When she stood, the bright, dying sun behind her back, she towered over him. "This morning my father was buried and now I spend the afternoon kissing some man I barely know."

"You can hardly say we spent the afternoon at it," Garrick answered harshly. "What's all the fuss about one kiss anyway? From the way you act one would think I tried to tumble you on the hill."

Laura's eyes opened wide in astonishment.

She was halfway down the hill before he caught her. Without thinking, Garrick treated Laura as he had always treated women—masterfully, rough. He pulled her into his arms quickly and ignored her hands pushing at him. He kissed her roughly. It was a battle to him and he meant to win. Laura's gradual response didn't surprise him, but the amount of passion that she came to display did. He was used to women who held something in reserve. Laura didn't. What she felt was clearly expressed. He drew back from her, both in surprise and to restrain himself. Laura's eagerness and obvious lack of experience had begun to excite him. Now was not the time to act out his plan.

Laura leaned against his encircling arms. She was dazed, and when she opened her eyes and looked at him, she saw his puzzled expression and was embarrassed. She had never reacted like that to a man's kiss, as few of them as there had been. "I . . . I have to go home. Clarry will be wondering where I am."

He didn't let her go but gave her a sweet, gentle smile. "You won't forget me?"

She strove to regain control of herself. "Not in the next few minutes anyway." She was trying to hide her red face and started down the hill, but again he caught her.

"What about tomorrow? When can I see you again?"

"For supper maybe?" she said, then realized she didn't know where he was staying. "You have a job?"

"Yeah. At the Red Rooster." He dismissed it. "What about earlier? What are you going to do in the morning?"

"I'd planned to go to the lumberyard. I haven't been there since . . ."

"I'll be there then."

Laura forced a smile, then turned and like a schoolgirl,

47

ran down the hill and mounted her horse. She waved at him before setting Lady into a gallop down the dirt road.

Garrick stood on the hill smiling down at her retreating horse. He reminded himself to go more slowly, that this was one deal he didn't want to harm, gave one last look of disgust at the ruins, eerie now in the half-light, and went to the old Ford. He was already late for his first day on his new job.

"You the new singer Bertie hired?"

Garrick looked up from the sticky, scarred table to the woman standing over him. She was short and thin, her arms like pipe cleaners sticking out of her cheap rayon blouse. The light was behind her and he couldn't see her face.

"You gonna stare all day or invite me to sit down?"

"It's a free country," he said without concern. He was on his fifth beer. He hated the stuff, but for some reason the town of Montero didn't serve hard drinks on Sunday.

"You're a friendly one, ain't ya? My name's Ruby and yours is Garrick, right? Real high-class name. You make it up or you born with it?"

He gave her a level look over the half-empty glass. She was probably young under the makeup but it was impossible to be sure.

"Bertie," she yelled, "give us a couple of teas."

"Save it for somebody else," he said. "This is bad enough."

She gave him a broad wink. "You'll like this tea. Thank ya, Bertie."

As Garrick stared into the chipped china cup he knew that he was looking at a double shot of straight Scotch. For the first time he looked at Ruby with some warmth. "You're not so dumb after all, are you?"

She smiled, unoffended. "I ain't dumb at all." She lifted her cup. "Here's to you, Gary."

"It's Garrick," he said flatly.

"Oh, my, we are touchy. I guess it's from mixin' with all the high-ups of Montero."

He ignored her.

"Who you after anyway? That Clarry Taylor's the only one in town with looks to match yours." She paused but he didn't answer. "Of course the Strombergs got a daughter and they're rich. Or maybe it's somebody else. I heard you been out all afternoon with Laura Taylor, though what somebody like you would see in her is—"

"I don't think it's any of your business."

Ruby laughed. "Laura Taylor! She's nice enough, I guess, but she's sure no looker and the family's broke, too. You know the whole town's been takin' up collections to put her through art school?" She took a big drink of the Scotch and became serious. "I could make it, too, if somebody paid my way through school."

Garrick downed the last of the Scotch. It was time for him to sing again. He rose from the bench, then leaned over Ruby. "You would never make it. If someone gave up ten thousand dollars tonight, it'd be gone by morning. And who would want to give you anything? Laura's one in a million. People want to help her but the real difference is that she will succeed—whether anybody helps her or not, Laura will make it to the top."

"And just what makes you so sure? You only been here three days. You couldn't know so much about her or anybody in this town."

"I knew all about her the first time I saw her, just as I know about you. There's only one thing you can do and that's lie flat on your back and I doubt if you're particularly good at that."

Ruby was still unoffended. "You're welcome to find out."

He didn't answer her but went to the four-inch-high platform at one end of the room. The Red Rooster was a roadhouse, four miles out of town on the Taos Road. To get the job he'd had to convince the owner, Bertie, that a crooner would be good for business. At least it couldn't hurt. It was a large room, the bar along one end, booths along two walls, and tables in the center of the floor. The fourth wall had the platform where Garrick now stood beside an out-of-tune piano, the only accompaniment he had to sing with. The room was painted in a motley array of brilliant colors—a green section of wall next to a pink one, red chairs and black tables. There was no pattern. It looked as if something had been painted with whatever was on hand.

Looking out through the thick smoke, Garrick listened to the opening notes of "Stardust" and began to sing. He tried not to think about where he was. It was only temporary.

Chapter 4

Scott Stromberg gazed out the train window at the barren land. He had been told that the scrawny bushes dotting the sandscape were called trees, but he looked at them with contempt. So far nothing he had seen had interested him even mildly, or for that matter, was not repulsive to him. Dry air made his skin itch; even the inside of his nose felt as if it were cracking. He'd had to eat in his compartment because he found the conversation of the locals unbearable. They were concerned with farms and pigs, and half of them didn't even speak English very well. The place was called New Mexico but he felt the 'new' could have been omitted.

Reaching inside his worsted silk suit jacket, he pulled out a monogrammed sterling silver cigarette case. The cigarettes were from France, tipped in gold foil. They were imported expressly for his father and himself. Scott lit the cigarette, watched his reflection in the window, and tried not to think of his father and murder at the same time. The thought was too tempting. A knock on the sliding doors interrupted his musing.

The porter slid one open. "Anything else you need, Mr. Stromberg? We'll be stopping in Montero in about twenty minutes."

Scott didn't look up. He didn't like to acknowledge a servant's presence. "No. Nothing."

He was hardly aware of the door closing. Montero, New Mexico! The end of the earth, or at least his father hoped so. He figured it was a place too small for his son to get into trouble.

Scott finished the cigarette and ground the gold tip into the carpet. Maybe he had been a little crazy when he had asked his mistress to marry him. He realized that now. He saw it so clearly. She was forty-two years old, desperate, and Scott was her last hope before her looks went. If he hadn't been so irrational, he'd have seen that. But he was fool enough to think he loved her and had asked his father for permission to marry. The old man threatened to disinherit Scott. Scott talked to her, said he didn't see why they couldn't go on as before, but she—she walked out on him, laughing every minute, calling him a naive child.

Scott put his heel on the cigarette stub and ground harder. He was not a child or naive any longer. But his father wouldn't believe him and Scott couldn't tell him of his humiliation. His father still believed Scott loved her and sent him to New Mexico to a branch of the Stromberg family, a poor branch, if he remembered correctly, a fat stupid little cousin and a fat stupid aunt and uncle.

"Clarry?" the young man behind the soda fountain said. "Would you like to go out with me this Saturday night? Some of the kids are getting together for a scavenger hunt."

Before Clarry could reply, Marian answered. "Bill Matthews! I don't know how you can be so insensitive. Don't you remember where Clarry was yesterday?"

Bill's face turned red. "I'm sorry, Clarry," he said. "I'm really sorry about your father. I didn't mean to be disrespectful."

Clarry continued to sip at a strawberry shake. She nodded but didn't answer.

When Bill had gone to the other end of the counter to wait on some other customers, Marian leaned forward. "You didn't want to go, did you?"

"No." Clarry glanced out the window again. The light that signaled the train's arrival still wasn't on. "No, I thought we were going to do something together."

Marian sighed in relief. She felt comfortable only with Clarry. When she was in a group of young people, she felt awkward, out of place. Her father said it was because they were her social inferiors. Once he had started to say something bad about Clarry, but Marian had defended her friend so violently that he never attempted it again. Sometimes he raised his eyebrows when Clarry walked across a room, but he said nothing.

"Aren't you hot in that?" Marian asked. Clarry had borrowed her dark gray wool jersey knit dress. Funny how they wore the same size yet were built so differently. The clingy jersey knit molded to every curve of Clarry.

"No, it's not hot. Tell me again. You're sure your cousin's coming on today's train?"

"Yes, Clarry, you saw the letter. Look, there's the train now. Are you ready?"

"Not just yet. I think I'll stay and finish this."

Marian looked at her in disbelief. There were hardly two teaspoonsful of soda left. "I thought you couldn't wait."

Clarry concentrated on her straw, moving it idly up and down. "Why don't you go on ahead so someone will be there to meet him? Then when I'm through, I'll follow you."

Marian didn't try to understand Clarry. She picked up her purse and left the drugstore.

Clarry waited a moment until she was sure Marian was gone. Then she slowly slid off the bar stool and went to the window. She couldn't see the train station from where she stood, only the light that signaled the train's arrival. She caught herself in the reflection in the window and smoothed her perfectly arranged hair, then ran her hands down the cashmere skirt. There were no wrinkles. The seams of her silk hose were perfectly straight.

It wasn't that Clarry wasn't anxious to meet the train and Marian's cousin, but she knew better than anyone how to make an entrance. Men looked at her when she was standing still but men watched her even more when she walked. She had no intention of covering her eagerness at meeting him. She knew how men liked to feel wanted, but the first impression she made had to be one of note. She patted her hair again and left the drugstore.

Scott glanced down at his cousin. She was even more of a frump than he had imagined. She dressed like the schoolgirl she was: pleated skirt, overblouse with short, puffy sleeves. The silk did nothing to disguise her lumpy body.

The porter stood quietly beside Scott, the many suit-cases piled on the wheeled truck. As Scott listened dis-dainfully to his cousin's chatter, his attention was caught by a young woman walking toward them. She was blonde, her figure superb, and she walked slowly, with an air of sophistication and self-knowledge.

Marian noticed Scott's glance and turned. "Oh, Clarry, there you are," she called. "Come and meet him." Marian sometimes got very angry at Clarry because she moved so slowly. There were times when there was a need for speed, but nothing made Clarry hurry. "Scott," she said when Clarry stood beside her, "this is my friend, Clarry Taylor. You'll be seeing a lot of her. She's my best friend."

"How do you do, Mr. Stromberg?" Clarry said quietly and extended a gloved hand. She looked up from under the brim of a fedora, knowing the shadow over one eye gave her a mysterious look.

Scott took her hand and held it for a moment. "I'm doing a lot better than I was a moment ago."

Marian looked from one to the other. Signals were passing from her cousin to her friend that she didn't understand, but she was glad they liked each other. "I drove the car down myself. Daddy said you might like to drive around and see Montero."

Scott turned back to his cousin and released Clarry's hand. "Possibly, but I doubt it. Where is the car?"

Marian pointed to a Cadillac convertible, new, washed and polished. It was quite noticeable amid all the Fords and Chevrolets parked along the street.

He started walking, leaving the two women and the porter to follow. Marian flushed at his rudeness but Clarry didn't seem to notice. She followed him to the car. Barely were they seated in the car, Clarry in the front seat beside Scott, Marian in back with the luggage, when Scott rammed the car into low, slipped the clutch, and sent rocks and dust flying as he sped down the dirt road.

"Scott!" Marian screamed, her hands on her hair as the wind tore the careful arrangement to shreds. "You're driving too fast. Stop it at once."

He looked across at Clarry. She pulled her hat lower on her head but said nothing. "Too fast for you, Clarry?" He threw it at her as if it were a challenge.

She turned to him, her eyes sparkling. "No, I like it."

"Well, it's too fast for me," Marian shouted.

He slammed on the brakes and the two women had to catch themselves to keep from falling forward. Scott reached back to the handle of the back door and flung it open. "There's the road. Did you hear me? If you don't like my driving, you can walk."

"Walk! But this is my car."

"Not while I'm driving it. Then it's mine."

"That's ridiculous. Clarry," she protested, "tell him that what he says is stupid."

Clarry sat facing straight ahead. Scott turned to her with great curiosity. "Yes, Clarry, I'd like to hear your opinion."

A moment of silence passed before she answered. "I don't think you were driving too fast." She continued to look ahead.

Scott watched her in speculation. The profile was magnificent, her figure lush, and obviously she was going to side with him. He turned and slammed the back door, leaving Marian in the back seat bewildered by both her cousin and her friend. "All right, Little Cuz, where's your house? Let's get you there, then maybe Clarry and I can have a look at your town."

"But Daddy said—" She stopped because Scott had again started abruptly and thrown her back against the seat.

Minutes later he skidded into the Stromberg driveway. For a moment he gaped at the house. It had been built in 1911, a Victorian mansion, the second story dominated by a round tower that took up over a third of the facade. At the turn of the century, the residents of New Mexico had considered the native building materials of stone and adobe declassé. Later, with the arrival of visitors and artists, the houses that had been there for centuries returned to fashion. The majority of the Victorian houses were torn down and adobe structures built in their place. The Strombergs were one of the few families who still clung to the old belief that adobe was for the poorer class. Besides clashing with the landscape, the uninsulated house was impossible to heat in the winter and swelteringly hot in the summer.

"Ghastly," Scott said at last. The three stories of the house dwarfed the piñon trees that covered the landscape for miles behind the house. In the East, the Victorians, set amid towering oaks and elms, were beautiful, but this was a giant's house in a Lilliputian land.

"Absolutely ghastly," he repeated. "So this is the Stromberg's New Mexico outpost?"

Marian was almost too insulted to speak. She felt superior in her tall house when she looked out over the town's low flat-roofed "mud houses"—as she preferred to think of them. "Our house is not ghastly. It is the only three-story house in Montero and—"

"Let's hope so," he interrupted. "Look, can you get someone to get these bags out so we can go?"

"But Mom and Dad are waiting to see you," she said as she let herself out of the car. She stood beside his door.

"Oh, hell, forget the bags and forget mummy and daddy, too." He threw his arm across the back of the seat, and before Marian could say another word, he backed the car out of the driveway.

He had driven a mile, much too fast and having no idea where he was going, before he spoke. "Where to?"

Clarry had sat silently through the exchange between Marian and Scott. She had given no opinion nor had she formed one. All that mattered to her was who Scott was, that he was a Stromberg, that he wore a suit that had obviously been tailored expressly for him, that his shoes were of rare leathers, that he was used to the handling of expensive cars. If asked about his looks or his personality, she could not have given an opinion. She saw only what she wanted.

"Any place to get a drink around here?"

"There's a roadhouse, but I don't believe it opens until the evening."

"Don't believe, huh? I take it that means you don't go there very often."

"No." She looked at him with only a sidelong glance. She was in awe of him.

He was watching her and glancing only occasionally at the steep dirt road. He made no effort to protect the car from the many ruts and potholes. "What do you do for excitement in a town like this?"

Clarry's first thought was that mostly the people of Montero waited. At least she felt like that was all she had ever done. And what she had waited for was this man in this car.

"There was a dance three nights ago. A band from New York came and played." Even as she said it she knew it sounded naive but then men sometimes liked women to be naive.

"A New York band, huh?" Scott said mockingly. "A New York band for a dance three nights ago and a roadhouse that may be open at night. What else is there? Church socials?"

"What do you do in New York?"

"Anything. Absolutely anything on earth at any time. Just before I left we—I—went to a nightclub. You do know what that is, don't you?"

Clarry nodded, taking no insult.

"There was a man playing there and his band made Dorsey sound tame."

"Really?" Clarry asked, eyes wide.

"Really," he mimicked. "It was a man named Benny Goodman, played the clarinet. The reviewers in the papers next day blasted it, called it newfangled jazz, not fit for human ears, but—" He stopped, slammed on the brakes, and brought the car to a halt. "Good Lord, what's that?"

Clarry hadn't paid any more attention to where they were than Scott was. They were on the Old Mission Road and before them loomed the towering adobe ruins. "It's just an old mission."

"Just, the lady says," Scott said with sarcasm as he gunned the heavy Cadillac. "The thing looks bigger than all of Manhattan. That whole thing was a church?"

Clarry couldn't understand his interest or his amazement, but then she was used to New Mexico's open spaces. Scott thought of land as precious. The massive, rambling structure before them, unused and decaying, amazed him.

He stopped the car in front of the worn stone steps that led into the roofless chapel. "This must have been the church," he said quietly as he left the car, leaving Clarry to help herself out. The strength and size of the place had its effect on him. "What about the rest of the place?" He gestured to the thick adobe walls that seemed to go on for miles.

Clarry shrugged. "I don't know. I think the priests or whatever lived there." She had never liked the Mission and had rarely visited it.

In spite of his studied sophistication, Scott was only twenty years old, away from the northeastern United States for the first time, and his interest in the new sights were betraying him. "God! but this place is old."

Clarry was willing to be interested in anything Scott was. "No, I don't think so. Laura says it's because it's so young that the state won't take care of it. She says that if it were old then it would be made into a national monument and we'd have lots of tourists and Montero would be rich."

"Does she now?" He was slipping back into his role of bored passivity. "And who is Laura?"

"My sister." Clarry looked at him openly.

Scott was puzzled by her. The only woman he had ever really known was his former mistress, and her constant hauteur was what he expected from a beautiful woman. Clarry wasn't distant or disdainful. Instead of being pleased, he felt a touch of contempt. How many times had he looked at a woman just as Clarry was now looking at him? He took a step toward her. She should have retreated but she didn't. Even when his arm slid about her waist she didn't move away from him. She was ready for whatever he offered; she had decided that long ago. He kissed her without much interest; he was more interested in her reaction than in the actual kissing.

"Are there any more like you in this town?" he asked when he moved away from her, still holding her.

"No," Clarry said simply, honestly, humorlessly.

He let her go abruptly. He had found out what he wanted to know. "Let's go back to town. I assume there is a town." He ignored her as he walked past the walls to the car and Clarry followed silently. He didn't open the car door for her.

They were silent as they traveled at high speed down the narrow dirt road. Clarry was content with where she was, what she was doing. She had no idea that Scott was angry. But he saw himself in Clarry, the way he had acted too many times. The way she accepted him, without any complaints of his treatment of her, made him want to abuse her trust, as he had been abused. No wonder she— that woman—had laughed at him. He deserved it.

He brought the car to a screeching halt in the middle of flying dust and bits of asphalt. "I take it this is the center of town." The green plaza was ahead of him, cottonwood trees lazily dusting the top of an ornate white bandstand.

"Yes." Clarry smiled at him. "There's the theatre," she pointed. "And over there is—"

"Spare me. If we can't get a drink of something real, maybe a coke, then?"

"There's a drugstore across the plaza."

"Will wonders never cease? I can't believe you have running water in this place."

Clarry was silent. Again, he did not open the car door for her and she let herself out.

The townspeople were very aware of the stranger walking with Clarry. Since he drove the Stromberg's Cadillac, they had an idea who he was but they wanted to be introduced.

"Good morning, Clarry," several people called. "Nice spring day, isn't it?"

Clarry wanted to introduce Scott to them, to let them know that he was hers, but Scott walked ahead, ignoring everyone. She nodded to her friends and followed him.

The bell jingled as Scott opened the door to the drugstore to let Clarry enter before him. No one was behind the counter. Scott walked to the magazine rack and picked up a copy of *Vanity Fair*.

Bill Matthews came through the curtain that led to the back of the store. "Clarry, I didn't know you were here. Change your mind about the scavenger hunt next Saturday?"

Clarry turned her head slightly so she could see Scott. He had stopped flipping the pages of the magazine and seemed to be listening. "No, I didn't. I...I think I might be busy Saturday."

Scott began flipping the pages again.

"Oh, well, if you change your mind, let me know. Hey, I just saw Laura. You know that singer from the band last Friday? He's still here and he's been followin' Laura around like a little puppy dog. Laura's great, I'd be the first to admit it, but she's not, well, you know..." Bill's face began to turn red. "What'll you have?" he asked quickly, to cover his embarrassment.

Clarry slid onto a bar stool. "We'll just have a couple of cokes, I think."

"We?" Bill looked around the store and for the first time noticed Scott as he walked toward Clarry.

As Scott walked past her he said, "Don't you think a booth would be better?"

Obediently, Clarry followed him to a booth.

Bill stood for a moment staring at Clarry's back. He'd known her all of his life. They had been in the same grade in elementary school and, even then, the boys had lined up to be allowed to do things for her. It was Clarry who told the boys where she wanted to sit, where she wanted to go, and they fell all over themselves in obeying her. But he had never seen her follow a man before. Of course, no one in Montero had dared to try leading her. Clarry was always *the* date to take anywhere and a guy didn't dare risk offending her.

Bill remembered the cokes, then added a dash of cherry juice to Clarry's, the way she liked them. On second thought, he served two dishes of his mother's homemade ice cream, much better than the kind the drugstore usually served. He put them on an advertising tray and carried it to the booth.

Clarry looked up when Bill arrived, but Scott did not.

"I thought you and...your friend might like some ice cream, too. On the house." It wasn't generosity that made Bill serve the ice cream. On the contrary. He wanted to know who the intruder was. The gift would force an introduction.

Clarry was very aware of Bill standing and waiting but she was more aware of Scott's silence. "Thank you, Bill. That was very nice of you."

After a moment he realized that he was not going to find out who Clarry's friend was. He turned and went behind the counter.

"Admirer of yours?" Scott asked.

"More or less."

"Anybody steady?" His eyes fastened on hers.

"No one."

Scott took a sip of his coke, then looked around the table. "And how are we supposed to eat your little friend's gift?"

"I'll get some spoons," Clarry said immediately and went to the counter to ask Bill for them. She ignored his look of surprise.

"Clarry!" someone behind her said.

"Hello, Emmett."

"You remember Louise, don't you?" he asked, possessively holding a pretty young woman's arm.

"Ignore him, Clarry, he just likes to remind me constantly that I spent too much time in Dallas." She left Emmett and walked closer to Clarry, taking her hand.

"I was so sorry to hear about your father. He was a good man."

"And how is Laura taking everything?" Emmett asked, his hand on Louise's shoulder. "Is she still angry?"

"No, I don't think so. She's not going back to school."

Emmett frowned because Clarry's tone revealed how glad she was that Laura would remain in Montero. "And what's she planning to do if she stays here?"

Clarry looked down at the spoons in her hand. "I...I don't know. You'll have to excuse me. Someone's waiting for me." She turned and went back to Scott, who let her know what he thought of being kept waiting.

"Garrick, I need your help again," Laura called from the back of the warehouse.

He stopped picking at the splinters in his hands, sighed, and followed her voice. They had been working for four solid hours, making an inventory of the Taylor Lumber Company. Yesterday, when he volunteered to help her, he had had a vision of her crying on his shoulder again and of his offering comfort, but today he was sure he had never worked so hard in his life. Twice he tried to get her to take a break and turn her mind elsewhere, but she dismissed him as if he were a troublesome insect.

"Garrick!"

"I'm coming," he called in a spiteful tone. He could only see the tip of her boot sticking out of an enormous wooden rack several feet above his head. "What can I do for you?"

She stuck her head out from the stacked lumber, ran her hand through her hair, and looked a bit guilty. "I knocked the ladder down. Would you put it back for me?"

He leaned the ladder against the scaffolding and watched her agilely back down. She wore faded, baggy Levi's, a plaid cotton shirt, an ancient concho belt. He grabbed her arm when she stood beside him. "Let's take a break."

"I can't right now. I still have that rack over there to go through yet."

"Yet! Before what? What's rushing you?"

"You don't understand. I don't have that much time."

He dropped her arm. "If you're talking about that silly vow of yours, doing something within a month, then it's just that—ridiculous. This town won't let you starve. If

61

you don't find a way to support yourself within a month, they'll understand."

"But I won't understand and that's who counts. I couldn't live with myself if I were a burden to others."

Garrick started to speak but began to smile. "You're a burden to me because you're working me to death and not feeding me. You think maybe we could stop for lunch?"

She smiled, too. "I put a pot of green chili on the stove this morning. It should be ready by now."

He grimaced. "Green chili.... Sounds awful but anything's preferable to the smell of all this sawdust."

A half hour later they were seated at the kitchen table, eating grilled cheese sandwiches and green chili stew, with Garrick enjoying both. Laura studied pages on a clipboard, the inventory of the lumberyard.

"Laura," Garrick said for the third time, "will you put that away and look at me?"

She finally did, with resignation.

"Not so hard, was it?"

"I'm sorry. I know I'm not very good company but I told you this morning I wouldn't be."

"And I had no idea you meant it," he said under his breath. "Any ideas yet?" he nodded toward the clipboard.

"No, nothing special. It looks like very little has been sold in the four years I was away. There's a lot of inventory, especially framing lumber."

"Not to mention bags of cement and all that pipe," he broke in. "It looks like your father was going to build a new town."

"I think he must have started getting into the plumbing side of the business, then something happened and he was left holding the supplies with no purchasers. You ready to go back?"

"Back? Oh, Laura, surely you must be kidding. I thought maybe we'd...stay here awhile." He reached across the table and took her wrist. "Surely you can't work all the time."

A knock on the screen door made Laura pull her hand away.

"Come in," she called, starting to rise.

"Laura, is Clarry here?" Marian Stromberg walked into the kitchen. "We met Scott this morning and I haven't seen her . . . Oh!" She stopped when she saw Garrick at the table.

He nodded at her over his coffee cup.

"I didn't know you had company, Laura," Marian's voice suddenly took on a purring quality.

"Sit down, Marian," Laura said heavily, "and have some coffee. Or maybe you'd like something to eat?"

Marian didn't take her eyes off Garrick as she slid onto the kitchen chair. "No, coffee will be fine," she said in a whisper.

"Marian," Laura said sharply as she poured the coffee, "tell me about Clarry. You mentioned somebody named Scott."

"Oh, yes. Scott's my cousin." She watched Garrick as if she were in a trance.

"For heaven's sake, Garrick, put a newspaper or something over your face or I'll never get any sense out of her."

He nearly choked on his coffee and Marian's face turned a brilliant shade of red. She gave Laura what she hoped was a withering look. She was too embarrassed to even glance at Garrick. "My cousin Scott is spending the summer with us and he arrived today so Clarry and I met the train. Scott dropped me off at the house, then he and Clarry went sightseeing."

"And you haven't seen her since?" Laura was alarmed.

"Well, you know Clarry." Marian waved her hand. "She and Scott acted like they'd known each other for years."

"What kind of boy is he?"

"He's not a boy, he's a man," Marian said arrogantly. "And after all, he is my cousin."

"And Clarry's my sister."

Garrick put his hand over hers. "Laura, don't get upset. I'm sure Clarry's all right." He was sure Clarry could handle any situation involving a man. "Don't worry before you have something to worry about."

"I guess you're right. More coffee, Marian?"

"No." She stood. "I really have to be going. I came because I wanted to invite Clarry to dinner tonight, a welcome party for Scott." She seemed to have a sudden idea. "And you, too, Laura, and . . . Mr. Eastman, if he'd like to come."

"We'd love to," Garrick said before Laura could answer. "Let me walk you to the door."

63

When he returned to the kitchen, Laura was clearing the table.

"Why did you have to tell her we'd go? The Strombergs' dinners are the dullest things imaginable. And besides, I still have a lot of work to do at the lumberyard."

"But she seemed so sincere," Garrick said, his eyes dancing.

"Sincere! She asked me as a second thought and only in the hope I'd bring you for her to drool over."

He caught her waist. "You sound almost jealous," he said quietly, his face close to hers.

"I have no right to be jealous."

"What if I gave you the right?"

She pushed at him to release her but he didn't. "I don't know what you're talking about. I still hardly know you."

"When are you going to stop saying that? What is it you want to know about me? I had a boring childhood. My parents died when I was very young and I have very few cavities. Now, what else?"

She laughed as he pulled her closer into his arms. "Those aren't the things I mean. I don't know *you* very well. What's inside you? How you think?"

He kissed her briefly, softly. "What if I said I think I may be in love with you, would that make a difference?"

She stared at him, eyes wide. "Love? But how can you? We only met a few days ago and then my father—"

He put a finger on her lips. "I know. I mean to give you time. Your father's death was a shock to you, but I'm patient, I'll give you time."

She pushed away from him, put her hands on the back of the chair. "I can't think. Too many things are happening too quickly."

He held her shoulders. "Laura, I said I wouldn't rush you and I won't. I have a job in Montero and my days are free. They're yours. Let's not talk about it anymore. You have any soapsuds around here? Let's get these dishes washed. Maybe the water will soften up these damn splinters in my hands and I can get some of them out before you replenish them."

"He's wonderful, Laura," Clarry was saying again. "He's handsome and he knows all about music and—"

Laura's thoughts cut Clarry off. She smiled to herself

because she was pleased to see Clarry so excited. Never before had she shown even the slightest interest in any of the hundreds of young men swarming around her. It was good to see her happy and excited. Laura was glad that one of them had something to be happy about. Clarry had returned only an hour before from a day spent with Scott Stromberg. She apologized that he hadn't come in, but, of course, he wanted to hurry back to his aunt and uncle. Laura didn't question the fact that Scott had spent his first day in Montero with Clarry rather than with his relatives. Too often men made fools of themselves around her beautiful sister.

A knock on the door stopped Clarry's chatter.

"I wonder who that is."

Laura quickly put the comb down. "It's probably Garrick. He's going with us."

"Why does *he* have to go?" Clarry blurted.

Laura frowned in puzzlement and annoyance. Clarry's tone sounded jealous.

"You look lovely," Garrick said, then bent and gave her a quick kiss on the corner of the mouth.

Laura drew back quickly, embarrassed at his familiarity. She turned and saw Clarry standing behind her. Clarry's face was a mask, revealing nothing of what she thought.

Both Clarry and Laura wore the same dresses they had worn to the dance. Clarry had insisted they dress in their finest for Laura's meeting of Scott. Laura had second thoughts about going into public so soon after their father's death, but she was swayed by the loneliness in the house now that her father was gone and by Clarry's excitement. Never had she seen Clarry so animated.

"It looks like we're all ready," Laura said. "We might as well go." When Clarry's back was turned, she whispered to Garrick, "And get this over with."

Garrick drove the old Ford pickup through town to the south side where the Stromberg's house loomed.

"Clarry and Laura," Mrs. Stromberg said cordially but insincerely. "It was so good of you to come tonight, although I didn't really expect you since it's so soon after your father's passing."

Laura looked down at the woman. She refused to be

baited. "I'm sure dad would have expected us to go on living." She used the cliché as if she meant it.

"But, of course, dear. I'm sure you've made the right decision. And who is Clarry's new young man?" She smiled up at Garrick. Mrs. Stromberg was a vision of what Marian would be in a few years—a lumpy figure, a disdainful look for everyone.

Garrick stepped forward and gave her one of his most winning smiles. "I'm Garrick Eastman, a new resident of Montero, and I believe I'm Laura's young man."

She stopped to give Laura a look of appraisal. "Laura's?" She made no attempt to hide her surprise.

Just then Marian and her father entered the room, a man trailing slowly behind them. Laura had her first glimpse of Scott. Her initial thought was that he wasn't handsome at all, then she reminded herself that she spent much of her time looking at such perfect creatures as Garrick and Clarry. No one could compare with them. He was short and slim, blond, with a hooked nose that he seemed to look down, as if he were searing at everything around him. She found it hard to believe that this was the boy Clarry had raved about for a solid hour.

Mr. Stromberg shook hands all around and led them into the living room, where a butler served sherry. So far, Scott had not spoken to anyone, but Clarry followed him closely. "Eastman," Mr. Stromberg said, "thought you might be interested in my gun room." He had orders from his daughter to make Garrick feel welcome, one of the family. "We've got some time before dinner, so maybe you'd like to see them now."

Garrick set his glass on the mantel, winked at Laura, and left the room, Marian right behind them.

When they were gone, Scott sauntered toward Laura. "So, you're the wondrous Laura I keep hearing so much about." Before she could answer, he continued. "You certainly don't look like your sister." He watched her to see how she'd take the insult.

She looked at him squarely. "But then few of us can live up to Clarry's beauty, can we? I assume you are Mr. Scott Stromberg."

"Oh, my goodness." Mrs. Stromberg jumped up. "Didn't I introduce you? I somehow thought you already knew each other."

Laura was taller than Scott, and since she stood close to him, she had to look down. After the introductions she tried to make conversation. "Are you staying in Montero for long?"

"Only as long as necessary." He downed the last of his sherry. "Clarry," he said commandingly, "see if you can find me some more of this." He had not spoken to her before, or even looked at her.

Laura watched in fascination as Clarry obediently filled Scott's sherry glass. Still he ignored her. Clarry stood by him silently.

When Scott had taken a drink, he finally looked up at Clarry. He put his hand on her neck and caressed it, his thumb running along the collarbone.

The gesture was too intimate and embarrassing. Laura started to protest when Clarry's eyes met hers. She was startled at the warning that was clear in Clarry's look.

"Here we are again," Mr. Stromberg said. "Is dinner ready yet?"

Marian clung to Garrick's arm. She avoided looking at Laura. "Oh, mother, Garrick just loves Father's collection and he said so many witty things." She rolled her eyes up to Garrick, attempting to give a look of conspiracy. She smiled slyly at Laura, who tried to keep from laughing.

"So you're Eastman," Scott said loudly. "The band singer Marian keeps gushing about?"

"Scott!" Marian said.

"Oh, don't worry, Little Cuz, I won't give away any secrets."

Garrick gave Scott a bland look. "Yes, I sing."

Scott set his empty glass down. "Maybe you'd favor us with a song after dinner. Oh, but, of course, you will be paid—whatever you're worth."

"Dinner, madam," the butler said before anyone else could speak.

Garrick untwined Marian's arm and went to Laura. They stood together while the others went ahead of them into the dining room. "What an obnoxious little brat," Garrick said. "A spoiled little boy."

"That's what I thought, too," Laura said. "Maybe he's just angry because he doesn't want to be in New Mexico."

Garrick stared at her. "Are you always so forgiving?"

67

"I'm not sure if I am or not, but Clarry's spent more time with him than I have and she likes him."

"Clarry would like anything in hand-tailored suits."

"Garrick!" she warned. "I'll not have you saying things about Clarry."

He put up his hand. "I know. I apologize—again. Let's not quarrel, let's just go in there, eat, and get this over with."

The meal was a long one. The Strombergs had an idea of what people of their position should eat, but they had palates of cardboard. They had found a cook in California who had represented himself as a French chef. They had believed him. The food was monotonous, overcooked, undercooked and greasy. Scott never missed a chance to make a snide remark about both the food and the service.

Laura was more interested in what was going on between Scott and Clarry. Clarry's eyes never moved from him. Yet Scott ignored her, totally and completely. The more she watched the two, the angrier Laura became. As soon as the meal ended, she wanted to get away, quickly. At the door, Scott surprised her by saying he'd walk them to their car. Outside, in the dim moonlight, standing very close to Laura, he pulled Clarry to him and kissed her. Not an ordinary good-night kiss but one deep and intimate, his hands running over her body. Garrick's grip on Laura's arm kept her from breaking them apart. Scott released Clarry abruptly, then turned to Laura and gave her a snide smile before returning to the house. No one spoke.

To Laura the drive across town to their house was endless. All she could think of was what a fool Clarry was making of herself. Clarry was her responsibility and she meant to take care of this unhealthy infatuation as soon as they got home. She ignored Garrick's protest when she refused to invite him in. She didn't see his anger because her own was blinding her.

Clarry was already in her bedroom when Laura got there, her dress hung carefully away. She wore a long satin slip. She glanced up at Laura. "It was nice, wasn't it? The Strombergs give such elegant parties."

Laura was struck again at Clarry's naiveté. She was so innocent, she needed protection so badly. "Clarry, I want to talk to you."

Clarry tensed, paused for a moment before dropping the

shoe she'd removed. "I'm awfully tired right now and to-morrow Scott and I—"

"That's just what I want to talk about. Clarry," she said gently as she sat beside her sister and put her arm around her shoulders. "Just how much do you know about Scott Stromberg?"

Clarry angrily shrugged Laura's arm away and went to put her shoes in the closet. "I know all I need to know about him."

"How can you say that?" Laura's voice was still gentle. "He only arrived this morning. How could you have learned enough about him in that short time?"

Clarry turned on her sister and Laura was surprised at the anger she saw. "I knew all about him before he ever came to Montero. I knew all I need to know."

"What in the world are you talking about?" She couldn't remember ever seeing Clarry angry before. Clarry was a docile, sweet, golden-haired doll, a bit selfish at times but never angry.

"I'll tell you what I'm talking about—money. Scott Stromberg has money and I plan to get it. I plan to use any way I can, any method necessary. I'm going to have him *and* his money."

Laura was stunned. "Clarry, you can't mean what you're saying!"

"Oh, can't I? Look at you, so damned pompous. You sit there ready to tell me about my behavior tonight. Oh, yes, I saw you. I'm not as stupid as you or anybody else thinks. I may not have the brains of the wondrous Laura Taylor but I have something no one else in this town has and that's men. Young or old, fat or thin, I can have them. Any man I want and now I know which one I want."

"Stop it!" Laura stood up, her own anger rising. "I won't have you talking like...like a..."

"A whore? Is that the word you're too good and clean to say? Well, I'll be that too if it means getting out of this place. Do you know what I think of it?" She waved her hand. "This whole state you're so in love with? I hate it. I hate the land, the people. Yes, I hate everything here."

Laura felt as if someone had hit her in the stomach. She sat down on the bed. "You can't mean that."

"Oh, can't I? And you know something else, Laura? I hate you—and *your* father. Year after year I've lived in this house with the two of you and watched you, and been an outsider. The two of you always laughing together, sharing everything. I was always left out. When you decided you wanted to be a painter, you got to be one. Whatever dear Laura wants, Laura gets. Do you know what it was like while you were gone? Always begging, everything given to us, and we had to say please and thank you. All for you. Everything for you."

"But I've tried since I found out," Laura said quietly. She was too weak to say much. How could Clarry not hate her?

"Oh, yes, you've tried all right, now that you know. For years you came home and you and Dad ate a month's groceries. When you left we'd have to go begging some more or do without. And it was all for Laura. *Be sure you don't let Laura know.* I heard that hundreds of times. We were starving, yet all anybody cared about was you and your damn paints. *When's Laura's show?*"

Clarry took a deep breath. She had never let her anger out before and now it was bursting through. "Scott's a way out of here and I mean to take it. For years I've had to put up with these local hicks pawing at me, sweating on my clothes, but Scott's a gentleman and he—"

"No, Clarry," she had to protest, "he isn't. That's what I wanted to tell you. Can't you see what he's like? He's spoiled. He treats you badly." She was beginning to get some of her confidence back. She stood and walked closer to her sister. "I know it's been hard on you and I have promised I'll make it up to you. Today I inventoried the lumberyard. There's lots of material there. We'll build something and—"

"And sell it to whom? Who would want to live in this dump? Not anybody with any sense, not me, not Scott. And speaking of him, what makes you think you've a right to judge men? Look at that parasite who's latched onto you."

Laura was puzzled. "Parasite?"

"You've always been great at handing out judgments, haven't you? But you can't see the nose on your face. I'm talking about your pretty-boy singer. Did it ever occur to you to ask yourself exactly why he stayed in Montero after the dance? What does he want? Why's he hanging around you every day?"

"I...I don't know." It was amazing how little she had thought about Garrick.

"Well, maybe you should ask yourself what it is he wants. Take care of your own life before you start trying to manage mine."

"But, Clarry, I don't want to see you hurt."

"Hurt! You don't know the meaning of the word. You spend a couple of years accepting people's leftovers while your father sends every penny to his beloved daughter and see if maybe you get a clearer understanding of what it means to be hurt. And you know what's really funny? The townspeople all love *you!* You wouldn't know the meaning of sacrifice, you who've had everything—art, laughter, love. And what have I had?"

Laura's eyes were beginning to fill with tears. "People love you, Clarry."

"Who? Marian? Dad? He devoted his life to you, never mind what he did to me. He never cared."

"But he did." Laura was desperate. How could she have lived with Clarry and never have known she felt like this?

"You know what, Laura? It's made me strong. I know what I want and I'm going to get it."

"You mean Scott?"

"I mean Scott. For once I'm going to have enough money so I don't have to worry again. I'll do anything—anything. You understand? But I'll never be poor again."

Clarry was not a person of great energy. Right now she was deflating. "I'm tired. I want to go to bed now."

Laura wanted to talk. "Clarry, please." She put her hand out.

Clarry moved away. "Leave me alone. Just leave me alone." Thoroughly exhausted, Clarry flopped onto the bed. She was asleep in seconds.

Laura hesitated, her vision blurred with tears. She started to cover Clarry, an old habit, but stopped herself. She left the room, closing the door behind her.

Bit by bit, her life was falling apart. Her art gone, her father gone, and now her sister slipping away. Or maybe she had lost Clarry before the others. The idea of being alone frightened her. She could face going to a school hundreds of miles away from her home but she had always had the security of a home and people who loved her. Her family and Montero were a magnet to her. But Clarry hated her, had hated her for years. And she had a right to. That's what hurt, that Clarry was perfectly right in her hatred. Laura had been given everything.

She didn't want to stay in the house any longer. She hurried into her bedroom, changed from her dress into her Levi's and cotton shirt, a wool Mexican sweater over them. When she started the truck she had no idea where she was going, but it wasn't long before the Mission ruins came into view. Its silence, the feeling that hundreds of people had walked where she was walking, always helped, no matter her mood. She ran through the labyrinth of broken walls to the first courtyard. The cottonwoods rustled in the wind. Crickets made loud noises in the blackness. She began to cry, at first slowly, then harder. She let herself slip down to the flagstone path, her head on the stone bench, and she cried.

When the sun rose, the early light woke her. At first she didn't know where she was, then the shadows showing a weathered corbel, a horned toad looking for the first bit of sunlight, reminded her. Being at the Mission made things less awful than they had been the night before. Her face felt swollen and hot, but the sun and the atmosphere were relieving her.

Her first thought was how could Clarry hate the land? She could understand her hatred of people, but how could she hate New Mexico? To Laura it was God's Garden of Eden. Why, even Garrick had been impressed. And last night at dinner Scott had mentioned the Mission.

She straightened. What was it she had told Garrick? To the people of the East the Mission would be old, built before the American Revolution. She looked around the courtyard. How would the people she knew in Ohio look at it? They thought a house built twenty years ago was old. She stood. A lot of the students at the school had been wealthy, very wealthy. Their parents had houses all over the world. The Depression hurt millions of people but there were thousands making a fortune out of it.

She started walking, beginning to look at the ruins with new eyes. How much of a ruin was it, really? Could it be repaired? She stopped in the second courtyard. She could envision it as a dance floor, with rooms opening onto it. Everything was whirling and she put her hands on her

72

head as if to steady it. "Think, Laura, think!" she whispered. A guest ranch. Why hadn't someone seen it before?

She went into the friars' rooms. Each one was large, often with a storage area attached. "Bathrooms," she said aloud and thought of all the toilets stacked in the lumberyard. She stopped and leaned against the adobe wall. The Mission nestled against the National Forest—hunting and fishing. There was skiing in Taos and Santa Fe. Tennis courts! There was plenty of land.

She walked outside, then began to run. There was a stone granary, the top of it carried off by the wind. The old orchard was a tangle of weeds, the trees half dead from lack of care, but with pruning...

"A guest ranch." She said it softly at first, then louder, until she was shouting and whirling around and around. A guest ranch!

Chapter 5

Laura limped along the trail, the reins to the horse in one hand, her hat in the other. She wondered if she had ever been so tired in her life. Four miles back, Lady had stepped into a pothole, and Laura, half asleep in the sun, had slid out of the saddle and landed on the ground with a bone-shattering thud. She stood up, dusted herself off, then started walking. She was sure she was closer to the cabin than to the town, so she plodded on. Now she sat down on a rock, rubbed her sore calf muscles, and looked over the surrounding land. She could hear a stream running somewhere in the distance, swollen with water washing down from the melting snow on the mountains. The forest was quiet and she felt like an intruder, as if there were thousands of eyes watching her.

Lady whinnied. Laura pulled the reins and stroked the horse's soft nose. "I know, girl. Quiet," she soothed, feeling that Lady was as nervous as she. She liked the forest, had lived near it all her life, but she'd never been so completely alone in it before. Camping trips had been with her father or a group of girls. Now, with the sun just about to set and the gradual change in sounds brought on by the coming of night, she wanted to get back on her horse and return to town. But she knew she wouldn't do that; she couldn't.

Three days had passed since that awful night when Clarry screamed that she hated her sister. Later that night, Laura had had the idea of creating a guest ranch of the old mission. So many things had happened since. Clarry pretended nothing had been said. The next morning she kissed Laura's cheek and smiled at her, then went on to talk about what a delightful man Scott was. Laura sat and listened, more stunned than anything. She never doubted that the things Clarry had said the night before were true; she knew they were. And now Clarry acted as if she were challenging Laura to say anything against

Scott. She was flaunting him to her older sister. Laura could see Clarry's side, that she thought Scott and his money could keep her from the poverty she had known and feared, but Laura could also see Scott, himself.

She couldn't imagine the pompous little Scott Stromberg marrying anyone from a remote mountain town in New Mexico. But Laura didn't dare say this to Clarry. She didn't think she could handle hearing Clarry tell her again that she hated her. She could let herself associate the awful words with the darkness, but if Clarry said them in the bright daylight... No, Clarry was right, and she knew she deserved every hateful word.

For three days the weight of her responsibility had pressed down on her. She began to feel that her father's death, Clarry's insane adoration of the arrogant Scott, and the reality of no longer being in art school were all her own fault. In a way, she felt that the punishment for her four years in art school was having to give up art. She hadn't felt that way before. Even after her father's death, when she had said a lot of noble words about giving up school, she hadn't believed she would really have to. That's why she hadn't written the letter to the Jules M. Grey Gallery. But she did write it after Clarry's outburst. Clarry's words of hate had made her see the truth. Her sister had given up a great deal for her. Now it was Laura's turn to sacrifice for her sister. She was going to make up for the past to Clarry, or die trying.

She stood now and started walking again. The light was getting dimmer, and she knew that before long she wouldn't be able to see her way. She didn't let herself think about what might or might not be waiting for her at the end of the trail. She had done a lot of growing up in the last few days. The Laura Taylor of a week ago wouldn't have set out on an all-day trip on horseback to a man's cabin deep in the National Forest; this new Laura was. She needed this man and she was going to do her best to get him.

The night she had gone to the Old Mission and first thought of the guest ranch, the idea seemed to have dropped from heaven. It was the answer to all her problems—how to repay the people of Montero, how to give Clarry the security she needed to prevent her from seeking a man like Scott. It was a way to get money to continue her art. The next day, the fragile dream shattered.

She went first to the Montero National Bank and explained it patiently, containing her excitement, to the president, Mr. Greene. When she finished, he sat quietly for a moment before answering.

"Laura," he said with great patience. "All in all, it sounds like a fine idea, and if someone had come to me with it before the Crash, I might have been willing to gamble, but—"

"Gamble!" Laura interrupted. "It's not a gamble! The easterners would love the Mission."

"I'm sure you're right and I agree *that* part wouldn't be a gamble. What would be is the loaning of money for *any* reason right now. And you're not talking about a few hundred dollars—you're talking about thousands."

"But most of the structure is already there. Surely it couldn't cost too much."

"There's plumbing and—"

"I have fixtures, pipe, lumber, tools, everything we need at the lumberyard."

He paused. "Who is *we,* Laura? You and Clarry? I can see you in the forest with a chain saw cutting down trees for *vigas,* but what about Clarry?" Laura started to interrupt him again, but he put up his hand. "This is a business, Laura, and I have to look at it as such. Before I could loan you any money, I'd need collateral, and of course that would have to be the lumberyard. Now, if you use the supplies for the building, then that leaves me with nothing but those two warehouses and the shop. Not exactly worth the amount you want me to give you. And another thing, you have no idea how much you need or even what you need to make the Mission into a guest ranch. You come in here with some lovely ideas but nothing concrete. You have no plans for renovation, no contractor to run the work for you, no labor to do the building. All you have is a dream and a stack of bathroom fixtures." He hesitated, then continued. "I'm sorry to be so blunt but you'll have to learn that there's a great distance between a dream and reality."

Laura returned to the present. A great distance between a dream and a reality. For the next few days after talking to Mr. Greene, she began to see what a distance it was.

She drove two hundred miles south to Albuquerque and talked to the president of the bank that owned the Mission land. The bank would be glad to get rid of the property. Laura had to sit through the banker's barely concealed smirks when she talked about making it into a guest ranch. Clearly, he thought her too young and too inexperienced to be able to carry off a project the size of the one she was talking about. On the long drive back to Montero, Laura wavered between frustrating tears and teeth-gritting determination.

In both talks with the bankers, she learned only two things of importance. One was that the bank would be glad to unload the Old Mission. Since the Depression, they had had to foreclose on hundreds of pieces of property so they were willing to sell any of it for ridiculously low prices. The second was that the bank was quite willing to trade for the land. Laura was aware that everyone traded for everything since the Depression. A carpenter would fix his neighbor's door in trade for a bushel of garden produce, or a lawyer would make a will for someone in trade for new shoes for his children. But she had thought the banks would be exempt. When she left the bank, the president had escorted her to the door, and she noticed the paintings by local artists on the wall. The president began to explain that they had been taken on trade for land. He hinted rather strongly that he was a good judge of art and that the paintings would someday be worth much more than the land.

Laura didn't say anything then. She wanted to think for some time before she carried out the drastic plan that had occurred to her. She thought about it all that night. She was frightened by the finality of what she planned but she also knew that once she did it she would go forward. No longer would she continue to consider the possibility of making the showing at the Grey Gallery.

The next morning she loaded every painting she had into the truck. She kept nothing. She took every letter, every award, every newspaper clipping she had ever saved and put them into a large envelope. She dressed carefully, a severely tailored suit, a fedora, the brim tilted over one eye. She wanted to look older than her twenty-two years, a woman who knew her business. Today her business was to sell herself and her talent. She meant to convince the

77

Albuquerque bank president that she was an artist of unusual talent and recognition, that her paintings were worth a great deal. She tucked a piece of canvas over the paintings to protect them and started the long drive. All the way she refused to let herself think that she was selling her life's blood or that she was giving up something that meant as much as life itself to her. She had to do it. And she did it.

Later, she was amazed at herself. She had raved to the bank president about her talent and her future. Overriding any objection he had, she soon had him agreeing that her portraits were magnificent. He almost agreed that she was doing him a favor. In the end she walked away with the deed to the mission and twelve acres of what the banker considered worthless land in a dying town. Both were sure they had come out ahead on the exchange.

Clarry was appalled when Laura showed her the deed to the Mission and told her the ideas she had. For some reason, Clarry seemed frightened by Laura's purchase of the land. She said little; in fact, she had said surprisingly little since the Strombergs' dinner, but she looked at Laura as if Laura had lost her mind.

Now that Laura owned the Mission, she went back to Mr. Greene at the Montero bank. He said Laura's ownership didn't change a thing, that she was still inadequately prepared. She began asking people about a builder. She knew most of the contractors in Montero from the years she'd spent in her father's office, but none of them felt confident in taking on what they called Laura's harebrained project. They agreed it was a good idea but they had families to support and they couldn't walk away from them just to take a stab at Laura's Mission, as it began to be called around town. And Laura couldn't pay them. She had no money to hire a contractor, and no contractor meant no money from the bank.

It was Mr. Martinez, her father's foreman, who first mentioned Ross Kenyon. "I think he used to live in Albuquerque, but he bought a place in the forest a few years back and lives up there alone now."

"And he's a builder?" Laura asked.

"From what I hear, he may be one of the best builders in the Southwest. When the Depression hit, I guess he just retired rather than fight it."

"Retired? Then he must be old."

"About forty-five, I guess. I only saw him once. Ask over at the IGA, somebody will know. He comes in for groceries every now and then."

It took Laura a day to find out anything about Ross Kenyon. It was amazing how a town the size of Montero could know so little about one of its residents. But then Kenyon was considered a newcomer, and since he kept to himself, no one was really interested. Laura had driven to the forest supervisor's office and he had shown her a contour map which gave the location of Kenyon's cabin.

And that's where Laura was going now. She had gotten lost once, then Lady had thrown her, or rather *dumped* her, to be exact. And now it was getting dark, but she was determined to find the man who could help her. It was her last hope for making the guest ranch.

She almost ran into the wall of the cabin before she saw it. It was bigger than she had expected, but the natural stone and the skinned logs blended so well with the darkened landscape that it was difficult to see. She tied Lady to a porch post and knocked on the door, but no one answered. "Hello," she called out as she opened the wooden latch and entered the cabin. It was one enormous room and she could barely see the outlines of furniture. Inside the cabin was even cooler than outside. An enormous stone fireplace took up the narrow end of the rectangular building. She felt like an intruder, but she warned herself that now was not the time for timidity. She knelt to put a match to the wood and shavings. The dry logs caught instantly. The fire was much better than any she had ever built.

From the light of the fire she could see the interior of the cabin. It was neat and clean with pine furniture, fat pillows covered in Mexican cotton, sheepskins everywhere. In one corner of the cabin was a kitchen, separated from the rest of the room by a long, maple-topped counter. An enormous galvanized tank held water over the enameled sink. Laura tried to form an opinion of the man who lived in this place but she couldn't. She was too nervous. She worried about how he was going to feel about her intrusion. On the back of the big wood stove sat a pot of pinto beans, generously laced with chunks of meat. To keep busy, she put more logs in the stove, stirred the beans, and began to look for the ingredients for corn bread.

79

Ross Kenyon smelled the smoke from his cabin from a long way off. It wasn't unusual for a ranger to stop and spend the night. He enjoyed the company, as long as it wasn't too often. But as he approached the cabin he saw an unfamiliar horse. It was a fat horse, more used to city ways than the long climb to the cabin. Still, the horse didn't deserve to be left standing in its own sweat, still saddled. More as a reflex than a conscious thought, he unsaddled his own horse and his guest's, wiped them down, and led them to the shed in the back. It was too late now for his visitor to return to town.

When Laura heard the front door open, she was bent over the oven door, just removing an iron spider filled with hot, golden brown corn bread. She stood and turned quickly, the hot pan in her hand. For a moment she just looked at him. He was a heavy man, his arms well muscled from many years of construction. His face was weathered by sun and wind and he looked every bit of his forty-eight years. He wore a sheepskin vest over a heavy wool shirt, Levi's and a thick leather belt. Two dead rabbits were slung over his shoulder.

The heat from the iron pan began to burn her through the pot holder. "Ow!" she yelped and quickly dropped the pan onto the counter top. "I . . . I made some corn bread," she said nervously. "I hope you like corn bread."

He walked to the counter and tossed the rabbits on top of it. "I take it you're from town. Get lost?" His voice was slow and deep.

She liked him. He had a way about him that made her feel comfortable. He reminded her of someone, but she couldn't think of whom. She smiled at him across the counter. They were the same height. "You are Ross Kenyon, aren't you?"

"Yes." His eyes were very alive, though he did not return her smile. "And you are—?"

She extended her hand to him. "I'm Laura Taylor." His hand was hard, calloused. The fear she had felt at meeting this man was rapidly leaving her. "I didn't get lost. I came all the way up here to see you. Are you hungry? The beans and chili are hot and so's the corn bread. I thought maybe we'd eat while—" She suddenly stopped. "I mean, that is, if you don't mind. After all, I have invited myself."

A hint of a smile appeared in his eyes. "I'll let you know

after I taste your corn bread." He was true to his word and only spoke again after he had started to eat. "You didn't come up here just to cook my supper, so tell me what's on your mind."

She talked through their meal. She talked to him as she hadn't talked to Clarry, Garrick, or even to herself. She was able to sort things out as she talked, to put them in order.

"So now you own the Mission," he said as she finished.

"As of yesterday."

"And you did this before you were sure you could get the work done?"

She looked down at the last of the beans on her plate. She had been hasty. She looked up again. "That's why I came to you. I heard you were the best builder in the Southwest. Together we could build it."

"*Together*, is it? I'm not sure you know what you're getting into. You need subcontractors, supplies and a heavy labor force."

"Half the men in Montero are out of work, and now that school's out we can get some kids to help make adobes. I own two warehouses full of supplies."

He liked her enthusiasm. Of course she had no idea what she was taking on. "And who's going to pay these people?"

Laura always came to this stumbling block. "I don't know. I don't have a cent. Mr. Greene at the bank hinted that he might give me some money if I got a builder to back me."

"No bank anywhere is loaning money," he said flatly.

She stared at him. "What about you? Do you have any money?"

He waited a while before answering. "Yes, I have money, but I'm not sure I'm willing to dump it into a long shot like this. Who knows if anybody will want to visit this place?"

"I'll take care of that. You can leave it to me. If you'll be my partner, I'll make sure we have guests."

"Partner?" He shook his head at her. "Are you always like this? You haven't known me more than an hour but you're asking me to go into partnership with you. You really ought to think things out a little more before you rush into them."

Laura suddenly realized that this man reminded her of her father. His steadiness, his offer of advice, made her realize how right she had been in asking him to be her partner. "No, I'm not usually like this," she said honestly. "I have spent a life of selfishness and now I have quite a few debts that need to be paid. I know I must sound like a scatterbrain, but I *have* to do something to earn some money and I really don't know what else to do. I don't have much in the way of assets but I have a good brain and I can work, as hard as necessary. I really believe in this project and I believe you're the one to help me. If not, I'll...Truthfully, Mr. Kenyon, I don't know what I'll do but I plan to make every effort on earth to build this guest ranch."

Ross watched her for a moment, then went to the fireplace mantel, took his pipe and packed it. "Have you ever done any drafting?"

"You mean with a T-square and triangle?"

"Exactly."

"I did some in high school but not much since."

"Think you can brush up on it?"

She began to smile, seeing where he was heading. "If I can get on a horse and ride to the middle of the forest to meet a man I never saw before and ask him to be my partner, then drafting's going to be a cinch."

For the first time he smiled back at her.

Laura thought again how much he was like her father, but Ross's view of Laura was far from fatherly.

She made a pot of strong coffee and went to get the inventory she had made of the lumberyard. When she found Ross had taken care of her horse, he endeared himself more. For the first time in many days, since the night of the dance, things were beginning to look up.

The two of them spread the inventory on a big pine table before the fire and reviewed it. Ross talked of supplies they would need that weren't included in the warehouses. They made lists of possible workers. Laura wanted to include first the people who had helped pay her tuition.

It was late when Laura began yawning. Ross removed the back cushions from the couch and gave her some blankets. He had to laugh to himself at Laura's trusting nature. In spite of himself, he was almost eager to build again. He had spent three years in nearly complete solitude, seeing only an occasional forest ranger. The prospect of taking on a project the size of the Mission and working with this young girl, who seemed to think the cares of the world were her responsibility, was exciting. It had been a long time since he had looked forward to anything at all.

Ruby turned her head so she could look at Garrick. He was sitting up in the bed, a cigarette in one hand, a full whiskey glass in the other. It wasn't the first night she had spent with him. If she'd made a guess about what kind of lover he'd be, she would have been right. She'd had worse, but then again she'd had a lot better. She thought it had something to do with his looks—handsome men rarely made good lovers; they were too used to adoration to give much to anyone else.

She raised herself on one elbow. "What time is it?"

"What do you care?"

She turned over and sat up, pulling the sheet under her thin arms. "No reason. It just seemed early." She looked around him to the clock. "It *is* early. How come you're not with your virginal Miss Taylor tonight?"

He didn't respond to the jibe.

"Oh, yes." Ruby smiled at him in the half-light. "Somebody said she was spendin' the night in the woods with some man." She couldn't resist baiting him. His smug coolness asked for it.

"This is the goddamndest town! Isn't there anything private?"

Ruby was startled. She had made an effort to find out about the whole Taylor family. She had heard Laura was trying to find a builder for some wild notion about the Old Mission, but she was making up the part about spending the night. She smiled to herself. "You know, I saw that man Kenyon once. Not at all bad-lookin'. Sometimes those older men are great in the sack."

Garrick threw back the cover and stalked across the room naked. She had an idea he had done the same thing in lots of women's rooms. She watched him refilling his glass. "What is it about her anyway? She's not good-lookin'. She's not rich. As far as I can tell she's got nothin' worth havin'."

Garrick faced her. "That's where you're wrong. You hear about her buying that Old Mission?"

"Sure. Who hasn't? Everybody in town is laughin'. 'Laura's pile of mud.' Who'd want it but a fool?"

"You're the fool and everybody else is too if they don't believe in her. She's going to do just what she says she'll do. She's going to turn that place into a guest ranch, one of the richest places on earth. People from all over the world will travel here to this little hick town, just to go to Laura's *mud pile* as you call it. Movie stars, ranchers, politicians, anybody rich and famous. And my dear Laura is going to sit back and rake in the dough." He lifted his glass. "And yours truly is going to be right there helping her."

Ruby frowned at him. "What makes you so sure? I heard she didn't have a chance."

"You heard! Since when did you believe anything you heard? I knew from the moment I saw her she was headed up."

"And you decided to hang onto the kite string?"

"Now you're beginning to understand."

"If she's so smart, what makes you think she'd want somebody like you? Why wouldn't she hold out for a millionaire of her own?"

He finished the last of the whiskey and poured another glassful. "Because I don't plan to give her a chance. I'm going to have Miss Laura Taylor hook, line and sinker before she ever meets a millionaire or a movie star or whatever."

"Pretty sure of yourself, ain't ya?"

"Look, I've been carrying this face for twenty-eight years. I know what it can do. I've missed a lot of chances before but I'm not going to miss this one."

"And after you get her, then what? You gonna settle down in Montero and raise babies? Somehow I can't see you dangling a kid on your knee."

"Not any under seventeen anyway."

"You know, I almost pity her. She gets her dream of a guest ranch but she gets a lifetime of puttin' up with you."

He frowned at her. "You can get out any time you want."

"Not me. But then I ain't like her. I ain't wantin' a man who'll come home every night, who'll stay off the booze. Somehow I don't think she's gonna like findin' out she's been used. A woman like that—"

"Shut up! Nobody asked you your opinion. There's only

84

one thing in life I know about and that's women. You just keep your opinions to yourself and I'll handle my women. Now, either lay down or get out."

Ruby stopped talking and obeyed him but she wondered if he knew women as well as he thought he did.

"Sixteen feet, two and five-eighths inches," Ross called to Laura.

She dutifully recorded the numbers, then marked out the five-eighths inch. It hadn't taken her long to realize that Ross was a perfectionist, but she had no intention of trying to convert the five-eighths inch down to the quarter-inch scale she'd be using on the drawing. They had left Ross's cabin very early, too early for Laura's taste, ridden straight to the Mission, and had started measuring.

First, they had to draw a plan of the Mission as it was. After the measurements were taken, Laura would make a drawing to scale and Ross would use that time to return to the forest with a few men and cut down tall, straight trees that had to be skinned and dried for the *vigas*. The trees could dry while the adobes were going up. Now she was trying to sketch an approximation of the contours of the walls and mark the numbers Ross yelled at her as fast as she could. He was being quiet and efficient, and expected Laura to be the same way.

Suddenly someone kissed the back of her neck. She was so startled she jumped, dropping her pad of grid paper and her pencil.

"Garrick!" she gasped as she whirled and saw him. She held her hand on her neck as if a bee had stung her. "You nearly scared me to death."

He reached out and grabbed her wrist, pulling it away from her neck, then he pulled her into his arms. "I think you've been avoiding me," he said, his face buried in her neck, his teeth running along her skin.

"I...I don't think so. I've been busy."

"Too busy for me?" he asked as he began to kiss her mouth. He watched her, made sure she was responding. He moved and pulled her closer to him. "Miss me?"

She couldn't help her thoughts, but she had missed him. Since the night Clarry had gotten angry and thrown Garrick up to her, she had avoided him. For a while she tried not to think of him but she couldn't stop. What Clarry had said had to be wrong. What did she have that any man could want? Did Clarry think he was after her for her money or for her looks?

"Yes," she said wonderingly, "I did miss you." She had been cautious with him before but she had so little to lose and everything to gain by returning this man's love.

"Laura!"

Abruptly, she dropped her arms from Garrick's neck. She didn't see his frown as she turned toward Ross.

"Oh, excuse me," he said as he looked at Garrick.

"I would like you two to meet. Ross, this is Garrick Eastman, a...friend of mine."

Garrick wanted to meet Ross after what Ruby had said about him. He saw an old man. "Glad to meet you...sir," he said as he held out his hand. He wanted to let Ross know where he stood. "But, Laura, I think we're more than friends."

Ross watched the two of them, Laura blushing, Garrick, flawlessly handsome, holding onto her in a possessive way. "You want to take off for the day?"

"No, I want to work while there's still light." She moved away from Garrick, picking up her pad and pencil. "I have to go now. Maybe I'll see you later."

He didn't mind her working. He had other things to do. "How about if I bring supper out here tonight? It's my night off."

"Yes. That would be nice."

He bent and gave her a quick kiss.

She stood and watched him leave through the maze of the Mission walls.

"He your boyfriend?"

She turned back to Ross. The two of them had made no personal remarks to each other. "I guess so. I haven't known him very long. He sings at the roadhouse on the Taos Road."

Ross arched one eyebrow. "That so? Glad he does something for a living. For a minute I thought he was a hood ornament."

Laura blinked twice, then began to choke on her laughter. It was such a fitting description of Garrick. "I rather think he's like ice cream—not especially nutritious but oh, so delicious." Suddenly she was embarrassed and felt like a traitor, but what she had said was true. She just never put it into words before. She didn't look up at Ross again.

He grunted as he went back to his measuring. "Wonder if anybody could live on a diet of ice cream?" he mumbled just before he called out another number.

"What's your sister doing lately?" Scott asked Clarry. "Marian keeps talking about how she bought that old place we went to on the first day."

Clarry didn't want to talk about it. Everywhere she went, someone made a snide remark about "Laura's mud pile." When Clarry first heard the phrase, she was horrified. She had had faith in Laura, that she would do *something*, but buying that awful Mission was a waste.

"She plans to make a guest ranch out of it."

"Not a bad idea if she can pull it off. My mother spends a month every year at some resort in Northern California."

"Tell me about your mother."

Scott gave her a look of contempt. That first day when he had met Clarry, he had been flattered that she so clearly was attracted to him. After all, she was incredibly beautiful. Right now she was lying on her back, languorously stretched out on a quilt spread on the forest floor. Her soft, shapely body was revealed completely under the thin silk dress that he knew was Marian's.

But after that first day, his vanity stepped aside and his reason took over. He made an effort to find out about the Taylor family. Clarry and her sister were poor, dirt poor, and it was easy to figure out why Clarry was so interested in Scott. At first it made him angry. One woman had used him and now a second one was trying. He thought of dropping her cold, but the more he thought of Clarry, the more he thought of the woman who had been his mistress. When he had loved her, she had stuck a knife in him. He felt like Clarry could be his revenge. He planned to make Clarry fall in love with him and then leave her, but the girl was impossible. No matter what he did or said he got no real response.

"Scott?" Clarry asked. "What were you thinking?"

"Are you sure you want to know?"

"Of course. I want to know everything about you. I love you."

She had said it many times before. "Do you, Clarry? Do you love anything at all?"

Her eyes widened in an appealing way. "What an awful thing to say. I love you and I love my sister and I loved my father."

"What about your mother?"

"I hardly knew her. She was always in and out of hospitals."

He didn't believe her, or at least he didn't think he believed her. He had been in New Mexico hardly a week but he could feel himself changing. He had never been away from home before, from his family and his friends. He had planned to be so aloof from everyone in New Mexico, as if he could punish them for the anger he felt. But now he was beginning to regret his earlier actions. He had alienated everyone, everyone except Clarry, and even with her, or maybe especially with her, he felt so alone. He didn't know whether he loved or hated her.

Nothing seemed to get a response from her. On his second night in Montero, he drove her to Taos, rented a room in a travel court. Clarry never said one word, either in complaint or encouragement. He wanted to humiliate her, as he had been humiliated. In the room, he demanded that she remove her clothes and lie down on the bed. He knew she was a virgin but she obeyed without a flicker of emotion. He made love to her, much more gently than he had intended, but he was the one who felt like crying. He felt sorry for himself. Poor little rich boy. Been to bed with two women and the only thing either of them cared about was his money.

He stretched out beside her, put his arm around her, and pulled her close. "What are you thinking about?" he whispered against her neck.

"About us. What else is there to think about?"

He moved his hand down to her breast. He forgot his loneliness. He was young; she was beautiful and willing.

"We did almost half of the measurements today," Laura said, her mouth full of the fried chicken Garrick had brought. She washed it down with a swallow of sweetish wine. "Ross says that a full day tomorrow and we should have it done."

"Ross says!" Garrick said in disgust. "For somebody who
88

doesn't talk very much, he sure says a lot. Or maybe you just repeat every word he says. By the way, what did the two of you do last night in his cabin?"

"Do?" Laura gaped at him.

"Yes. Do!" Garrick was losing his temper. "Don't tell me he didn't make a pass at you. He's not that old."

Laura glared at him in the darkness. They sat on the hill overlooking the ruins. She threw the chicken down and stood up. "You're disgusting."

Instantly he was beside her, putting his arms around her as she tried to push away. "I'm sorry, Laura. I can't help it. I'm just jealous of everyone around you."

"Jealous? Of Ross?"

"Of anybody. I told you I love you. Laura, please sit down again. I really wanted to talk to you tonight."

She didn't know what to think of Garrick's declarations of love. She'd never been one to daydream of dragons and helpless maidens. Those stories would have disgusted her. She believed people, men or women, created their own destinies. Garrick's avowals of love bewildered her. She hadn't the time or the leisure to sort out her own feelings.

"What did you want to talk about?" she asked as she sat down again.

"I'd like you to marry me," he said quietly.

She was astonished. Marriage had never entered into her plans for her life. But then her plans had meant for her to be an artist.

"Don't look at me as if I'd lost my mind. People do get married, you know. In fact, eventually nearly everyone does."

"It's just that I hadn't thought of it before."

He took her hand. "Of course not. You've never met the right man before, not someone who loves you and who you love."

"But how would we live? Where would we live?"

He chuckled softly and kissed her hand. "My dear practical Laura. A man at your feet declaring undying love for you and you think of ways of making a living." He squeezed her hand. "But I wouldn't have you any other way. In fact, that's one of the things I love about you. To answer you, we'll live just as we are now. I'll continue singing at the roadhouse and you'll work on your Mission. Since you own a house and I don't, I'll move in with you. The only difference really will be the nights." He moved closer to her. "We'll spend all our nights together."

When Laura didn't answer, he took her silence for encouragement. He gathered her into his arms and began to kiss her. She responded, not as he wished, but some. He began to lower her to the quilt, his thigh moving along hers.

Laura was an innocent when it came to sex or even love, for that matter. She liked Garrick's kisses, liked the feel of his slim body along hers, but it began to frighten her, too. She was frightened of losing control and of the unknown.

She moved her face away from his. "No, please. Don't," she murmured. "Let me go. Please, Garrick."

His instinct was to slap her. Damn little bitch! Always telling him no, always taking the upper hand with him. He had never asked a woman to marry him before, although several had asked him. He controlled his emotions. There would be time later to show her who was the man.

"Of course," he said gently. "I didn't mean to rush you. It's just that—" He grinned crookedly at her. "Well, you're a very desirable woman, Laura."

She sat up, smiled timidly back at him but she didn't want to look at him. She wondered if she were normal. Maybe the only thing she was good for was painting pictures and running a lumberyard. What was wrong with her that she couldn't respond properly to the moonlight and a handsome man who said constantly he loved her?

Ross Kenyon stood as a silent observer to the little scene on the quilt. He sensed, more than saw, the man's anger when Laura pushed him away. Once he almost stepped forward, as if to protect her, but he stopped himself.

The last thing he wanted was to become involved again. He had enough memories haunting him, too many hurts, too much guilt. He liked the girl Laura, but not enough to take on any responsibility. Responsibility was the last thing he wanted out of life. He turned silently and walked away into the woods. The trees and the animals were the only thing he wanted. People and their problems only led to trouble and he had had more than enough of that in his life.

Chapter 6

For the next month, Laura worked harder than she ever had in her life. During the day she shoveled dirt through a screen, then mixed it with straw and water, poured it into a form, and set the adobes to dry in the sun. Hundreds of adobes, thousands of adobes. At night, her shoulders aching, she bent over a makeshift drafting table, a board propped on top of the kitchen table. She was constantly with Ross. After she finished the drawing of the Mission as it was, she used a transparent overlay and began making changes. Ross talked endlessly about such things as traffic patterns and the grouping of plumbing. Laura began to see how much she didn't know. There were storage problems, gas lines, fire exits, septic tanks, and above all, an incredible, extensive plumbing system. She soon learned that a bathroom was a great deal more than a few porcelain fixtures in a small room.

Yet she enjoyed it all. She felt less helpless than she had; she was more in control of herself again. Ross's patience was something she needed and came to depend on. He never belittled her lack of knowledge but always first listened to what were sometimes impossible schemes. Then he showed her why her ideas wouldn't work. She designed an aesthetically pleasing kitchen; he showed her how the door couldn't be used while the refrigerator was open. Then she designed beautiful cabinets that he proved would take months to build and be impossible to clean. Yet he never made her feel foolish.

They rarely talked about anything personal and never about Ross's life, either past or present. The first time Ross saw Clarry, he studied her with dispassionate honesty. Clarry barely looked at him, then went to her room.

"I take it she's your sister?" he asked Laura. "The one you're doing all this for?"

"More or less. I also owe a lot to the people of Montero."

"Laura," he said, hesitating, "nobody at twenty-two owes the world as much as you think you do. You just plain haven't had time to accumulate so many debts."

She didn't answer him. She didn't know how much he knew but obviously it wasn't enough or he would agree about her debts. And she was worried about Clarry, who spent altogether too much time with Scott Stromberg. Sometimes Clarry wouldn't get home from a date until the early hours of the morning. Laura would be so tired from a 14-hour day at the Mission that she wouldn't have the energy for the talk she knew she should have with her little sister. Clarry seemed strained since Scott had come to Montero. She had never been given to much humor but now even the little she had seemed to be gone. She seemed intent on one goal in life and she was going after it. In a way she was as dedicated to her project of acquiring Scott as Laura was to renovating the Mission. Laura hoped she was wrong in what she saw. Clarry's anger that night had frightened her more than she wanted to admit. She wanted to trust her sister, feel confident that Clarry knew what she was doing.

The more Laura worked, the less she saw Garrick. She was pleased with his marriage proposal, but the truth was she was too tired and too involved with the renovation of the Mission to give him much thought. She had no idea how this affected the singer, how his anger toward her was building daily. She saw only his sweetest side, but each day Garrick's sense of urgency about Laura increased. He saw her growing attachment to Ross Kenyon, even if she didn't. The two of them were constantly together. She quoted him at every opportunity.

And the more Garrick watched Laura, the more he drank.

Laura was right about Clarry's dedication. In fact, in the last month, she had become obsessed with Scott Stromberg. Never in her life had she had to go after a man, they had always come to her. And now that she wanted someone, she was surprisingly uneducated as to how to go about it. She watched him constantly, studied what he liked, what he seemed to want in a woman. If he admired an actress's hair, Clarry would attempt to copy the style. If he looked at a dress in a magazine for longer than usual, she badgered Marian into purchasing one like it. She had no qualms about using Marian. Clarry had tunnel vision; she saw only one thing ahead and that was Scott. She pursued that goal blindly. She blocked out all the things in her life that frightened her, that brought back memories of a past she couldn't bear to think of. Scott was her way to get away from the poverty and she zeroed in on the single goal of becoming his wife, of making herself indispensable to him. It never occurred to her that he wouldn't want her. There was nothing she couldn't, wouldn't or didn't do for him and she meant to have him at all costs.

"Oh, Marian," Laura said as she walked into the kitchen. "You startled me." She was tired from a long day at the Mission. Ross had put her in a supervisory position and she wasn't at all sure she liked it. He had more faith in her than she had in herself. "Clarry isn't here." Clarry was rarely at home anymore.

Marian looked down at her hands and shook her head. She held a long envelope tightly.

Laura suddenly realized that Marian was crying. She sat down beside her and asked quietly, "What is it? Is someone at your house ill?"

Marian only shook her head.

"Clarry! Has something happened to Clarry?"

She managed to whisper, "No."

Laura felt too tired to play Marian's game of charades. "Do you want to leave a message for Clarry? I'll tell her whatever you want when she gets back."

Marian put her head on her arms and began to cry seriously. "Oh, Laura, it's so awful. It's just so awful. Scott's my cousin, my own cousin. And Clarry's the only friend I ever had. How could they?"

Laura stared for a moment, then took the envelope from Marian's hand. It was a letter from a travel court in Taos. It seemed an earring had been left in Mr. Stromberg's room and they were returning it. The letter was dated nearly a month ago. Laura knew immediately whose earring it was and who had been wearing it. In a way she felt she had asked for it. She had been so busy with her own problems and with the Mission that she had left Clarry too much on her own. A young man like Scott could have easily swayed Clarry. Clarry had no one to turn to for guidance. "Are they together now?" she asked.

"I don't know. I haven't seen much of Clarry since Scott came here. They're always together, always going away in the car." She sat up and sniffed, wiped her eyes. "I tried to tell Clarry, but she—"

"Do you have any idea where they are?" Laura interrupted. She clutched Marian's arm tightly.

"None. Laura, you're hurting me. I thought Clarry might be here. I told you I never see her anymore."

Laura dropped her arm. "I'm going to your house. Maybe your mother will know." She left the room, Marian still at the kitchen table.

Mrs. Stromberg was annoyed at the way Laura demanded to know the whereabouts of Scott and again she wished Marian wouldn't associate with such people. Laura was filthy in her denims, adobe mud in her hair, on her face. When she finally told Laura that Scott was in the garden, Laura didn't even thank her, just took off in that horrible unladylike stride of hers.

"Well, if it isn't the phantom sister," Scott said cheerfully when he saw Laura. "I hear a great deal about you, but for all I see you, you might be a ghost."

Laura thrust the crumpled letter at him. "What do you have to say about this?"

He looked at it but he didn't touch it. "So, little cousin has been snooping through my things. Look, I'm sorry you had to find out."

If Laura hadn't been so angry, she would have been surprised at his statement. "Sorry!" she said. "You're sorry! So you admit what you've done to my sister." She sat down in one of Mrs. Stromberg's lacy wrought iron chairs. "My sister is ruined, destroyed, and you're sorry!"

"Don't take on so. You sound like a bad actor in a melodrama."

"Bad—" She glared at him. "Ever so smug, aren't you? Big New York City man. What does it matter to you about the peons in the lower sections of the country? After all, they're poor. They couldn't have the same feelings as a rich 'white' man. That's what it is, isn't it? The plantation owner's right to his slaves."

Scott drew himself up. He knew he couldn't defend himself to her. "Of course. You don't think it was anything else, do you?"

She raised her fist at him, tears in her eyes, then she dropped it again in her lap. She bent forward, trying to control her sobs.

Scott stood over her a moment, watching her shoulders shake. She was right, he thought. He reached to his inside pocket, withdrew his cigarette case and a gold-tipped cigarette. As he tried to light it he realized his hands were shaking. He had thought of Clarry with revenge, but he had found revenge an empty emotion. As empty as Clarry's words was her lovemaking. He had been so angry at his father for sending him to New Mexico, and angry at himself for being under twenty-one, not legally a man. He was beginning to realize that it took more than age to make a man.

He tossed the cigarette to the ground, crushed it. It was time he faced some of his responsibilities rather than run away from them. He sat down by Laura. "You're right in everything you said," he said quietly. "I was angry when I came here and Clarry was available. I took my anger out on her."

Laura turned and looked at him, beginning to see something besides an arrogant boy.

"I've been wrong." He looked out across the green garden into the piñon trees. He gave a small smile. "I don't guess I've ever said that before. I think I've always felt my money gave me a right to whatever I wanted, but the time I've spent out here—" He stopped and looked at her. "There's no need for you to listen to my problems. Clarry says she loves me. If you like, I'll marry her." He waited for her answer.

"*Does* she love you?"

He slowly removed another cigarette from the case. When it was lit, he spoke again. "No, I don't believe so. You may not like the truth, but I believe Clarry only loves my money. I think she thought that by going to bed with me it would force me to marry her."

It was Laura's turn to look away. For a full minute she didn't breathe. She knew he was right. "Do you love her?"

"No," he said honestly. "She's beautiful, she always wants to please me, but no, I don't love her."

"Yet you'd be willing to marry her?" She looked back at him.

"Laura, I know quite a bit about you. My aunt and uncle talk about you a great deal. And I've learned a lot from you. If I'd been in art school and as good as they say you are, I'd have continued. No one on earth would have stopped me. Yet you gave it up to stay here and work. I hear you have fifteen people from Montero employed on that Mission of yours. And I know you stayed here for Clarry, too. You must love her a great deal."

"Yes. I do. I've been as much of a mother to her as a sister."

He bent forward, put his hand over hers. "I would give a great deal to have a sister like you—or a mother or a wife for that matter." He looked at her mud-begrimed face. "I almost wish—" He stopped, then leaned back against the chair arm, inhaling deeply on the cigarette. "So where do we go from here? Am I what you want for dear Clarry?"

She was beginning to get some of her reason back. "A loveless marriage? How long would that last? How long before you'd be seeing other women and Clarry would— I don't know what Clarry would do. I don't think she knows herself. She thinks that getting a rich husband would solve all her problems, but she can never think past the wedding ceremony. What about five years later? What would you talk about? What do the two of you have in common?"

"About the same as my parents, absolutely nothing. And they've made it together for twenty-five years."

"Are they happy?"

He tossed the cigarette away. "No, they aren't."

"Is that what you want?"

"I didn't think that was what you wanted. You said I'd ruined Clarry, destroyed her was the way I believe you put it."

She leaned back against the cold iron of the bench. "I'm so tired. I don't know what I mean or say. Realistically, you're right. This is 1935, not the Middle Ages. Of course she's not destroyed. It was the shock of it all and feeling it was my fault for leaving her alone so much."

"Leaving her alone? You do sound like her mother. You're what? Four years older than her? You shouldn't feel so responsible for her."

"Now you sound like Garrick. Maybe I shouldn't but I do. You were right, we have to decide what to do now."

"We? Shouldn't we ask Clarry what she wants?" he asked.

"I know what Clarry will say if you tell her you will marry her. She'd jump at the chance and two lives would be ruined, and maybe mine since I could have prevented the inevitable."

"What makes you so positive we'd be so miserably unhappy? There's always a chance."

She glared at him. "Everyone thinks I'm stupid when it comes to Clarry but I'm not. I know what she's like. I've always known. She's...she's really very simple, more of a child than a woman. In school she did just enough to get by, nothing ever creative or extraordinary, yet she did the best she could. There's a nursery story that always reminded me of Clarry. It was about a young girl who had several geese which she loved very much. These geese were her whole life. So for Christmas she wanted to give them a feast and gifts and a big tree, but she couldn't afford it. Since the only thing of any value she owned were the geese, she sold them and bought everything for the party. Only on Christmas morning, when she woke up alone, did she realize what she'd done. The story was called "The Girl Who Could Think Of Only One Thing At A Time.'"

They were silent for a while.

"Yes, I do think you know her. You think that if she marries me she will someday wake up and find she has her Christmas tree but the things she loves will be missing?"

"Yes. Clarry needs someone who will adore her. I don't think she could handle anger."

Scott smiled at her in irony. "You don't see me as the patient, doting husband, do you?"

"No." Laura wasn't in a mood to smile.

"Laura," he said quietly, "if you make this decision for Clarry, how's she going to feel about it? Do you think she's going to thank you?"

Laura stood up and walked a few steps away, her back to him. "I don't want to think about it. I have two alternatives. I could let her marry you, then stand back and watch her fall apart, disintegrate, inch by inch. Or I could prevent her marriage and watch her hate me. Of course she'll hate me anyway if she marries you and finds herself miserable. She'll say I should have stopped her."

He moved to stand beside her. "I don't envy you."

"I don't envy myself either." There were tears in her eyes again.

"So what are you going to do?"

"I'm going to lose either way, aren't I? All I can do is hope maybe she'll find someone who will love her and make her happy, then..."

Laura was taller than Scott and larger than he liked a woman to be, but he pulled her into his arms. "I'm sorry. I can't say it enough and I know it means nothing. You've taught me a lot and all I've done is complicate your life. Now all I can do is try to help in some way. Don't tell Clarry anything about today, about the letter from the travel court or that you talked to me. Tonight I'll talk to her. I'll be such a heel you'll never believe it. And tomorrow I'll leave. I can face my father now. I'm sure of that. Clarry will be hurt but at least she'll not hate you. She'll hate me and I'll be hundreds of miles away."

She moved her face away from his cheek. "You'd do that?"

"I owe you that much."

She hugged him tighter and Scott thought that large women weren't so bad after all. And that's how Clarry saw them, from the door of the house across the length of the garden.

Laura sat up late that night, nervous about what she had seen when Clarry returned from her date with Scott. She had trusted him when they talked, but now, alone, she wasn't so sure. If he told Clarry the truth, Clarry would hate her sister—more than she did already. Yet Laura knew it was for her own good.

When the screen door slammed, Laura jumped, her nerves frayed. "Clarry?" she called somewhat timidly. There was no answer, so she went to the kitchen. It was empty. Clarry was in her bedroom, slowly removing her clothes. Laura wasn't sure what she had expected but ordinary behavior was not it. "Are you all right?"

Clarry didn't look at her sister as she carefully hung Marian's dress away. "Why shouldn't I be?"

Laura couldn't tell her what she knew about Scott. "No

reason, really. We've hardly seen each other much lately. I thought we might talk."

Clarry looked at her sister, her eyes devoid of any emotion. "It's late and I'm tired, so if you don't mind I think I'll go to bed. Besides, don't you have a lot of work to do at your Mission?"

"Yes, of course I do, but—?"

"Then maybe you ought to get some sleep, too."

Laura knew she had been dismissed. Maybe she had been wrong about Clarry's attachment to Scott. Maybe she wasn't so dead set on catching a rich husband after all. Laura went to bed, worried, but relieved at Clarry's lack of hysterics. For some reason she'd expected accusations about what she and Scott had plotted against Clarry. But nothing happened.

A month passed and Laura began to relax. Clarry's lack of anger, the little time they saw each other, and the tremendous amount of physical labor Laura was doing made her too tired to spend much time worrying about anything. Marian told her Scott had left the day after they had read the letter. Otherwise, she would not have known it, because Clarry never mentioned Scott. Laura tried to get Clarry interested in the progress at the Mission, but Clarry either wouldn't go or went and sat silently on a bench while Laura worked. Laura's guilt over her sister's lethargy increased. After a hard day of lifting flagstone slabs, she went home, cleaned the house for Clarry, then made her a nice supper. Yet nothing seemed to lift Clarry from her daze.

The work, combined with her attempts to rouse Clarry, gave Laura little time for anything else. She was on her hands and knees, marking the position of the flagstones in a guest room floor when Garrick walked up behind her. He ran his hand along the side of her neck in an almost painful way.

She turned and smiled up at him.

"What are you doing now?" he sneered.

"The tiles have to be taken up for the plumbing, then replaced exactly as they were, so they have to be marked first."

"How very interesting."

She was beginning to get used to his sarcasm. She had been infatuated with him at first, and with the fact that such a handsome man was paying attention to her. But lately she found that she wasn't pleased to see him. Right now she could smell liquor on his breath. That was becoming a common occurrence also.

He reached out, encircled her waist, and pulled her close.

She pushed at him. "Please, Garrick. Leave me alone. I have work to do."

"Work! You always have work to do. You never have any time for me."

She thought he sounded like a spoiled child.

"Who is it? That Ross you're so fond of? Is he the one you want?"

She pushed harder but he didn't release her. She began to suspect that he was drunk. "Ross and I work together. That's all. I have to go back to work."

He put his hand on the back of her neck and began to pull her face toward his. She struggled against him. "No woman's ever turned me down. You hear me? No woman's ever—"

"Laura!"

Garrick stopped when he heard Ross's voice.

"Laura, are you all right?"

She felt her face turning red. She pushed away from Garrick, smoothed her hair.

Garrick gave one angry look at Ross, then left the little room.

Ross went to Laura. "Did he hurt you?"

"No, of course not. He was just..." She didn't know what to say.

"He was drunk and you know it. It's none of my business but why do you put up with him? One of the men said you were going to marry him."

She occasionally forgot how everyone in Montero knew everyone else's business. She sat down on an adobe *banco* along one wall of the room. "I don't know what I'm going to do. He asked me."

"And that's reason enough to get married, just because he asked you?"

"No, I guess not, but then I don't see many men pounding my door down with marriage proposals."

"A bunch of fools then," he murmured.

She laughed. She was beginning to get over her embarrassment. "That's what I think and my father thought, but look at me, I'm old maid material if there ever was. Always a bridesmaid but never a bride. Who'd want a wife who could lay adobe and run a crew of fifteen men? Every time I see Mr. Greene at the bank he shakes his head at me, then hurries into his office as if he were afraid of me. Men like sweet soft women like Clarry, not truck drivers like me."

"Will you stop it! I've never heard you like this before. What's wrong with you? Why this barrage of self-abuse?"

She forced herself to smile at him. "Don't get me started on my problems or I'll flood us out of here. There's nothing wrong with me. A sublimely handsome young man wants to marry me and I don't want to marry him but I can't for the life of me figure out why. My sister is sweet and loving toward me but I somehow get the impression she hates me. And I'm so tired all I want to do is sleep."

"Does marriage mean so much to you?" he asked quietly. "I thought women didn't mind having a career these days."

"Maybe I'm just greedy but I want it all, a career, a husband and a whole houseful of kids."

He stared at her for a moment. "I think you could handle them, too."

"Sure," she said angrily. "Laura can handle anything. Laura can do anything she wants to do. She can—" She broke off when Ross walked away from her.

"When you quit feeling sorry for yourself, you can go back to work. There are three more rooms to do before the light goes." He walked out the door.

Laura realized immediately he was right. She turned and went back to marking the flagstone floor.

Garrick brought the old pickup truck to a screeching halt on the dusty, rutted road. Clarry was walking beside the road, her walk and figure unmistakable. Ordinarily, he would have passed her but today he stopped, threw the door open to her. "Want a ride?"

Silently she got in beside him. When he started again, he took the flask from his coat pocket and offered it to her. She accepted, taking a drink of the cheap whiskey as if she were used to it.

"Had some practice, huh?" Garrick asked, looking from
101

her to the road. He glanced at her body. "You know, you look different somehow. Or maybe you're just looking better to me."

"Better than what? Dear sister Laura?"

"Ah ha! Do I detect a touch of sarcasm in your tone? I thought you'd be grateful for the supreme sacrifices of your dear sister."

"What sacrifices? That mud palace of hers? Don't let her fool you. She loves it. Everybody in town talks about what a martyr she is, giving up her art school for poor dumb Clarry. I wish she'd gone back to art school!"

She said the last so vehemently that Garrick gave a low whistle. "I thought you didn't want her to go."

She took the flask from the seat, took another drink. "I thought she'd make things better but all she's done is ruin my life."

"I didn't know you had much of a life. Here, give me that before you drink it all. How'd Laura ruin your life?"

"It doesn't matter. It's not anybody's business but my own. But she's going to pay for it. I swear she'll pay for it."

"And how do you propose to do that? Blow up that ranch of hers?"

"I wouldn't know how," she said seriously.

Garrick was startled. "You really do hate her, don't you?"

Clarry didn't answer his question. Something else occurred to her. She turned toward him. "Is she in love with you?" she asked pointedly.

Garrick's pride wouldn't let him be honest. "Sure. Most women are," he grinned. The drink was making Clarry look better and better. "She's going to marry me."

Clarry looked back at the dusty road. "Scott was going to marry me until she stepped in."

He wanted to laugh. So that's what she was angry about. She was a fool if she thought Scott Stromberg would marry a small town girl like her. But he wasn't about to say so. He was beginning to see where Clarry's thoughts were headed. It wasn't difficult.

He stopped the truck. "So now you want to get back at her for doing whatever she's done to come between you and Scott?" A plan of his own was starting to form. He had known for some time that Laura wasn't going to marry

102

him, and as the guest ranch began to take shape, he could see the money it would bring slipping away from him. "Clarry, honey, maybe we can work out something."

But Clarry wasn't about to let anyone in on her plans. She wanted to hurt Laura in the same way Laura had hurt her. For a month she lived in the same house with her sister, and her hatred had taken on a single-minded purpose. She wanted revenge. She heard Garrick's questions but she didn't answer him. She had never confided her problems to anyone and she wasn't about to start now. Garrick said Laura loved him. That's all that mattered to her. She had loved Scott and Laura had taken him away from her. Now Clarry was going to take Garrick away from Laura.

When Laura drove into the driveway that night and saw Garrick's old truck parked by the house, she frowned. It had been an especially long day and she hadn't yet forgiven him for his drunken actions of the morning. But as she started toward the house she began to smile. Poor Marian still drooled at the very sight of Garrick and here Laura was regretting that he was visiting her.

Inside, the house was dark and at first it seemed silent. Then she heard a noise from the end of the hall, toward Clarry's bedroom. It seemed like a long walk to the half-open bedroom door. She heard the low murmurs of a man, a voice that had become familiar to her over the last couple of months. She wanted to turn around and leave the house but she couldn't.

Slowly, she pushed the door open. Garrick looked around in surprise. The sheet had fallen away from his dark shoulders and back. He had a sleepy, half-lidded look that made him even more handsome. Beneath him Clarry looked up at her sister—in triumph. That look hurt Laura more than finding her sister in bed with a man.

"Laura," Garrick said, his voice slurred, obviously by drunkenness. "Look, we—"

She turned away without waiting to hear any more. She was in the truck before she realized where she was going. She turned automatically toward the Old Mission Road, but this time it was Ross she sought.

Chapter 7

Laura had no idea what she expected when she reached the Mission but when she saw Ross outlined in the moonlight, she felt a surge of relief sweep through her. He was strong, solid, dependable, something she needed now.

He turned when he heard her running toward him. He rose, and opened his arms to her. Her heart was beating madly. "What's wrong?" he asked as he ran his hand across the side of her face. "Has something happened?" He hadn't realized how much this vulnerable young girl had come to mean to him. He had watched her for a month, saw her daily do the work of three men, saw her torn apart by her lazy, selfish little sister, seen the drunken Garrick hound her constantly.

"Laura, honey, what's wrong?" His shirt was by the stream and he wanted desperately to put it on, but her tears were beginning to wet his shoulder. Hiding his scars was secondary to Laura's problems.

He knew her well enough to know that self-indulgence was not for her. He held her away from him. "All right, Laura, let's sit down and I want you to talk to me and tell me what's wrong."

She sniffed. "Clarry, she's—oh, Ross, it's so awful!"

Ross had doubts that anything Clarry did could be worse than what he thought her capable of. Too many times he had seen her sulking around the Mission, too lazy and snobbish to lend a hand to her overworked sister. Laura looked so forlorn right now that he wanted to smile. At twenty-two, nearly everything seemed like a catastrophe. But at forty-eight, Ross knew that rarely was anything as bad as it first seemed.

They sat down and he pulled her against his chest, holding her close to him as much for his own pleasure as for her comfort. "Now start at the beginning and tell me what happened."

"Scott," she whispered. "Clarry's angry about Scott."

"Then tell me about him."

She was glad for the release. She had had no one to talk to since her father died and Ross was so much like him. Her story was disorganized and at times incoherent but she told him everything.

"And you and Scott decided what was good for Clarry?" he asked.

"But she doesn't know. At least I don't think she does."

"I'd be willing to bet she does. There isn't much that's a secret in this town. You said Mrs. Stromberg was there. Maybe Marian was, too. Or even Clarry herself. Any number of people could have seen you talking to Scott. And it wouldn't be hard to figure out what was said since he left town the next day."

"But Clarry would think—"

"Clarry would think that you'd kept her from marrying him, which is exactly what you did."

"But it was for her own good!" she defended herself.

"Laura, everyone on earth has certain rights and one of those rights is to make his own mistakes."

"But Clarry would have been miserable."

"How can you be sure of that? I've lived a lot longer than you have and I've seen stranger marriages work."

"But Scott didn't love her."

"Laura, I'm on your side. You don't have to defend yourself to me. You're in a mess now because you tried to play God with someone else's life and you had no right to do that."

She lay quietly against his bare shoulder. She realized he was right. How like her father he was. If her father had been alive, she would have sought his advice and taken it.

She was no longer crying and she saw the moonlight cast strange shadows on Ross's other shoulder. She touched the shadows but they were rough. The odd light was caused by scars, great thick striated scars covering Ross's shoulder. She pulled back from him to look at his face. His eyes were calm. She saw that all of his chest, shoulders, and, she assumed, his back, were marked. "How...?"

She looked back at his face. He moved away. The moment of intimacy was broken.

Quickly, he took his shirt from the ground and put it

105

on. "It's a long story." His tone left no room for further questions. "Come on in the Mission and I'll make some coffee. We can plan tomorrow's work while you're here."

He walked ahead, leaving Laura to follow or stay as she pleased. She followed, slowly.

He had already set the coffeepot on the Coleman stove by the time she got there. The air between them was heavy.

"Ross, I'm sorry. I didn't mean to offend you. I guess I've lived in Montero too long and I think everyone's business is my own."

He didn't answer her or absolve her, as she needed. She felt herself start to cry again. She had found a friend and lost him all in the space of a few hours.

He glanced at her, then stopped, astonished. "You really do take on the responsibilities of the world, don't you? Sit down and drink this while it's hot. It'll do you good."

She obeyed him, watched him as he turned away.

"There was a fire," he said so quietly that Laura wasn't sure at first that she heard him. "I was drunk, as usual, and smoking in bed, also as usual. The house caught on fire and unfortunately I was saved. My wife and daughter burned to death. Sometimes, on very quiet nights, I can still hear their screams."

He stopped, as if he wanted to say more but didn't dare. He turned and looked back at her. "I was a young man who played with others' lives also. Sometimes we're let off easily but sometimes the price is more than we can handle."

She knew better than to say she was sorry. He wouldn't like that. "And you never remarried?" she finally asked.

"Unlike you, responsibility is something I want to avoid. More coffee?"

She held out her cup to him. "It must have been a long time ago. Yet you still feel it was your fault?"

"Feel!" he said angrily. "It *was* my fault. I was constantly drunk, just like that boyfriend of yours. She'd be alive today and my daughter would be . . . your age, I guess. If I hadn't killed them."

Laura set her cup down and went to stand beside him, her hand on his arm. "Maybe I am your daughter." She tried to smile. She would try anything to take away some of the hurt.

Suddenly his mood did change but not the way she

expected. His eyes were bright in the dim light. "It's never crossed my mind to be your father, Laura."

His arm went around her waist, and when he brought his mouth down on hers, she found herself clinging to him, returning his kiss. He was not like Garrick, playing her emotions for what they were worth. Ross gave as much as he took.

She was out of breath when he moved away from her and began to kiss her neck. He was what she needed— strength, understanding, love. "I love you, Ross," she murmured. "I love you."

Only the slightest hesitation in his movements let her know he had heard her. She remembered Clarry in bed with Garrick, how Clarry had spent nights with Scott. What was it like? What was it like to have a man love you, want you? She moved her head and sought his mouth again, this time with passion.

He put his hands on the side of her head, looked at her in question.

"Please," she whispered. "Let me stay with you tonight."

He stared at her for what seemed to Laura a long time. He nodded finally, bent and lifted her into his arms. He carried her outside the ruins into the cool night air, into the dark sweet-smelling forest.

When Laura arrived at her house the next morning, an idiotically sweet smile on her face, the first person she saw was Garrick. There were dark smudges under his eyes, as if he hadn't slept in days. She didn't want to see him or think about the time she had last seen him. All she wanted to do was take a shower, eat an enormous breakfast, and go back to Ross.

"Laura," Garrick began almost before she was in the house. "I want to explain about last night."

"There's nothing to explain." It didn't take long to lose her euphoria. "It was none of my business."

"None of your business! Your sister and your fiance in bed together and you say it was none of your business!" He was losing his caution.

Laura swallowed hard, determined not to allow him to hurt her. "My sister, yes, but we're not still engaged, if we ever were."

Garrick stared at her in anger. Then, as he began to realize he was defeated he knew there was no longer any reason to play up to her. There was a way he could still get what he wanted from her. "Did you know your baby sister is pregnant?"

Laura's face lost all its color.

He took her arm, extremely pleased with her reaction. "Maybe we'd better sit down in the living room." He led her to the couch, and when she was seated, he went to a cabinet along the wall, took out a bottle of whiskey and a glass. He filled it, then went to sit beside her.

"Is it your child?" Laura asked.

"No. I imagine it belongs to that Stromberg brat. That's probably why he left."

"No," she said as she looked down at her hands.

Garrick watched her as he drank the whiskey. So she did have something to do with Scott's leaving, just as Clarry said, he thought. "So what are you going to do now? Baby sister's pregnant with no sight of a husband anywhere."

"I don't know," she said quickly. She had been so happy after the night spent with Ross.

"I have a proposition to make," Garrick said as he drained the glass. "I figure it's going to be pretty hard to find a husband for Clarry, at least one who'd take the responsibility of another man's child. So I thought I might take her off your hands."

"You? You mean you want to marry Clarry?"

"Possibly. For a price."

"A price! You want me to pay you to marry Clarry?"

"Now you're beginning to understand."

"But what do I have? How could I pay you even if I agreed? And what about Clarry? Does she love you? Do you love her?"

He went to the cabinet and refilled his glass. "When are you going to get your head out of the sand and stop daydreaming about love? Is that why you got Scott to leave town, because he was fooling with your sister and didn't love her?" He laughed when she looked so guilty. "Don't you understand that Clarry's never going to love anyone but Clarry?"

"As Garrick is never going to love anyone but Garrick?"

He raised his glass to her. "*Touché*. That's why I think
108

Clarry and I would make an ideal couple. Neither of us would need the other. All we'd need would be a little of your money."

"Money!" She stood up. "I don't know where you got the idea I was rich, but right now Clarry and I are living on Ross's money."

"Laura, you underestimate yourself. You have an air about you that says you're someone special, different. And that air includes the look of money. I recognized it the first time I saw you."

She sat down, heavily. "And that's why you were first interested in me?" she said flatly.

"Of course. What other reason could there have been?"

She didn't like to think how much his words hurt. "So you want me to pay you from any money I make in the future?"

"Yes. Let's say thirty-three percent of the profits of the Mission."

She didn't agree to his scheme. "I have to talk to Clarry and see what she wants."

"Then you can agree right now," Clarry stated as she walked across the room and slid her arm around Garrick's waist. "I love him," she said defiantly.

Garrick looked down at her in surprise, then he understood. She thought Laura loved him and she thought she was taking him away from her older sister. If she could ever look at anything from more than one angle, she would see that she was only hurting herself. He couldn't care less. As long as he got Laura's agreement—on paper—he didn't care what happened to Clarry, or to the bastard she was carrying.

When Ross awoke the next morning, his first thought was that something was wrong. He lifted himself on one elbow, then smiled at the indentation in the pine needles beside him. Laura. He thought of her sweet young skin, her eagerness to please, to learn. But as soon as he remembered the night, he thought of what the day would bring. She was too young and too innocent to accept what had happened as a mere tumble. She would think of marriage and a permanent relationship. And he wasn't ready for that again.

He had been miserable while he was married before.

109

He hated the idea of someone always waiting for him. He hated not being free, the idea of being part of a couple rather than a whole unto himself. Suddenly, he felt closed in by the adobe ruins at the foot of the hill. Laura knew what was to be done for the next few days. He had taught her how to supervise the subcontractors and the high school boys who worked as laborers.

He had to get away, be alone for a while. "Enselmo," he called to the man just leaving his truck, ready to begin the day's work. "I'll be gone for a few days. Laura will handle everything while I'm gone. If you have any problems just stop and go on to something else until I get back."

Enselmo nodded in agreement, but Ross was already walking toward the granary that was being converted to riding stables. He kept his horse there.

"What do you mean, he's gone?" Laura asked for the third time.

Enselmo patiently repeated what Ross had said to him. Laura knew his leaving had to do with her, and she began to look back with bitterness on what had been a wondrous night. Ross did not return in a few days. Weeks passed and still he did not return.

And those weeks taught Laura some vital lessons in self-reliance. She had no one to turn to for help in decisions, yet she found she could survive on her own. She used the subcontractors' knowledge of building to help her with the Mission and she became very good at giving orders. She could command respect from the men, settle disputes, act as a go-between for abrasive personalities. She began to see herself as a more complete person rather than a struggling, helpless art student.

Each day she spent at the Mission, alone, unsupported, made her see her homelife more clearly. She was able to talk to Clarry without feeling crushed and wounded when Clarry looked at her with cold, hard eyes. She never went as far as to talk about Scott, but it was understood between them that Clarry knew. Laura offered to send Clarry away so she could have her baby but Clarry was adamant about marrying Garrick. Laura knew they would be unhappy and told Clarry so, but Clarry seemed to become more firm in her resolution every time Laura talked to her.

Clarry Taylor and Garrick Eastman were married in
110

late July 1935, and went to live in Clarry's and Laura's house. It didn't take long for anyone to realize what a mistake the marriage had been.

Clarry, who had always slept a great deal, saw no reason to change now that she was married. It got to be a habit that Garrick waited each night for Laura.

"Hard day?" he asked as she collapsed on a kitchen chair.

"No worse than usual," she said as she dropped her head in her hands.

He stood behind her, massaged her shoulders, felt her begin to relax. Lately he had been drinking very little, and as much as she hated to admit, Laura enjoyed these quiet times alone with him.

"Have you heard from Ross?"

"No," she said as she began to tense up again. "And I don't expect to. I'm afraid I scared him off for good."

He ran his hand up the side of her neck. "How could you scare anyone, Laura?" he asked quietly.

She moved her head away from his hands.

He turned away from her, went to the refrigerator and brought out a cold pitcher. "Margueritas," he said as he held it up to her.

Laura had never drunk much in her life. She had always been too busy living to want to lose a moment to the blur of alcohol. But in the last month, between her anger at Ross, her fatigue, and night after night hearing the quiet sounds from Clarry's bedroom, she had begun to enjoy the strong, sweetish drinks Garrick prepared for her.

In the living room he smiled at her. "You look more down than usual." He poured her a glass of the Margueritas, tart with lime and icy cold. "Tell me what you're doing at the mission now," he urged.

She hadn't eaten since noon and the tequila hit her stomach hard. She began to feel relaxed, the weariness slipping away from her. Garrick had lit candles about the room and now she stared at his handsome face. If things had worked out differently, he would be her husband now and not Clarry's. As she drank more tequila she began to wonder exactly what it was that had made her decide not to marry him.

"Are you going to answer me?" he asked softly as he smiled at her.

111

"Oh, yes." She sat on the floor, leaning back against the cushions of the couch. "Today we started on the kiva. The walls have to be relaid, some of the stones have fallen out and in a few days I have to engineer a round roof. That should be interesting since I have absolutely no idea how to go about it."

He refilled her glass, moving so that he sat beside her. "That would be Ross's job, wouldn't it?"

"It would be." She looked at him. "I don't want to talk about him."

"What do you want to talk about?"

The drink was making everything fuzzy. "I'm not sure I want to talk at all."

She turned her head away but he put his hand on her cheek and made her look at him again. "You're changing, Laura. I can see it every day. It seems like it started when Ross left. Did he hurt you?"

She glared at him. "What do you care? What does anybody care? You have thirty-three percent safely in writing. Clarry has the man she loves and a baby on the way and Ross is free. All of you have what you want, so what does it matter about me?"

"It matters to me, Laura," he said softly.

Later, she didn't know exactly what happened. One minute they were talking and the next minute she was in his arms. Clothes were shed quickly and Laura didn't know whether it was her loneliness, the liquor or her pent-up desires but she and Garrick made love passionately that night. She forgot who she was, who he was. All she knew was that for a moment she was not alone.

Two days later, Ross returned to the Mission. Laura arrived early, before the men, to find him peering down into the enormous stone-walled pit that was the kiva. For a moment she stood and stared at him, feeling that her heart had jumped into her throat. She took several deep breaths to try and calm herself. For the last few days she had lived in a sea of remorse over what she and Garrick had done. One night she even slept at the Mission, afraid to go home, afraid of what she might do again. Her loneliness was more than she could handle.

Now, as she watched Ross, she forced herself to smile. She walked toward him briskly, clipboard in hand. "Welcome back," she called cheerfully. "You're just in time. I have no idea how to put a roof over this. One of the men said it had to be calculated according to the weight of the dirt on top and how many people would be walking on it. I looked in the library but I couldn't find anything on it. Of course, I don't know how we could guess the number of people who'll be walking on it or their weight. I mean twenty fat people wouldn't be the same as twenty skinny people."

"Stop it!" he commanded.

She obeyed him. A few months ago she might have cried at his sharp words but now she faced him defiantly.

Ross saw immediately what he had lost. She wasn't the same young girl he had left. She had grown up a lot, experienced a lot of pain in a short time. "I want to talk to you."

"I'm listening," she said flatly.

"I know you must think I deserted you and I guess I did, but I needed time to think."

"How nice. I'd like a month alone somewhere to think, too, but I have work to do."

He gave her a half smile. "Still angry?"

"Why should I be? You deserved a vacation." She started to walk away but he caught her arm.

"You frightened me, Laura. I'm old enough to be your father and I should know better, but you frightened me. I told you I was afraid of responsibility and I meant it, yet you asked me to be responsible for more than myself."

"I didn't ask anything of you."

"You did, whether you know it or not. You said you loved me, and when someone loves you, it is a duty to the loved one."

"I'm sorry I bothered you. Now let me go so I can get back to work."

"Laura, will you stop being so hostile? I came back to tell you that I love you, too. And if you don't mind having an old man for a husband, I'd like you to marry me."

She stood and stared at him but didn't answer.

"Are you going to let your pride stand in your way or were you lying when you said you loved me?"

She was angry that he had left her alone, angry because she blamed her loneliness on what had happened between Garrick and herself. But she did love him. "Yes," she said slowly. "I'll marry you."

113

He grabbed her hand and started pulling her toward the truck.

"Where are we going?"

"To wake up the court clerk and get a license, what else?"

She grinned at his back and hurried after him.

They were married three days later and nine months later a daughter, Julia, was born.

Garrick counted the months and wondered whose child Julia was. Sometimes he thought he saw a resemblance in the little girl to his own family.

PART II
1946

Chapter 8

Six men sat at the long walnut table. The walls of the large office were paneled in the same walnut. Every eye was focused on the map at the end of the room and on the man who was pointing to a spot in northern New Mexico. Before the men were booklets describing the proposed venture, an American playland.

Since the end of the war there had been a boom in business. The men coming home wanted peace and families. They felt they had seen all the action they needed and now they wanted to settle down, raise children, and do all the things families do together.

Industry was watching this trend and knew there was money to be made. Middle-class America was creating a new industry—tourism. Vacations were being written into workers' contracts.

These six men had pooled every cent they could find on the hope that they could gain something from this new tourism. They had formed a syndicate for the express purpose of creating a kind of playland the world had never seen before.

After several months of searching, they found the perfect spot: a little town in the mountains of New Mexico, surrounded on three sides by national forest. An old mission was there that, ten years before, had been turned into a resort. The syndicate wanted to change the resort into a motor court. They knew the age of the Mission would satisfy parents' need for an educational trip for their children. The rest of the town could be transformed into a tourist's heaven, complete with wax museums, rides and exhibition gunfights. Since the town was quite remote, the syndicate could buy all of it and have no fear of competitors.

The syndicate's first approaches were met negatively by Mrs. Laura Kenyon, the resort owner. The syndicate considered buying all the town around the resort but they knew the land would be useless without the Mission. The syndicate wasn't above forcing her to sell but they wanted to choose the right man to do the forcing. Jack Galloway seemed made for the job. Who better than a handsome young war hero could force a woman, any woman, to sell?

The man by the map was extolling the virtues of the young war hero, and the men of the syndicate nodded in agreement. What the man did not say was that he knew Jack for what he was—a ruthless, cool killer. Jack had been told not to return until he had secured the purchase of the Mission at Montero. Losing this job would cost both Jack and his sponsor security of their future business life.

Jack smiled at the nervous man who had everything he owned tied up on this venture. During the war when Jack was given an order, he obeyed, no matter what methods he had to use to carry them out. He saw nothing different in this order. He would use whatever methods were needed to secure the purchase of the resort.

Chapter 9

Laura Kenyon paused before the bulletin board outside her office. She carefully reviewed the list of daily activities available to the guests of the Mission. There were a couple of horseback rides, an all-day one and a sunset ride. There was a putting-green tournament, a table tennis contest, shuffleboard, tennis, a hayride and a barbeque. There was also an announcement of a three-day camping trip, a list of movies to be shown that week, and lessons in gardening and cowboy arts for the children. A large poster advertised a rodeo to be held at the end of the summer.

Laura frowned and ran her hand through her hair. She didn't realize it, but at thirty-three, she was a striking woman. Her years of work and responsibility had given her character and her eyes showed it. She never worried about her appearance and had no idea of her raw beauty.

She looked down at her clipboard just as two guests strolled past her.

"The first time I was here," one guest was saying, "I knew I'd starve to death. I'd start out an hour before meal-time just so I'd have enough time to find the dining room."

The other guest laughed. "I keep finding the oddest little places. Yesterday I found a tiny courtyard down a narrow little alley. Tell me, is this place *really* made of mud?"

Laura smiled to herself as the guests went past her. For years, she had heard the same comments. The entire Mission was a rabbit warren of rooms and courtyards. The guests seemed to think they had discovered each nook and cranny. One man, a federal judge, said he'd stop coming as soon as he learned his way around.

But for Laura, the Mission was home. She knew every brick, every curve, every bit of adobe mud. She had hardly left the place in the eleven years since it had been re-modeled. There were many nights when she didn't go home to Ross and Julia but slept on the couch in her office or in an empty guest room, if such a rare vacancy occurred.

"Laura!"

She turned to Mrs. Martinez. The woman was the head housekeeper of the entire Mission. She had said that she cared for her children for so long that a few more wouldn't make any difference. And that's how she treated Laura's distinguished guests—like children. She didn't believe the guest was always right. One rather well-known actor kept burning cigarette holes in the sheets. Mrs. Martinez upbraided the tall young man for nearly an hour. She told him he was a disgrace—and didn't his mother teach him any manners? The bewildered young man, accustomed to everyone jumping to do his bidding, was so astonished, he could do little more than say, "Yes, ma'am" and "No, ma'am." He stopped burning holes in the sheets and he returned to the Mission at least once a year.

Laura turned to her housekeeper. "Any problem?"

"No more than the usual. The Italian actor pinched one of my girls this morning."

"Should I speak to him?"

Mrs. Martinez put her hand up. "I will. No need for you to worry. What time did you get here this morning? The light was on under your door when I came at six."

Laura laughed. "I didn't get here too early if that's what you mean."

"Mrs. Martinez," someone called. "I didn't get enough towels this morning."

"That one!" Mrs. Martinez said in disgust. "I'm going to find out what she does with all those towels and I'm going to see her red face."

Laura watched her housekeeper walk away toward the big linen closet. Laura turned toward the lobby.

The lobby had once been part of the church and its high ceiling was impressive. The tile floors were polished and many Indian rugs were scattered about. Enormous bouquets of local roses graced the tables and corners of the room. Mr. and Mrs. Woodman, who had once helped Laura in art school, grew the flowers for the Mission. Laura had given them the money to build a greenhouse on their land, then bought all the flowers they could grow. Laura made an effort to find out what flowers each regular guest liked and supplied his or her room with them. The greenery ranged from cacti to orchids, violets to sprays of chamisa. The Woodmans supplied them all.

The lobby was fairly empty now. In an hour the Mission's private plane would be landing on the airstrip outside. It brought guests from the airport in Albuquerque at regular intervals.

To the side of the lobby was the big pine reception desk, built locally. Behind it stood Irene Anderson, the new receptionist. Irene had just graduated from Montero High School, one of the top students in her class. In spite of her youth, she seemed much older. Her manner with the guests was calm, patient, controlled. In the month since Irene had worked there, Laura had never seen the girl agitated in the least. She always seemed to be in control.

Laura looked about the room, checked to see that everything had been cleaned perfectly during the night. The guests arriving today were royalty from some country Laura had never heard of. The White House had called and asked that these guests be especially well treated. Laura smiled and hoped that they didn't burn holes in the sheets, or else Mrs. Martinez might cause an international incident. But she knew that these older families rarely made trouble, it was the newly wealthy who created problems.

She looked up as Garrick entered from the dining room. He didn't even notice Laura, although she stood just a few feet from him. He walked straight toward Irene, his eyes alight as he watched the pretty young girl.

What she saw had already happened too often to upset Laura. She had dealt with Garrick for the past eleven years and she knew what he was like. There wasn't a pretty young woman whom he didn't go after, and that included guests as well as employees. Laura had found that the women were pleased and honored by his attentions. At first she had tried to stop his flirtations but she soon found that Garrick was as much of an attraction at the Mission as the Olympic-size swimming pool.

She had to admit that he was still handsome. The little lines by his eyes only seemed to add to his good looks. But the years and his constant drinking were beginning to take their toll. He had put on some weight and was developing a paunch. He so seldom got any exercise that his body was no longer the lean, well-muscled form she still carried in her memory. At thirty-six, he had the face of a movie idol and the body of a much older man.

But Laura didn't offer advice to Garrick. She had tried that long ago, but he had his own ideas about her interest in his body. He couldn't believe that every woman in the world didn't love him. Or maybe, Laura sometimes thought, he believed none of them did.

She watched as Garrick leaned on the desk and talked to Irene. The girl ignored him as she straightened the keys in their boxes. Garrick smiled slowly and lit a cigarette. She noticed that his hands were shaking.

Laura sighed and walked toward them. She knew better than to try to stop Garrick. No doubt she would have a tearful Irene in her office complaining that Mr. Garrick was so cold to her.

"Well, if it isn't my sister-in-law," Garrick said as he inhaled deeply on the cigarette.

"What brings you here so early? Irene, could I see the guest list?"

"I never left," Garrick said, his eyes daring Laura to ask him where he had slept.

Laura didn't ask. She didn't want to know which guest he had spent the night with. Nor did she ask about Clarry. Long ago she had stopped worrying, and interfering. She had offered Clarry money for a divorce after she lost the baby for which Garrick had married her, but Clarry had only glared at her older sister. Clarry finally said that she'd like to control her own life for a while. Laura had backed away and over the years tried to stay out of Garrick's and Clarry's marriage.

She looked at Irene. "When the prince and princess arrive, give them the Princesa Suite. Find out if they want separate beds."

Irene nodded and put the list back in its place. Laura knew the girl would do a good job. For all Garrick's faults, he was a good judge of people. She thought it was perhaps because he was so lazy himself. He could choose people who would get the job done. That's why Laura had put him at the head of personnel. Of course, all the people Garrick hired were physically attractive, but they also had brains. And Laura found it never hurt to have a good-looking staff.

"Irene, send for me when the plane arrives. I'll probably be on the north side for most of the morning."

"Yes," Irene said quietly, solemn as always.

"Garrick, I think the cook was saying he needed some more waitresses and one of the lifeguards from last summer isn't available this year. Could you find some people?"

Garrick leaned on the desk, watching Irene. "You know, I've been thinking about female lifeguards. I'll bet Irene here would look good in a swimsuit. With those legs..."

"I can't swim," Irene said without turning.

"What does that matter? We can..."

"Garrick," Laura interrupted, disgusted. "I need some people, and in the next few days. I want a lifeguard who can swim, not one who looks good in a suit. Are you going to do it or do I have to get someone else?"

"All right!" Garrick said. "Get off my back." He turned and eyed her. "Sometimes I think you're jealous. Is that it, Laura? Are you jealous of pretty little Irene here?"

Laura closed her eyes for a moment and prayed for strength. This surely must be the most repeated conversation in the world. Next would come Garrick's reminders of the night she got drunk and they made love in the living room, if you could call something so quick, love. Over the years he'd blown the event into a emotionally charged affair. She looked away from him. "Don't forget, Irene," she said as she started toward the exhibition gallery. Irene was welcome to Garrick.

The long exhibition gallery was lined with the work of New Mexico painters. In the corner of each painting was a discreet price tag. The turnover in the paintings was tremendous. The guests thought nothing of paying five or six hundred dollars for a souvenir of their trip to New Mexico. Of course, Laura never allowed anything but quality work to be exhibited. Sunday afternoon painters and housewives with a hobby were not for her. No, instead she selected the Indian artists and other painters who were serious about their work. Three years ago, she'd invited, at her expense, four art dealers from across the United States to spend a long weekend at the Mission. Her purpose had been to show some of the local work. One of the dealers had been interested in a Montero boy's paintings. Laura had sent the boy to art school in the East and now the boy had an exhibit in San Francisco. He was repaying

123

Laura at twenty-five dollars a month. The New York dealer had scheduled a showing of Indian works and the pieces had sold very well.

She turned left out of the gallery onto the deep portal that faced the open courtyard. The glass doors that sheltered the portal in the winter had been stored with the first warm weather. Several guests sat under the shade of the trees in the courtyard. Mrs. Woodward was giving lessons in growing orchids at the west end of the portal.

All the doors in the Mission had been brought from Mexico. They were old and weathered, adding to the historic feeling of the Mission.

Outside, the sunlight dazzled her. There was no sun in the world like that of New Mexico. The mountain air made the air crisp and clear and the sun made it sparkle with a diamond's brilliance. The guests were always commenting at how clean everything in New Mexico seemed. There was no mist to cloud the air, no mold to destroy their possessions. Something about the air invigorated them. Flabby wives found themselves agreeing to five-mile hikes in the forest.

Of course, Laura thought with a smile, after their hikes they had to be pampered. And the Mission was well suited for that. Sore muscles could be soaked in the hot mineral baths.

While she and Ross had been remodeling the old Mission, one of the lumber trucks had dislodged a pile of loose rock. It had taken five men most of the day to get the big truck out. They found that the truck had fallen into what looked like an old well. But the water from the well was hot and bubbling.

Dr. Thomas, who had attended Laura's father and who was an amateur historian, went to Santa Fe to do some research on the Mission. It took him a month to dig through the old Spanish documents and even longer to polish his Spanish so he could read them. The documents revealed that the Mission site had been chosen because of the natural hot springs in the area. The brothers had walled the springs with stone and used them for soaking. The doctor also found that two children, in 1872, had drowned in one of the old wells. The townspeople had filled and sealed the wells after that and they had been hidden until the lumber truck dislodged some of the stones.

The Mission was already taking guests when Laura heard about the mineral springs. With glee, she hired several brawny high school boys and cleared the springs of debris. Two years after the Mission opened, the lovely little grotto baths were ready. Laura left them natural, each spring directed into a lovely stone pool, open to the sky, enclosed by a private wall. Even when there was snow on the ground, the guests could use the hot baths. Connected to the baths was a large building of massage cubicles as well as exercise rooms where classes were given twice a day. There were also lectures by a well-known nutritionist and help with dieting, if a guest desired it. A small movie theatre was attached to the building.

As Laura walked toward the swimming pool she stopped to check on a group of high school students setting tables under the trees. Each year she took several of the top students from Montero High and hired them to teach the children of the guests. The students were wonderfully patient and enjoyed their work. A biology student took children on nature walks. A math student was tutoring a child for three hours a day, a child who otherwise would have had to remain at home and attend summer school. There were art lessons, music lessons, a creative writing class and drafting lessons. Laura waved at a couple of students. She knew that more than one adult would join the classes.

As the sun rose higher in the sky, the guests began to waken and the day started. There was an air of complete peace at the Mission. A guest could do absolutely nothing or one of hundreds of activities. All around the resort were hammocks stretched in private places. The kitchen was glad to prepare sack lunches for anyone who wanted to wander about alone. A guest could choose between the crystal and silver of the dining room or the wildness of the forest.

During the day, Laura rarely sat down. She was always ready to answer any questions or work to make anyone more comfortable. She oversaw everything from kitchen deliveries to the problem of Miss Betty Grable being asked for her autograph while she was on vacation.

"Laura."

She turned to Emmett Romero. Emmett was Laura's general manager. She had hired him years ago, on Ross's

125

advice, but Emmett complained she never let him do as much as he should.

"Have you seen these?" he asked, waving a couple of bunches of lettuce at her. "The kitchen people are refusing to serve this, Laura." He looked down at her with an expression of extreme patience. "You've got to stop buying everything locally. We could get much better quality if we had it flown in from California."

"Please, Emmett," she smiled. "You know how I feel. I'll talk to the cook."

"No," he sighed. "I'll do it." He tossed the insect-eaten lettuce to the ground. "Think you're ready for another summer?"

She closed her eyes and turned her face toward the sky. "I'm more than ready." She looked back at him and they shared a smile. The winter season brought guests who went to ski in Santa Fe and Taos. It seemed that in every couple who came, one skied and one didn't. The one left behind wanted to be entertained. Sometimes during the winter, the Mission felt very small to the staff.

"Did you get the prince and princess settled?" he asked.

"Finally," she sighed. "We had to rearrange the furniture in the sitting room and the prince went to talk to the cook about his wife's allergies. By the way, the writer in the courtyard suite complained that the gardener woke him this morning when he was getting his tools. And the chimney in Room 6 is blocked."

"It's too warm for a fire," Emmett frowned.

"Not to the Sandersons. They're from Miami."

Emmett laughed. "What else?"

"Do you have a couple of hours?"

Emmett and Laura walked together back inside the Mission. The feeling at the resort was that it practically ran by itself. There was a smoothness, a fluidity about the entire enterprise that belied its complexity.

But Laura and Emmett knew the work that went into the place. Because of the relaxed atmosphere, everyone felt free to complain about the least inconvenience. If a maid missed a corner, Laura was told about it. If a guest had a problem with his bill, he went to Laura. There was something so accessible about Laura that everyone brought their problems directly to her. Several times she had spent the night listening to a woman pour out all the problems

126

of her troubled marriage. During the war, she had comforted more than one widow. Ross constantly told her she took on too much of other people's problems. And though Emmett tried to take on as many problems as he could, people knew who was really in charge.

Betty Gomez, one of the three secretaries, met Laura and Emmett in the exhibition gallery. "I think we have a problem."

Laura merely sighed while Emmett groaned aloud.

Betty continued. "The princess is allergic to, as far as I can tell, nearly everything in the world. It seems she can eat only certain seafoods. I called the White House and they're sending a fresh shipment out but it won't be here until after midnight."

"We have seafood," Emmett said. "Did someone tell the prince that seafood is flown in every Wednesday morning?"

Betty rolled her eyes. "This is Friday. The prince said the seafood was too old, that it must be fresh daily."

"Daily!" Emmett said. "Why the hell did she come to New Mexico? Why didn't she go to Maine?"

Laura put her hand on Emmett's arm. "I'll stay and meet the plane. Betty, arrange for daily shipments while the prince and princess are here. And send some of your little brothers into the forest after some trout. I imagine the princess won't object to fresh mountain trout. Anything else?"

"Not at the moment," Betty smiled. "I need your signature on some checks later today. The dairyman is raising his prices again." She turned to go back to her office across from Laura's.

Emmett turned to Laura. "I'm sorry I blew up like that. I guess I can't get used to the fact that so many of our guests are spoiled children. Listen, I'll stay and meet the plane tonight. You go home and spend some time with Ross and Julia."

Laura knew how much she wanted to go home at a decent hour tonight. She had arrived at four this morning so she could make sure everything was perfect for these special guests. "I think I'm going to take you up on that suggestion. Do you think Louise will mind?"

"Of course not. She understands that I don't have a nine-to-five job."

"Good." Laura looked at her watch. "Oh, no! I'm late

for lunch with Clarry again. Why don't you call Louise, and if there's any problem, let me know." She turned and went toward the dining room.

As soon as she was gone, Emmett grimaced at the thought of calling Louise. They'd been married for ten years and during that time he had seen her change from a sweet, loving woman into a shrew who, lately, took to having a few too many drinks in the afternoon. At the first of their marriage, she'd been understanding about his work, even interested. She liked to hear about which movie stars were visiting the Mission and sometimes she even dropped in on Emmett and was introduced to them.

But after the children were born, Louise lost her interest in the Mission. Her whole life became absorbed in the children and she seemed to expect Emmett to feel the same. When he had to work late, she said it was because he didn't want to come home. For a year or two he had been able to make her laugh and see the foolishness of her thoughts, but in the last few years, she had developed a new idea.

Louise decided that the reason Emmett stayed so long each day at the Mission was because he had fallen *in* love with Laura, and *out* of love with her. Emmett had been shocked at this idea and had been too speechless to even deny it. The last woman in the world he could love romantically was Laura. How could a man love a woman who made him feel inadequate, as Laura so often did? He had tried to explain this to Louise but whatever he said only made matters worse. She would always twist his words in such a way that they were praising Laura and belittling of Louise.

Emmett had thrown his hands up in frustration, giving up all hope of trying to talk to her. In the last year he began to spend even more time at the resort than before. And Louise started to drinking. It wasn't a problem yet but he knew it could be. But the truth was, he didn't know if he wanted her to stop. After a few drinks, she could laugh again, and love again. Maybe he should help her, but for right now, her drinking was almost a relief.

He went to his office, closed the door, and asked the Montero operator for his home number. Louise answered after four rings. He could hear their five-year-old son, the youngest of the two, crying in the background. Her hello sounded agitated, harassed.

He took a deep breath and tried to make his voice sound light and happy. "Louise, I just called to tell you that I won't make it home for supper tonight. I have to meet a plane at midnight. I have the funniest story to tell you. The White House called and—"

"You don't have to try and impress me," she said flatly. "Do you know that we're invited to dinner at your parents' house tonight?"

"I'm really sorry. I want to go but I can't. If you'd listen, I'd explain it to you."

"Of course, please do explain. Maybe I'm not too stupid to understand, that is, if you use simple words and don't talk too fast."

"Louise, I don't know what you're talking about."

She lost her false calm. "I'm talking about you and your damned Laura, that's what. She owns that fancy resort. Why can't she stay and meet the plane? Why do you have to always do your work *and* hers, too?"

Emmett clenched his teeth. "She does more than her share of the work! She pays me a damned good salary, as you well know, and I don't earn half of it. Any time I can help her, I'm going to."

"Help her! You practically live with her. Laura asks you to do something and you jump. Like a monkey on a chain."

"For your information, Laura didn't ask me to do this. In fact she was going to stay herself. I don't know what time she got here this morning but she was already here at six when the kitchen people arrived."

"Dear, holy Laura!" Louise sneered into the telephone. "When will any of you learn that she isn't the Holy Mother's sister? She runs this whole town! I can't even go to the grocery without hearing Laura this and Laura that. I'm the only one who sees through her. She likes power. She likes controlling everyone's lives."

Emmett felt anger roar through him. Laura was more a servant than a queen. Why couldn't Louise see that? "I won't listen to any more of this. You're acting younger than the children."

"And what would you know of our children? It's been
129

so long since you've seen them that I'm not sure you could pick them out in a crowd."

Before Emmett could reply, a quick knock sounded on the door and Garrick entered. "I don't know if it matters to you," Garrick said, "but we can hear your shouting outside."

Emmett gave a quick nod and turned away from Garrick's amused expression. He didn't like the man and didn't want him to hear any of his personal problems. His voice lowered, "I have to go now, dear. I'll eat supper here so don't worry about me."

"I take it you want me to shut up," Louise screeched. "You don't want to hear the truth. Tell me, did your dear Laura just walk in?"

Emmett smiled into the telephone. "Good-bye, dear," he said sweetly. He hung the receiver on the cradle even as he heard Louise's angry words start again.

Emmett began to straighten the papers on his desk. "Did you want me?" he asked without looking at Garrick.

"Just passing." Garrick looked around Emmett's office. It was half the size of Laura's, but at least he had his own. Garrick had a corner in the secretary's office. It wasn't that he needed the space, especially since the girls did all his paperwork, but he would like to see his name on a door. "Your wife giving you trouble?"

Emmett didn't answer but sat down in his chair and pointedly opened a ledger.

"Let me give you a little advice about women," Garrick said. "All they need now and then is a good screw. You make 'em happy in bed and they'll worship you. Of course, the way to go about it is to make 'em come to you. You just hold out on Louise and she'll come to you. Then when she does, give it to her good and hard."

Emmett looked up at Garrick in disbelief. His philosophy didn't make sense, much less help his situation. He could smell whiskey even across the big desk. Perhaps all the women fell over themselves for Garrick now, but what would happen in a few years when his looks were gone?

"Did you find a new lifeguard yet?" Emmett asked, dismissing his personal problems.

Garrick smiled knowingly. "Yeah. One of the high school girls said her brother would like the job."

"High school girls! You aren't—!"

130

Garrick's look silenced Emmett. "I have enough to do without any kids. You know, Emmett, you might teach Louise a lesson. Try some other women. It'd be good for you. That Irene Anderson is just dying for a man. I can see it in her eyes." He put his hand on the doorknob. "I'll hold off on her a while, give you a chance." He winked in conspiracy and left the office.

Emmett leaned back in his chair and shook his head. He didn't believe he'd ever get used to Garrick and his women. What did they see in him? He dismissed Garrick and looked back at the ledger. It wasn't easy keeping the resort in the black. Laura hired so many people from Montero that there was very little profit margin. The high school kids alone ate up a big chunk of money. And anyone who needed work had only to go to Laura and she'd create a job for him. There wasn't a family in Montero that wasn't employed in some way by the Mission. They either worked here or supplied goods. Mrs. Gomez and five of her eight children baked pies for the resort, while her oldest, Betty, was a secretary. Mr. Gomez was the head gardener.

He sighed as he looked at the new dairy bills. They could bring milk from Albuquerque cheaper than what the local man charged. It was no use talking to Laura. She would only say she owed everything to Montero.

In spite of her good intentions, it was almost sunset when Laura left the Mission. The days were getting longer and there was a promise of summer warmth in the cool mountain air.

It was only a short drive from the resort to her house. It was the same house that Laura had lived in with her father and Clarry. Ross kept it in good repair. They had bought an empty lot next door, and six years ago, Ross had built himself a workshop. Over the years, he had made some beautiful pieces of furniture. During the war, he had worked only with the local pine, but now he was ordering rosewood and vermilion from New York.

For a long time, Laura worried about feeling that she had deserted Ross and, for that matter, her daughter, too. She tried to interest Ross in the running of the Mission, but he just smiled and said he had no intention of baby-sitting a bunch of children. Sometimes he'd lead a small group of guests on an elk hunt or a fishing trip, but even

131

then, he'd take only experienced people with him. He wanted no hunting accidents caused by ignorant tourists.

She pulled into the driveway and walked to the back of the house. At this time of day, her husband and daughter were usually outside.

Ross and Julia were playing croquet on the patch of lawn Ross had planted. "Hello!" Laura called to them.

Ross looked up and smiled. "There's iced tea on the table. We'll be through in a minute. Just as soon as I finish beating Julia."

Laura sat down on one of the leather chairs from Mexico, took a glass of iced tea, and watched them. Ross was fifty-nine now, but he didn't move like a man that age. He still worked, still kept in shape. His hair was dark gray, his face that of a man who had done and seen all he wanted. His was a quiet strength which more than once had kept Laura going. He was the rock that supported her so she could deal with the people at the Mission. No matter what the turmoil at the resort, she could come home to relative peacefulness. Ross would hold her in his arms and comfort her. Sometimes she thought that he had two daughters, one thirty-three and one ten.

Laura sipped her tea and concentrated on Julia. She rarely looked at her daughter without feeling a twinge of conscience. She knew so little about Julia, had spent so little time with her. When Julia had been younger, Laura had taken her to the Mission with her but Julia preferred to stay at home with her father. As Julia grew older, Laura hoped her daughter would come to like the resort more, especially since it would be hers someday. But even with the enticement of meeting one movie star after another, Julia didn't like to go to the resort. She stayed at home, read a lot, and rode her horse, which she kept at a neighbor's house. Other than those interests, she had few.

Laura realized how very little she actually knew about her own daughter. She had tried hundreds of times to talk to her, to find out what she wanted. But she got nowhere. Ross had told Laura to stop pushing Julia, that all Julia wanted was to be herself.

Laura looked at her daughter, at the small body, fat pigtails and large brown eyes. She was pretty, or was going to be. She was a mixture of Clarry and Laura. She had Laura's coloring, but the delicate evenness of Clarry's features. She had Ross's quiet solemnity and never let anyone know her thoughts, except, perhaps, her father. She never caused any problems, made excellent grades, yet sometimes Laura got the feeling that Julia was angry.

"She beat me again," Ross said as he put his arm around his daughter's shoulders.

Julia smiled and put her mallet in the rack.

Ross walked to Laura and kissed her heartily. "You're home early. I figured we wouldn't see you until midnight, what with all the calls from the White House."

"How in the world did you know about that?"

Ross sat beside her. He shrugged. "I heard it in the drugstore this morning. Something about a prince and princess."

"Julia," Laura said, "would you like some tea? It has mint in it."

Julia smiled winsomely at her mother, looking up at her through her thick lashes. Like Clarry at that age, Julia knew how to use her prettiness to advantage. "I made the tea," she said in a soft voice.

"Come on," Ross said. "Sit with us."

"I have homework to do."

Laura grabbed her daughter's hand as she walked past. "Couldn't you stay and tell us what you did in school today?"

"The same old stuff. I need to go now. I'm giving a report on Pancho Villa."

Laura released her daughter. "Yes, of course. Maybe Sunday we can all go on a picnic. Would you like that?"

"Of course, Mother," Julia smiled prettily and left the porch.

"Why do I get the feeling that I'm the child and she's the adult?"

Ross gave a snort of laughter. "Maybe it's true. It's not easy being a celebrity's daughter."

"Celebrity?" Laura laughed. "Celebrities are people who sit around the pool and have drinks brought to them." She stopped and frowned.

"What happened?" Ross asked, immediately aware of her change in mood.

"Nothing really. Just something that I know shouldn't bother me. Garrick, blast him! Couldn't wait to tell me. There's a plane coming in at midnight tonight and Emmett

133

said he'd stay to meet it. Garrick overheard him and Louise screaming at each other on the phone. I hope I'm not causing any problems."

"Once again you're trying to take on everyone else's problems. Louise is just jealous."

"Jealous? Of Emmett's job? I've told Louise that I would give her a job, something part-time if she wanted."

Ross took Laura's hand from the chair arm. "She doesn't want a job. She's jealous of you. Next to her, you're a femme fatale. She's scared to death she's going to lose Emmett to you."

"Ross, surely you must be kidding. Emmett and me? And what does she think I'm going to do with you?"

"She isn't thinking, she's just feeling. If she had any sense, she'd know I'd blow Emmett's head off if I thought he had a chance with you."

Laura laughed, then got up and sat in Ross's lap. She snuggled against him. "What would I ever do without you?"

"Nothing. You'd probably die from worry or else let the people of Montero eat you alive."

"What does that mean?" she asked, looking up at him.

He kissed her instead of answering. "How about a quickie before dinner?"

She laughed at his little-boy expression. "Your place or mine?"

He glanced at the light in Julia's window. "The shop. You're so damned noisy, I don't want to frighten our daughter."

"Are you complaining?"

"Of course. Haven't I got a lot to complain about?"

He pushed her off his lap and they walked hand in hand toward his shop.

Chapter 10

Clarry Eastman sat at the breakfast table alone, a sketch book open before her. The early morning sun came in through the sparkling clean French doors that led out onto the patio. The round table was set with Balleck china with a delicate pattern of blue flowers. The sterling was traditional without being ornate. A bowl of fresh tulips sat in the middle of the table.

The room was not large but it was beautiful. The early sun made the white plaster walls gleam. Through the doorway could be seen the living room, a large gracious room, comfortable but elegant. The furniture was a combination of the finest modern and the most cherished antiques.

The rooms fit Clarry perfectly. She had changed a great deal in the last eleven years, not just physically but emotionally also. But that wasn't so apparent to the casual observer. Her hair was no longer bleached to white blondness. It was its own honey blonde color and fell softly to her shoulders. Her face and her entire body had lost its coat of plumpness. Instead of looking like a sexy child she had the look of a mature and beautiful woman. At twenty-nine, Clarry was at the peak of her beauty.

She wore a white linen dress, tailored yet feminine. She made a few more marks in her sketchbook before slowly closing it and then beginning her breakfast of juice, a boiled egg and black coffee. Over the years she had learned the discipline of weight control. She was not like Laura, who could eat whatever she wanted. Clarry existed on salads and fruit.

The door from the kitchen opened and Garrick entered. She gave him only a brief glance before turning back to her breakfast.

"Good morning, Clarry," Garrick said quietly. He leaned toward his wife to kiss her cheek but she pulled away. He frowned, then took a chair across from her.

"There was a lot of work at the Mission last night. I'm sorry I missed dinner."

Clarry didn't bother to answer him or give credibility to his lie. She felt he knew she was aware of his other women but it was never openly referred to between them. Clarry suspected Garrick was afraid of losing her.

"Are you going in to the shop today?" he asked over his coffee.

"Of course," she said coolly.

He reached across the table and put his hand over hers. "I said I was sorry about last night. You know how busy Laura is and Emmett..." He stopped when he saw her expression. "What are you drawing?" He nodded toward her notebook.

She closed it. "Nothing important. I have to go now or I'll be late." She rose. "I hope you have a good day."

She didn't look back when he called after her. After eleven years of marriage, she felt she knew his weakness. Perhaps even when they were first married he had sensed that Clarry had some of her sister's strength. And over the years that strength had emerged. Clarry had changed from an insecure, frightened girl to a confident and secure young woman.

But it had been a long, difficult process of changing.

She walked gracefully through the living room, down the hall with its floor-to-ceiling windows and into her bedroom. Her bedroom was an example of Clarry's perfect taste. The large bed was draped at the four corners with soft apricot silk, the edges and hem hand-embroidered with a delicate flower pattern in the same shade. The bed itself was covered in cream-colored tussah silk, the headboard upholstered in a floral design of apricot and cream. The floor was brick, waxed daily to achieve its dull lustre. There were three rugs on the floor, handwoven in Peru to Clarry's specifications, using a simple design of ivory and deep blue. The few pieces of furniture, the desk, two chairs and a chaise longue were eighteenth-century Italian antiques, upholstered in blue and green stripes. The walls were plaster, barely tinted to a soft, glowing butterscotch. The three paintings on the wall were seventeenth- and eighteenth-century English portraits, all of women. Four large baskets of pink and white phalaenopsis orchids were set on the floor, the flowers making a pattern against the light-colored walls.

She couldn't look at the room without thinking of Ross, for he was one of the people who had helped her change over the years.

She had commissioned the building of the house five years after she had married Garrick. It had been one of their few outright quarrels. He wanted to continue living at the Mission, to keep his share of the profits from the resort to spend on trips, cars and expensive clothes. It was amazing how much money Garrick could spend.

Clarry began to show a strength no one suspected she had. She carefully sought advice about investing money from those guests she respected and followed their advice. She bought land in Los Angeles. She invested in the municipal bonds of several growing western cities. Garrick laughed at her but Laura gave her money to invest for her. Clarry often felt Laura gave the money to her out of guilt, but Clarry nevertheless doubled it for her.

When Clarry had cleared enough of a profit that she felt she could afford a house, she again asked a guest for his advice. He was a prominent architect and chose the hillside site, making a sketch of a house that was fitted to the slope of the land.

Later, Clarry took the sketch to Ross. It hadn't been an easy thing to do. She knew Ross never cared for her. To her surprise, Ross was happy to make working drawings for her. He simply said, "Good!" when Clarry stated she wanted her bedroom at the other end of the house from Garrick's.

It came as a surprise to everyone, but Clarry and Ross worked well together. Clarry was so pleased to be around a man of Ross's quiet strength that she relaxed for the first time in years. And Ross was delighted with Clarry's uncanny eye for beauty. She had the ideas; he knew how to make them work.

Together they created a beautiful house, large, low, hugging the side of the hill, built of adobe, stone and redwood. When it was done they shared a six-pack of Schlitz, sitting on the flagstone floor in the empty living room, watching the sunset through the big windows.

"I envy Laura," Clarry said quietly, after her third beer.

"There's no reason you should," Ross answered. "Your

only problem is that you don't put enough value on yourself. Look at Laura. Now Laura believes she can do anything in the world. It doesn't occur to her to think she can't do something. I think if Laura decided she wanted to pitch for the Yankees, she'd go after it."

"And get it!" Clarry laughed.

Ross's eyes twinkled. "She probably would. But you, Clarry, you're probably just as talented as Laura, maybe even more so, but you don't have the drive that she has. You don't believe in yourself."

"I couldn't have created the Mission out of nothing like Laura did," Clarry protested. Ross's words had a ring of truth to them.

"Probably not, but then neither could I. I don't have Laura's belief in the goodness of life either. But you could do something. You could use some of all this talent you're hiding."

"Hiding!" Clarry laughed, then glanced at her reflection in the mirror.

Ross's tone changed from a laughing one. "Yes, hiding! Hiding behind Laura and that creep you married. And hiding behind your looks. When are you going to start liking yourself?"

Clarry stared at him. She wasn't ready to hear the truth about herself. She laughed and ignored his words. They never again spoke like that. They remained friends but the closeness they had had while building the house didn't last.

Yet over the years Clarry had changed. She had her hair tinted to a shade closer to her own color, then let it grow out. She lost weight and began swimming every day. And her close association with Garrick made her realize that men were not the answer to her problems.

As she changed externally, the way she felt about herself also changed. Once she had thought that marriage to a rich man was the answer to all her problems. But years of working at the Mission with the wives of rich men had made her see that that wasn't the answer.

She thought of Ross's words about her talent and she began to wonder seriously if he were right. She always had had a flair for clothes, had always liked them. Over the years she had collected a small library of books on the history of costume. During the war, when everyone was
138

wearing "utility" dresses, she had looked with longing to the beautiful gowns of the past. At first she was only doodling, but then she took a few of those dresses with their soft curves and adapted them to fit the image of the postwar woman. After a few months she began looking at her designs seriously. She took a correspondence course in fashion illustration so she could draw the ideas she saw in her mind.

She had never worked so hard at anything in her life. She set up a drawing table by the windows in her bedroom. She bought paints, inks, illustration board. She studied the designs of the past and incorporated them into the modern woman's life-style. She drew evening clothes, play clothes, swimsuits, clothes for working women. She designed for particular figure types. As a challenge to herself, she set herself the task of designing a wardrobe for some ungainly guests. She liked trying to camouflage a big belly or heavy legs or an aged throat. She felt anyone could design for the perfect Paris mannequins, but what woman was shaped like them?

Yet, for some reason she couldn't explain, she kept all her drawings secret. She had an oversized filing cabinet in her office in her dress shop and another one in her bedroom. They were always kept locked and she carried the only keys with her.

She turned at a soft knock on her door.

Garrick waited until she asked him in before he entered. "Clarry, I think we should talk."

She picked up her sketchbook and hat. "I really do need to go. Couldn't this wait until later?"

He caught her arm. "Something's wrong. I can feel it," he said, his eyes searching hers. "If you're angry about last night..."

"I'm not angry," she said with great patience. "It's just...I don't know what's happening to me. I feel like something's going to happen or maybe that something *needs* to happen." She could hardly stand to look at him. She knew that for all his bravado, his numerous "love" affairs, he really needed her. He needed her strength, the security their marriage represented to him. Once long ago, when he was drunk, he told her he had a fear of being alone.

"We'll talk later," she said, then walked past him and

left the house. She knew he could sense changes in her, perhaps even before she was aware of them. But lately she was restless, asking herself a lot of questions about her life and what she wanted to do with it. For so many years she had been struggling just to earn a living and to get over her great fear of poverty, but now she was wanting more. She had money, a home, and people always told her she was beautiful. She had a husband who was good to her, in his own way, and he certainly made no demands on her. For many years that had been enough. A few months ago one of the guests at the Mission said Clarry ought to have an affair, or better yet leave Garrick and get herself a man who'd drive her wild at night.

The idea had intrigued Clarry. For years she had been so busy trying to prove that she could do something on her own, without Laura's making the decisions for her, that she hadn't thought of men and passion. But lately she had begun to wonder what it would be like to have a man help her make decisions, a man to lean on instead of one leaning on her.

At the Mission she parked her small white sports car under the trees between the Mission and the individual guest houses, and went into her dress shop. There was no sign outside, nothing to announce the shop. The guests referred to it as Clarry's or as Laura's sister's shop. It was a large, open room decorated in white and champagne. The clothes were discreetly displayed. Once a month Clarry staged a fashion show with the female guests as the models. She chose the clothes for each woman, and the guests nearly always bought what they wore. Twice a year Clarry flew to New York and bought clothes for her shop. She chose only the best, only the top designers. First time guests were surprised to find such elegance in—as they said—the middle of nowhere.

The front of the shop had French windows and doors with antique brass latches. Inside, hints of gold glowed amid the quiet elegance. Clarry's two saleswomen were young, slim, pretty and intelligent. Dena and Jill were local women, chosen and trained by Clarry. She paid them well and treated them with respect.

As she entered her shop, she saw Jill standing quietly by as Mrs. Duncan turned and twisted before a triple mirror. Mrs. Duncan was forty years old, the wife of a man
140

who had made a fortune building airplanes during the war. She hated getting older and tried to hide her lumpy body with childish clothes. She was trying on a simple long gown of bright pink satin. Jill looked up and gave Clarry a look of desperation.

Clarry set her purse, gloves and sketchbook down. "No, Mrs. Duncan," she said firmly. "That dress is not for you."

Mrs. Duncan looked indignant. "But I had a gown very much like this when I first met Walter."

Clarry didn't say a word but unzipped the dress. "Jill, bring that new Dior that just came in. The navy blue silk one with the low back."

Before Mrs. Duncan could protest again, she found herself undressed and redressed in a gown unlike any she had ever worn. Clarry had instantly seen that the woman's best feature was her long-waisted back. She was used to showing her large breasts, but the years and lack of exercise had made them sag, and a low front dress made her appear even heavier than she was.

"Now straighten your shoulders, please," Clarry instructed. "Remember that your back is your most beautiful feature."

The woman was nearly speechless as she stared at herself in the mirrors. The sleek gown had changed her from an aging overweight woman to a sophisticated matron. She did indeed straighten her shoulders.

"Will you take the gown, Mrs. Duncan?" Jill asked politely.

The woman laughed and turned to Clarry. "What else do you think I could wear? I just may buy my fall wardrobe here."

Clarry smiled graciously and went to the storage area behind her shop. She was instructing Jill in what dresses to give to Mrs. Duncan when Dena entered. "There's a man outside who wants to see you, Clarry."

"Did he give his name?"

"Bill Matthews. But he said you probably wouldn't remember him."

Clarry paused with a blue linen playsuit over her arm. Bill Matthews. Of course she remembered him, a tall skinny boy who had a crush on her. Not long after she married Garrick, Bill and his family had moved away.

She handed the suit to Jill and went into the showroom.

If she hadn't known who he was, she wouldn't have recognized him. He was still tall but certainly not skinny. He wore the green jacket and brown pants of an army officer. And he leaned on a cane.

"Bill, I wouldn't have known you."

His deep brown eyes looked at her hard, as if he wanted to remember her always. He was a good-looking man, not startlingly handsome like Garrick but clean-cut and wholesome. "I didn't think you'd remember me. You know, you're even more beautiful than I remembered. Not so..."

"Flashy?" she laughed.

He smiled down at her. "I just remember you as being the most beautiful young lady in the world. I was on my way to visit my parents in Arizona and decided to make the extra drive to Montero."

"To see how it'd changed?"

"No," he said seriously, his eyes searching hers. "To see if you were still here. I wanted to see if you were as pretty as I remembered or if I had been dreaming."

"And?" she asked lightly.

He grinned at her. "And you know the answer to that." He turned and looked about the shop. "This yours?"

"The shop is. The whole place is Laura's."

He shook his head in bewilderment. "This is some place! Was that Betty Grable I saw in the hall?"

"Claudette Colbert was here last week."

"You know, we left just as Laura was starting this place. My father said it was proof that the town was dying when its citizens started going crazy. I never would have believed she could have made this out of an old pile of adobes."

"No one believed it. I was so scared that I was ready to do anything to escape Laura's madness. Have you seen all of the resort?"

"I think I only saw a corner. I came in the lobby and a girl gave me directions to you."

She paused for a moment because she was very pleased that he had come to see her. "Could I take you on a tour?"

"You can take me anywhere you want," he said seriously. "Tell me, do you still like cherry juice in your coke?"

"That's been a long time," she smiled. "I can't believe you'd remember that after all these years."

"I remember everything about you. I've had a lot of time to remember." He nodded down toward his cane.

"If you need assistance, you can lean on me."

"Don't say that or you'll undo two years of therapy. But perhaps you'd take my arm just the same."

"Yes," she smiled. "Yes, I'd like that."

Clarry took Bill through every corridor of the Mission. She introduced him to everybody that they met. He remembered only a few of them besides Laura. Garrick left his post of leaning on the registration desk, making propositions to Irene Anderson, and demanded to know who Clarry's friend was. Clarry lifted one eyebrow at Garrick and he retreated. He liked to pretend, in public, that he controlled his wife. Clarry saw that under his blustering he was worried, but for once she didn't stop to reassure him.

She turned away and walked rapidly into the dining room.

"Hey!" Bill called. "I'm not up to races yet."

Clarry stopped. "I'm sorry." She looked up at him. "Your leg is hurting you."

He looked at her in astonishment. "How did you know that?"

"The blood vein at your temple is enlarging by the moment. If you've seen enough of the Mission, how'd you like to drive into the forest and have a picnic lunch?"

Bill sat in the dining room while Clarry made the arrangements for lunch. He smiled when she returned.

"You've changed, you know that?" he said as they drove into the forest.

She laughed. "Everyone changes in eleven years. I had to grow up and I had to face poverty and the death of my father all at once."

"And your marriage," he said, studying her.

She didn't answer but kept her eyes on the dirt road ahead.

"Could I ask some personal questions?"

"How personal?"

He leaned back in the seat. "I want to be honest with you. This isn't just a chance meeting." He took a deep breath. "I don't know where to start. Did you know I've been in love with you for as long as I can remember? All through the war I dreamed about you. I built the picture

143

of you up until no woman could come close to you. Then I got hit by six machine-gun bullets and through years of surgery and therapy I thought about you. Clarry Taylor became an obsession with me."

She stopped the car but she didn't move and he continued talking.

"I came back to get you out of my system. I figured you'd be fat and have six kids by now. I've been in Montero for four days asking questions about you. Instead of a hag I find you more beautiful than you were at sixteen and you've created a thriving business all of your own and built the most beautiful house in town. The townspeople keep saying they didn't believe you could do anything, but you've proved otherwise."

He stopped speaking and turned toward her. "You're married, I know that, and you've accomplished more in your life than I probably ever will, but I want to ask you straight off: could there ever be a place for me in your life? I know it's sudden and it must seem as if I've come out of nowhere but..."

She looked away from him, her heart pounding. It was true that she knew nothing about him, but one sentence kept echoing through her mind: it's time. It's time. It was time to try something new, to stop hiding from life, to think of something besides municipal bonds and dress designs.

She turned and smiled at him. "There could be a chance," she said teasingly.

He grinned, then grabbed her hand and kissed it enthusiastically. "Now how about some food? I've waited days to find out if the Mission food is as good as everyone says."

"It's better!" she laughed, then reached for the basket.

Bill had a difficult time forcing himself to keep his hands off her while they ate, but he reminded himself that he had been in love with her for years while he was virtually a stranger to her.

They didn't return to the Mission until the sun was already setting. Bill told her how his life had always revolved around her, and Clarry told him of her fears and of the awful time after her father's death. He made her talk about herself in a new and open way. She told him about her dress designs.

144

At sundown they drove back to the Mission and ate supper in Clarry's office. She unlocked the file cabinet and spread out her sketches for him to see. He made a few comments about the excellence of her drawing, and then as they looked at each other they slowly moved toward each other. Suddenly they were in each other's arms.

Clarry had never before been made love to. Not real love, not where the man gave as much as he took. She had been too young to abandon herself to Garrick and she had never really loved him. But now she responded completely to Bill.

"I never felt so good in my life," she whsipered. "Nor so tired. I think I may die."

Bill only laughed and poured champagne between her breasts. "We've only started," he said as he began to drink the wine.

Chapter 11

Jack Galloway stood before the mirror and grinned at himself. He wore a heavy denim shirt, denim trousers and a wide leather belt. He ran a comb through his hair. The denim he wore was just the right touch. He had the look of a rich man at play. The last thing he wanted was to look like a businessman or that he needed Mrs. Kenyon to sell the place.

"Good morning, Mrs. Kenyon," he said when she opened the door to her office. "I hope I'm not disturbing you."

She motioned him to a comfortable chair in front of the big desk. She took a seat across from him. "I'm always available to my guests. Now, how can I help you?"

He smiled at her directness. "I'd like to make you an offer, but first I'd like for you to hear my ideas." He settled back in the chair and watched her. She was calm, relaxed in the way that only great confidence allows. She wasn't going to be an easy person to deal with. But Jack had his own confidence. A good-looking woman like her would no doubt love to get rid of the burden of this place.

He explained his plan slowly, with several smiles. He told her how the syndicate planned to make Montero, New Mexico, one of the best known spots in the United States, maybe in the world. He talked about the syndicate's plans for the town, the incredible attractions they'd bring. He talked about how they'd make the Mission itself more productive.

Laura interrupted him before he had finished. "Let me see if I understand, Mr. Galloway."

"Jack," he grinned. "Everyone calls me Jack."

"All right," she said somewhat impatiently. "Jack. As I see it, you not only want to purchase the Mission but the town also."

"As much of it as we can, yes."

146

"And then you plan to turn it all into some sort of Vacationland, USA. Am I correct?"

"Yes," he smiled, completely relaxed. He had the deal in the bag.

Laura stood up and walked to the side of her desk. "In the last eleven years since the Mission opened, I have had twenty, maybe twenty-five, offers to buy the Mission, but this is by far the most ambitious."

Ambitious, a good word, Jack thought. "Of course it's ambitious. My employers are no small businessmen. If I told you some of their names—" He waved his hand and laughed. "Listen, we really have plans for this town. The people here would make a fortune. And you, you'd be set for life."

Laura put her hands on the desk, leaned forward, and stared at him. "Who would make the fortune? Didn't you just say that your employers would buy the land from the citizens? Land in Montero is cheap because there's no industry here. Your syndicate could buy the land for practically nothing, then build whatever they wanted, and they'd make the money from the tourists, not the citizens of Montero, isn't that right?"

Jack lost his smile.

"Now, as for what your people would do for Montero, I don't happen to believe neon lights, Ferris wheels and bears drinking Coca-Cola have any beauty in them at all. I think Montero is beautiful the way it is and doesn't need what you offer. As for my resort, the last thing I plan to do is cut it into tiny little rooms so I can take care of a hundred more guests."

Jack rose and went to stand across from her, the corner of the desk between them. "But look at this place," he said patiently. "It's too big. It's..." he chuckled. "It's like a woman's mind, creative but a bit disorganized." He smiled seductively at her. "You're too young, too pretty, to be saddled with a place like this. I'm prepared to offer you enough money to make you comfortable for the rest of your life." He moved his hand so his fingertips just touched hers.

Laura leaned closer to him and didn't move her hand. "Jack, you aren't the first man to make a pass at me to try to get me to sell," she said with a smile. "Let me make this clear. I am not interested in you or your offer to buy my resort. I will not sell."

He straightened. "I'm sure that once you've had time to think about my offer—"

"Mr. Galloway, if I did decide to sell, I'm afraid you'd be number ten or eleven on my waiting list. One man from Texas wants the place so badly, he's deposited fifty thousand dollars in the Montero bank in my name. If I decide to sell, all I have to do is call the bank president and the money will be delivered to me—in cash."

Jack stepped backward. "But you don't take it?" He took a deep breath. "But I want to use the whole town of Montero."

"*Use* is exactly the correct word. Now, Mr. Galloway, if you'll excuse me, I have work to do. I hope you enjoy your stay with us. If you need any assistance, please feel free to ask." She sat down behind the big desk and began going through the morning's mail.

Jack left Laura's office and started toward his room. One approach had not worked, perhaps another would. Perhaps other people could persuade Laura Kenyon to sell.

He spent the day beside the pool. At one time or another, nearly all the guests visited the big pool. Besides, in swim trunks, his scars could be seen. He had found some time ago that next to wearing his medals his scars were the best reminder of who he was.

It didn't take long for the word to spread about his war heroism. He quietly acknowledged everyone who thanked him for personally saving them during the war. And he asked questions of them all. He found out that the blonde doing laps in the pool was Laura's sister. He started to make his move when he saw some muscular guy hovering over her. The guy gave Jack a couple of looks of warning and Jack backed away.

Later in the day, he found out that the guy with Laura's sister was only an "old friend." Jack actively sought to find her husband.

He saw Garrick leaving a guest room. Garrick stopped in a shadow, pulled a hip flask from his pocket and drank deeply.

"Mr. Eastman," Jack called, "allow me to introduce myself."

"You don't have to," Garrick said. "I've been hearing
148

about our boy hero." The men were about the same height but Garrick's dark good looks were different, more mysterious than Jack's.

"And I've heard more than my share about you. From the women."

Garrick grinned at the young man. He felt no jealousy. There were certainly enough women to go around. Maybe he could even get a little rest. "I've met my share of them," he said confidently.

"Could I buy you a drink? That is, if you can find the place. I get lost every time I take a step."

"Disgusting, isn't it?" Garrick agreed. "I told Laura when she was building it that it was wrong, but she's the stubbornest female ever made."

The men started walking toward the Kiva Bar and Lounge. "I met your Laura this morning and I don't mind telling you that I find her a little intimidating."

"Laura?" Garrick laughed as he led the way down the stairs into the circular pit that was the bar. "She likes people to be afraid of her, that's all. I could tell you some stories—"

"I wish you would," Jack said seriously. "What's your pleasure?"

"They know," Garrick said, not bothering to look at the bartenders. He led Jack to a dark table. "Okay, what do you want to know?"

Jack debated whether to tell the truth or not. "I was sent out here to buy the place."

"Buy!" Garrick slammed down his empty glass. "Did you know she's had about a hundred offers? And she's rejected everyone!"

"You sound disappointed."

"I should. I own a third of this place. You look around here at all the rich people and you'd think anyone owning a third would be rich, too. But we're not! Laura gives every deadbeat in town a job. If he has Montero written on his birth certificate, Laura will give him a job, whether we need somebody else or not. She hires at least one member of every family in this town."

Jack turned his whiskey glass about in his hands. "You couldn't be making very much if there are so many extra salaries to pay."

Garrick downed another glass. "Very little. That's why
149

I've urged her to sell. She could make a mint from the sale of this place and a third share of the profits could set me up."

"You know," Jack said slowly, "this Laura seems too good to be true. She foregoes her own profit to help the townspeople. From what I hear she practically lives here, working constantly. What about her family? Does everyone love her?"

Garrick snorted and poured both of them another drink. "She has a family. She's married to some old guy." Garrick wouldn't let anyone see how he felt about being jilted by Laura, or his fear that he was losing Clarry. "She has a daughter." He smiled to himself. He had never mentioned it to a soul, but he continued to believe that Julia might be his daughter.

"As for loving her," Garrick continued, "not everyone does."

"You wouldn't mind sharing some of that information, would you?"

Garrick stared at the younger man. "I get the feelin' I'm being set up."

Jack smiled. "I knew you were a smart man. Let me level with you." Jack told Garrick about the syndicate that wanted to buy the resort and as much of the town as possible. He watched the man's dark eyes light from within and knew Garrick liked the whole idea. "You know, the syndicate's going to need a general manager for the resort, somebody who knows the place."

Garrick leaned back in his chair. He'd like to be manager of the Mission, just for a year maybe, just so he could show Laura, and Clarry, too, that he could do it. They treated him as if he were of no consequence. Damn Laura for hiring that Emmett Romero over him! If he were manager of the Mission, then no one would look down on him.

"Why do you want to know who's against Laura?" Garrick asked.

"I just thought maybe I could talk to them. I want to talk to her friends, too, but sometimes a person's enemies..."

Garrick smiled. "The manager's wife, Louise Romero, is jealous of Laura. Thinks she's having an affair with her husband. And Louise has been hittin' the bottle lately, too, I've heard."

150

"Is she? Is Laura having an affair with Romero?"

"Lord, no! I'll bet every man who's ever visited here has made a pass at Laura and none of them has succeeded."

"Are you sure of that?"

Garrick laughed. "Very. If you're thinking in that direction, you can forget it. If you had gray hair and one foot in the grave, she might consider you but not any other way."

"Who else?"

Garrick closed his eyes for a moment. "Marian Stromberg. How could I have forgotten her? She was the town rich girl until Laura opened the Mission. She still has money but Laura has the prestige. Marian takes it as a personal affront." He stopped for a long drink. "You know, this town always says it loves Laura, but I wonder if they really do. If they thought they could get rich, I wonder if they'd let anyone stand in their way."

"I've been wondering exactly that. In fact, that thought has been in my mind all day long. Could I get you another bottle?"

"No," Garrick said, rising unsteadily to his feet. "I've got to go home. With a beautiful wife like mine waiting, a man likes to go home," he smiled, winking.

Jack returned his wink. "I envy you."

"Yeah, everyone does," Garrick slurred, frowning.

Julia Kenyon sat quietly on a swivel stool in the drugstore, concentrating on her Coke.

"Julia," Sheriff Moya called. "Did you know your mother has a prince and princess staying at the Mission?"

Julia smiled sweetly at the sheriff, even blinking her eyes rapidly a couple of times. She looked all innocence, and extremely interested in what the sheriff was saying.

"That Laura!" the man behind the counter said. "It was sure a good day when she bought that mud pile. Julia, did anyone ever tell you how she traded all her paintings for the place? No one believed in her then. We all thought she was crazy."

Julia kept smiling and lifted the straw up and down in the ice in her paper cone. No one noticed that her hand gripping the edge of the counter was white knuckled or that even as she smiled her teeth clenched and unclenched.

Sheriff Moya came to sit beside her. He started telling

Julia how Laura worked in her father's lumberyard after school, how Laura never had time to drink Cokes. And did Julia know that Laura was out collecting bills when she was Julia's age?

Julia listened with such intensity that an outsider would never have guessed she had heard the stories nearly every day of her life. She was concentrating on the sheriff so hard that she didn't see her Uncle Garrick enter the drugstore.

Garrick's head was whirling from too much whiskey and from Jack Galloway's news. It would be nice to be general manager, very nice indeed. It just might make up for some of the rotten things Laura had done to him. And if he were general manager, maybe Clarry wouldn't be so cool to him. It didn't help his ego any to see his wife spending so much time with another man.

While he waited for the cigarettes, he absently listened to the conversation around him. Julia was smiling prettily at a couple of old windbags, and Garrick looked at her with pride. She was so pretty, always so interested in everybody, such a sweet little girl.

As he watched her he became aware of what the people beside Julia were saying. Some fat old man was saying Laura had single-handedly pulled Montero out of the Depression. Then the sheriff started going on and on about the great career Laura had given up so she could help the people of Montero.

Garrick thought he was going to be sick. The people talked about Laura as if she were a saint. For God's sake, she was only a woman.

His glance went to Julia and he realized the girl looked like she was hypnotizing herself. He snatched the cigarettes off the counter, told the man to put them on his bill, then walked over to Julia and took her hand. "Come on," he said gruffly. "I'm going to take you home." He ignored the people who were saying it had been nice talking to Julia and they hoped she'd come back tomorrow.

"Go on, get in," Garrick commanded as they reached his convertible. He slammed the door and skidded away from the curb. "Damn them!" he began. He was just drunk enough and just angry enough to give full vent to his feelings. "Who do they think they are? This whole town makes me sick. You can't go anywhere without hearing
152

Laura this and Laura that. Too bad she isn't Catholic so they could give her name to the Pope and try for sainthood."

Julia sat quite still, her hands folded in her lap. She had never liked her Uncle Garrick. He always smelled like whiskey and he said mean things to her pretty Aunt Clarry. And once, one awful day, she saw him try to kiss her mother. She hated them both that day. Later she forgave her mother because she had, after all, laughed at Uncle Garrick. But she still remembered how he had touched her mother.

Garrick kept on talking. He was thinking of how Laura had turned down Jack's offer without even consulting anyone. It wasn't just her resort that was involved but the whole town as well. And he owned a third share. "Who does she think she is?" he asked, not caring if he made any sense to Julia or not. "Laura's just an ordinary woman. She didn't do anything anyone else couldn't have done in the same situation. She just had a lot of luck, that's all."

As he pulled into Laura's driveway he remembered that no one in the drugstore had given him any greeting. "I could have showed them. I could have married Laura once but I decided not to."

He felt better after having said that. Maybe it was true. If he hadn't given up on Laura so soon, if he hadn't jumped at marrying Clarry and getting the third share, maybe...He smiled as he stopped the car and looked at Julia. He was taken back at the look of horror on her face, so different from her usual sweetness.

Julia was horrified. "My mother would never marry somebody like you!" she gasped. There were tears coming to her eyes. "You...you stink!"

Garrick's mouth dropped open. Here he'd been so nice to the haughty little bitch and this is how she repaid him. The afternoon sun on his head and too much whiskey were giving him a headache. He ground his teeth together. "I may not have married your mother but I could be your father," he said in anger. "She's cheated me more than once but she's not going to do it again. Maybe you'll think differently when she sells the Mission and *I* start running it."

Tears were running down Julia's cheeks. "You're not my father," she whispered.

153

Garrick ran his hand across his eyes. He was already beginning to regret what he had said. He didn't believe he was Julia's father; Julia had too much of the look of Ross for him to really believe it. Today had been too much. "You're right, kid, I'm not your father," he said heavily. "You better go in now."

Julia slowly opened the door and got out. She clutched her schoolbooks to her as she walked inside the house.

Later that night as Julia and Ross were grilling hamburgers for supper, Ross put his hand on his daughter's shoulder. "You're too quiet tonight. What's bothering you?"

Julia only shook her head and closed her eyes against the tears.

Ross knelt in front of her. "Did something happen at school today? You didn't get into an argument, did you?"

She flung her arms around him. "I love you, Daddy."

He held her close to him. "And I love you. So tell me what's the matter."

She shook her head against his neck. She couldn't tell him what Garrick had said. She couldn't tell him about Uncle Garrick kissing her mother.

Ross pulled her little face around to look at him. "Does it hurt too much for you to tell me now?" he asked quietly.

She nodded, looking at his shirtfront.

"Maybe later then. Sometimes time makes things hurt less. Then you can tell me. Is it a deal?"

"Yes," she managed to whisper.

He stood. "Okay, go get the ketchup and I think we're ready." He watched her run into the house and wondered what could be bothering her. It wasn't easy getting things out of her. She tended to bottle everything up, hiding behind her prettiness. He looked toward the back gate as he heard Laura's car pull into the driveway. He smiled, put down his spatula, and went to meet his wife.

Later, over hamburgers, Julia startled them both by asking if Laura were going to sell the Mission.

"Where in the world did you hear that?" Laura asked, astonished.

Julia shrugged, picking at her hamburger bun.

Ross watched his daughter, perhaps this was what was bothering her. But then there were always rumors that Laura was going to sell.

"Actually," Laura continued, "I did get another offer today. You remember that man who was decorated so much during the war? The good-looking one whose face was on all the magazine covers?"

"Jack Galloway," Julia supplied. "My teacher hung his picture in our room."

"The very one. He's staying at the Mission and this morning he offered to buy the place. Not a bad price, either."

"I didn't know war heroes had a lot of money. Seems I remember that he came from a poor family," Ross said.

"He's representing some eastern syndicate of men. He not only wants to buy the Mission but the whole town as well. It seems they want to turn the town into a tourist attraction, wax museums and that sort of thing."

"You aren't going to sell him the town, are you?" Julia asked in dead seriousness.

Laura laughed. "That's not for me to say. I don't own the town."

"But you own the Mission and the Mission owns the town, doesn't it?" Julia asked almost desperately.

Before Laura could speak, Ross put his hand on his daughter's. "You are right in a way. I'm sure the people don't want the town without the Mission. Would you like for your mother to sell the resort? We'd have lots of money and we could move away from Montero."

Julia considered seriously for a moment. Here, she was always *Laura's daughter,* but what would she be if her mother didn't have the Mission? Here, everyone knew her, spoke to her. "No," she said quietly. "I don't want to leave."

"Good," Laura sighed, "because I don't plan to sell. I just thought of something. Maybe we could get Mr. Galloway to speak at your school. He seems like a nice man."

"Yes, that would be nice," Julia said brightly, smiling up at her mother, so that she didn't notice the way Julia was shredding a paper napkin.

Marian Stromberg patted her hair and tucked a stray wisp back into the neat roll around her head. She turned and checked to see if the seams in her stockings were straight. It wasn't easy for her to turn to look at the backs of her legs. She'd put on some weight in the last few years. Of course that was only natural. A woman should look like a woman instead of being obsessed with being young, as Clarry was.

She looked about the big dining room impatiently. How she hated coming to the Mission! It was almost like admitting defeat to Laura. Of course Laura was probably very glad to have a Stromberg visit her establishment. After all, someone from Marian's family was sure to give the place a certain amount of prestige.

"Are you meeting someone, madam?" a young man in a dark suit asked her.

She gave him a cold look. She knew he was from Montero and she was sure he knew her name. He was just being obstinate in pretending he didn't know her.

Before she could speak, a male voice came from behind her. "Miss Stromberg?"

She turned and smiled up into Jack Galloway's blue eyes. "It's so good to see you again, Mr. Galloway." She held her hand out to him and gave a smug smile to the hovering headwaiter near her.

It had been a pleasant shock this morning when the handsome, famous, courageous Jack Galloway had come to her house and invited her to dine with him this evening. He had said he was interested in purchasing land in Montero and had heard that she was the one to contact. He'd gone on to say that he had had no idea she was so young and so attractive. Marian almost suggested they go somewhere else besides the Mission, as if there were anywhere else to go in this boring town. Then she thought she should show Laura's guests that there were people of class in Montero.

"I've reserved a table for us in the greenhouse," Jack smiled, holding out his arm to her.

She took it and walked with her head up as she went through the lush greenery aisles of the greenhouse dining room. The stars in the black New Mexico sky were visible through the glass overhead. Around them were tropical palms, fern trees, cyclamen, bougainvillea vines draping from the ceiling, and great pots of hanging fuchsia and tuberous begonias. Each table was almost private, surrounded by greenery. All the furniture was white, the crystal and silver of the finest quality.

"It's a beautiful place, isn't it?" Jack offered, unfolding his snowy napkin.

156

"A bit overdone, but all right. Of course, what can you expect from the Taylors? Not that Clarry isn't the loveliest girl, but Laura sometimes..." She smiled as if she were holding something back and looked down at her gold-and-white handlettered menu.

"I guess you've known them a long time, haven't you?"

"The Strombergs have been in Montero for a very long time."

Jack ordered for both of them, pleasing Marian with his selections. It was so nice to have a man do things for her again. Ten years ago, when her parents had been killed in a boating accident, she had lost a lot. She had been alone in a town of strangers. She had had to stand by and watch Laura Taylor marry, have a child, and build this resort.

"This morning you said something about buying some land, Mr. Galloway."

"It's Jack, remember?" he smiled. "I was sent here as a representative of a group of eastern business men. We'd like to buy the Mission and a great deal of land in Montero and open a sort of vacationland."

She sipped at a martini. "You mean bring industry to Montero?" The idea excited her. As it was, Laura owned nearly everyone in the town. But if other businesses could come to Montero, then it would break her monopoly.

"She won't sell," Marian said flatly. "I don't guess you'd like to buy land unless she does sell."

He leaned across the table. "May I be absolutely honest with you? I think it would be good for this town if Laura did sell. As it is, she's making all the profits. If this place were opened up to the tourists, then everyone would benefit. Of course there'd be those who didn't like the idea of tourists. Those people could sell to us and they'd have money to move elsewhere."

Marian thought for a moment. "Of course! As it is now, everyone works for Laura. If there were other businesses, they could work for themselves."

Jack smiled. "You're as intelligent as you are lovely."

Marian blushed shyly and began to adjust the ruffle at her sleeve. "But it all depends on Laura selling, doesn't it? She'll never sell!"

Jack leaned back in his chair. "I thought perhaps the people of Montero could help me persuade her."

157

"You don't know this town! They think the earth would fall if Laura willed it."

"I'm not so sure of that. There's a lady in town who makes pies for the Mission. Laura buys them at a price, then nearly doubles her money by selling the pies by the piece here in the dining room. I wonder how that pie lady would feel if she saw a way to sell her pies retail?"

"And make the profit instead of Laura," Marian finished. She dipped her artichoke leaf in drawn butter. "It seems to me that the best thing to do would be to let the people of Montero choose their own futures. They aren't all stupid."

"My sentiments exactly."

Marian carefully studied the artichoke leaf. "I just had a thought. This place is awfully expensive. I'll bet the average tourist couldn't afford it."

Jack waited patiently.

"Did you know that I own twenty acres right next to the Mission? Laura's tried to buy it several times, but I'd rather let it go to waste than give it to her. Perhaps I should start building something for the tourists, a motor court perhaps."

Jack smiled in admiration. "You can't be sure that she'll ever sell. You might be wasting your money."

She ignored him. "Did you know that Montero is set on solid rock? To build anything, you have to dynamite. I just wonder if Laura's guests are going to like waking to the sound of dynamite."

Jack settled back in his chair and sipped his wine. He smiled over his glass at Marian. "Yes, I, too, wonder how much Mrs. Kenyon can take."

Two days later, Jack was in the Montero drugstore. He lingered over coffee and a chicken sandwich while he listened to the gossip around him. Everyone was speculating as to why Marian Stromberg had just ordered several thousand concrete blocks. Not that Marian ever bothered to speak to any of the townspeople, but they knew she was up to something.

"What does Laura say, Louise?" the druggist asked.

"How would I know?" Louise snapped as she stared at a row of aspirin bottles.

The druggist shrugged and turned to Jack. "Anything else I can get you?"

"No," Jack said, tossing coins onto the counter. "That Laura you mentioned, is she the one who owns the Mission?"

"Sure," he grinned. "Laura Kenyon."

"You know, I've heard about how she built that place from a ruin. I expected her to be older. I certainly didn't expect a stunner like she is. How can any woman be so young, so beautiful, and smart as well?"

The druggist grinned possessively. "She's a Montero girl. We raise 'em like that."

"Well, you certainly do a good job. She's got every guest and every employee eating out of her hand."

Louise suddenly ran through the store and out the door.

"She must have left something on the stove," Jack said amiably.

"Naw, her husband works for Laura. I think the green-eyed monster bit her."

Jack gulped the last of his coffee. "Thanks for telling me. I'll keep my big mouth shut from now on." He grabbed his hat, and as he left the store he was whistling. He took a piece of paper with an address on it from his pocket. Garrick had told him of a convalescent soldier who would be able to make a model of Montero for him. He kept whistling as he walked toward the man's house.

Chapter 12

Irene Anderson was just leaving her typing class. The streets were dark, but it was only a short walk from the high school to her house and her old car was in the shop again. She walked quickly, not afraid really, but wanting to get out of the darkness.

When the big car started following her, she didn't even turn to see who it was. There was no need. At times she couldn't remember when Garrick Eastman wasn't near her. At work, he always seemed to be close to her desk. His breath, always smelling of whiskey, circled her head like a black cloud. His hands, so soft from his easy life, clutched at her. They ran up her arms, across her shoulders, touched her hair, and even once, across her thigh.

She shivered and quickened her pace. Why didn't he call out to her? Why did he just have to follow silently, like the death angel in the Bible? At work, he rarely spoke to her, just stood there watching, his hands coming from nowhere.

When she had first gotten the job as receptionist, she had been indignant at Garrick's behavior. At lunch one day, she mentioned to one of the secretaries that she was angry at Garrick's attentions. The secretary looked at her as if she were ill. How in the world could she not adore Garrick? He was so good-looking, so rich, and he was Laura's brother-in-law. The woman hinted that Laura would not like to hear complaints about someone so close to her.

Irene didn't know where to turn. She couldn't do anything to risk losing her job. She had to support her mother, and soon Dave, her brother, would be home from the hospital. The army helped with his expenses, of course, but her mother often said it wouldn't be enough. Irene went to school four nights a week and Saturday morning. She

160

was working to get a secretarial job at the Mission and hoped eventually to work up to head housekeeper.

At the sharp sound of the horn beside her, she jumped, then began to run. She could hear Garrick's laughter behind her.

She ran into her house and slammed the door behind her. She leaned against it, her heart pounding wildly.

"I don't know why you can't enter a house like a normal person," came her mother's voice. "Other women get nice, ladylike daughters, but I get a door slammer. And where have you been?"

"To my typing class," Irene said patiently. "You know I go every Tuesday and Thursday."

"Don't you get smart with me, young lady!" Mrs. Anderson snapped. She stepped into the living room wearing a cheap, flowered robe and furry house shoes. She was a small woman, a constant frown on her plain face.

"I don't know what I've done to be cursed with a back-talking, smart-mouthed daughter like you. I stay here all day and work my fingers to the bone, and what gratitude do I get for it? What do you have to go to a typing class for anyway? Why can't you get a husband like other girls?"

"I don't want a husband," Irene said heavily. "Was there any mail?"

"You don't want a husband because you can't get one. Who wants a door slammer? And you can't even cook. Who wants a wife like that?"

Irene closed her eyes for a moment. "Was there any mail?" she repeated.

"Don't you look at me that way! I know what you're thinking. You think you're too good for your poor old mother after spending the day at that hoity-toity place where you work. Well, I'll have you know that here, in the real world, you have to work for a living. Don't you think you can come home and get waited on like you do there. You don't make enough money for me to buy food, much less afford personal maid service like you get all day long. I work too hard to make meals for you and keep them hot under silver covers like you want."

Irene walked past her mother to the hall table. It was no use arguing with the woman. She had learned that long ago. The only thing that modified her mother's tirades was Dave. He could make their mother stop complaining.

When Dave was home, everything ran more smoothly. Sometimes Dave took Irene away, just the two of them, for a drive or a picnic. Dave told Irene she was smart, encouraged her to get good grades in school. He protected Irene from their mother, kept her from screaming at Irene twenty-four hours a day.

But when Dave was away, Mrs. Anderson gave free rein to all the venom she had stored. No matter what Irene did, it wasn't right. But Irene had Dave's letters to sustain her. He encouraged her to go to school at night, to work toward a good job, to believe in herself, not to sell herself short.

Then, eighteen months ago, Dave had been wounded. He was paralyzed from the waist down and would spend the rest of his life in a wheelchair. His letters stopped abruptly. Irene wrote him daily, telling him how much he was loved and needed. Six months ago, he started writing again.

There, on the hall table lay a new letter. It had already been opened, although it was addressed to Irene, but it didn't matter. Tears blurred her eyes as she began to read it.

Her mother started again. "You're wrong if you think you can get out of work here. There's dishes to be done and the kitchen needs to be cleaned. This isn't your fancy Mission. I don't have servants to wait on me like you do."

Without thinking about what she was doing, Irene took the letter to the kitchen. She propped it against the window as she ran hot water into the sink and started washing the dishes that her mother had left all day.

The first sentence of the letter told her what she wanted to know. Dave would be coming home in ten days. She closed her eyes for a moment in relief. Soon everything would be all right. Garrick would no longer bother her, not when her brother was home.

The army had sent a detailed account of Dave's illness and had even included some comments about what to expect from his morale. But Irene didn't think much of the army's pessimism. Dave still had his mind and his hands and he had people who loved him. Irene smiled to herself. Now she had no worry that Dave would ever leave her. Now she felt no rush to get married. She could wait until the right man came along, someone gentle and tender, someone who would love her. Until then, she had Dave.

She heard her mother's voice in the background, but she didn't really listen. Her mother no longer slapped her as she had when Irene was a child. When their father had left them when Irene was a baby, her big brother Dave became both father and brother to her. Now, at last, she'd be able to do something for him. She worked hard at the Mission, put in extra hours, took on extra duties, because she planned to ask Laura soon to give Dave a job. When he came home, they would discuss it, decide what he'd like to do. Then Irene would ask.

After she finished the last dish, she began to wash the greasy stove. Soon everything would be good again. She would drive Dave to work each morning and in the evening he would tease their mother out of her bitterness. Yes, it was all going to be wonderful. Just ten more days.

Garrick slammed into his house, his face mirroring his black mood. Damn the bitch! he thought repeatedly. Irene Anderson acted like a queen instead of the two-bit tease she was. What made her think she was so special?

He grabbed a decanter of Scotch, poured himself a triple, downed it in one gulp, then poured another. Maybe she was one of those women who wanted to be courted. Maybe she expected flowers and candy. He snorted as he drank the second glassful. He'd get her, without courting.

"Garrick, has something upset you?"

He whirled. He hadn't realized anyone else was in the room. Marian Stromberg sat on the couch beside Clarry. He ignored his wife.

Marian was another matter. Now, at twenty-eight and looking at least forty, Marian still looked at Garrick as if he were a famous movie star. Right now, he rather liked her attentions. He had never made a pass at her because he thought she would find bedroom activity repulsive, but he always wooed her. It paid off once when she gave him two thousand dollars to pay off a few people in Albuquerque.

He walked across the big room, took Marian's hand from the back of the couch and kissed it through her short white cotton gloves. "Whatever was wrong with me is now
163

soothed. May I say, Marian, that you look as lovely as always?"

"You may," she smiled, lowering her eyes, then looking at Clarry from under her lashes.

"If you ladies will excuse me...," he said as he walked toward the end of the room where the door led to his bedroom wing.

Marian stared after Garrick as if in a trance.

"Would you like some more coffee?" Clarry asked quietly.

Marian gave an enormous sigh. "Oh, Clarry, you're so very, very lucky." She turned back to look at her friend. "Garrick is such a gentleman." She put her hand over her mouth and giggled. "I know he's rather naughty at times, but he is so very, very gallant."

Clarry's hand tightened on the handle of the coffeepot. Yesterday she asked Garrick for a divorce and he merely laughed at her. She had expected nearly any reaction except laughter. He said he liked their marriage. It left him free but at the same time gave him an excuse when the broads at the Mission came on too strong. Besides, he wasn't about to lose his reason for Laura to pay him a third of the profits.

Clarry hadn't yet recovered from Garrick's announcement.

"Oh, Clarry! I nearly forgot. I got a letter from a distant cousin of mine. You may remember him. Scott Stromberg."

"Yes," Clarry said, her voice little more than a whisper. "I remember him."

"Well, I never did know what happened that summer. I never could see why you liked him so much. He was so rude. Anyway, after he left here, I never heard a word from him again for all these years. Suddenly, last week I got a letter from him."

"What did he have to say?"

Marian waved her hand. "Nothing but the most disgusting trivia. He left New York and moved to some midwestern state, married a perfect nobody, and had three kids. He even sent a picture of them! Isn't that a scream, Clarry? We were such schoolgirls then and we thought Scott was so sophisticated, but he wasn't at all."

Clarry's hand shook as she put her cup back on her

saucer. She would not allow herself to think of "might-have-beens." "Did he say anything else?"

Marian gave her friend a sly look. "He said he'd heard about how well the Mission was doing since he had an aunt who visited it once." Marian set her cup down angrily. "And to think she didn't even bother to visit me! Anyway, Scott wanted to know how you were." Marian continued before Clarry could reply. "Of course I sat down immediately and wrote him and told him how immensely happy you were. I told him all about your wonderful husband and your lovely house. Of couse I did leave out the part about the dress shop. You know, Clarry, you really shouldn't work. You have a wonderful husband and you should devote more time to him."

Clarry stood. She didn't want to hear Marian's tirade again. "It's late, Marian, and I have some work to do."

Marian gave Clarry a reproachful look for her rudeness. Of course one could never expect a shop girl to have better manners. "I can take a hint. It just seems to me that once in a while you'd listen to me. Someday, when all this is over, you'll thank me." She shut her mouth abruptly. She didn't plan to tell Clarry or anyone else about her scheme to force Laura out of the Mission. Yes, she thought, she was doing it in part for Clarry. If Clarry had money from the sale of the resort, she wouldn't have to work and she could relax and learn to appreciate her husband.

"I do need to go anyway," Marian said quickly to cover her error. She looked around the lovely room. "You were so lucky to get Garrick instead of that boring Scott. Imagine! He plays softball with the kids on Sunday." She shuddered delicately. "If I were to marry, I'd want a husband like Garrick."

Clarry braced herself as she listened to Marian, and once she was gone, she leaned against the door for a moment. Laura had once asked Clarry why she still put up with Marian and Clarry couldn't really answer. Marian was more than sad. She lived in a dream world and saw little of what happened around her. She still saw Garrick as a handsome, suave man on a pedestal. Year after year, Clarry had to listen to long speeches about how lucky she was and how wonderful Garrick was.

She walked toward the hall leading to her bedroom. She wouldn't let herself think about Marian's words about

Scott. She wondered what Scott would think when he heard how wonderfully happy Clarry was.

She closed the bedroom door behind her and thought that maybe Marian wasn't so far wrong after all. She had spent many hours and several nights with Bill Matthews in the last few days. And she was beginning to think she was in love with him.

Whether or not it was love, she was certainly beginning to catch fire from Bill's enthusiasm for her designs. He was appalled that she was hiding them, that she had so little belief in her talent. Bill said that as a man he was sick of women's broad-shouldered dresses and he wanted to see women look like women again. He thought Clarry's designs could start a fashion revolution.

Clarry didn't believe all Bill said but she began to have confidence, enough, she felt, to withstand the laughter if she were ridiculed.

She turned on the light over her drafting table. She was designing a dress for Laura and she already had one at the seamstress's. Poor Laura, Clarry thought, she probably wouldn't ever realize she was being used as a guinea pig for some revolutionary fashion. But Clarry knew some of the guests who would notice.

She picked up her steel pen and set to work.

Chapter 13

"Mother," Julia asked once again, looking up from the comics of the Sunday paper, "are you going to sell the Mission?"

Laura put down her coffee cup with such a clatter that Ross looked at her over the paper. "If one more person asks me that, I may go crazy," she said as she stood up. She whirled toward Ross. "This is that awful Jack Galloway's fault."

"Awful?" Ross said, one eyebrow raised. "I thought he was very kind when he agreed to talk at Julia's school."

She flopped into the overstuffed chair. "The man's trying to drive me crazy. Even my own daughter—" She put her head in her hands.

Ross folded his newspaper and went to sit on the arm of her chair. He put his arm around her. "What's been bothering you lately? Are you sure it's this Jack Galloway or are you just tired?"

She leaned against him. "Tired mostly, I guess. It's just that lately everyone seems to be urging me to sell. Garrick must mention it three times a day, and now the guests are asking me."

"The guests? Has Galloway been talking to them?"

Laura glanced at Julia, seemingly intent on the comics. "He moved out of the Mission yesterday so it's hard to know what he's up to now. Marian Stromberg has surveyors on that land she owns next to the Mission. Last week one of the surveyors told a guest the Mission had already been sold."

Ross gave his wife's shoulder a squeeze. "If it hasn't, then you have nothing to worry about. If they give you too much grief, why don't you post a sign or clip a notice to the menus?"

Laura laughed. "That isn't a bad idea. What is it, Julia?" she asked as her daughter looked up at her, her eyes wide.

"Look at this!" she said, pointing to the inside of the entertainment section of the Sunday paper. "Mr. Galloway is giving a free picnic for everyone in Montero. And here's a picture of him with President Truman. What does it mean, 'the wealth of the future'?"

Laura looked up at Ross.

Ross took the paper from Julia. In the center of the section was a full two-page ad and a very large picture of Jack Galloway being presented with a medal by the president. Large, bold letters invited the entire town to a picnic next Sunday. There was a long list of the food to be served.

"Do you know how much that's going to cost him?" Laura asked. "What does he plan to get out of this?"

"I think this may give you a hint." Ross pointed to the bottom of the first page. It stated that the purpose of the picnic was to give the citizens of Montero a chance at the wealth of the future. It talked about education for the children, culture for the adults, comfort for the older citizens. It asked whether the people of Montero were free or whether they lived in a dictatorship.

"Just what is that supposed to mean? Is he insinuating that President Truman is a dictator?" Laura asked.

Ross didn't answer but he had an idea what Jack Galloway meant. He just hoped he was wrong.

There wasn't usually much excitement in Montero, New Mexico. Over the years the people had gotten used to the famous people who visited the Mission. Sometimes the druggist would have to fill a prescription in the middle of the night and even that would be enough to fill the town with speculation and talk.

Jack Galloway's picnic was the most exciting thing to happen in years. There wasn't a house or store where the picnic wasn't the topic of conversation.

"I bet they found oil in the town," one person said as he buttered his toast. Every cafe in Montero was full at every meal. The people talked across tables like one big family.

"Naw, uranium's the thing now," someone else added.

"Maybe it's something secret like the A-bomb they

made down in Los Alamos. Remember, Jack Galloway has connections in the White House."

"But in the newspaper, he mentions culture. There's no culture in Los Alamos. Those people have to have a pass to leave or enter. I'm leavin' if the government wants to do that to Montero."

"But I bet you hold out for a good price, huh, Sam? Those scientists make a lot of money."

The banter went back and forth. There wasn't a person who didn't have an opinion. For a while, the Mission was nearly forgotten. People began to think of wealth, real wealth, where they could fly to places like the Mission and be a guest rather than supply goods for the resort.

By Thursday, everyone had exhausted the possibilities of what Jack Galloway planned. All that was left was the idea of wealth. They began to talk about what they'd do if they were wealthy. Over the years they had seen a great deal of wealth at the Mission and they had an idea of how they'd handle their own money, if they had any.

It was surprising how much the people of Montero knew about wealth. They talked competently about the different types of caviar, and where the best oysters came from— Maine or Louisiana. The women knew about the latest clothing designs from the Paris designers. The children sat down with the Sears catalog and started choosing the toys they would buy when they were rich.

By Saturday, the excitement was at a fever pitch. The women were becoming mildly resentful at spending their days cleaning and cooking. If they were rich, they would have someone else do it for them. The men kept daydreaming about fishing trips to Utah or, better yet, for salmon in Scotland. The children neglected their homework. When they were rich, they'd have someone else do it for them.

By Sunday morning, a great calm had spread over the whole town. The people were quite serious as they took their best clothes from the closets and dressed with special care. They didn't know whether or not some of the guests from the Mission were going to be there, but they didn't want to look like country hicks.

They attended church in the morning and there wasn't one person who didn't pray for his wishes to come true. It seemed that it was time for them to *get* instead of always giving.

169

Laura and Ross, their daughter beside them, walked quietly out of the church. "I feel like a pig on my way to the slaughterhouse," Laura said as she observed the un- natural calm around her.

"Just remember that you own the Mission and no one else. If you don't want to sell, you don't have to," Ross said, also very aware of the people.

"Hey, Julia!" a child called. "Are you going to the picnic?"

"Are we?" Julia asked. Her big eyes reflected the ex- citement the others were feeling.

"Of course!" Laura said in a false note. "I wouldn't miss this for the world."

Ross squeezed her arm, and they walked toward their car to begin the journey into the forest where the picnic was to be held.

Of course the townspeople had made numerous trips during the last week to the place where the picnic was to be held, but they were always disappointed. There were no advance preparations of any kind. Now they realized that many people must have worked all night to create the sight that awaited them.

In the center of the big opening was an enormous, open tent, more a canopy. Hundreds, maybe thousands, of brightly colored oilcloth flags ran from the tent to the trees. Big tables covered with food were set under the trees.

But what caught everyone's attention was what was under the canopy. There was a large table with something on it, and the people realized immediately that this was the important attraction at this picnic.

"What's under the tent?" Julia asked from the backseat as her parents pulled into the place designated for parking.

"I don't know but I have a feeling I'm not going to like it," Laura answered.

Laura and Ross had to practically fight their way through the crowds to get under the canopy. The towns- people were staring with quiet fascination.

It was a model, an enormous scale model of Montero. Every road, every house, and Laura suspected, every tree, was accurately displayed. But the big model wasn't of Montero as it was but as it could be.

There was a sign over the gate over the Santa Fe highway that said: "Montero, New Mexico. Vacation Capitol of the World. Welcome." The road into town was covered with small businesses, motels, an old car museum, a doll museum, restaurants.

"You know," Mr. Woodman said, next to Laura, "I own that land on the west side of the Santa Fe highway. I always thought it was worthless. I wonder what they'll give me to build on it?"

His words were a catalyst for the people to start. There wasn't a piece of land that didn't have a hotel or pony ride or restaurant on it. The northeast section of town was replaced with a big midway. There were rides, sideshows, games of chance, and a long, complicated roller coaster.

"I'll sell my house to 'em," someone laughed. "For a price."

The voices began to grow more and more excited. Everyone found his or her house and exclaimed over what additions had been made. Property that a week ago had seemed useless now seemed to be worth a fortune. The Chevrolet dealer's lot had tripled in size and was covered with little shiny metal cars. The plaza had one dress shop after another on it. One woman laughed and said she knew where she was going to spend a lot of her money.

"Laura," Clarry said quietly, beside her sister, "look at the Mission."

Laura could hardly see anything else. As far as she could tell, the resort was untouched. Even on the scale of the model, it looked elegant and serene amid all the bright signs and modern buildings. It was like a rich old lady looking over the flashy younger generation.

"It doesn't make sense, does it?" Clarry asked. "Why would they change everything except the Mission? Surely they must know that a town *like that*," she motioned toward the model, "wouldn't attract the type of guests who usually come to the Mission."

"They!" Laura said under her breath. "I think *they* know exactly what they're doing." She turned and began to maneuver her way through the crowd.

"Laura!" Ross caught her arm. "Where are you going?"

"Home. I don't want to see any more of this."

He pulled her around to face him. "You can't run away."

"Run away? That's just what I want to do! You heard them in there. They think that just because there's a little

171

cardboard motel on their land that someone is going to pay them big city prices for the land. I don't want to be around when they find out differently."

"You're not being honest with me," he said, looking hard into her eyes. "You and I both know that's not what you're afraid of. Galloway's going to say it all depends on your selling the Mission, isn't that true?"

"Yes," she whispered. "He already told me that. But Ross, I can't sell. I don't want to sell."

"Then don't! It's your choice."

She looked at the ground between them. "But the people... They deserve a chance, too."

Ross ground his teeth together. "I'm tempted to smack you. What happened to your brain? Galloway's syndicate is trying to force you to sell. Do you think they're going to treat you like this, then give buckets of money to the townspeople for their land?"

"No, of course not."

"I have a feeling they plan to do about half of that building at first. They'll buy what land they can, as cheaply as they can, then force the rest of the people out. Who wants to live next door to the world's largest roller coaster?"

"But I don't have any right to decide for them. If they want to sell—"

Ross gave her a little shake. "Sometimes you carry your gratitude too far. I've never minded that you poured all the profits back into the Mission and that you hired half again as many people as the Mission needed, but I do mind your selling out just to please the people of Montero. Do you want to sell?"

"No! You know I don't."

He put his arm around her shoulders. "Then no more discussion. You don't want to sell and you're not going to. Now, let's get something to eat."

"I couldn't, really—"

"Come on, there's time enough for misery later," he said, grabbing her hand. He had an idea the people of Montero were going to be pretty angry when they saw their dreams of wealth go down the drain.

The people of Montero were in an extraordinarily good mood as they sat down to a big meal of fried chicken and baked ham. They felt like country squires, seeing their own safe, comfortable futures rolling out before them.

Jack Galloway circulated and spoke to everyone, asking if the food were all right, if they needed anything.

At two o'clock, several men, out-of-towners, began announcing a speech to be given at three. Ross took Laura's hand as they walked to the wooden platform which had been set up. Jack Galloway mounted the stairs and stood behind the microphone.

The sun shone through the trees and flashed off Jack. He wore his uniform, full dress, every medal he had been given dripping down the front of his jacket. There was more than one sigh from the women. He smiled at the crowd boyishly and said he wasn't used to this sort of thing. The crowd laughed adoringly and Jack looked down at his feet in shyness.

"I'm just a small town boy," he began. "I've not been to school much and I don't know all that much but I do have some things I believe in."

The humble words coming from a man who had obviously done and seen a great deal were endearing. Everyone smiled as if they shared a secret with this modest young man.

"I believe in America," he said quietly, but the words could have been shouted. "I believe America is the greatest nation on earth." He had to wait for the applause to stop. "That's why I took on this job, because I see a way for Montero to serve her country."

"I think I'm going to be ill," Laura said rather loudly, and several people turned to glare at her.

In spite of Jack's declarations that he was a humble man, he was an excellent speaker. He talked about the progress of America, hinting that the hated Japanese and Germans were planning more wars, and progress would be the only thing to save America. He talked of America's children, how all wars had been fought to save them, and that education was part of the future. He spoke of the men who had "fought and died for us," that the ones left behind needed a way to express their gratitude for America still being a free nation.

He spoke for nearly an hour, even once pausing to wipe a tear from his eye. The audience, even the children, listened in rapt attention. Everyone wanted to help keep America great, they all wanted to do their share.

Jack paused for a while and lowered his voice. He quietly asked if Montero were ready to help her country. The shout from the crowd rustled the tree leaves overhead. Jack smiled at them and shook his head in wonder at such a self-sacrificing crowd.

He continued with his speech. This time he talked faster and only for a short while. He said that making Montero into a vacationland for all America to play and learn in was almost noble. He spoke of schools for the children, relaxation for the adults, progress for the country as a whole.

When he saw the happy, excited look on everyone's faces, he took his microphone and walked down into the crowd. "Now, I'd like to hear other people's opinions of my ideas."

He held the big microphone before a woman's face. She grabbed it eagerly. "I'm Della Anderson and I for one agree. It's time we helped America—and ourselves!"

Jack put his hand fondly on her head and nearly grabbed the microphone from her. "Of course this all depends on one person," he said laughingly. "Montero was chosen because of its historical value." He tossed the words off as if they were of no great consequence.

Laura saw him coming toward her, but short of running from the place, she saw no escape. She was angry, very angry. This man was using patriotism to get what he wanted.

"Laura!" Jack smiled, thrusting the microphone before her. "How do you feel about America?"

Laura looked at him with all the anger she felt, and the people of Montero grew quiet. They wanted to know what Laura felt about this wonderful opportunity Jack was offering them.

There were a hundred things Laura wanted to say to Jack. She wanted to talk about greed and his use of patriotism on a group of people who were too close to the war to think clearly when the word was mentioned. She stood, very slowly, and looked out at the sea of faces. They were her friends and neighbors, people she had known all her life. A great many of them worked for her. They looked at her expectantly.

"I will not sell the Mission," she said firmly.

The people looked at her with a puzzled expression. Who had asked her to sell?

Jack gave an exaggerated shrug of helplessness and began to walk back to the platform. The people didn't quite understand what was going on but they knew something had happened.

Della Anderson, Irene's mother, stood up. "Do you mean that whether we get the vacationland or not depends on Laura Kenyon selling the Mission?"

Jack looked at them again, an expression of great sadness on his face. "I'm afraid so. It wouldn't be good for them to have it as a resort where there were . . . well, adult things happening."

Laura opened her mouth to speak, but Ross grabbed her arm. "Let's go now, Laura." He'd been watching the people turn toward her, one by one, their expressions going from happiness to sadness to coldness as they saw Laura blocking what they wanted.

Laura allowed herself to be led away. She didn't want to see the people's faces, the few she had seen were more than enough.

Julia followed her parents, then Clarry and Bill Matthews. The townspeople stared and then began to whisper. They'd seen Clarry and Bill together a lot lately. And Clarry a married woman! It seemed to emphasize what Jack had said about the things going on at the Mission. That place was getting downright decadent lately.

Garrick stared open-mouthed for a moment at another man escorting his wife. So that was why the bitch had suddenly asked for a divorce. Several people looked up at him in sympathy. He nearly dropped his cigarette. He didn't like their looks and he wasn't about to accept them. He wasn't going to be cuckolded by another man.

Emmett Romero also stood to follow Laura. He, too, had seen through Jack's passionate speech. Louise grabbed the hem of his jacket, but Emmett ignored her.

All together there were an even dozen people who followed Laura to the cars. Irene Anderson started to go, but her mother elbowed her sharply and she sat down again. Dave sat in his wheelchair, his eyes hard and unseeing, his mouth twisted into a line of grimness. He didn't care what happened to anyone in the town, himself included. His life might as well be over.

Chapter 14

Clarry jumped slightly when Bill kissed her neck, then she bent so he could have better access. He put his arms around her and ran his lips up to her ear.

"Are you always so delicious in the morning?" he murmured.

"Always," she laughed. "And are you always so... energetic?"

"Spend the whole night with me and find out."

She turned on the swivel stool and faced him. "You know I wish I could, but—"

He kissed her to silence her. "Now show me what you're doing. If we keep this up, we'll wind up rolling around on the floor again, and I don't think your salesgirls would care for that."

"I might, though," she whispered, kissing him again.

"Nope!" he said firmly, twirling her to face her drafting table where she was working on a new dress design. "Who's this for?"

"I don't know. It was to be for Laura, but..."

Bill leaned on the edge of the table. "Things pretty bad, huh?"

She set her pencil down and looked at him. "A week ago everyone was full of what Laura had done for them. Now they seem to think Laura's doing something *to* them."

"How's Laura taking it?"

"As well as can be expected. A couple of people quit, but generally everyone who works here has been fairly understanding."

He picked up a drawing and studied it. "That's not the way I hear it in town. People keep saying Laura needs a rest and it might be for her own good if she sold."

"Damn them!" Clarry said angrily. "This is Laura's life. She'd be lost without it."

Bill put the drawing down. "And what's your life, Clarry?" he asked quietly.

She couldn't meet his eyes. If he knew what was being said about Laura, he knew what the townspeople were saying about them. Every time she saw Garrick, he delighted in repeating a piece of gossip about Clarry's immorality. People were beginning to remember her and Scott Stromberg. They talked about what a little sexpot Clarry had always been. They didn't seem to remember that there had been eleven years without a hint of scandal.

Bill put his hand under her chin. "Is it that bad?"

She tried to be calm. "Worse," she smiled but felt the tears beginning.

He put his arms around her. "This thing will blow over in a few weeks, and ten years after we're married, who'll ever remember the Montero Vacationland?"

Clarry pushed away from him. "It's not just the gossip. Garrick says he'll never give me a divorce. He's afraid Laura will cut off his percentage from the Mission."

A week earlier, the night after the picnic, Clarry had told Bill why she had married Garrick. The whole thing had made him ill. To think that someone would take money to marry his Clarry!

"Perhaps if we talk to Laura, maybe she can arrange for Garrick to keep on receiving payment."

Clarry looked up at him, startled. "I can't take my problems to her now. She may seem all right, but I know her, she's really upset by this thing with Jack Galloway. Every time she steps into town someone starts talking to her, 'for her own good.' The creeps want her to sell so they can be rich. Or at least they think they will be."

Bill ran his hand up her arm. "You really care about her, don't you?"

Clarry was quiet for a moment as she studied the pencils on the table. "A long time ago I used to think I hated her. Maybe I did hate her because I was so selfish and she was so generous. She gave up her art career for me and for this rotten town. And I hated her for it! I guess I wanted her to be as selfish as I was."

"You've certainly made up for it now."

"I want to. The last thing I want to do is add more problems to her own. You know," she looked at him. "Everyone thinks Laura is very strong but sometimes I
177

think she's almost delicate. She needs people, people supporting her and loving her. This may sound silly but sometimes I wish she'd be more selfish and stop giving so much to everyone. She should show this town that they need her and not the other way around. She ought to fire about half the staff and bring in some people from Denver. She'd probably get more work done for less money."

"About how likely is Laura to do that?" Bill smiled.

"About as likely as I am to try and take over the Mission," she laughed. "Maybe we could mix us up. I need some of Laura's self-sacrificing and she needs some of my selfishness."

"You are not selfish!" Bill said firmly.

"And you are blind!" Clarry laughed.

Before Bill could speak again, Jill came into the big storage area. "Excuse me, but Louise Romero is out here and she's making a fuss. She says she wants to see you."

Clarry walked toward the door to the shop.

"She's a little..." Jill said.

"Drunk?" Clarry added, her face serious.

Jill nodded curtly.

"Good morning, Louise," Clarry said solemnly. Louise had lost a lot of her youthful prettiness, and now too many drinks had made her facial muscles sag. There were dark circles under her eyes. "Could I help you?"

"You sure can!" Louise said loudly. "What do you have that can help me compete with your dear, sexy, rich sister?"

Clarry took Louise's arm. "Perhaps we should go into my workroom."

"Of course. A native of Montero would give a bad name to your elegant store."

Clarry closed the heavy door to the shop and was thankful for the soundproof adobe walls of the Mission. "Bill, would you get Louise some coffee?"

"Hiding him, are you, Clarry? I wish I had a man I could keep hidden away and then take out whenever I wanted."

Clarry practically pushed Louise onto the sofa and handed her the coffee. "You *do* have a man but you prefer to drive him away."

"Like you do Garrick?" Louise asked sweetly over her coffee.

178

Clarry and Bill exchanged looks. Bill nodded, then quietly left the room.

"Trying to hide me?" Louise asked.

"Emmett may put up with you and Laura may feel guilty about you, but I won't! There's nothing wrong with you except self-pity. You have a home, lovely children and a husband who loves you."

"Loves me! He spends day after day with another woman! Could you stand by and see your husband do that?" Too late, Louise realized whom she was talking to.

"I have and I do," Clarry said quietly. "I believe I've stood by through a great deal more than your imagined slights."

"Imagined! What about last Sunday when Emmett followed *her* instead of staying with me?"

"Why didn't you go with your husband? Jack Galloway was wrong to try to embarrass Laura so she'd have to sell. You've spent enough time here. You know Laura doesn't make a lot of money. Why didn't you stand up for her—and your husband?"

Louise looked up at Clarry with hate. "Because your sister wants my husband. Why do you think she keeps him so late every night?"

Clarry couldn't reply for a moment. She stared at Louise in astonishment. "You are driving yourself insane, do you know that? Emmett works late so Laura can go home to her own husband. Don't you have a grain of common sense? Why would Laura want Emmett when she has Ross?"

Louise jumped to her feet. "You're disgusting! Are you having an affair with Ross as well as Bill? You two sisters are just alike."

Clarry didn't realize she was going to slap Louise until she had done it. Louise grabbed her cheek. "You'll regret that. Both of you will regret what you've done to me." She turned on her heel and left the room.

Clarry watched the door slam and stood for a moment, shaking. It seemed like the whole town was going crazy. Jack Galloway's picnic had stirred up a hornet's nest of trouble. She poured herself a cup of coffee and went back to work. Maybe in another week it would be all over.

Irene Anderson was sitting at her small desk behind the big reception desk. She put her elbows on the desk to support her aching head. Her body was trembling and tears blurred her eyes.

Suddenly, arms slid around her, lips nuzzled her neck. A strong smell of whiskey made her upset stomach turn over. She sent her elbows backward, hard into Garrick's ribs.

"Leave me alone!" she gasped, unable to control her anger.

Garrick released her abruptly, glared at her. He was getting sick of her cat-and-mouse games. "What the hell's wrong with you? I think I've been damned patient with you."

She was shaking too badly to even answer him. Garrick Eastman was the least of her worries.

"It seems like you'd be grateful since I got you a raise. It wasn't easy, what with Laura so upset about this Galloway thing. But I did it for you, baby. I know about that crippled brother of yours. I figured you'd need the extra money."

Irene looked down at her hands. The young man who had left for war and the one who had returned in a wheelchair bore very little resemblance to each other. "I...I am grateful," she stammered. "Thank you. We do need the money."

Garrick stepped closer to her, put his hand on her neck. "That's more like it. I don't know why you seem to think I'm such a monster." He chuckled at the idea but he was very aware of Irene's stiffness under his touch. "You know, this Galloway business may be a good thing for you. About four people have quit since the picnic. I was thinking that there might be a job for your brother."

She looked up at him with hope in her eyes. Maybe if Dave had a job, some of the hate would leave him.

Garrick smiled at her and ran his hand down her arm, his thumb running along the side of her breast. "Of course, if I did this for you, I'd expect something in return. I scratch your back, you scratch mine. You get my drift?"

She jerked away from him. "I understand you," she said, letting all the repulsion she felt show in her voice.

Garrick curled his lip at her. "You just remember, honey, who hands out the jobs around here. There's nobody in town who'll give a job to a cripple like your brother. When you get tired of playing the princess, let me know.

You know where you can find me." He turned away angrily and left her.

She wouldn't be able to save anymore. The army had sent a male nurse home with Dave, just for a few weeks until Irene and her mother learned to take care of him, and so Irene had an extra mouth to feed. Her salary barely supported her and her mother, much less two more. Garrick had gotten her a five dollar a week raise, and Irene had waited a week before telling her mother. She first spent a whole five dollars on herself, eating in the dining room with the other employees and buying a silk scarf from Clarry's shop. Now she felt guilty about even that small expense.

"Irene, are you all right?" Betty Gomez, one of the secretaries, asked. "You don't look well at all. Why don't you go home?"

"I can't. It's too early." Irene busied herself, straightening the already neat desk.

"Early? Are you kidding? It's after six and you get off at five."

Irene stiffened. She didn't want to face the fact that she didn't want to go home, that she'd rather stay at the Mission.

Betty put her hand on Irene's shoulder. "Something's really upsetting you lately. Want to talk about it?"

Irene gave a forced little smile. "There's nothing wrong. I just forgot the time, that's all."

Betty frowned, not believing her for a moment. Irene was a quiet, solitary person. She never joined the other girls at lunch, never invited them to her house, never even seemed to date, although Betty knew several of the guests had asked her out. Irene kept to herself, never complaining, always doing her work, never asking anyone for anything. Betty shrugged. "Maybe you're coming down with a summer cold. Go home, get in a hot tub, and drink a little rum and lemon juice. That'll make you feel better even if you don't have a cold."

Irene tried to keep her smile. She'd have to go home, clean the house, listen to her mother's screaming at her, watch Dave's sulky silence, and then go to bed late and start all over again tomorrow. She had had to drop her secretarial class at the end of the semester. There was no more money for what her mother called "frivolities."

181

She got her purse and left the resort. Her car was still in the shop so she looked for someone to catch a ride with. She didn't have to wait long before she saw Emmett Romero walk to his car. The two of them rode in silence, each absorbed in his own problems.

He let her out before her front door, and she took a deep breath before she entered the house.

"Where have you been?" her mother greeted her, as she always did.

To the king's ball, Irene thought to herself. Her brother sat in his chair, silently staring out the window. He didn't bother to look up in greeting. Irene set her things down and went to clean the kitchen. It wasn't that her life was any different now—she still did most of the chores, still supported all of them—but now there was no more hope. Before, she thought that if Dave came home everything would change. Things had changed all right, but for the worse. She had had dreams of getting married someday, having children, getting away from her mother. She had hoped both she and Dave could help support their mother but now she saw no possibility of that. Her mother wouldn't work and Dave couldn't, so the burden fell on Irene. How could she marry and leave the two of them to fend for themselves?

As she began to wash the dishes, she knew she was not being honest with herself. If she had no hope left, why did she turn down the offers of the men at the Mission? Some of the other girls slept with the men and came away with some very nice souvenirs. But Irene wouldn't. She didn't have much left but she did have her self-respect. She always dreamed that someday some handsome young man would come along, and she wanted to be pure for him.

It was late when she finished the kitchen. Her mother had gone to bed early, complaining of a severe headache. Lately she had been saying that her headaches and back-aches were caused by Irene's boss, that greedy, power-hungry Laura Kenyon. Mrs. Anderson said that if Irene were a good daughter, she'd force Laura to sell the Mission so the town could be rich. She said Laura liked being a big fish in a small pond and didn't want anyone else to have any money.

Irene went into the living room. It was nice to have a few moments of quiet before she went to bed. She turned

182

quickly at a sound behind her. "Dave! I didn't know you were still up. Can I get you anything?"

He looked at her as he looked at everything—with hatred. "How about a new pair of legs?"

The tears rushed to her eyes.

"Sit down," Dave growled, "and stop looking like I've hit you. Did you hear anything at the Mission?"

She knew what he meant. He wanted a job, wanted to feel useful. She knew that a great part of his problem was having to be supported by his little sister.

Irene put her face in her hands and began to cry. She was so very, very tired.

Dave rolled his chair close to her and touched her hair. "What is it?" he asked quietly. "Are you sick of looking at your crippled brother?"

She held his hand to her cheek. "You know it's not that. Oh, Dave, I don't know what to do. Garrick said today that he might have a job for you."

Dave jerked his hand away. "A job!" he breathed. "Oh, God, you can't imagine what that would mean to me. It does a lot to a man to have to be supported by a woman."

She looked up at him, tears still in her eyes.

"A job would make me feel like I was alive again. Irene, you don't know what it's like, sitting here day after day, feeling helpless, worthless even." He clasped his hands together as if he were praying. "A job would help replace some of what I've lost."

"It . . . it isn't certain yet," she stammered. "Garrick said it . . . the job depended on some things."

Dave's jaw hardened. He looked years older then he did before the war. "Like what? That I run a mile and a half each day?" He started to turn away.

"No!" she said, putting her hand on his arm. "It's nothing about you." She looked down at her hands. "He wants me to . . . to . . ."

Dave stared hard at the top of her head for a moment, then rolled his chair away to his customary spot by the window. "I see. I get a job if you come across for him, is that it?" He looked at the curt nod of her head. He gave a derogatory little laugh. "It's almost hard to remember what it's like to be desirable to the opposite sex. Remember Jeanie, that girl I went with in high school? She came by the other day and patted my shoulder like I was an old man. She was so careful not to say anything that hurt me, but everything she said hurt. She is alive, so full of life, while I sit here day after day and..."

He stopped and took a deep breath. "Do you think I don't see what goes on in this house? Mother is a sick woman, I know that. And I know she takes her sickness out on you, but what can I do? As long as I can't make any money, what right do I have to make demands?"

He slammed his fist down on the arm of the wheelchair. "You know, you're lucky, Irene. You have everything going for you. You're young and pretty and healthy. No wonder this Garrick wants you. Isn't he Laura's brother-in-law? He'd have some power then. Isn't he that good-looking guy all the women want?"

He turned and looked back at the window. "You're lucky a man wants you. What woman would want a cripple like me? I can't even get a job, much less make love to a woman."

Dave kept on talking, but Irene didn't hear him. She got up quietly and slowly left the room.

Chapter 15

Laura shut the door to her office behind her and leaned against it for a moment. Here she could find the peace and quiet she needed. She sat down heavily in the big leather chair behind her desk. She felt like she had been living in a nightmare for the last two weeks. If Jack Galloway had announced that gold had been discovered under the Mission and Laura refused to let anyone dig, the reaction couldn't have been worse.

Laura had just been confronted by Della Anderson. The woman had said that a hotel was being planned for her property and she had already started tearing down her garage. Laura had tried to reason with the woman but it was futile. The woman jutted her chin out and said Laura wasn't going to keep her at the door of the poorhouse.

Now, in the calm of her office, Laura wondered if Irene was anything like her mother. Laura didn't know the receptionist very well except that she was one of Garrick's latest conquests, or so he said. She made a mental note to keep an eye on Irene. She didn't like the feeling of being surrounded by people who were so openly against her.

She called, "Come in," to a quick knock on the door.

Emmett entered. "I think we may have some trouble, Laura," he said.

"May?" she laughed. "Aren't things bad enough? I don't guess there are five people in town talking to me. Even some of the employees look at me as if I were their personal enemy."

He sat down across from her. There were circles under his eyes. He wouldn't tell her about the last several nights that he and Louise had stayed up late, arguing about whether Laura should sell or not. Louise said Emmett couldn't bear the thought of being away from Laura, and that was why he didn't want her to sell.

"What is it?" Laura asked. "I guess I'm as ready as I'll ever be."

He handed her a piece of paper, a typed letter with the logo of the Montero Chamber of Commerce across the head. Laura was requested to attend a meeting at eight o'clock tomorrow night. The purpose of the meeting, the letter said, was to discuss the future of Montero.

Laura groaned and tossed the paper on the desk. "It's like the Spanish Inquisition sending out invitations. Just what do they hope to gain by this? I've already said I wasn't going to sell."

Emmett grinned at her. "You know how women are. They change their minds with the wind. Maybe the people want to know how the wind's blowing today."

Laura was too tired to join in his laughter. Perhaps the meeting was a blessing in disguise. The people of Montero were sane, intelligent people, and she'd tell them the truth about the syndicate, that *it* would make the money and not the people. It would be good to get a chance to explain her side.

The town meeting was held inside the Masonic Lodge. As soon as Laura walked into the building she knew this was more serious than she had realized. On one side of the room were a couple of hundred chairs, then across from a long table about ten more, vacant and obviously meant for Laura, Ross and their few followers. The townspeople were seated, silent and waiting.

"They must have been told a different time," Laura said indignantly to Ross. He took her arm and they walked past the hundreds of staring eyes to take their places on the other side of the room.

When everyone was seated, the mayor rose. He smiled warmly toward the small group on the far side of the dividing table. "Laura," he said gently, "we've called this meeting only after a great deal of thought. As I'm sure you can guess, the picnic given by Major Galloway was a shock to us. For days, we didn't quite know what to think. After the first numbness wore off, we began to think, and we began to discuss the pros and cons of Montero becoming a Vacationland. Now, we'd like to present you with some of our findings."

The mayor sat down, still smiling graciously, and

turned the floor over to the high school science teacher. He said that he had spoken with Major Galloway, and the war hero had told him that the increased taxes would be able to supply the schools with better equipment.

The English teacher spoke about higher education, the hope that Montero's children would someday go to the very best colleges and universities. And of course the better financial condition of the parents would allow the adults to send them.

One of the school bus drivers spoke for better transportation, more paved roads. One of the clinic nurses emphasized the need for a hospital and the danger of Montero's isolation. The art teacher named famous artists who would visit Montero, and the music teacher spoke of symphonies to be given on the plaza.

Laura sat quietly through all of it. Each speaker smiled sweetly at her, and each statement concerning the "good of the children" was politely applauded. Laura clenched and unclenched her hands, and she felt her anger rise.

Ross watched her, pleased by her anger. He had been afraid she would give in to the people, let them sweet talk her into selling. He leaned back in his chair. He had been on the receiving end of Laura's anger a few times and he knew she could hold her own against anyone.

When the townspeople were done, they sat back and smugly waited for Laura's agreement with them. How could she refuse to help the children?

Laura stood slowly. "Are you finished?" she asked quietly. "Have you had your say?"

No one answered her rhetorical question.

She walked toward the table, put her hands on it, and leaned toward the people. "I have never before seen an example of mass delusion until this moment. I wish you could see yourselves, listen to yourselves."

The mayor rose, began to gather his papers. "There's no reason for you to be insulting."

Laura whirled toward him. "Sit down! You called this meeting and I've listened to you for an hour. Now it's my turn.

"First of all, let's go over what you think the children of this town need. Two years ago the Mission donated several thousand dollars' worth of science equipment to the school, equipment I had gotten through a manufac-

187

turer. Eight years ago I set up a scholarship program. Any student who's willing to work can go to college—free."

She turned toward a couple in the back of the room. "John, how does your son like Harvard?" she asked. She didn't wait for an answer. She looked at the nurse. "You make it seem as if Montero is so isolated that people would die if they needed a doctor. Has the Mission's plane ever been denied to anyone in an emergency? I lost several regular guests a few years ago because I used the plane to fly Jimmy Gomez to Albuquerque after he swallowed his sister's marbles."

She paused, watched their faces. In spite of her words, their expressions were still cold. She lowered her voice. "Don't you see? You're hiding behind the children. The children of Montero are fine, they're great. We have a clean, crime-free place to live and I don't want it to change."

She took a deep breath. "Jack Galloway wants you to sell so he can make money, so his bosses can make money. I deal with these kind of people daily. I hear them laughing at the way they manipulate people. That's what they're trying to do here. They'll buy a few pieces of land for very little, build some ugly commercial buildings, and ruin Montero. The rest of us won't want to live here anymore. That's when the syndicate will buy more land, for practically nothing. Then where will we be? We'll have no town, no homes, no..." She stopped, feeling her energy draining away.

"I will not sell the Mission. I do not want to see Montero turned into what Jack Galloway wants to create. That's all I have to say." She sat down heavily in her chair. Ross took her arm, Emmett gave her shoulder a squeeze.

The mayor stood after a moment, his face red with emotion. "I know we're not sophisticated like you, Laura," he said with heavy sarcasm. "We don't have the privilege of hearing the big shots laugh at poor country fools like us."

Laura started to speak, but the pressure Ross put on her arm stopped her.

"But we're not all completely stupid," the mayor continued. "We do have choices. We're not going to sell our land for just any price, as you seem to think we will. I imagine a few of us have at least a grain of sense." He

188

looked out at the people as they nodded their heads in approval.

Mr. Woodman stood. "I think this whole meeting is about choices. Everything in this town is controlled by the Mission. Every business sells to it. At least one member of every family works there. I'd like to start controlling my own life. I'd like to sell my flowers to a bigger market."

There was a chorus of "Me, too," and various nods of agreement.

"And another thing," soneone else said. "I'm tired of hearing Major Galloway's name dragged through the mud. He's a good man and I'm pleased he chose our town to honor."

There was more agreement.

Laura stood, her eyes blinking back tears. It hurt her to know they felt she controlled them. "No one has to work for me. I'm trying to be fair. If I thought it was for the good of the town, I'd sell in a minute. But if Montero becomes a Vacationland, it'll be a slum in five years. I don't think you want that anymore than I do."

Della Anderson stood up. "We don't want you controlling us!" she fairly shouted. "You like being the richest person in town. You like owning everything and everybody. You couldn't bear the thought of having your peons become equals, could you?"

"That's not true, I—" Laura began.

"We helped your family once, Laura," someone else said loudly. "We never expected any payment in return, but it sure seems like you have a short memory."

"I have tried to repay you! I've given you jobs, bought your goods—"

"And made yourself rich in the meantime," someone shouted at her. "You get to hobnob with all those fancy bigwigs you keep braggin' to us about, while we do the work that supplies the goods. Now we see a chance for a better life and you laugh in our faces like we're stupid, blind children."

Before Laura could speak, someone else began shouting. Half the room seemed to be on its feet. "Maybe you don't control us as much as you think. Maybe we can make some of our own decisions."

Ross stood beside Laura, put his arm around her shoulders. "The Mission will not be sold," he said, his voice carrying over the rising noise. "You can tell yourself what you want, but the Mission belongs to Laura and me and we're not selling." He turned to his wife. "Let's go home."

Laura nodded in agreement, cast her eyes down, and gave herself up to Ross's protection. She wouldn't look at the people around her. They were her friends, people she had known all her life, but right now they seemed like strangers.

She felt numb, bewildered, unbelieving of what she had heard, as they drove home. Once inside he fixed her a tequila and honey. She drank it without thought.

Ross watched her and knew he could have easily choked each and every citizen of Montero to death. The bastards had said she controlled them by giving them jobs! It wasn't that he had expected anything different, not when money was involved. People the world over were a greedy lot— he knew that, but Laura didn't. He could kill them for hurting her, for throwing in her face all she had done for them, all the sacrifices she had made for them. When they had first married, he had urged her to spend more of the money on herself, but she refused.

He took Laura's empty glass away from her. "Let's go to bed," he said quietly.

Laura smiled up at him. The drink had been very strong, nearly half a water glass of straight tequila. "At least it's over," she said with relief. "They know now that I won't sell and there's nothing they can do. They're mad at me now, but in a few days they'll see my side."

Ross didn't answer. He had an idea that Montero was just beginning to fight. He pulled out her of the chair and guided her to the bedroom.

Chapter 16

Laura woke late the next morning and her head ached slightly. She smiled in memory of Ross's drink. He made it for her whenever she was worried and wouldn't be able to sleep.

Her smile vanished immediately when she thought of last night's meeting. She glanced at the time and dressed quickly. Ross had breakfast ready for her.

"How do you feel this morning?" he asked.

"Fair," she answered, gulping coffee. "I'm trying not to think. Did Julia get off to school all right?"

"Sure. She's glad this is the last week. You know, I was thinking. Maybe we could take a trip this year."

Laura looked up over her eggs. "To some Vacation-land?"

He smiled at her, glad to see that some of her humor was returning. "Anywhere. I just thought it might be nice to get away for a while."

"And spend some of all the money I have?" she asked bitterly. "No, I'm not going to think about it. I have to go." She put her arms around Ross and kissed him. "Thanks for last night. Thanks for taking care of me."

"Any time," he said seriously, then walked her to the door.

Laura was able to relax as she drove to the Mission. The clear day, the clean sunshine, took away a lot of last night's pain. In fact, she could almost believe the meeting hadn't taken place.

Her hopes were short-lived.

The minute she stepped into the lobby, she knew something was wrong.

"I will not stay where there is no food!" said a woman indignantly. Her husband was a Hollywood producer. "I must have cream for my coffee and no eggs! Whoever heard of such a thing!" She looked up and saw Laura. "I'd always

191

heard this was a well-run resort but they were wrong. You'll not see me again." She slammed her room keys on the reservation desk and a boy strode out of the main doors, carrying her bags.

Laura went straight to the kitchen where she was greeted with a torrent of words from all the kitchen staff. It took a while to piece together that the dairyman, butcher and greengrocer, all local people, had not delivered this morning. "Did you call them?" Laura managed to wedge in between their words. Another flood of words followed.

Within minutes, Laura was in her office and on the telephone to the dairyman.

"I want cash in advance," he said as soon as she had identified herself.

"Cash!" Laura said. "Since when have I not paid my bills? Since when has my credit not been good?"

"Everybody has to do what they must, you know what I mean? We all gotta stand up for our beliefs and my belief right now is cash in advance," he said coolly.

"I understand you perfectly," Laura said and slammed down the telephone. She knew before she called the others what their answer would be. All of them wanted cash in advance before they would deliver food.

Laura realized that the townspeople must have stayed late last night and planned this. She rushed out of the office and ran to her car. She didn't have much time before preparations had to be started for lunch. The Mission relied on daily fresh deliveries all year, even flying in green goods in the winter. There was very little stored food.

At the bank, she asked to see Mr. Greene, the president. She had always dealt with him in her business for the Mission. A clerk told her Mr. Greene had suddenly been called out of town.

"I can imagine what called him," she said sarcastically as she followed the clerk into a vice-president's office.

"What can I do for you, Mrs. Kenyon?" the man asked.

Laura saw the remoteness in his eyes. "I need to cash a check," she said. "About ten thousand cash, I would guess."

The man leaned back in his chair, put his index fingers together to form a temple. "Ten thousand dollars is a lot of money," he said patiently.

She slapped her check down on his desk. "I didn't come

here for a lecture on the value of money. I need the money and I need it quickly."

"The truth is, Laura," he said in an honest, companionable tone, "I just can't give you the money."

"You what!" she gasped.

"I'm afraid we've been hearing some reports about the Mission's financial status that aren't what we'd like."

"Just what the hell are you trying to imply?" she demanded.

"Please, this is hard enough for me as it is. There have been rumors lately that the Mission is about to go bankrupt."

"Bankrupt!? That's the most absurd thing I've ever heard."

"I'm sure it is, but until we have proof, I'm afraid you will not be allowed to withdraw funds. Were the Mission to declare bankruptcy, we would, of course, need the funds to pay the resort's many creditors."

Laura opened her mouth to shout at him but closed it again. It was no use trying to reason with someone who was talking nonsense. She could get a lawyer, but the arguing would probably take weeks, and in the meantime her guests needed to eat.

There was nothing to do except take her check and leave. Every minute she lost was precious. She called Emmett from a pay telephone, told him of the situation, and said she was driving to Santa Fe to see if she could get groceries. She asked Emmett to do the best he could to keep the guests content.

She stopped by the house, jumped out of her car, and ran to Ross's woodshop. "I need the pickup," she said. He looked up from the piece of wood he was planing and tossed her the keys. She was out of the door before he could ask a question.

He stood in the doorway, watched her spin out of the driveway in the old pickup. As he turned back to his shop he thought he had better finish what he was doing and get to the Mission. Laura needed help.

Laura drove to Santa Fe in record time. She went straight to a wholesale market and spent an hour talking about deliveries to be made to Montero. The owner was unsympathetic about her plight; he sensed her desperation. He asked an outrageous amount for making deliveries to Montero. Laura was ready to agree to anything to get back to Montero with a load of groceries. She didn't want the man to call the Montero bank and be told the Mission's credit was no good.

After what seemed to be an eternity, the pickup was loaded and Laura was on her way back to the Mission. She was greeted near the mineral baths by Ross.

"Don't tell me it's gotten worse," she said, grabbing a box from the back.

The next moment she was rocked against the lowered gate of the truck by the reverberations of an explosion. She would have dropped the box if Ross hadn't caught it. She stared, horrified. "What now?"

"Marian," he said, taking the box from her. "She's building a hotel and she's blasting to lay the foundation."

Laura grabbed another box. "How long?"

"According to the contractor, it's going to take three to four weeks."

Laura clenched her teeth together. "How many guests have left so far?"

"Five," he said flatly.

Laura put her head up and started walking faster. At least they'd be able to serve supper and tonight she would talk to a lawyer and see what could be done about the dynamiting.

Julia sat quietly at her desk. She was bewildered by the events of the last few days. Over the years she had learned how to mask her feelings with a smile and a flurry of her thick eyelashes. She had friends and was popular, but everything had changed since the town meeting.

She hadn't even been aware of the town meeting until the next morning when she was fully informed. It seemed that all the parents except hers had discussed the meeting at breakfast. Julia first heard of it when the other children started saying her mother was keeping them from getting rich. They taunted Julia, laughed at her, and excluded her from their games. Since the meeting she had been an outcast.

"Julia," Mrs. Walsh, her teacher, said quietly. "Would you like to come sit at my desk and grade papers?"

Julia was startled by this request. It wasn't her turn to receive such an honor nor had she done anything to deserve it. In fact, she had missed half the spelling words on her test this morning.

"Julia?" the teacher repeated gently. "Would you like to grade papers?"

"Oh, yes," she breathed as she started forward.

"Teacher's pet," someone hissed as she went by.

Julia kept her eyes on Mrs. Walsh, smiling her most enchanting, and didn't look at her classmates. She took her place on Mrs. Walsh's oak chair and began to check the arithmetic against the answer sheet.

Even though she didn't look directly at them, she could feel the angry, hostile stares of the other children. She would not cry! She wouldn't let them see how they hurt her. But then they always hurt her, whether they meant to or not. She was never a part of them, always an outsider. She wasn't Julia Kenyon, she was Laura's daughter. One girl said her mother felt sorry for Julia because Laura was never home.

Julia didn't know how she felt about her mother. Lately, since her Uncle Garrick had said he could be her father, she had begun to look at Laura differently, not so much as a mother but as a person. She saw a woman who could do anything, who had everyone's love. People expected Julia to be as perfect as her mother, and when she wasn't, they lost no time in telling her so.

Now everyone seemed to be angry at Laura and for some reason they were angry at Julia, too. She wasn't trying to keep them from being rich and she couldn't understand why they said that. She wanted the other children to feel rich, too, so she wouldn't be different.

She carefully checked each paper, making a neat check by each correct answer, an X over the incorrect one. At least, Mrs. Walsh liked her. All her teachers had liked her, not because she was Laura's daughter but because she made good grades and worked hard. School was the only place where she felt good.

"Recess, children," Mrs. Walsh announced. "Julia, would you like to lead the girls' line today?"

Julia smiled because she knew Mrs. Walsh was trying to make up to her for the way the children were treating her. Mrs. Walsh knew that Julia was Julia and not just an extension of her mother.

Once out on the playground, Julia almost wished Mrs.

Walsh hadn't been so nice to her. The children circled around her.

"You think you're so smart just because your mother owns the Mission!" one little girl hissed.

"My mother said your mother was going to regret being so greedy. She said the people of Montero were going to close the Mission."

Julia backed away from them. "My mother won't sell," she w　ered. "She said she wouldn't."

"Your mother is a liar!"

"She isn't!" Julia gasped, tears starting in her eyes. "She always tells the truth."

"Then how come she said she wasn't going to sell when she is? My daddy said she didn't have any money and he wasn't going to give her any," said one girl whose father worked at the bank.

"She won't sell!" Julia said loudly, then pushed through the girls to freedom. Tears were running down her cheeks, but she saw Mrs. Walsh walking toward the group. Here at last was a friend! She ran to her teacher and threw her arms around the woman's waist. With the comfort of someone strong and loving, she began to cry in earnest. She sobbed loudly and wrenchingly into Mrs. Walsh's skirt.

"Julia, what is it?" Mrs. Walsh asked. "Have the girls been bothering you?" She pulled Julia from her, then knelt and began drying her tears with her own handkerchief.

"Julia, listen," Mrs. Walsh was saying, even though Julia was crying too hard to hear her. "The children are upset. They didn't mean anything. It's just that you have so much and they have so little. They don't have a rich and famous mother to give them everything. Their parents love them, too, and they want to be able to give their children as much as your mother gives you. If Laura sold the Mission, then the children could go to the universities; they could meet the right people. Perhaps you could speak to your mother."

A few of Mrs. Walsh's words were getting through to Julia.

"You could tell Laura about how kind all the teachers have been to you and—Julia, what's wrong?"

Julia pulled away from the woman as if she were diseased. One fact went through her mind—*all the teachers.* Had all the teachers been nice to her only because she was

Laura's daughter? Didn't anything she had ever done count on its own?

She turned and started running and didn't stop until she got home. The house was empty. She cried for hours. The phone rang constantly, but she didn't answer it. Someone kept knocking on the front door, but she stayed in her room and didn't look up.

Ross received a call at the Mission that Julia had run away from school and no one could find her. He tore through the streets of Montero like a wild man. When he reached home, Julia was sitting at the kitchen table, calmly eating a peanut butter and jelly sandwich. Her calmness did not fool him.

"What happened?" he asked, sitting down across from her.

She shrugged. "The other kids are mad at Mother."

He watched her steadily. He knew her as well as he knew himself. She was like him, and he knew how she hid what hurt her most. In a few days he'd get her to tell him what was wrong.

He took her hand and squeezed it. "There's been a lot going on the last few days. What if we sat down together and talked about it? It's easier to deal with something you understand."

"Do I have to go back to school?" she asked, holding her breath.

"Since this is the last week, how'd you like to miss all of it?"

"But my report card! I'll get bad grades!" she looked down at her half-eaten sandwich, a lump forming in her throat. Maybe her mother should go to school since the teachers were actually grading her instead of Julia.

"I'll pick it up and get all your things like your scissors and whatever else. Now, how about it? Think you could spend a few days with me?"

All the love she felt for him showed in her eyes.

Ross could see she had been crying and was about to start again. "Hey! How about fixing me a sandwich?"

She smiled and went to get bread, and Ross started telling her about the Mission and the people of Montero. He wasn't a parent who believed children should be left ignorant. He knew the world of fear that children could create. He told her about the town meeting and the problem of getting groceries and money. For two days, Laura had been fighting Marian's dynamiting with no success. One by one, the guests were leaving.

When Laura came home, Julia was in bed, exhausted after her emotional day. Laura, too, was exhausted. She told Ross that the IRS had called in the afternoon. They had had a tip that the Mission had falsified certain records and wanted to look over the books.

But the ledgers were missing! Laura, Emmett and half the staff had spent hours looking for the missing account books but they were nowhere to be found. The IRS was coming in the morning, and Laura had nothing to show them.

Ross ran a hot tub for Laura and helped her into it. He didn't tell her about Julia's running away from school.

Chapter 17

The next week passed without incident. In fact, a few new guests arrived. The groceries arrived promptly from Santa Fe, and Ross had some money in an Albuquerque bank so they were able to pay enough of the bills to get by.

After a week, though, the peacefulness ended. Marian's contractors began to dynamite twenty-four hours a day, and the explosions rattled windows and frightened guests.

On Monday, ten days after the town meeting, half the staff called in sick. Ross and Julia went to work with Laura. A third of the Mission was empty, but for whomever was left, the remaining staff acted as maids, janitors, cooks, or anything that was needed.

Several of the guests were wonderful. They all knew the people of Montero were trying to force Laura to sell and they encouraged her to stick to her guns. They helped by tending to their own needs as much as possible.

Julia had never spent much time at the Mission because she hated feeling like an outsider, but now she was glad to help. She chopped vegetables in the kitchen, baby-sat, cleaned bathrooms. At least, at the Mission no one taunted her.

More things began to happen after the staff called in sick. The keys to the wine cellar were lost, and when the door was taken down, they saw that many of the wine bottles had been shattered by the explosions from Marian's dynamiting.

The laundry refused to deliver clean linen, so Mrs. Martinez began trying to do the wash at her house. It was a slow, inefficient method. The liquor distributor said his truck was down and the mechanic didn't know when it could be repaired. Garrick viewed this as a personal loss and made a trip to Albuquerque to buy liquor.

By Wednesday, Laura was too tired and too confused to think. The IRS was calling her daily and making nasty threats. She sat at her desk, her head buried in her hands. She didn't hear the knock at her door or the door opening.

"Laura? May I talk to you?"

Laura looked up to see Irene Anderson. "I don't really have much time to talk now. You know how busy everyone is."

"Yes." Irene looked at her steadily. "I know we are quite shorthanded now and that's why I was thinking of asking for a job for my brother."

Laura fell back against her chair. "You're asking me to hire someone now?" She grabbed a handful of papers from her desk. "Do you know what these are? They're bills! I can't pay them because the bank won't let me have my own money. Some of the guests are paying me in advance so I can buy groceries, otherwise we wouldn't be able to eat. And now you come here and ask me to hire someone new."

"I'm sorry, I didn't mean—" She turned to leave.

"Irene! I'm the one who's sorry. I've had a lot on my mind the last few weeks. See Garrick and maybe he can find your brother a place. We can certainly use help, but his salary may be late. Can he drive a car?"

"He...he's paralyzed from the waist down."

Laura felt like crying. How could this girl try to add this new responsibility to her? A handicapped person would need training and no one had the time right now. "See if you can work something out with Garrick," she said as she turned back to her desk. Irene was a good worker and she wanted to help her, but she just didn't have the time right now.

Irene thanked her and left the room. Instead of going back to her desk, she went to the Kiva Lounge. "Make me something strong, will you?" she said to the bartender.

"It's a little early, isn't it?" he asked, raising one eyebrow.

She glared at him. "I'm old enough, if that's what you mean. Make it with tequila."

The bartender obeyed and she drank her drink in one gulp.

"Another one," she said, "only this time make it stronger."

A hand touched her shoulder. "You left your desk," Garrick said. "Betty's looking for you."

She smiled up at him as she took her other drink. "Why don't you sit with me? I'm celebrating my freedom."

He frowned at her but took the stool next to hers. "It's a little unusual for you to be hittin' the bottle, isn't it?"

She leaned forward and smiled at him. "Early and unusual. You know, I've never been drunk before, never in my whole life. But today I plan to get smashed." She ran a finger across his cheek. "And you know what else I plan? I plan to get out of this town, to leave my adoring mother and my pimp of a brother."

Garrick motioned to the bartender for another drink. "I've heard about your family. As bad as I've heard?"

"Worse," she said, gulping a third drink. "I've been the good, dutiful daughter and—" She stopped. "Let's not talk about me. I want to hear about you. I want to hear about everyone. Little Irene is no longer the sweet little thing she was. Today," she said, lifting a fourth drink, "Irene is a free woman."

He caught her arm before she could drink. "You're going too fast. You'll get drunk too soon and you won't be able to enjoy it."

"Enjoy it," she breathed. "What a lovely idea. I'd like to enjoy something. I'd like to do more than work all day and work all night."

She dropped her head in her hands, tears coming.

"What is it?" Garrick said, touching her hair. He looked up at the bartender and motioned him to leave. He put his arm around Irene and led her to a booth. They were alone in the lounge. "What's happened to you?"

She was just drunk enough to really relax. The strength of Garrick's arms around her felt good. "I'm tired of being alone," she said. "I'm tired of waiting for someone to come along and take care of me, but all I end up doing is taking care of everyone else."

He stroked her hair. "I know how you feel. I think I've been alone all my life."

She pulled back to look at him. "You? You have everything. You're rich. You have a beautiful wife and home."

He pushed her head back down. "My wife married me because she was going to have somebody else's kid. I blackmailed my sister-in-law into giving me money and now . . . now Clarry wants a divorce and I'm facing everything going up in smoke."

"You mustn't let it!" she said fiercely. "You can't be like me and let everyone use you, take from you all the time. You've got to stand up for yourself. Don't let them do that to you!"

Garrick laughed throatily. "I thought you and I were enemies. How come we're on the same side now?"

"I just found out my family was my enemy," she said flatly. She sat up. "Let's get out of here, could we? I'd like to go someplace and have some fun, know what I mean?"

"I know exactly what you mean. Want to stop at your desk and get your things?"

She put her hand on his neck. "I don't want to stop for anything."

Garrick drove her to Santa Fe in her car, to some places he knew there. He looked at Irene and he thought of Clarry's leaving him. He thought of his world about to end. He remembered how Irene had once been repulsed by him and he wondered what awaited him in a world outside the Mission. He knew his looks could no longer get him women as in the past. He knew that young, pretty Irene only wanted to be with him because he was available and she was drunk. The time was coming when the only women who would want him would be the drunk ones.

"Don't look sad," Irene said, smiling at him. "This is a day of emancipation. Tomorrow I'm going to pack my things and leave this town forever. Tomorrow I'm going to be free." She lifted her glass. "Here's to the freedom of the virgin."

Garrick laughed. "You can always do something about that."

Irene set her empty glass down hard. "Make love to me," she whispered. "Take me somewhere nice and make love to me."

He nodded solemnly. There was nothing he wanted more than to make love to this angry, hurt, drunken girl. He took her hand. "Come on, let's go."

Outside the bar it was night and he had to practically carry Irene to the car. He realized he was drunker than usual. When he backed out of the parking lot, he banged the car into the one behind him.

"Be careful," Irene giggled.

Garrick drove south toward a motel on the outskirts of

Santa Fe. As he drove, Irene began to hum, and when he glanced at her, she was unbuttoning her blouse.

"Wait till we get there, honey," he said, but he couldn't seem to keep his eyes off her.

He was drunk and he was watching her so that he didn't see the sharp curve in the road. One minute they were on the road, the next they were sailing through the air into black emptiness.

Garrick felt he must have blacked out for a moment while the car tumbled down into the arroyo, turning over a couple of times. He sat up, shook his head. There was blood on the side of his head.

He turned toward Irene. "We're going to have some headache tomorrow, aren't we?"

She lay peacefully against the door, looking as if she were sleeping.

"Irene?" He pulled her forward, but her head lolled about on her shoulders. Her neck was broken.

For a moment he couldn't think. He glanced around him. Above the car was the highway, the car headlights whizzing past, not stopping. No one seemed to be aware of the car below them.

Garrick's head began to clear and he thought of Clarry. She would get her divorce when she found out about this. Laura would cut him off completely from the Mission. And the police! No doubt he'd be up for a manslaughter charge.

As he went over these thoughts he knew what he must do. He offered a silent prayer of thanks that he had used her car and not his own. He hadn't wanted anyone to see him driving away with another woman, not when Clarry was bitten by this divorce idea.

He again looked to see if anyone was near, then tried the door. It was wedged but he managed to open it. He gingerly stepped onto the soft arroyo sand, testing his weak, shaky legs. He tried not to think about what he was doing as he pulled the lifeless Irene into the driver's seat. When he had propped her into place, he slammed the door and began to walk down the arroyo. When he was at least a mile from the car, he climbed up to the highway and caught a ride. By morning he was in his own house, shaved, showered—and scared. He knew he had to make Laura sell the Mission. If it were sold, he could bank the money and get out of Montero, because he knew that sooner or later someone would find out he had been with Irene. If he stayed in Montero, he could end up broke and in prison.

Clarry was bent over the dryer door, removing sheets, in the Montero laundromat when Jack Galloway took a sheet from her. She looked at him for a moment, then pulled the sheet from him, turned her back, and went to a big folding table.

"Could I help you?" Jack asked. "I'm quite good with sheets."

"You're good with a lot of things, especially manipulating people. And no, I don't need your help."

He picked up a pillowcase and began to smooth it. "Things pretty bad at the Mission?"

She didn't answer him but kept folding.

"I don't know why you're being so hard on me. It's not me who's causing the problems but the people of Montero."

"You offered them money," she snapped. "No one can withstand that!"

"And what about you? I've heard an awful lot about you. I hear you're in love with Bill Matthews, but Garrick won't give you a divorce. And I hear you have some dress designs that are good, maybe even great."

Clarry paused in her folding. It was no use asking him where he had heard this. She knew there were no secrets in Montero. She jammed the sheets into the big wicker basket and started toward the door.

Jack caught her arm. "I could help you. I know some people in L.A. I could get them to look at your dresses. And I know Garrick, too. Maybe I could talk to him.

Clarry pulled away from him. "Let me make this very clear, Mr. Galloway. *I* am not for sale." She pulled away from him and went out the door.

Jack was shaking as he lit a cigarette. Last night he had had a call from the syndicate. They thought he was taking much too long to persuade Mrs. Kenyon to sell.

At night, as she left the Mission Laura felt as if she were fighting a losing battle. Was it worth it to see so much hatred around her, to see her own child working six hours a day? Ross said Julia was more content at the Mission than he had seen her in a long time. But Laura wasn't sure.

Ross met her at the front door, his arms open to her. "Anything new happen?"

"We got the laundry done," she said sarcastically. "Two more guests left because of the lack of service. The pilot quit, so until I can get someone else, there will be no more seafood."

He held her close to him.

"I've been thinking about Scotland all day."

Ross held her away from him. He knew what she was going to say. "You could spend the whole summer in Scotland if you sold the Mission," he finished for her. "Is that what you really want? Are you really so afraid of a little anger?"

Laura could only gasp at his understatement.

"You know, I fell in love with you because you were a fighter. Of course, then you were fighting something impersonal—poverty. Everyone was behind you because you were the good guy in the white hat. Now, you look like the villain and you're ready to fold."

She pulled away from him. "Maybe I *am* the villain! You once told me I had no right to make other people's decisions for them. I broke up Clarry's romance and because of me she married Garrick." To her surprise, Ross gave a low chuckle.

"You certainly have a high opinion of yourself. From what you told me, Clarry decided to marry Garrick on her own, and she could have divorced him long ago. When Clarry realizes she's worth something, she'll get rid of that husband of hers. What the hell has any of this to do with Clarry? I thought you were trying to decide whether or not to sell the Mission."

Laura ran her hand through her hair. "Everyone in town seems to think I should. Maybe they're right and I'm wrong. Maybe I am holding them back, keeping them poor."

Ross walked away from her. "You've been in this town too long," he said bitterly. "No one has the power you seem to think you have or that they think you have. If they wanted a Vacationland, they could organize and do it themselves. They don't need the eastern money."

"I...hadn't thought of that before. What do they want then?"

He didn't want to tell her. The people were jealous of

205

her strength, her security, her accomplishments. There was a naive, innocent quality about Laura that he didn't want her to see. He smiled at her. "They want all your money, your jewels and furs. They want a car like that wreck you drive."

Laura smiled back at him. "How can you laugh at this? This is serious."

"The only thing serious is whether or not you want to sell. Make your decision and stick to it."

"Even if every guest leaves?"

"You can afford an empty Mission longer than the citizens of Montero can. They'll wise up in a few days."

"What would I do without you, Ross?"

"Die of worry probably," he said flatly. "Now come into the kitchen. Julia and I baked a cake for you. If you're real good and eat it all up, I'll drive you out of your mind with passion later on."

She laughed. "I'll hold you to that promise."

"Can I pick the place where you do the holding?" he leered.

She laughed again and followed him into the kitchen. Her day at the Mission could be hell, but home and Ross provided a haven of quiet pleasure.

Chapter 18

Jack Galloway sat on the edge of the hospital bed in the Montero Clinic. Dr. Thomas was holding an X-ray in front of him, but Jack wasn't paying much attention.

"You should be more careful, Major Galloway," the doctor said. "You came close to killing yourself on those stairs. Look at this, that broken rib missed puncturing your lung by a hair."

"Yeah, sure, doc," Jack said in a distracted way. He got down from the bed, his breath taken in sharply as his taped ribs hurt him.

"I wish you'd let me keep you here overnight."

"Thanks but no thanks. I promise I'll rest for a couple of days, but you know how it is with soldiers and hospitals. I guess I had enough during the war."

"Of course," the doctor said. "Just be sure you do rest."

Jack left the clinic, walking stiffly. *Stairs,* he thought.

This morning, before he was awake, while it was still dark, he half jumped from his bed when someone started pounding on the door. He opened it quickly, before he even thought about who it could be. Three men, well dressed, stood there. He knew who they were without asking.

"The bosses want to know when the woman's going to sell this place."

"Soon," Jack said. "It's almost sewed up."

"Almost ain't good enough. You were sent here to do a job, you understand, Galloway?"

He gave a little wave of his hand and the two men behind him stepped forward.

Before Jack could react, four fists plowed into his ribs. He could hear them crack. As he lay on the floor, barely able to see for the pain, the man looked down at him.

"You got one more week, Galloway. At the end of that

week, we want the deed to the Mission or the money back, you understand?"

He didn't answer, just sat silently as they left the motel room.

Now, he knew something had to be done. There was no time for talking the townspeople into helping him. He went back to his motel and called Garrick from there. Garrick was the only one to help him now. He needed someone on the inside.

Later, when he met Garrick in a bar, he realized he looked much older, perhaps something was bothering him, too.

"You look like the one with the broken ribs," Jack said.

Garrick frowned. "I've been doin' some thinking. I thought maybe I'd start working out, maybe a couple of times a week."

Jack almost laughed aloud. He had one week to find out if he was going to live or die, and this man was worried about getting old. "Maybe if you had a little more time, you could do whatever you wanted, even get out of this place."

Jack had Garrick's attention. He offered Garrick half of whatever he made if he would help him. Garrick could afford to retire, get out of this hick town, live in the south of France or wherever he wanted.

Garrick agreed instantly.

Betty Gomez stuck her head into Laura's office. "Irene Anderson's mother just called and said Irene didn't come home last night."

"That's a good excuse," Laura said sarcastically. "Isn't Irene's mother the one tearing down her garage?"

Betty stepped inside the office. "I wouldn't judge Irene by her mother. That woman's enough to drive anyone insane. If I were Irene, I'd have left long ago. You should have heard her this morning. She said Irene stayed out all night, just like she was a whore. Can you imagine a mother saying that about her own daughter?"

"I can imagine anything lately. Get someone else to handle the desk, will you?"

"Sure. I hope Irene comes in. I don't think any of us realize how much she does around here. She's such a sweet girl. She doesn't deserve to be treated like that—by her own mother yet." She shrugged and left the room.

Laura returned to the bills in front of her. She had been able to persuade an Albuquerque bank to give her an open account until her lawyer got her money from the Montero bank. A court order kept Marian from blasting from six P.M. to eight A.M., so at least the guests left could sleep in peace. It looked as if things were going to work out. She and Emmett had been able to show enough canceled checks to the IRS to persuade the government that the Mission kept honest books. Things were staying on an even keel for the moment.

She looked up as Garrick entered. "I wanted to ask you about something," she said. "Irene Anderson asked me for a job for her brother. Did she talk to you about it?"

"Oh, yeah, she mentioned it." He licked his dry lips.

"Good! Then find him a job. See what he can do, then use him somewhere."

Garrick nodded curtly, as if he intended to help her not sell the Mission.

That afternoon every toilet in the Mission backed up. The contents of the sewage system spilled out from the toilets, the sink drains, the bathtubs. The resort reeked.

Ross pulled on overalls and began his search for the source of the problem. It was easy enough to find. Someone had unscrewed the cap to the clean-out to the main drain leading to the septic tanks and stuffed it with plumber's oakum, a combination of jute and asphalt. It had taken moments to destroy, but it would take days to dig and clean out.

While Ross and a couple of high school boys worked on the drains, several of the most faithful guests checked out. The sight and smell of the toilets regurgitating all over the floor was more than they could take. Mrs. Martinez, Clarry and Bill began mopping floors. Several Navajo rugs were hopelessly ruined.

The next morning, the reservation list was misplaced. Two prominent guests arrived and both expected the Caballero Suite. Both had talked to a man at the Mission and had their reservations confirmed. No matter what Laura said, the guests would not be appeased. They both left in anger, vowing never to return.

Two days later there were only a handful of guests left.

Then the worst thing happened: six guests were taken to the hospital with ptomaine poisoning. The state health authorities traced the cause to animal droppings in the salad dressing and urine on the towels the employees used to dry the dishes at the Mission. The kitchen was closed for three days.

There was very little that went on at the Mission that the people of Montero didn't know about. They felt they had been right all along when two of the guests nearly died from the food at the Mission. They almost felt justified in the things they had done. Imagine using towels soaked in animal urine!

Jack Galloway at first offered his certificates casually, as if they meant nothing to him. They were beautiful things done on parchment paper, handlettered with a deeply embossed seal in the lower left corner. The certificates gave the owner a share of the Montero Corporation, a real estate developing business, and could be bought for a hundred dollars each.

The townspeople saw the certificates as a way to prove Laura wrong. She said the syndicate would make all the money. Now the townspeople were forming their own syndicate. They would own the town jointly.

Jack sold five hundred of the pretty certificates in four days. The syndicate had called on him again last night, but this time he flashed some green under their noses and told them to be patient, that Laura Kenyon couldn't hold out much longer.

Jack carefully hid the money and began to wait. He would give Laura three more days, and if she didn't agree to sell, he was going to Brazil. He'd have the fifty grand from the sale of the certificates and he'd hide so no one could ever find him. Of course, if she did agree to sell, he'd return the money to the people. Either way, he was covered.

Laura found out about the certificates through Louise. Emmett had been spending nearly all his time at the Mission for the last few days. Louise waved the certificate under Laura's nose. "You won't own him anymore—I will."

Laura didn't even know how to answer her. This woman was worried Laura was having an affair with her husband
210

and it seemed so ridiculous. As if it weren't enough with the Mission's problems, this morning she had heard that Irene Anderson had been found dead in a car at the bottom of an arroyo in Santa Fe. Mrs. Anderson called Laura to say it was her fault because Irene couldn't bear the idea of being poor all her life.

The call had made Laura numb. She didn't know how or why, but she did feel responsible for the young woman's death. Perhaps if things hadn't been so hectic and she hadn't been so involved in her own life, she could have helped Irene.

"You're not even listening to me!" Louise said. "You think you're so good—" She broke off when Emmett entered Laura's office. Louise put the certificate behind her.

"What are you doing here?" he asked wearily. The Mission was empty; only a feeling of doom was left.

"Protecting my family!" Louise snapped. "I decided that I was going to buy you back if I had to."

Emmett looked at her with suspicion. Sometimes he worried about her sanity. "What's that?"

Louise pushed the certificate toward him triumphantly.

Emmett took it, read it, then handed it to Laura.

"How can Jack Galloway sell shares to Montero? Has he incorporated a company? What are his assets?" Laura asked.

Louise looked bewildered.

Emmett grabbed her by the shoulders. "How much did you pay for this?"

Louise still looked puzzled. "A hundred dollars."

Emmett gave her a shake before Laura came between them. "How many other people in Montero have bought these?" Laura asked quietly.

Louise backed away from them, her eyes wide. "Hundreds," she whispered. "Nearly everyone has bought at least one or two."

Emmett called Ross and together they began a search on the certificates. They were worth only the paper they were printed on.

Louise was confused. "He couldn't use that money to buy the Mission because then the people of the town would own the resort and not the syndicate."

Ross was the only one with an answer. "I have a feeling

211

Galloway began to realize Laura wasn't ever going to sell. Maybe he wanted the money so he could get out of the country. My guess is that the syndicate will do more than just fire him if he doesn't get Laura to sell."

Louise leaned back against her chair. "And to think we all believed him. I think it must have been all the medals. He looked so...so trustworthy standing there at the picnic." She stopped and looked at Laura. "God! How you must hate us!"

Laura looked at her with sympathy. "No, I don't hate anyone."

"Well, I do!" Emmett said as he jumped up, knocking his chair over. "This whole damned town should be shoved into the ocean for what it's done to Laura! It's been hell standing by day after day and watching them destroy this place. And what did Laura do? She—"

Ross's laugh interrupted him. "Come down off your soap box. Everybody is greedy. This town just had a chance to show it in mass form. What we've got to do is worry about the future." He looked at Louise. "I guess we're agreed these certificates are worthless."

Louise nodded, her mouth tense. "The Woodmans put their life savings in those things, and I know several other people who have invested heavily in them."

Laura groaned. "Didn't they think? Didn't they even let a lawyer look at them?"

"We all trusted him. He just seemed so trustworthy, a war hero and all. What can we do, Laura?" Louise asked.

"You could have stood behind her when she needed you," Emmett snapped.

"Louise," Ross said. "You can help us. I want you to start calling the townspeople, anyone who bought these certificates, and tell them they're worthless. At least that'll make them doubt Galloway and keep them from shelling out more money." Ross's mind wasn't fully on the problem of the phony certificates. He kept thinking of the clogged drains and the more serious problem of the pto-maine poisoning. Jack Galloway hadn't done those things because they took someone who knew the inner workings of the Mission. Ross had an idea who that person was.

"Good idea," Emmett said, "I'll help you."

"No one will believe you, will they, Ross?" Laura asked.

"Huh? Oh, no, I guess not. Does anyone know where Garrick is tonight?"

Emmett snorted. "There's no telling since all the female guests are gone."

Ross stood. "Laura and Emmett, I suggest you get some sleep, and you, Louise, I think you should start calling. It'll probably take you all night."

"And what about you?" Laura asked.

"I think I'll just check the premises and maybe even sleep here tonight. I hate to leave it empty. You go home, maybe pick up Julia at Mrs. Martinez's house."

"Sure," Laura said absently. She had a few plans of her own.

As soon as Laura got away from the others, she went in search of Jack Galloway. She found him at his motel. He greeted her warmly.

"I am so very, very glad to see you, Laura," he said. "Won't you come in and please forgive the mess?"

Laura wasted no time. She thrust Louise's certificate at him. "How many have you sold?" She watched his face, saw the color leave it.

"It's not what you think," he began.

"Save it for your patriot/children speeches. Look, Mr. Galloway, we know the certificates are worthless. I want the money returned to the people of Montero."

"The money's in the bank," Jack said smoothly. "I can't get it until the morning. Is that soon enough?"

"I'll meet you there when they open the doors. The people already know that the certificates are worthless, so I wouldn't try to leave town with the money."

He smiled at her as she turned and left the room.

Laura didn't go home but back to the Mission to tell Ross of her talk with Jack. Now the man knew he was caught and he wouldn't be able to escape.

Laura wasn't prepared for Ross's anger.

"You did what!" he bellowed. "What do you think, that he's some little schoolboy you can smack on the hands? Don't you realize his life may be in danger? And damn you, Laura, when are you going to stop fighting for this goddamn town? One day this place is going to eat you alive and you won't say a word. They've done everything they can to force you to sell, yet you stick your neck out for them."

213

He stopped suddenly and grabbed her. "I love you! Don't you realize that? Jack Galloway is a desperate man. He could have harmed you."

She leaned against him. She wasn't heroic so much as ignorant. She hadn't thought of the possible outcome of confronting Jack. "Do you think he'll show up at the bank tomorrow?"

"I doubt it. I can't imagine he'd put the money in the bank. He wouldn't be able to get to it fast enough." He stepped away from her.

"Where are you going? You're not going after Galloway, are you?"

"No," he said sarcastically. "One fool in the family is enough. I want to look around the Mission. I have an idea Garrick is around here."

"What's Garrick have to do with anything?"

He clenched his jaw for a moment. "I believe Garrick was working with Jack. I think he's the one who sabotaged the drains and poisoned the food."

"But two people nearly died! Garrick isn't a murderer."

"He wouldn't be on a one-to-one basis, but he could have contaminated the food. I'm afraid he may be planning something else. He's been drinking even more than usual the last few days. I want you to stay here in the office, keep the door locked and the lights out."

"Ross! You make this sound dangerous. You don't think Galloway—"

"I don't know what he'll do. I think the man's being pushed pretty hard. There's a pistol in the desk."

"Ross, don't go out there. Let's both stay here until morning."

He touched her cheek. "Jack Galloway is probably all the way to Las Cruces by now. I just want to talk to Garrick and I'm sure as hell not afraid of him. Now sit down and I'll be back in a few minutes."

Jack Galloway did some quick thinking after Laura left. He had to force her to sell and he had to do something to give himself a few days' cover. He could use the money from the sale of the certificates and get out of town, but he had to create some commotion so he wouldn't be missed for a day or two.

He drove to the shed on Marian's land, broke open the

lock, stuffed dynamite and caps under his shirt, and began to run toward the Mission.

Ross found Garrick in the big exercise room by the mineral baths. Garrick was drunk, sprawled across a leg extension machine.

"Well, if it isn't Laura's husband. Hello, Mr. Laura."

Ross grabbed Garrick's shoulder, half pulled him, half pushed him from the padded table. "You bastard!" Ross growled through clenched teeth, then sent his fist into Garrick's jaw. He felt things snap and give under his knuckles.

Garrick slammed against the edge of the machine, his shoulder plowing into the chromed steel.

"What did he offer you to do it?" Ross asked.

Garrick wiped at the blood streaming from his nose. "Half," he whispered.

Ross grabbed the side of the table. "Get out of here." His voice was quiet. "Get out of this town and I never want to see your ugly face again. You understand me?"

Garrick rolled to a standing position, his eyes wide with fear. He turned and half ran, half stumbled from the building.

Ross stood for a moment in the silence of the building. His body was shaking with the violence of his emotion. That the man could have hurt Laura after all she'd done for him! It was all he could do to keep from killing Garrick. At least now, Laura would be rid of him forever.

He left the building slowly, his footsteps almost silent. He didn't see the shadow that clung to the walls of the Mission until he was very close to the man. He opened his mouth to shout because he thought it was Garrick, but the shadow moved too quickly to be Garrick.

He stood silently and watched as the man broke away from the walls and began to run. The moonlight gleamed on Jack Galloway's blond hair.

Ross knew instantly that Galloway had done something inside the Mission. He ran into the kitchen. At first glance everything seemed to be undisturbed. Then he caught the faint hiss of something. He listened for several seconds, then went through the doors into the dining room.

In the faint light, he could see the red glow of the fuse

on the dynamite as it burned across the hearth of the dining room fireplace.

He watched it for just a moment's breath because he knew it would be the last thing he ever saw.

The explosion tore out the dining room and kitchen, shattered the greenhouse, collapsed the roof over the entire southern wing of the Mission. A beam from the ceiling of Laura's office came crashing down onto her desk.

The people of Montero were already awake since they had been on the telephone all night learning the truth about Jack Galloway's phony certificates. Some of them were already on their way to the Mission to ask Laura's help when they saw the roof travel skyward.

When they got there, a fire had started from the broken gas lines in the kitchen. Laura was sitting in what had been the dining room, Ross's mangled body cradled in her lap.

Chapter 19

Dave and Della Anderson were standing in the cemetery, staring down at the fresh grave site. A small headstone bore Irene's name.

"I told her she should have some insurance," Mrs. Anderson said. "But Irene never did believe in helping anyone else. Just look at what she did. She'd have done anything to keep from helping her poor old mother and her crippled brother."

Dave turned to face her. He held his fist up to her face. There were tears running down his cheeks. "Irene was better than either of us could ever be, and if you ever so much as say one word against her, so help me God, I'll kill you."

Mrs. Anderson looked startled for a moment. But she had a built-in protection against hearing what she didn't want to. She sniffed in martyrdom and began to wheel Dave's chair across the gravel path.

"Let's go see to that nice Mr. Kenyon now," she said, ignoring his outburst. She didn't mind having her son all to herself now. Irene had always interfered before. "Now there was a man," she said. "A real man. He stood behind Laura through everything."

Dave felt his guts tighten. He had never seen before how distorted his mother's mind was. She was haunted by feelings of persecution, living in a fantasy world. Twenty-four hours ago she had hated Laura Kenyon. Now she looked to Laura to save her from all the money she'd paid for the worthless certificates.

He ran his hand across his eyes as they neared the big funeral group gathered around Ross Kenyon's grave.

Garrick was so drunk he could hardly stand. Two nights ago he had barely escaped death—twice. First at Ross's hand, then from the explosion itself. He hid in the trees and rocks until the townspeople arrived. Tentatively, he went toward the debris. The main gasline had been shut off and the fire was out.

His first thought when he heard of Ross's death was that now he wouldn't have to leave, now that no one knew of his part in Ross's death, or about Irene.

Clarry had come to the Mission, Bill close beside her. People had called her all night, begging her to get Laura to help them with Galloway. It was during the calls that she heard of Irene's death. When she saw Garrick standing in the rubble of the Mission, she began to ask herself what he'd had to do with the young girl's death.

The townspeople, scared by their own losses, heavy with their realization of what Laura had paid, stared in numb silence. The sun was just rising and the daylight let them see to what extent the Mission had been destroyed. A newsman from Albuquerque began to realize there was a story here. He began asking questions, and the people were too hurt and weak to shield their answers. They told the truth.

Now, standing at the funeral, Garrick told himself that no one's death was his fault, and it didn't mean a thing that he lost Clarry—she was only a facade anyway. What he needed was the real thing.

He moved closer to Laura. She hadn't said much of anything for days. Oh, well, she'd get over her grief. After all, Ross was an old man, almost sixty, and he, Garrick, was only thirty-six. Laura would like having a young husband. Now that both of them were free, he'd have a chance at her again. Then he'd *own* the Mission.

He smiled and stepped even closer to Laura.

Julia watched Garrick's movements through cold, hard eyes. She knew her mother had killed her father. He had died trying to protect the Mission. Always the Mission! It was like something that needed sacrifices and her mother had thrown Ross to it.

She stared up at Garrick. He was not her father! Her father was good and kind, not this smelly, mean man who her mother let near her.

She didn't cry but only gazed at the flower-draped coffin. She wouldn't let her mother get away with killing her father.

Laura was walking alone in the forest above the Mission. From the top of the hill she could see the major destruction of the resort. Over a third of it was devastated. The roof was gone, the walls charred from the fire, some walls destroyed. As far as a hundred feet away were pieces of china, silver twisted by the explosion.

It would take thousands of dollars to repair and months of labor, and Laura didn't care. She no longer had any interest in anyone or anything. Immediately after the funeral, she had turned to her car and driven to Ross's old cabin in the forest. There she could pretend she still had him, that she wasn't alone.

After a day, her fantasizing stopped and her anger began. It was the greed of the people of Montero that had killed her Ross.

As she was leaving the funeral Sheriff Moya handed her a note. It said that Jack Galloway had driven his car over an embankment. The car exploded with its contents.

Laura looked at the sheriff with hate and dropped the note to the ground. What did she care about Galloway's death or that the townspeople's money had burned with him? For all she cared, the whole town could burn with him.

Now, as she looked down at the Mission, she realized the irony of it all. The people had wanted the place so badly, and they had killed Ross to get it. And now what did they have? It wasn't far from where it had been eleven years ago, a pile of mud. The people had killed their own dreams as well as Ross.

She looked down at the place, her eyes full of tears and her heart full of hate.

It was some moments before she saw the trucks and cars coming down the road. The dust blurred the outlines.

"Damn them!" she cursed aloud and began running down the hill. They were vultures, trying to steal what was left from her, ransacking the place. Ross's death wasn't enough for their greed.

By the time she got close enough to see clearly, she stopped, bewildered. It looked like every man, woman and child in Montero was there. They were unloading what looked like a fleet of trucks. There were flatbeds full of lumber, the truck doors painted with the name of an Albuquerque lumberyard. There was a cement truck, three pickups full of flagstone, a long flatbed of massive beams.

A pickup was full of hand-carved corbels. There were at least a dozen loads of adobes.

The people were all working, shouting, a man she recognized as an Albuquerque contractor bellowing orders, cursing so many useless people in his way.

One by one, the people began to see her and they stopped and stared at her in silence.

Della Anderson was the first to recover. "You know that garage of mine I took down? I brought the studs to use. Only this idiot says they're only good for concrete forms." She sneered at the contractor.

Louise Romero held up a shovel. "I'm helping dig dirt to make more adobes. And Laura, when I'm done, I'm applying for a job at the Mission. Think you could use a new waitress?"

It took Laura a moment to realize that they were starting to rebuild the Mission.

Everyone began calling to her. Mr. Greene, the bank president, back from his mysterious trip, said the people of Montero were paying for everything, that they owed her that much. The contractor asked her to get rid of half the people—but could she first answer a few questions, please?

Laura felt her hate leaving her and with it her strength. Her knees buckled under her and she sank down onto a rock. The tears that had been held inside her since Ross's death came out in a wrenching, bucking way. She dropped her head in her hands and began to cry.

She didn't stop until she felt arms around her. She clung to her sister. "Clarry, I loved him so much."

"We all did," Clarry said. "He was a better man than any of us."

It was some time before Laura could stop crying. She looked out at the town. The people were standing with their heads bowed, their guilt and misery showing. Laura looked up at Clarry and an understanding passed between them. They would talk later, talk as they had never done before.

Clarry stepped back and handed Laura a shovel. "Ross always loved your strong back. I don't think he'd like your sitting there while the rest of us worked."

Laura took the shovel and rose very slowly. She looked at the people one by one. She might forgive them but she would never, never forget. She straightened her shoulders and went toward them.

No one seemed to notice that Garrick and Marian were not with them. In fact, they were the only townspeople absent that day.

PART III
1956

Chapter 20

Laura Kenyon sat behind her big desk and stared absently at the list of reservations in front of her. There were two photographs of Ross on her desk and six more on the walls. On the end wall was a small collection of his hand planes, a tool Ross had loved. Above the door were the horns from a nine-point elk that Ross had shot.

She looked up from the papers to gaze at Ross's photograph, as she did several times a day. Sometimes she remembered how Emmett had said, years ago, that she was trying to canonize Ross and to make the Mission a shrine to him. She and Emmett had started quarreling then and hadn't stopped until he and his family left Montero. She had heard he had an excellent job at a major hotel in San Francisco.

She shook her head at the memory. She couldn't please anyone. For so many years people had advised her to stop hiring so many people and to start running the Mission as a profit-making business. When she started to do that, more people turned against her.

After the explosion, Laura changed and with her, the Mission. She didn't rehire the many local people who had quit. She began looking into competitive merchandising. The deep anger she felt because she believed the people of Montero had killed her husband was further flamed when she found that the Montero people had been overcharging her for years. She could import goods and products for less than she had paid locally. For flowers, she built her own greenhouses and hired a man from Japan. He lived at the Mission and supervised all the plantings. When Emmett told her the Woodmans had to sell their house and leave Montero, she smiled. She remembered Mr. Woodman at the town meeting, telling Laura she had to sell.

Laura withdrew funds from the local schools. She began

to look at the work of artists outside of New Mexico. Within two years, she had cut the Mission staff in half and doubled her profits. Very few people from Montero worked at the resort now. Mrs. Martinez had retired as head housekeeper and in her place was a young woman from Ohio, who had studied hotel management in college.

To the guests, things were the same: there were still artists in the big corridor, paintings in the gallery. In the summer, students still gave lessons. But the difference was that Laura now hired people for their qualifications, not because they were from Montero. For her part, she didn't care if the town dropped off the face of the earth. She was as isolated from the people as if she had moved the entire resort to Albuquerque.

She set Ross's portrait down and went back to the papers. She ran her hand through her hair. It was still dark, still thick. At forty-three, she was very good-looking. She had been awkward as a young woman, but as a mature one, she was extraordinary. Her figure was as good as it had been at twenty, and her face looked better for the addition of a few lines at the corners of her eyes. The only bad change was the lack of laughter in her face and her life.

Outside Laura's office, in the exhibition gallery, Julia was talking with the new manager of the Mission. He was the third one in the last three years.

"Laura's not going to like buying the new bedspreads locally," the man was saying. "She said to send someone to Mexico, that they'd be cheaper."

Julia smiled at him seductively. She was as tall as her mother and had much of Laura's authority about her, but softened by some of her Aunt Clarry's sweet looks. Too often people made the mistake of believing her to be pliable. "And I said to buy them locally. Now who are you going to obey?"

The man threw up his hands in disgust, then walked away. Working for the two women was like working in the middle of a war. Laura had the power, but she usually stayed in her office. Julia, on the other hand, had her finger in every corner of the Mission. The employees were divided down the middle. Half took their orders from Laura, half from Julia.

Julia's eyes followed the manager for a moment, then

she walked toward her mother's office. Her anger rose as she thought of how too many of the employees disregarded her. They seemed to think that because she was only twenty she couldn't know much about running the Mission. But she knew, and many of the employees did, too, that at twenty, she already had had ten years of experience.

After the explosion and her father's death, there had been very little left for her. Her mother disappeared for weeks, and when she did return, she worked harder than ever. Julia felt unwanted, as if she were the most unneeded person in the world. The school term finally ended, and with her father gone, there was no one to listen to her.

At ten, she discovered work. She was intelligent, responsible and willing, and she made herself useful. She helped in rebuilding the Mission. When school started, she began to ride her bicycle to the resort as soon as class was out. She even went to the Mission on weekends.

By fourteen, she was handling reservations and making sure the staff did their work. By sixteen, people were treating her as if she were an alternate manager. The guests found that if they wanted anything done, they could go to Julia.

When she graduated from high school, Laura asked her which college she planned to attend. It was the first of many, many quarrels. Julia refused to even consider going to school. She wanted to stay at the Mission and work. Laura talked for days, and for the first time she met with someone as unmovable as she herself was. Julia would not budge from her decision to remain in Montero.

After what came to months of arguing, they quit. Neither admitted victory or defeat. Julia stayed but she was given no power. Laura didn't want to give her the title of manager because then she'd have an excuse not to leave the town. And Julia refused to give in.

Laura looked up as Julia entered her office. Whenever she saw Julia she thought her daughter should be somewhere other than working at the Mission. Right now she looked at her and visualized her on a beach somewhere, surrounded by handsome young men.

"I think it's time we took the glass doors down," Julia said, sitting down on the couch across from the desk. "And we ought to have the chimneys cleaned this year. I think a couple of the Gomez boys could do it."

Laura looked up. "You could get someone cheaper in Albuquerque. Have a contract drawn up and get a couple of bids."

Julia just smiled at her mother, her long lashes shadowing her eyes. She had learned, when she was a child, the advantages of being agreeable. "Joe and his little brother are trying to earn enough money to go to school this fall. They'll do a good job and they can use the money."

Laura glared at her daughter, as always, disconcerted by her outward sweetness and her inner strength. "And they'll charge us an arm and a leg because we can pay. I'm not running a charity here, I'm trying to make a profit. Let the local boys make a bid, and if they're the lowest, we'll use them."

Julia stood. "You know they know nothing about making a bid. We'll pay them by the job, and they won't get paid until the job's complete and done to my satisfaction. I think that's fair for us and for them."

Laura gave a little snort that was meant to be a laugh. "I learned a long time ago how important it was to be 'fair'!"

Julia put up her hand as if to shield her face. "I've heard all this before. I'm tired of hearing what Montero did to you. I'm tired of fighting you for everything."

Laura was pleased when Julia dropped her flirty ways. "You're the one who's obsessed with Montero. This is a competitive world, and if your friends want to learn to live in the outside world, let them learn to compete just like everyone else."

Julia didn't bother to reply but turned and left her mother's office. She went into the secretary's office and picked up the telephone.

"You two at it again?" Betty Gomez asked.

Julia didn't answer but listened to the busy signal on the telephone. She hung up. "Call your cousins in a minute and tell them they have the job." She turned to leave, then looked back at Betty. "And if you want them to work here, I wouldn't mention it to the boss."

Betty looked after her for a moment. She hated being caught between the two women. Someday, she thought, it was going to come to a showdown. She picked up the
228

phone to dial her cousins' house. The boys needed the job, and she'd let Julia handle Laura's wrath.

Julia went down the artisan's corridor and then outside. She headed across the shuffleboard courts toward the guest houses. Three years ago, she had moved out of her mother's house and into the most remote guest house. It was half hidden under the trees at the edge of the forest, a small adobe building consisting of a sitting room, bedroom and bath.

Julia gratefully shut the door behind her. The little living room was a mess of books, magazines, clothing. She never let the staff clean here, saying it was a waste of money, but the truth was, she wanted her privacy. It was nice to have someplace where she wasn't under inspection, where she could be herself and not Laura's daughter.

On the north wall, hung her only picture, a photograph of her and her father. Sometimes Julia remembered that little pigtailed girl with sadness. Ross had his hand on her shoulder, and Julia thought she could remember everything about her father, his kindness, the way he always listened to her.

She looked away from the photograph. She wondered if there was a day when she didn't ask herself if he really was her father. She went into the bedroom and changed into her swimsuit, then drew on a terry cloth cover.

Outside, the hotel manager was waiting for her. He was young, handsome and blond, and Julia had gone out with him a few times. But there her interest died.

"Hello, Carl," she said pleasantly, then kept walking.

He grabbed her arm. "Julia, will you stop it!"

"Stop what? I don't know what you mean."

"We just had a quarrel and you're acting like nothing happened."

She gave him a look of exasperation. "Why do you consider a difference of opinion a quarrel? And besides, what difference does it make? I just think we could get the bedspreads locally without a trip to Mexico, that's all."

"Julia, it's not the bedspreads and you know it. It's us, the two of us. You know that when I took this job it was because of you. I thought we cared for each other."

Julia smiled at him. They had met at a six-week seminar for hotel management. Julia had been asked to speak about the problems of running a resort the size of the

Mission. Maybe it was because she had felt so alone away from her home, but she had been quite miserable. Carl had sensed her misery and asked her out. During her two weeks there she had almost thought she was in love with him.

But the pull of the Mission was too strong. Once home again, she could hardly remember Carl's name. Yet he persisted, called her, wrote her, and four months later, when the manager's position was open, Julia persuaded Laura to hire him. Maybe she wanted to love him. Sometimes she imagined being married and living at the Mission. But as soon as she saw Carl, she knew he wasn't right. There was no authority about him, no confidence. And the Julia he wanted was the one who smiled and flirted. He didn't like it when her decisions were better than his.

"I'm sure I don't know where you got that idea," Julia said, still smiling, and pulled away from him. "You were hired as the manager here, and as far as I can tell, I have to do most of your job." She turned away from him and walked toward the door to the Mission.

Carl glared after her for a moment. What hurt most about her words was that they were true. Most of the time he felt ineffectual, caught between two strong women. He had no power, no possibility of acting on his own decisions. Lately he'd been tossing a coin to see which woman he would agree with.

He watched Julia, gave one last admiring glance at her incredible legs, and went toward the mineral baths. Somehow he didn't mind losing her. He didn't want to spend his life engaged in a power struggle. He had a friend in Denver. Maybe he'd call him tonight and talk about the possibility of another job. Suddenly, the idea of leaving the Mission was wonderful.

Julia continued toward the pool, her head high. Long ago she learned to mask her feelings. Sometimes she wondered why she turned down man after man. She met people from all over the world, yet somehow, none of them interested her, at least not for very long. Men were attracted to her because of her looks and her mature manner, her ability to cope. Yet at the same time, they found her intimidating. She had never met a man her own age who had half her self-assurance. The older men were all married or were so unattractive physically she couldn't care for them.

She dived into the water in a clean arc and swam methodically back and forth across the pool. Her Aunt Clarry had taught her the importance of a daily exercise program, and Julia followed the advice with great self-discipline.

Laura stood by the pool stairs, holding a towel for her daughter. "I came to apologize," she said as she wrapped the towel around Julia. "I hate it when we quarrel. I told Betty to hire her cousins."

Julia removed her bathing cap and pulled on her robe. She wouldn't start another quarrel by telling her she had already hired the boys.

"Julia, I wish we wouldn't quarrel so much," Laura said. "I was just thinking that it's because we're together so much of the time. Did I tell you that last week I got some brochures from the University of Delaware?"

Julia tried to calm herself so her anger wouldn't explode. "Perhaps I can see them later."

Laura grabbed her daughter's arm. "Don't give me that! You know you have no intention of looking at them!" She lowered her voice. "Can't you see what you're doing to yourself? You have buried yourself alive in this isolated little town. You never meet anyone, never get to see any of the life outside of here. All you do is work! Julia," she said, "I'm only thinking of you. I don't want you to spend all your youth here like I did. I've given you money, why don't you use it? Go to Paris or Venice. You can afford it."

Julia gently pulled away from her mother. "Why do I get the feeling you're trying to get rid of me? Why are you trying to buy me off?"

Laura could only look at her daughter in astonishment—and hurt. All she wanted for Julia was more than what she had had. She didn't want Julia destroyed as she had been. She knew too well the pain of loneliness.

Julia tried to control her anger as she walked back to her little house. She and her mother were always quarreling. Then, like clockwork, Laura would apologize and start urging her daughter to leave Montero. The idea of Paris had no intrigue for her at all. What was challenging to her was keeping the Mission running smoothly and the guests happy.

She dressed hurriedly to get back to the resort before

dinner. There were always a hundred things to do to get ready for the big meal. Tonight there was a barbeque as well as the more formal meal inside. The big covered grills were covered with pork, and hickory smoke poured across the lawns. A barbeque seemed like an informal event, but Julia was well aware of the work and organization that was required.

It was many hours later before she was able to climb into bed. Carl had told her of his plans to resign, and now Julia needed to look for a new manager. Laura left the choice to her since she had been pleased with Julia's choice of Carl.

She had set her alarm for six. Tomorrow she had to drive to Albuquerque to meet a plane that was bringing six paintings for exhibit and a new guest. The artist refused to ship his work unless either Laura or Julia personally picked them up. The guest was arriving an hour before the paintings, and if he didn't mind riding in a pickup, Julia would bring him back. Otherwise, he could fly with a local airline.

Chapter 21

Julia arrived at the Albuquerque airport a half hour before the guest's plane was due to arrive. It was still only nine A.M. and the air was cool and crisp. She first arranged for the small local airlines to be ready in case the guest wanted transportation. Most of the time, the eastern guests were prepared to "rough it." They half expected to be driven to the Mission in a covered wagon. A few were surprised that a place as wild as New Mexico had indoor toilets.

On the other hand, guests from west of New Mexico thought they were traveling closer to New York, the world's cultural center, so they expected great luxury. They wouldn't consider riding in a pickup.

Julia checked her card about this newly arriving guest. For years now, Laura had made it a policy to find out about her guests. She kept open contacts with people who could find out whatever she wanted to know.

Bradley Northrup was forty-five years old and head of a large, extremely successful architectural firm. He and his wife were divorced five years ago, and since then, Mr. Northrup had become rootless, living close to whatever job he was supervising. A month ago he had made a reservation at the Mission, asking Laura for permission to study the architecture and talk to her about running a place the size of the resort. He had been commissioned to design a resort somewhat like it and he needed advice.

Julia waited impatiently for the plane to land. As the passengers disembarked, she looked for her guest. Usually, they were easy to spot: the newness of their expensive clothes always gave them away. Sometimes the easterners sported cowboy hats and shiny ostrich-skin, high-heeled boots and the Californians, anxious to appear fashionable, wore Paris originals. Whatever they wore, they looked out-of-place amid the simple, well-worn clothes of the natives.

There were two men who looked as if they were her

guests. Both wore handtailored three-piece suits and carried elegant new briefcases.

"Are either of you Mr. Bradley Northrup?" Julia asked, smiling at the men.

They gave her cool looks as they said they were not. They made a point of saying they were only passing through this part of the country.

"Excuse me, but are you Mrs. Kenyon?"

Julia turned to the voice behind her. No wonder she hadn't known him! He wore easy clothes, neither expensive nor new. He was a tall man, thick, with dark hair liberally threaded with gray. His blue eyes were bright and alive, his jaw square.

He smiled at her. "You look surprised. Are you disappointed that you didn't get one of them?" He nodded toward the backs of the men walking away.

"Of course not. It's just that after a while you get so you can pick out the guests."

"And I don't look like one?" He grinned at her. "I don't know why, but I think I've just received a compliment. May I say you don't look nearly old enough to have started building the Mission in 1936?"

"I didn't. My mother is Laura Kenyon. I'm Julia. Could I have your baggage tickets? I'll get your luggage."

He ignored her request. "Did you drive all the way down here for me?"

"Actually, no. We have someone who lives in Albuquerque who usually meets the guests and makes sure they get on the Mission plane. But today I had to pick up some paintings coming in later so I volunteered to meet you."

"And see that I don't get lost?"

She laughed. "Something like that." She was beginning to warm to the man. "You have a choice. You can fly to the Mission on a small plane or ride back with me. I have to warn you, though, that I have another hour to wait before I can leave and I'm in a truck."

"You make it sound like a threat. Are you picking up someone else?"

"No, just the paintings. Please, will you give me your baggage checks? We can get your suitcases loaded while we're waiting."

He nodded to a fat, rolled bag at his feet. "That's it."

He looked back at her. "I feel like I'm failing every test of a guest at the Mission."

"True, you are," she smiled. "But then you're also making your own set of rules. Are you hungry? There's a coffee shop just down the hall."

"Maybe I could buy you a cup of coffee, and afterwards I'll let you decide if you want me to ride back with you. I have a few thousand questions to ask about the Mission."

Julia laughed at his words, but he wasn't exaggerating at all. From his bag he withdrew a rigid tube and took out a rolled drawing. He spread it across the table in the coffee shop. It was a detailed floor plan of the Mission.

"Where did you get that?" Julia asked.

"Did you ever see a book called *The Great Resorts* by John Alexander?"

Julia shook her head.

"I should have guessed. It was published in 1947. Let's see, you were about..."

"Eleven," she smiled.

He smiled, then looked back at the drawing. "All of eleven years old. Needless to say, the book wasn't a best-seller, but several libraries still have copies." He put his finger on the dining room fireplace. "This was where the bomb was planted, wasn't it?" He looked up at her. "You may not remember that, either, since you were a little girl."

Julia stiffened and leaned back in her seat. "Since the explosion killed my father, I don't think I would be likely to forget it."

Brad looked blank for a moment, then turned pale. "I didn't know that," he said quietly. "The book only said a man, angry over something, had planted a bomb at night and blown a lot of the resort up. I took it for granted that no one was hurt. I'm really sorry."

Julia managed to smile. "It was ten years ago and I guess I shouldn't mind. Heaven knows I've answered enough questions about that night. It's just that... I don't know how to explain it, but things have a way of standing still in Montero. Maybe it's because we're so isolated. It may be ten years since my father's death, but to a lot of us, it seems like yesterday."

He watched her with an unusual intensity. "I grew up in a small town. I can understand how small they can get."

235

She tried to relax. "Somehow I doubt if your birthplace is as infamous as Montero."

"Infamous?" He frowned in wonder. He had no idea what she was talking about.

The last thing Julia wanted to talk about was that horrible time after her father's death. She looked down at the plans spread across the table. "You were right, the bomb was planted here."

He knew she wanted to change the subject. "How was the place changed when it was remodeled?"

"It wasn't remodeled," Julia said flatly. "It was rebuilt. It was rebuilt adobe by adobe exactly as it had been. My mother wouldn't allow any of it to be changed. Some of the walls were awkward and the kitchen needed modernizing but my mother refused to consider the idea."

He was still watching her. She talked as if she had been there during the rebuilding but she was a child. "What do you do at the Mission besides pick up paintings and guests?"

Julia smiled and leaned back, took a sip of her coffee. "That is a very difficult question to answer. Some people say I run the place and others say all I do is interfere. I guess it's however you want to look at it."

"And your mother? What does she say?"

Julia put her cup down with a clatter. "My mother wants me to go to college and become a cheerleader or something equally useful. She wants me to have all the fun she never had."

"And what in the world could a pretty young girl have against fun?"

Julia shook her head. "Absolutely nothing. Just my idea of fun isn't studying the Victorian poets." Before he could ask, she continued, "I happen to like the Mission. No, correct that. I *love* the place. Maybe it has something to do with my father giving his life for it. Maybe I want to give my life for it, too. I don't know, but I do know it's a part of me."

Suddenly she was embarrassed. She always tried to keep herself separate from the guests. And most of the time she kept herself apart from everyone. She looked about for something to say, something that would keep her from looking at this man's penetrating stare. "Goodness!" she said lightly, looking at her watch, "It's already time for the other plane." She stood abruptly. "Maybe I can answer some of your questions on the way to Montero." She turned and went toward the landing field.

Julia was very embarrassed about her revelations and tried to cover her awkwardness by ignoring Brad Northrup. But he refused to be ignored. He helped unload the paintings from the plane, and when he saw that the corner of one was damaged, he insisted she open and inspect it. The painting, thankfully, was unharmed, but it took quite some time to reseal the package.

Brad climbed into the truck and looked at Julia as she sat behind the steering wheel. "How about lunch?" He seemed fully aware of her nervousness.

At lunch, he again spread the plans across the table and again started asking questions. He wanted to know how the unusual design of the Mission appealed to the guests.

"We get a lot of complaints," Julia said. "They're always saying they get lost or they can't find the same place twice, but in the end they come to like it. The complainers are always the ones to come back."

He pointed to the courtyard. "I believe this is closed in the winter, right? How does that work? Surely you don't try to heat the place."

"I think heating would be impossible. There are half-inch cracks in the woodwork." She set her coffee cup down. "I can see you're unexposed to New Mexico building methods. Out here, because of the dryness, nothing rots. Back East you have to worry about the weight of snow on the roof and you have to make the windows fit tightly."

Brad looked puzzled. "You have buildings here that are hundreds of years old, surely—"

Julia gave half a laugh. "When we were rebuilding the Mission, one of the workers dropped his level off the roof and someone backed a truck over it. The man climbed down from the roof, got his level, then took his hammer and straightened it out. He continued to use it for the rest of the job."

Brad could only stare at her in disbelief. A level was a tool that had to be highly accurate. How could they roof a building if the walls weren't level? Brad solemnly began to roll his drawing and replaced it in the tube. "I think I'm going to have to see this place to believe it. Maybe it'd be better if you just told me about it." He watched closely as Julia began to speak of the Mission. She might have been a starry-eyed girl talking of her lover.

"It's a feeling really," Julia was saying. "The whole place is made of the elements of the land. It's as if the soil had risen up and made walls. It surrounds you and protects you, almost as if it were hugging you."

"Rather like making love," Brad smiled, then watched as Julia looked down at her plate, her cheeks flushed.

Julia recovered herself quickly. "It's a long way back, maybe we should get started."

Brad insisted on driving and only laughed when Julia seemed concerned. He said it was the least he could do to repay her for answering his questions. And he did ask questions, more and more of them. He wanted to know the history of the mineral baths, the history of the original mission, and with it he wanted to know about Laura Kenyon.

"It must have been scary to take on so much at such a young age. When I was twenty-two, I'd just finished school and I had a lot to learn before I could design my own buildings."

Julia tightened her jaw. "My mother has a way about her. She never worries about the consequences, she just does what she thinks should be done. I don't believe anything scares her."

Brad looked at her out of the corner of his eye. "That's hard to believe. It sounds to me like she was plenty scared."

"How can you judge someone you've never met?" Julia snapped.

"Because I've met her daughter and because of some of the things you've said. You told me she wanted you to go to college and not miss out on some of the fun she never had. She must have been aware of what she was missing back then. If she was intelligent enough to build the Mission, surely she was smart enough to see there were alternatives."

"I guess so," Julia said slowly. It was difficult to think of her mother as young and vulnerable. "She did have a choice. She was in art school when my grandfather died. The town offered to keep paying her way to school. She didn't have to stay but she felt Clarry needed her."

"Wait a minute! You're going too fast for me. The town

was putting her through art school during the Depression?"

Briefly, Julia told him of the events leading to the building of the Mission.

Brad gave a low whistle. "Some lady! She makes me feel guilty. The book said she hired people mostly from Montero. It makes sense now. She wanted to repay them for their goodness."

"Their goodness!" Julia exploded and then calmed. "Where have you been the last few years? Didn't you read in the papers about Montero?"

He turned and frowned in puzzlement.

"Does the name of my beloved uncle ring a bell? Garrick Eastman."

Brad looked at her in astonishment. "That happened here?" He looked back at the road. "I was in South America at the time, but when I came home, I remember hearing something about it. One day I was at my sister's house and her little boy wouldn't eat all of his oatmeal. She said if he didn't obey her, he was going to grow up to be another Garrick."

Julia kept staring ahead. "That was Montero. Garrick was married to my Aunt Clarry."

Brad kept glancing at her, watching the way her eyes never flickered from the road. "It must have been a difficult time for you and your mother."

Julia took a while to answer. "More than difficult. The entire town had united to try and drive us away from the Mission, my father had been killed, and then the press decided to tell the story to the entire world. It was due to their digging that they found out about my uncle."

"Wasn't there something about a girl who was killed?"

"Irene Anderson. She worked as a receptionist at the Mission. It was found out later that Garrick was driving the car when they went off the road. He walked away and left her in the wreck. Her mother tried to sue the Mission for taking away her sole means of support."

"And what happened?"

"Garrick was charged with manslaughter but he was acquitted. Irene's car had something wrong with the steering and no one could prove Garrick had been drunk that night. He claimed to be dazed from the wreck and later couldn't remember it clearly. He used every penny he had on lawyers."

"And the woman who was suing the Mission?"

"The charges were dropped. It was just some lawyer trying to make a case out of nothing. Garrick was discharged, and when my aunt divorced him, he no longer had any association with the resort. After about a year, Irene's brother left town and his mother went with him. We never heard of them again."

Brad sat in silence for a moment. "How did your mother take all this?"

Julia leaned her head back against the seat. "It changed her. She hates Montero now. She never lets them forget what they did to her."

"And you? You don't sound like you hate them."

"I did when I was a child. I hated everyone because they expected me to be like my mother and I wasn't. I don't have half her strength—or her determination. But later, I think I felt sorry for them. They've suffered a lot because of my father's death."

Brad wanted to ask more questions, but before them loomed the largest, longest structure he'd ever seen. He felt Julia lean forward and he glanced at the expression on her pretty face. She was a woman coming home to her lover. She leaned toward the dashboard and looked as if she'd never seen the place before.

"I take it that's the Mission," he said.

Julia only smiled in pride and wonder. "The tall part to the left is the old chapel. We usually have four or five weddings a year there and every Sunday we have services. The guest rooms are to the right. The new guest houses are behind the main building, closer to the forest."

"And where will I stay?"

"See that low wall just to the right of the big portal? That's the courtyard suite. You have your own private garden. We thought you might like to work there."

"How thoughtful!" he said, truly pleased.

Julia smiled contentedly. "We always try to decide what our guests will like and then match the accommodations to their needs."

Brad kept staring at the massive resort as he slowly drove toward it. He had seen pictures of it, of course, but nothing had prepared him for the sheer volume of it. It did indeed rise out of the ground as if it were part of it, a natural swelling. Its age and dominating presence were awesome. He felt like an intruder in the truck. He should be on horseback, bearing gifts, an offering, asking permission to approach.

Julia's laugh made him look at her.

"You feel it too, don't you?" she smiled. "It doesn't always affect people in the same way. Some hate it. One woman had us drive back to the plane; she wouldn't even enter it."

"I can understand that. I feel like Jonah walking into the whale's mouth."

"No, not Jonah," Julia said. "I always feel it's going to swallow me but I rather look forward to it. The Mission would never harm me."

Brad pulled into a parking lot half hidden by trees. Stepping out of the truck, he felt the utter stillness and serenity of the mountain air. He looked up at the Mission. He and Julia had spoken of the place as if it were alive and breathing, and now, closer to it, the feeling was even stronger. It wouldn't be difficult to imagine the big place picking up her skirts and walking.

Her, he thought, as he took a painting from the truck. He had no doubt that the Mission was a female. The very air around it seemed to breathe that here was a strong, proud, gracious woman. He turned and looked up once again. One woman had built this magnificent structure. One, very young, very alone girl had created this glorious building.

As he unloaded a second painting, he chuckled. Here he was a famous architect, who had built houses, hotels, skyscrapers, all over the world but had never come close to achieving what this inexperienced girl had. None of his buildings approached the awesome, almost holy quality of the Mission.

Laura Kenyon, he thought. Here was one woman he very much wanted to meet. If she had half the presence of what she had built...He stopped and chuckled again.

"Are you laughing?" Julia asked, curious.

"Maybe," he grinned. "Maybe it's this place. Maybe I feel like it's going to hug me, too."

Julia smiled happily at him. Anyone who liked the Mission owned some of her heart. People always reacted to the place, sometimes with animosity, sometimes with love, but no one was ever neutral.

She picked up a painting and headed for the entrance. "Come on. You're not going to believe the inside."

Brad followed her and with each step he felt more curious about the woman who had built the place. The huge expanse of the lobby had no supporting poles and he knew what a feat of engineering that was. The walls were massive, undulating gently toward the high ceiling. He wasn't sure what he had expected of the Mission but this wasn't it. It was much larger, much stronger than anything he had envisioned as designed by a woman.

He turned and gave a quick look at Julia's back as she registered him. He had spent too much of his life working and his wife had been a weak, clinging woman. She could no more have driven a pickup two hundred miles to meet a plane than she could have built the Golden Gate Bridge. Julia was obviously a strong, confident young woman but she was the copy. What was her mother like? What kind of strength existed in a woman that she could shape the earth and create this living, breathing structure?

"Brad?" Julia called. "Are you ready? Would you like to see your room now or maybe have a drink?"

"I'd like to see it all."

Julia smiled. "I'll take you myself. I'll show you every nook and cranny."

"No," he said as he glanced down the long exhibition gallery. The skylights made the hall glow with light and warmth. "I think I'd like to explore on my own. Later, when I get a feel for the place, maybe I'll ask for a tour."

Julia opened the door to his room for him.

Brad's first impression was that he could live here. The large bed, obviously custom-made, fit easily into the enormous room. The flagstone floors were waxed to a deep luster. A big fireplace was stocked with piñon wood and ready to be lit. French doors led to the outside courtyard, a private, walled area set with weathered wood benches and a four-foot-tall stone statue of Saint Francis holding a tiny birdbath. A robin sat on the saint's left shoulder.

"What do you think?"

He shook his head at her. "I think it would take all night to tell you."

"You're on! How about dinner with me tonight?" Julia

immediately looked embarrassed. "Of course you may have other plans," she faltered.

Brad saw her embarrassment and laughed. "Nothing could be more important than dinner with a beautiful young woman. How about eight o'clock?"

She relaxed and smiled. "Maybe I should show you where the dining room is."

"Don't you dare!" he laughed. "I made it around the South American jungles so surely I can make it through Laura's Mission."

Julia frowned for a moment at the name, then returned his smile. "I'll see you at eight then," she said as she left his room.

Chapter 22

"Julia," Clarry said quietly, "you look so preoccupied. Is something wrong?"

Julia looked up at her aunt from her position on the floor and smiled vaguely. They were in Clarry's office, Clarry at her big drafting table, Julia on the thick white carpet, her full skirt and several crinolines spread around her.

Clarry put her pencil down and gave her full attention to her niece. At thirty-nine, Clarry was beautiful, elegant, serene, her eyes always watching, always giving. After Ross died, Clarry had taken Julia under her wing, watched her, cared for her.

In return, Julia gave her aunt what she gave no one else—honesty. With Clarry she didn't always smile, didn't always coat her words with honey. Clarry understood Julia, sweet and feminine on the outside, intelligent and ambitious on the inside, and always wavering between love and hate for Laura.

"How are the twins?" Julia asked.

"The same as they were this morning when you saw them," Clarry said, speaking of her and Bill's six-year-old boys. "Are you going to tell me what's wrong or do I have to wheedle it out of you?" Clarry looked fondly at Julia.

Clarry smiled sweetly. "Could I guess that a man is at the bottom of all this?"

Julia gave a startled look at her aunt, then laughed. "I wish I could have secrets around you. How could you guess that a man has anything to do with my mood?"

"Maybe because I see some of myself in you. Now, come on and tell me all about it."

"This morning I went to Albuquerque to pick up some paintings and to arrange for a guest to get here, either on another plane or with me."

"I take it he returned with you. Now tell me, what's he like?"

Julia gave Clarry a sideways look. "He's not what you'd expect. I mean, he's not..."

"Why don't you tell me what he is?"

Julia rose and walked toward a big worktable. There were two bolts of vibrant silk on the table and a piece of seersucker spread out, pattern pieces taped to the fabric. Clarry had once had had a chance to show her designs at an international house in Paris but she'd refused the invitation. She decided she wasn't a business woman. All she wanted was what she had: a home, a loving husband, two perfect children and enough of a job to occupy her while the boys were at school.

"He's strong," Julia began. "And there's something about him that makes me talk to him. Oh, Clarry," she said as she whirled around. "I told him things I've never told anyone else. I told him about all the things that happened when Daddy died."

Clarry was serious. "That must have been difficult for you."

"Yes and no. There's something about him that made me talk. He seems so...receptive, I guess." Her eyes lit. "And he loved the Mission."

Clarry had to work to keep from laughing. Sometimes she felt Julia was so much like her, then she'd make a statement that was pure Laura. "When do I get to meet him?"

"I'm having dinner with him tonight. I've already had the table set, that one in the corner by the hibiscus."

"Julia, it all sounds heavenly. I hope everything works out well. By the way, did you know that Carl gave Laura his notice of resignation today?"

"Yes," Julia said in a hard voice. "He thought I came with the job." She waved her hand in dismissal. "I guess you'll be leaving for the day soon but maybe you can meet him tomorrow."

"I'll make a point of it." Clarry looked at her watch. "I *am* late! Please come by tomorrow and let's talk. Okay?"

"Sure, of course I will. I'll tell you all about dinner and all about Brad. You wait and see. You'll really like him."

She squeezed Julia's hand. "I'll like him if you do. Now, I really must go. The boys will think I've deserted them."

Julia laughed. "I doubt that. Give my love to the little monsters." She watched as Clarry left the office.

Clarry stepped out of the showroom, then realized she still wore her smock. As she removed it, three fabric samples fell out of her pocket. "Rats!" she muttered. She had intended to show them to Laura yesterday. She hurried down the artisan's corridor to her sister's office.

"Laura," she said, sticking her head inside. "Are you busy?"

"No, not especially. Come and talk to me."

Clarry stepped inside and shut the door behind her. "I only have a minute. I should have been home an hour ago. I wanted to show you these samples and see what you thought."

Laura looked obediently at the tiny fabric samples. For the life of her she could not visualize how they'd look as curtains. She looked up at Clarry with such a helpless expression that Clarry laughed.

"All right," Clarry said. "I can take a hint. I just thought you might like to choose them yourself for once." She put the swatches in her purse.

"Are you leaving?" Laura asked. "I hoped you could stay a few minutes."

Clarry smiled at her sister. She couldn't help glancing about the room. Emmett had called it a shrine to Ross and he'd been right. But Clarry never gave her opinion unless asked. She knew that the sisterly bond was too fragile and she didn't want to injure it. Laura was lonely, deeply, painfully lonely, but refused to do anything about it.

"Just for a minute," Clarry said, sitting down. "Julia came by a few minutes ago."

Laura leaned forward eagerly. "What did she have to say?"

Clarry looked away for an instant. It hurt her deeply to see the rift between Laura and Julia. She loved both of them, but the two women were so much alike that they did little else but quarrel. They were used to being stronger than other people, used to being able to manipulate others, so when they came against each other, neither knew how to compromise.

Now Laura was eager to hear anything about the daughter she loved so much. Julia would be horribly hurt if she knew Clarry told Laura all that her niece confided in her aunt. Laura had never betrayed Clarry's confidences to her daughter. It was a sad way for mother to learn about daughter, but Clarry knew that for now it was the only way.

"Julia picked up a guest from Albuquerque today."

"Yes," Laura said impatiently. "Bradley Northrup. He's some big deal architect. He wasn't aggressive to Julia, was he?"

Clarry smiled. "I think it may be the other way around. Julia took an unusual liking to him."

Laura frowned. "Isn't that rather quick? I mean, after all, she did just meet the man."

"Laura," Clarry warned. "If you do one thing to let Julia know I mentioned it to you, I'll..."

Laura gave her sister a withering look. "I've never done that in all these years so I don't believe I'll start now. I do think I'll introduce myself to the man, though. I should have done that anyway."

Clarry stood. She knew Laura wouldn't interfere. Laura had learned that harsh lesson too well. "I really have to be going. I'll see you tomorrow morning and I want a full report on Julia's Brad."

"It's a deal," Laura said as she followed her sister to the door. "Tell Bill and the boys hello for me."

Clarry smiled, waved, and walked toward the lobby.

As soon as her sister was out of sight, Laura frowned. So, Julia had started another of her seven-day-wonder romances, and this time with a guest. Laura and Clarry had argued quite a lot over whether to hire Carl or not. Laura knew Julia rarely stayed interested in a man for more than a few weeks, but she couldn't let Julia know that Clarry had told her about Carl. Now the young man, disappointed and not strong enough for Julia, had resigned.

Laura shut the door to her office and set out to look for this new man. At least if he were a guest, he'd be leaving soon and would have a way out when Julia inevitably threw him over.

She knocked on the door of the courtyard suite but there was no answer, so she started toward the big courtyard. She usually personally welcomed all the guests, but because she hadn't known when Brad had arrived, she had missed him.

She searched the entire Mission, looking for a new,

young face but had no luck. By the west wall, outside of the oldest part of the Mission, she saw a man with a tape, measuring the short wall. She stared for a moment at his back. His gray-flecked hair and the thickness of his body wasn't what she had expected. Perhaps he was a friend of someone and not Julia's new love interest.

She watched as he made notes on a clipboard, then began to measure again. She walked forward, took the end of the tape and held it for him.

He looked at her with surprise and interest as he walked backward. After he made more notes, he looked up again. "You staying here?" he asked.

Laura liked his looks, his warm air of confidence. He looked like a man who had worked in the outdoors instead of sitting behind a desk. "I live here," she said quietly.

"I didn't know there were any permanent guests." He kept looking at his notes. "Do you know that some of these walls are twelve feet thick?"

"Only the oldest ones. Most of them range from four to six feet. It's good insulation. It's never hot inside in summer, yet it's easy to heat in the winter. Most of the guests keep a fire going in the winter, saves on the gas bill. Of course, someone has to stay close to make sure they don't burn themselves."

· Brad was staring at her in open-mouthed astonishment. "You're Laura."

She laughed. "You make it sound like an accusation."

He tossed the clipboard to the ground. "Let me introduce myself." He held out his hand to her. "I'm Bradley North-rup."

Laura took his hand and felt some of his warmth flow into her. It was hard to believe this man was attracted to Julia; he was older than Laura. She withdrew her hand. "Your letter said you wanted to study the Mission."

He kept staring at her, not speaking.

"Mr. Northrup, you're making me feel like I have soot on my face."

"I'm sorry," he smiled. "It's just that I had conjured up a very different picture of you. Somehow I expected you to look like...," he gestured up at the Mission, "...like someone who could build something like this."

She laughed. "Is that supposed to be a compliment?"

"A very sincere one. Of course, I should have guessed
248

that it would take a beautiful woman to create something of such beauty."

"Thank you." She looked down the long wall of the Mission. "I guess it is a shock when you first see the place. Many of our guests think it's a bit overpowering."

"It does make you feel small, doesn't it?" He looked back toward the forest behind them. "I was just about to see if I could find someplace where I could look down in it, maybe a hill or something."

"There's a perfect place right up there, if you don't mind a climb."

"Not if you'd lead the way."

She pulled away from him because he was openly flirting with her. He wasn't the first man to do so, but he was the first man in a long time whose offer tempted her. "No," she smiled and then gave a look down at her skirt and heels.

"Maybe tomorrow."

She frowned. Was this man interested in Julia or was Julia's attraction one-sided?

"If you're wondering if I'm married and make passes wherever I go, then let me reassure you. I don't," he said. "I usually have too much work to do. And actually, I brought enough work with me to keep me busy most of the summer."

He took a step toward her. "I am divorced, forty-five years old, and I want to tell you that you are the most interesting thing I've seen in years."

"Thing?" she laughed, warming to him in spite of herself.

He looked up at the Mission walls. "You built that. You took a bunch of mud, some inexperienced laborers, and created this magnificent piece of art. I've never met another woman who could do a third as much."

"Then you must have not met many women. It was done out of necessity and I was far from being alone in doing it. My husband supervised all the engineering, all the construction."

"But it was your plan, your idea. I read how you fought the banks and how everyone said you couldn't do it."

His open flattery was getting to her. "They called it my mud palace," she said almost wistfully. "That was a hard year. I was so tired I was too tired to be tired."

249

He chuckled, his eyes dancing with admiration and respect. "I wish I could have been here. It must have been exciting, knowing you were building, creating something."

She thought for a moment. That summer had been horrible, her father's death, Clarry's screaming announcement that she hated Laura, Ross's abandoning her. "Yes, it was exciting. There were other things that happened that summer, but the building seemed to override everything. When I got here in the morning, all I cared about were those walls rising."

He was watching her with intensity. She was certainly a beautiful woman, not the classical beauty of a model, but she had a warm, strong look about her. He felt energy and intelligence coming from her. This was a woman to challenge a man. He had a brief vision of working beside her. He smiled as he thought that she would never let him win an argument easily.

"And now it's finished," he said, watching her.

"Yes," she said as she seemed to come out of a dream. "It hasn't been changed in years." She looked back at him. "Have you seen all of the Mission? There are some nooks and crannies that even I forget about."

He laughed. "About as likely as a mother is to forget her child."

The mention of a child brought Laura back to reality. She had come to meet this man because he was Julia's new beau. "I just remembered some work I have to do," she said abruptly. "I'm sure I'll be seeing you, Mr. Northrup, and please don't hesitate if you need anything." She turned and quickly walked away.

Brad stared after her in wonder, puzzled at her quick departure, almost as if she were offended. Or that she suddenly remembered that he was her guest.

He walked down the south wall of the Mission, and with each step and each thing he saw, he felt Laura's touch on it. If she could build a place like this when she was twenty-two, what could she do at forty-three? She obviously knew a lot about construction, and he had read that she had drawn the plans for the resort. If she had some more training, she could get her architect's license. With her sense of land and structure, she could be formidable.

He smiled as he thought of all the things he could teach her and all the things he could learn from her.

250

It was with regret that he realized it was getting late and he was to meet Julia for dinner.

Julia dressed carefully, wearing one of Clarry's designs. She hoped it made her appear older and more sophisticated. She looked in the mirror and tried to forget her latest confrontation with Carl. He had been nasty and immature. She smoothed the silk over her left shoulder and was glad her bare shoulder was smooth and tanned. Maybe what she needed was an older man, someone calm and knowledgeable.

She picked up her silk clutch purse, and started toward the dining room. It would be nice to have an older man around, someone to take care of her while she took care of the Mission.

Brad met her in the passage leading to the dining room.

"No trouble finding the place?" Julia asked.

"None. But of course I did have a map." He followed her as she led the way to the table she had chosen.

"You said you wanted to see the interior by yourself. Did you?"

"Every inch of it."

"And?"

He smiled at her because she was like a vain woman fishing for compliments. "You really love this place, don't you?"

"Of course." Julia was surprised. "Why shouldn't I?"

"Some people might consider it a burden. I would think there's a lot of responsibility involved in keeping so many guests happy."

Julia shrugged nonchalantly. "Sometimes it's a challenge, especially in giving them the food they like, but I certainly wouldn't consider it a burden." As she watched him, she saw his attention go to something behind her. She turned and saw her mother walking through the dining room, stopping at each table and speaking with the guests.

Julia frowned as she saw the light in Brad's face. "I take it you've met my mother," she said heavily.

Brad seemed unaware of her tone as his eyes never left Laura.

Laura looked at her daughter's rigid back, then at Brad as he rose to greet her.

251

"Won't you join us?" Brad said, motioning to the space between him and Julia.

"Julia," Laura said, "you look lovely."

Julia didn't look at her mother but studied the design on her empty plate.

Brad seemed oblivious to the tension between the two women. "We haven't started yet," he said. "There's room, and besides, I have several questions I wanted to ask you."

Laura frowned at him, tried to let him know he was hurting Julia, but he kept smiling in such a way that Laura was almost tempted to accept his offer. "I'm sure Julia can answer any of your questions about the Mission," she said curtly before turning away.

Brad took his time before sitting down again. "Julia, you should have told me your mother was so lovely," he said. "It was a shock to realize that a woman who'd built a place like this could be as beautiful as Laura."

Julia looked at him with big, stricken eyes. Suddenly she was transported back to her childhood. She was in a classroom again and the teacher was being nice to her because of Laura. The town treated her either good or bad, based on how they felt about Laura. Even now, as an adult, her life was entirely controlled by her mother.

She stood. "I don't feel well," she said.

Brad rose, too. "It's nothing serious, is it?"

"No," she said, gathering her things. "I think something upset my stomach."

"Could I get you anything?" He put his hand on her arm.

She jerked away from him. "No, nothing. I think I'll just go to my cabin."

Brad looked after her for a moment, guessing that she was angry about something but he couldn't imagine what. He caught a passing waiter and asked if Laura usually ate at the Mission. The waiter said she had just requested that a sandwich be sent to her office.

"Wait a minute." Brad took the menu from the table and ordered chicken kiev, asparagus with Hollandaise sauce, and a very old white wine to be put on a tray. "And charge it to my bill."

When the food was ready, he carried it to Laura's office and knocked.

She looked up in surprise when he entered. "Where's Julia?"

"She felt ill suddenly and left. I didn't relish the idea of eating alone."

Laura immediately picked up the telephone and dialed Julia's cabin. She wasn't surprised when Julia's voice was frosty, reserved. She hung up the telephone, upset by Julia's tone and by the presence of the man who was causing further problems between her and her daughter.

Brad was looking at some of the many photographs of Ross hanging all over the room. "I take it he was your husband," Brad said as he turned to face her. The sheer number of the pictures surprised him. It was almost as if she were afraid she would forget him if she didn't keep herself surrounded with reminders.

He was well aware of Laura's discomfort but he wasn't going to acknowledge it. Something was going on between mother and daughter and somehow he had become a part of it. But he wasn't going to allow himself to be used.

"I brought you some supper," he said, whisking off the cover to the enticingly arranged meal.

Laura picked up three folders from her desk and went to a cabinet in the corner. "I'm sorry, Mr. Northrup, I'm really not hungry. Perhaps you should return to the dining room."

"What is this?" he asked, irritated. "First your daughter leaves me and now I get the brush-off from you. I'd like to know what I'm doing to cause this hot-and-cold attitude from you."

"I can't speak for my daughter, but as for myself, I don't usually socialize with my guests. Now, if you'd please excuse me, I have work to do."

Brad didn't make a move toward leaving. He knew Laura was attracted to him; he could feel it. So there must be another reason for her coolness. He looked about the room at the photographs, the collection of hand planes. Everywhere there seemed to be some reminder of Ross Kenyon.

"It's quarter to nine but you're still working," he said quietly. "So I can't believe there's another man."

Laura closed the filing drawer loudly. "Just because I don't date guests doesn't mean I don't date anyone. Did it ever occur to you, Mr. Northrup, that I might not *want* your attentions?"

Brad looked at her and smiled. At least he had her attention now. "No, it didn't occur to me." He motioned toward the food. "It's getting cold and it's getting late. If you'll excuse me, I think I'll start eating."

Laura watched him for a moment, then laughed and shook her head at him as she took a chair beside him. "Are you always so pushy?"

"I prefer to consider myself dynamic and irresistible." He opened the bottle of wine and poured two glasses. "To us," he said, raising his glass.

Laura hesitated for a moment but she drank to his toast. For a while she told herself she should be pushing him out the door but she didn't feel she was strong enough, emotionally, to do that. She wouldn't let him know that he was the first man she had spent such an intimate evening with in a very long time.

"Let me tell you about my work," Brad began, watching her. He purposely talked about himself and his architecture to see how she'd react. It took a while, but he could see her becoming interested. Several times when he mentioned a problem with some building, Laura told how she had solved the same problem while building the Mission.

"But that was a long time ago," Brad said after a while. "Don't you miss the excitement of building?"

Laura wanted to defend herself. "Running a place like the Mission gives me all the excitement I need. It's one crisis after another."

"And all of which you could handle with one eye closed. Right?"

"Of course not!" she snapped. "Some of the problems take days to figure out an answer."

Brad snorted. "How long has it been since any problem took much thought at all?"

Laura refused to answer him. To cover her agitation, she took a deep drink of wine. He made her life sound almost dull. It was a challenge to run the huge resort. "What are you after, Brad?" she asked quietly.

He almost said *you*, but he didn't. "I guess I'm just puzzled by everything. I came here for a few days' rest and to get some ideas about designing a resort like this. I have a commission to do one near Tucson next year."

Before he could finish his thought, Laura interrupted him. "You do!" she said excitedly. "You must really look forward to that. If I had this to do over, I'd—"

"What?" He was fascinated with the way her eyes lit up.

"Are you going to design it from scratch?"

"Yes."

Laura closed her eyes for a moment. "I think the mystery is what makes a good resort. You want to feel isolated but at the same time you need to feel protected from harm. If I designed one, I'd make several small buildings rather than one large one. You could almost create little communities with the use of trees and walls. There would be separate guest cabins and larger houses with shared living areas."

Brad leaned forward. "And what about the dining room?"

Laura thought for a moment. "I'd make one central kitchen and three different dining rooms radiating out from it. Then long-time guests would have a choice of where to eat. One dining room could be a greenhouse like mine, then a very formal room, and the last one could be for lunches for the younger set, with a jukebox."

"What else?" Brad encouraged.

"A nightclub! I'd get singers and musicians to come. We can't here because the lounge is our only one. Too many people don't like loud music. That's the whole key to a resort—choice. People must have a choice of what they want to do."

"You're talking about millions! All those separate buildings cost too much."

"No, no, no," Laura said. "It's all a matter of illusion. The dining area would be only one building, but with a few interior walls you could divide it. A large area of guest rooms could radiate off the kitchen. Put in some plastered adobe walls and you can make each house seem private. It could all be done with four or five buildings at the most."

Brad leaned back in his chair and gazed at her in amazement. Her excitement was contagious. He hadn't been excited about a new job for a long time. "What about things to do? My client's worried his guests will get bored."

Laura threw up her hands. "Tucson is only an hour from the Mexican border. Half the guests will think

they've been abroad if you take them across the border.
Have some people put on dances, give lessons, set up an
old Mexican market, and let the guests buy themselves to
death."

"You sound cynical," he said.

"You get to be after a while," she said, coming down
from her excitement. "I've been exposed to so many
wealthy people over the years. They'll spend thirty-five
thousand dollars for a car, then haggle over the price of
a piece of jewelry made by an Indian who lives on beans
and tortillas."

They were quiet for a moment, Laura embarrassed by
her excitment about a resort that had nothing to do with
her.

Brad was aware of the way she changed in moments,
from wide-eyed, almost girlish enthusiasm to flat-eyed
cynicism. She had seemed much more alive when she was
speaking of something new, something to be created outside of Montero, New Mexico.

He put his wine glass down. "I'm staying here for two
weeks and I know you're busy, but I'd like to ask you to
help me."

"To do what?"

"I'd like you to help me design this new resort."

"Me?" Laura asked, surprised. "I have no idea how to
build a resort."

"That may be one of the stupidest things I ever heard
anyone say. Who in the hell built this place?"

Laura rose from her chair. "I told you this was done out
of necessity. And then I had my husband. He was the real
mind behind building the Mission."

Brad went to stand beside her. "From the story I read,
you already had the idea and the possibility for financial
backing before you even met your husband."

"Aren't you a little old to believe everything you read?"
she answered drily.

"I believe in what I see," he stated quietly. "You must
have had a great deal of confidence in yourself at one time
but somewhere along the line you've lost it. Maybe it's
because you bury yourself here and surround yourself with
memories."

She quickly defended herself. "Who do you think you
are to judge me? You haven't even been here for twenty-

four hours, yet you stand there and dare to talk of something you know nothing about."

"I've been in the building trades all my life and my father before me. I knew when I saw this place that it took one hell of a human being to create it. I met you and I was fascinated because you're beautiful as well as talented. But I keep running into your fears. You back yourself up against these adobe walls and try to fade into them."

"This is the most astonishing conversation I've ever had. You are the architect, not I. I merely said I would not be interested in helping you design a place I have no interest in. I am perfectly happy as I am and I have more than enough work of my own without helping you with yours."

He stepped backward, away from her. "I'm sorry I tried to pawn my work off on you. It was lazy and inconsiderate of me."

Without another word, he left Laura's office.

Laura stood still for a moment, her body feeling limp after her angry outburst. There was no reason in the world the man's words should have made her so angry. And she did have a lot of work to do and she couldn't really spare the time.

She began to clear the dishes and put them on the tray. She paused as she thought of that summer when she had designed the Mission. Of course, then she had had walls to work from, part of her design was already made for her. It would be much harder to design something from scratch.

She picked up the tray and headed for the kitchen. It was almost a shame to let Brad design the Tucson resort alone. Unless he had had intimate contact with a big resort, he wouldn't know how important privacy was. Resorts were the perfect place for corporation presidents to meet their mistresses.

She handed the tray to a waiter and started back to her office. On second thought, she turned left and went to Clarry's shop. In Clarry's office was her big drafting table.

Laura pulled out a clean sheet of paper and started doodling. She sketched her ideas for the kitchen and dining rooms first, then started adding clusters of guest quarters. When she had a rough idea down, she started looking for

257

grid paper. To space the areas out would give her some better ideas.

She was unaware when the moon set and later when the sun began to rise.

Chapter 23

Ryan Lowery shut the door of his small house behind him and started in the direction his mother had said the drugstore was. He took his time, walking slowly, getting the feel of the quiet town. He was used to new places, the constantly changing succession of towns and cities.

Montero seemed cleaner, and deader, than most places, but nevertheless, he held himself against it. He had learned through harsh experience that no matter what a town looked like on the outside, it was usually rotten underneath.

His mother worried about him, said he was too young to be so cynical. For Ryan it was an effort to keep his mouth shut every time she spoke of his cynicism. After all, she was the one who made him that way.

Ruby wasn't really a prostitute, she just liked an easy life. If a man wanted her on her back, she didn't mind. She liked people and harmony, and she did whatever was necessary to achieve a peaceful, harmonious life.

The burden of responsibility for minor things like rent and food fell on her young son's shoulders. Ryan started working when he was eight and he had never stopped. He saw to it that there was food in the house and that his mother ate. Too often she would be so interested in a new man she would forget everything. The men could beat her, steal from her, use her in any way, but she never stopped giving to them. She could never understand why Ryan had grown up with such a chip on his shoulder.

Now, Ryan walked down the north side of the Montero Plaza and passed a couple of townspeople. He frowned as the couple stopped and stared at him. He braced his shoulders and kept walking. He hated small towns! Everyone knew everyone else's business, and a stranger was gawked at as if he were something out of a zoo.

Not that he had ever been in too many small towns. At

least not since he was ten when his mother had been run out of town. The social workers had tried to keep Ryan, but he escaped them and went to Ruby. He knew she needed him more than those small-town hypocrites ever had. After that, they stayed in the cities, getting lost in run-down bars and dollar stores.

But in the last year, they had had to make changes. Ruby, always too thin and never really healthy, started coughing blood. It cost Ryan a week's wages, but he took her to a doctor, a real one, not one in the free clinics. The doctor told him, in a bored manner, that Ruby was dying and probably had only a few months to live.

Ryan hadn't told her, but Ruby knew and she knew where she wanted to spend her last months. She owned a house in Montero, New Mexico, a place she had spent a few years in and the place where she had conceived Ryan. She had never gotten pregnant again and so she remembered Montero as a place of dreams because Ryan was the most wonderful thing that had ever happened to her.

Over the years, they had collected rent for the little house, always letting the bank in Montero know where they were. Finally Ryan had notified the people in the house to vacate and three days ago they returned. He had managed to save enough money to afford a doctor for his mother and a couple of secondhand beds. Now he needed a job until... until the end came.

He frowned as two more people stared openly at him, this time two old men sitting across the street. The men paused in their conversations and gazed fixedly, their mouths slightly agog. Ryan calmed his first impulse to confront the men. He knew that in small towns a person had to hide any hostility under a cloak of superficial sweetness. Again he thought how much he hated small towns.

Inside the drugstore, it was worse. One by one the people stopped talking and fixed their attention on him. A couple of teenagers, sitting on bar stools at the far end of the bar, looked up and frankly appraised him. Ryan was used to the attentions of women and he knew that a lot of the jobs he had had were the result of his looks rather than his abilities.

But the reactions of the others made hostility surge through him. "Where can I get this filled?" he challenged as he pushed a prescription toward the man behind the counter.

"I'll do it," the man said quietly.

Ryan waited, exchanging glares with the other customers, daring them. One of the teenagers nudged the other and Ryan felt them share his confusion. They didn't understand the treatment he was getting any more than he did.

"It's ready," the druggist said.

"How much?"

When the man answered, Ryan shoved three bills over the counter and left the store. He was hardly outside before he heard the people burst into excited chatter. He clutched his vial of pills and started back to his house. His first thought was that a few police reports had preceded his mother and him, but he doubted it.

He glanced at the pills for a moment, then stopped dead. The pills were labeled for a Ruby Eastman. Eastman? he thought. Where in the hell had the man gotten that name?

Ruby was sitting up in bed wearing a cheap pink nylon bed jacket. There were movie magazines all around her. "Ryan, is that you?"

He stood over her bed and scowled down at her. "What's going on in this town?" he demanded.

Ruby patted the bed beside her. She was so thin, her emaciated body hardly lifted the covers. "Tell me what happened?"

Ryan sat down because he knew there was no use being angry with his mother. Anger frightened her. "They looked at me as if I were some sort of monster, that's what. The man in the drugstore must have called people all over town because they came running out of their stores to stare at me."

She reached up and caressed his cheek. He was so incredibly handsome with his high cheekbones and his dark, serious eyes, eyes that were nearly always angry and distrustful. He was only twenty-one but he had seen and done so much that he seemed much older.

"And this," Ryan said, holding the bottle of pills out to her. "It's made out to Ruby Eastman."

Ruby took the vial and smiled. "How kind of them. They assumed both of us had his name."

Ryan jerked his chin up. "Whose name?" he demanded.

261

She sighed and leaned back against her pillows. Ryan wasn't a man to forgive easily, and she knew all too well that he wasn't going to like the story that she now had to tell him. "Would you get me my box, please?"

Ryan handed her the large, locked metal box that was her prize possession. Once in Chicago when they had been thrown out of their apartment, their belongings confiscated for nonpayment, Ryan had climbed in a window and retrieved the box. He knew the box contained old love letters and all the silly sentimental things Ruby loved so much.

She rummaged in the box and from the bottom pulled out a fat, sealed envelope. Before he could take it, she put her hand on his arm. "Please look at these with kindness," she said.

"Why should I look at them at all?"

"Because they are clippings about your father."

Ryan wouldn't let her see how her words affected him. In all their years together, he had never asked and she had never mentioned who Ryan's father was. He always assumed Ruby had no idea which of several men it could be.

"The people stared at you because you look just like your father."

He looked down at the envelope and then took it slowly. He wasn't sure that he wanted to open it. He had seen enough of the way the people looked at him to know his father's reputation couldn't be good.

"Go on, take it," Ruby urged. "Go outside in the backyard and read it. Take your time and ... Ryan, please try to be forgiving. Whatever Garrick did, he's your father. He gave you life and your good looks. Remember that."

He took the packet from her and went outside as she asked. He broke the seal slowly because he felt that what was inside was about to change his life. He thought a couple of times about burning it sight unseen but he knew it was better to know the worst.

The first piece of paper he saw was from *Life* magazine and it was a large photograph—of himself. He stared for a moment at the phenomenon of seeing himself on an old, creased magazine page. The caption under the photo said that the notorious Garrick Eastman would go unpunished for his crimes.

Ryan turned the page and saw pictures of the big resort he had driven past on the night he and Ruby arrived. Only in the photo, a big part of it lay in rubble. There were more pictures, of Ross Kenyon, his wife and their sad-eyed little daughter.

There was only a short story with the photos, telling how Laura Kenyon's brother-in-law had plotted with an eastern syndicate to force Mrs. Kenyon out of the Mission. The entire article featured Garrick Eastman, saying he had caused the deaths of Ross Kenyon and an angel of a young woman named Irene Anderson.

Ryan closed the article and turned to the many newspaper clippings. It was hours later when he finally stopped, having found out a great deal about the man whom he resembled so much.

There had been a trial for manslaughter because Eastman had driven a car into an arroyo, killing a young woman. He had abandoned the girl and the car but he wasn't connected to the death until his picture appeared in the paper weeks later.

When Garrick was freed from the charges, the townspeople of Montero began a whisper campaign against him. They hinted to the press that he was the real cause of Ross's death and the bombing of the Mission. The wire services picked it up and exaggerated it until Garrick Eastman's name was synonymous with evil.

In one article, a war hero, Jack Galloway, was mentioned, but it only stated he had been in Montero at the time of the bombing and the girl's death. The article did mention his death, one of America's greats lost to the world forever.

About a year after the trial, when it seemed America was about to forget Montero, New Mexico, a new reporter came to the town. He wanted to write a book, a nonfiction account of what had happened. The people of Montero felt safe since the whole country had put the blame on Garrick and they had convinced themselves the papers were right.

The reporter was very young and wasn't hampered by sentimental feelings about war heroes. He dug through old files, listened to anyone who would talk, and gradually began to piece the facts together.

His book was a documentary account of what happened

in Montero but it read like sensationalized fiction. It spent ten weeks on The *New York Times* Bestseller List.

The people of Montero tried to sue, but there wasn't one word of the book that wasn't true. The entire story was there—how they had helped Laura go to art school, how she had built the Mission and kept the town from going bankrupt, then, with all the painful details, the story of how the town had turned on her. Jack Galloway's part was revealed in full, and Garrick was seen less as a villain than as a helpless, weak alcoholic. The real story was what a town had done to one woman and how she'd managed to overcome them, even though her toll was the life of her husband.

There were several long reviews of the book. One critic said it should be called a novel of American horror.

Later articles told of the popularity of Montero, how tourists came to gawk at the evil people of the town. The Mission had to hire a guard to keep nonguests from entering the grounds. Guests could stay no less than one week to discourage one-nighters who came to chip pieces of bathroom tile as souvenirs.

The last article, published two years ago, was written as a nostalgia piece, asking readers if they remembered the infamous Montero. It said the town was quiet now with only the old-timers remaining. The young people left Montero as soon as they could get out. It said Laura Kenyon was still running the elegant Mission, still unmarried. And the evil Garrick had married a local woman, Marian Stromberg, and lived in an old Victorian house in Montero. He was a recluse now, rarely ever leaving the house. There was some further comment on the wages of sin as the writer concluded that no one seemed to have been punished enough for his treachery.

Ryan slowly folded the articles and put them back into the envelope. He reached into his pocket and pulled out a pack of cigarettes. His hands shook so badly he had to use three matches to light the cigarette.

His father! he thought. Not just evil, but a weak, vain, stupid drunk as well.

Ryan felt hatred toward the man who was his father. He jumped up, smashed his cigarette butt into the ground, and ran his hand across his chin. Now he was cursed with a face so much like his father's that he was branded as being of the same mold. No wonder the people stared at him. They saw him as if he were his father.

He took his car keys from his pocket and went to the old Ford Ruby had insisted they purchase. She said Ryan must have transportation for his dates. He grimaced. He had never had much time for women and now maybe he could get a job frightening little children. Or maybe he should set up a tent on the Plaza and charge admission.

He spun the car out of the driveway. It was bad enough in the cities when he had to deal with Ruby's police record. He was twelve the first time he arranged to bail her out of jail where she had been picked up for prostitution. By the time he was sixteen, he was on a first-name basis with most of the cops.

Now it wasn't Ruby who caused him problems but his own face. He didn't know quite where he was going, but on that first night, when Ruby insisted he drive her around, they had seen a big Victorian house. Ruby made him stop, and she stared at it for some moments before she let him drive on.

Now, Ryan found the house on the outskirts of the town. He stopped the car, got out, then looked up at it with hostility. All these years he had wondered about his father, and now that he knew, he hated the old man.

All his life, Ryan had fought against being part of the underworld. His neighbors had laughed at him because he'd rather work than pick up the free cash available by robbing a liquor store. Wouldn't they laugh now if they found out his old man made theirs look like Snow White?

When a woman came to the window and glared at him, he looked back insolently. She drew the curtains and he left.

Chapter 24

Marian Eastman reluctantly gave the grocery boy a twenty-five-cent tip, then shrugged as she looked at the large box of groceries. It made her angry that she had to deal with such mundane things in life as groceries. Just yesterday, another of her cooks had quit. It had gotten so that people weren't even reliable anymore. No one wanted to work for a living, they wanted everything handed to them on a silver platter.

She started to leave the kitchen, then paused to take three cookies out of a package. She ate two of them on the way to the back door.

At thirty-nine, she was an old woman. Her shapeless figure had turned to fat, and her clothes were suited more to a teenager than an adult. She wore a stiff fifty-yard crinoline under her felt skirt. Her pink blouse bore a kitten on the pocket.

Marian paused for a moment outside the door, looking for Garrick. Sometimes it was almost as if he intentionally hid from her. Once, long ago, he looked at her and said he had certainly been punished enough for what he had done. It was almost as if he meant that Marian was his punishment. Of course that was absurd and she never allowed such a thought to enter her head.

She smiled as she saw his shoulder, hidden behind a big cottonwood tree. Just look at him, she thought, so calm and peaceful and not a worry in the world. And she had made him that way! she thought with pleasure. When everyone else was hating him, she stepped out of the shadows and gave him her love and support. She had been the only one to stand behind him during the trial. And Clarry! She had deserted her dear husband when he needed her the most. She had sat beside Bill through everything, even that whole ugly trial, never once caring about Garrick.

Later, that book had come out and proven that Garrick

hadn't done all the things people believed. By then Marian and Garrick were already married and no one could take him away from her.

And she had been good for him, oh, so very good for him. He had wanted to leave Montero but Marian wouldn't go. She wanted to show every last citizen how she could get a husband. And besides, if she left, Laura would think she had won and driven Marian from town.

Over the years, it had been easy to force him to stop drinking. All she did was tell the merchants not to sell to him. As for the other women, she hired a bodyguard to protect Garrick from himself.

Three years ago he had come to his senses. He no longer tried to fight Marian for his right to a little freedom. Now he just sat quietly, staring out at the mountains.

"Garrick," Marian said loudly, beside him. Sometimes he acted as if he didn't hear very well. "I brought you a cookie."

Garrick kept staring ahead, not even acknowledging her presence.

Marian took a chair opposite him. It made her angry to see what the people of Montero had done to this wonderful man. His once handsome face had fallen. There were deep circles under his eyes. His hair was no longer dark, and he was thin to the point of emaciation.

But to Marian, he was always the handsome crooner she had first seen with her father. Perhaps that was one reason she loved Garrick so much, because she connected him with the happiest time of her life, when her father had been alive.

"I don't know what we're going to do for lunch or for supper even," she began as she ate the third cookie. "No one wants to work. That ungrateful girl! All I did was suggest that since she knew no one in town anyway, I didn't see why she had to have all of Friday afternoon off. It really is inconvenient for us. Well, you should have heard her! I know if you'd been there, you would have silenced her, but me," she gave a little sniff, "I never can speak out to anyone. All I could do was stand there and take her abuse."

She looked at Garrick, saw the way he was looking at her. She didn't like it when he turned such a cold eye to her. She looked away.

"I went into town this morning to place a new ad for a cook, not that I think I'll find anyone better, but I can at least try."

Garrick looked away from her, still silent.

"Oh! I almost forgot. I saw a young man who could have been your twin."

She had his attention now and she liked it. At times like this she knew Garrick really loved her. He was just so quiet, yes, she smiled, the strong silent type.

"I stopped in the drugstore for a refill to my prescription. You know, the one for my backaches. I told the doctor about the pains but he didn't really care. He never seems to care. I could die in his office and I think he'd give that infuriating little laugh, like he didn't really believe I was dead."

"What about the man?" Garrick asked patiently.

"Oh, yes. Well, last week the druggist said he came in and you could have knocked him over with a feather. He said the man looked exactly like you did when you first came here."

She leaned forward. "Remember that night? I knew then we were meant for each other."

Garrick looked away, losing interest. He was used to Marian's long monologues about herself. Anything at all was a diversion. She was happy as long as he didn't drink, smoke, look at other women or live in any way. He had tried to leave her several times. Once he had been gone for three weeks, but the availability of drink had been his undoing. She found him, drunk in a gutter in Albuquerque. Now she rarely let him out of her sight.

She sensed Garrick's failing attention. She continued her story. "Of course I didn't pay any attention to the old man. You know what a terrible gossip he is, but then a couple of other people had seen the young man, too. They all said he looked enough like you to be your double. Of course I just couldn't believe anyone could be as handsome as my Garrick," she said with a flutter of her eyelashes.

Garrick looked away from her again.

"But I saw him!" She had saved the best for last. "Everyone said he'd been here nearly a week and they'd seen him several times, though he never spoke to anyone. Well, as I was walking past the theatre, there he was. It was the oddest thing. He really does look like you, except somehow he looks angry. He glared at me as if he hated me. He was quite insolent so that I had to walk around him."

"How old is he?"

"It's hard to tell. About twenty-six, I'd guess. I'm really not good with ages. He seemed quite young."

"What did you find out about him?"

Marian missed his sarcasm and his assumption that she had certainly asked for all the gossip about the young man. "Everyone was dying of curiosity so it was easy to find out about him. His mother owns a house here and has owned it since the Depression, although she hasn't lived here. The grocery owner went to visit her, to welcome her back, but he said the boy threw him out."

"Who is his mother?"

Marian waved her hand. "I don't know. No one seems to remember her. She used to work at a roadhouse, I think it was called the Red Rooster."

Garrick frowned. "I used to sing there."

Marian didn't like to think of her husband working in a cheap tavern. "I'm sure you had nothing to do with her. She was just a barmaid. Anyway, she's dying! I think she told the groceryman she had lung cancer. This was before he was rudely asked to leave, of course."

"What's her name?"

"The barmaid's? I have no idea. It was Lowell or something like that. No one really cares. We all agreed we were glad she didn't have something contagious and come back here to spread it. At least she won't be here long, then that dreadful son of hers can leave. He is really the rudest person you ever saw. Here he is the son of some syphilitic barmaid and he has the gall to force me off the street. Me!"

Garrick looked away again. There had been so many women in his past, so many quick tumbles in hundreds of beds. It was so long ago and his mind had been always a little hazy with drink then, but he seemed to remember spending some time with a barmaid at the Red Rooster.

He almost smiled at where his thoughts were leading him. If this boy did look like him, if by chance he could have been created in one of his many trysts, what kind of man could he be? He couldn't be much, not with him for a father and a barmaid for a mother.

Marian kept talking, going on and on about the cruelty of the people of Montero to her and her husband. She started in on Laura, as she did daily. To Marian, Laura was the cause of all their problems. If Laura would leave Montero, then Marian and Garrick would be the happiest people in the world.

He didn't listen to her. He had learned how to block her out over the years. It was his only defense; he was a prisoner, kept in continual solitary confinement.

It was two days before Garrick could get away to visit Ruby. He knew it was no use trying to escape the bodyguard Marian had hired for him, so he tried to reason with the man. Garrick had sometimes felt the man's sympathy for him but he had never tried to use it. Once again Garrick vowed not to drink, and the big man drove Garrick to Ruby's house.

Garrick stood outside for a while and wondered whether he should knock. He had lost nearly all his self-confidence over the last few years, and without alcohol to bolster him, he wasn't sure of himself. Finally he straightened his shoulders and knocked on the door.

Ruby forgot what Ryan had told her about letting strangers in. She wanted company, especially since Ryan now spent so much time wandering around the countryside. "Come in," she called as she patted her hair, wishing she had a mirror.

She recognized him right away. Ryan had his face, but in place of Ryan's anger, Garrick had the look of a man who had given up. She patted the bed. "Come sit beside me."

Even as she said it, she could hear Ryan's voice in her head. He was always telling her that she had no sense when it came to men, that a man could beat her, rob her, whatever, and she'd still take them back. Ruby knew it was true, but looking at Garrick, at her son's father, how could she turn him away? He carried the weight of the world on his shoulders.

"Do you remember me?" Ruby asked when he sat facing her.

"I came about the boy." He studied her, trying to remember, but all he remembered from that summer when he sang at the Red Rooster was Laura, and his wanting her so badly.

Ruby smiled, one thin arm lifting to point to a photograph on the old painted dresser. Garrick went to pick up the framed photograph.

"He looks just like you," Ruby said with pride. "I was hoping he'd get some of your good looks but I never expected so much. Even when he was a baby, he was pretty. Everywhere I went, women volunteered to baby-sit him."

Garrick continued to stare at the photograph. Had he ever looked that good? Had he possessed so much and thrown it away?

"Is he mine?" he asked quietly.

"Oh, yes," Ruby laughed. "You were the only man I had that whole summer. I was younger then and I guess I even thought about a home and marriage."

He put the photo down and walked back to her. "But I was too infatuated with Laura then to even give anyone the time of day."

"Laura and a bottle," Ruby laughed.

"What's he like?" Garrick asked softly. He was thinking that it was unbelievable that anything could have been created during that summer.

"Old," Ruby sighed. "Ryan is a twenty going on fifty. He's so afraid he'll turn out like me that he guards himself against any fun in life."

Garrick looked sharply at her.

Ruby just smiled at him. "I know what I am. Ryan sometimes thinks I don't have any brains, but he couldn't be as smart as he is and have a stupid mother. He thinks I should be like him and hold myself away from everyone, but I can't; I don't want to. I love people. I love women, men, old people, young people, and all my life I've tried to show people I love them."

"And Ryan resents that?"

"Oh, yes," Ruby laughed. "He tries constantly to save me from myself."

"Does he know about me?"

"He has for about ten days now. I kept clippings of the trial and he found a copy of that awful book that man wrote. I never read it myself."

"Why not?" Garrick asked bitterly. "The rest of the country did. Did you know they translated it into foreign languages so the rest of the world could see how horrible Americans were?"

She put a bony hand over his. "It hurt you, didn't it?"

271

He stood. "To see myself as I really was? I'd say it more than hurt." He glanced at Ryan's picture. "I was like him. From the time I could crawl, I had women all around me. They adored me. It didn't change as I grew up. Everything came to me so easily, I didn't have to struggle because I knew some broad would always put a roof over my head. The first time I got turned down was by Laura and I think it scared me. I wanted to prove to everyone that no one could turn me down."

Ruby was used to men pouring their hearts out to her. "What about your wife, Clarry? She was so pretty the last time I saw her."

Garrick leaned back against the tall dresser. "If you thought she was pretty then, you should see her now! When we got married, I thought we were two of a kind, and maybe we were then, but Clarry had some of the same blood Laura has. Clarry began to change right away, just like I did. Only I got worse and Clarry got better. It took her a long time to get up the nerve to tell me to go to hell but she finally did."

He stopped abruptly, looking down at his hands. This woman may be the mother of his child but he really didn't know her.

Ruby understood what he was feeling. She changed the subject to her favorite one. "Ryan's always had more brains than the two of us put together. He's always been the hardest worker you could imagine. I quit school in the sixth grade but not Ryan. Every morning he'd get himself up and dressed, then go off to school. No matter where we went, he found himself a school. He always kept a job, too. He worked after school and on weekends. When he got to high school, he'd study half the night, sometimes all night. You should have seen what he studied! I couldn't understand half of it."

Garrick was very interested. He was beginning to realize that this woman was talking about his son. "Didn't he ever play? What about sports? What about girls?"

Ruby laughed. "You haven't changed as much as you think. I'm afraid Ryan never had much time for girls. He had too much to do taking care of me. There was one little girl, though. I didn't know anything about her until one day she knocked on the door and asked to see Ryan. She was from a good family, you could see that right away,

272

and she was white as a sheet, I guess from walking through a neighborhood like ours. I asked her in but she looked like she was going to cry, then she ran away."

"I don't guess Ryan ever mentioned her to you."

"No. Ryan keeps to himself. He's never been one to share what he's thinking."

"I would think you'd be close, considering that he still lives with you. When I was a boy, all I wanted was to get out as soon as I could."

Ruby leaned back against the pillows. "Me, too." She looked at Garrick's sunken face, knowing hers was no better. The two of them had led hard lives. "I don't know how we could have produced someone like Ryan. He tries to act like he's a big tough man, but the truth is he really cares. Deep down inside he's as unselfish as you and I are selfish."

"You don't seem selfish. You could have demanded child support from me but you never did."

"And have you maybe try to take away my boy?" Ruby said fiercely, then smiled. "See what I mean? I think of him as mine and I didn't want to share him. But Ryan, he certainly had to share me with enough people. He had every right to hate them and me but he never did. Oh, it all made him angry, and hard-nosed about the world but he doesn't really hate."

She paused for a moment, gazing at her son's photograph. "Ryan's always been strong, not big, mind you, but wiry strong. I guess it comes from working since he was just a boy. Anyway, one day when Ryan was fifteen, he came home and found a sailor beating me. Ryan threw down his books and tore into the man like some enraged cat. Like I say, he was just a boy but he beat that sailor up somethin' awful."

She closed her eyes for a moment. "I was in a corner and my shoulder hurt a lot but I watched as Ryan stood over the sailor. I was afraid he was going to kill the man. But you know what he did?"

Ruby shook her head in wonder at the memory. "Ryan got a towel and dipped it in cold water and wiped the man's face until he regained consciousness. Then he got the sailor to talking. Ryan even called in sick at his job, something he just never did, and spent all night talking to the sailor. The man told horrible stories about how he'd been beaten

273

as a kid and how his old man had beat his mother to death."

"And Ryan listened to him, after what he'd seen him do to you?" Garrick asked.

"He's an amazement to me. He could get a good job somewhere but he doesn't. He's always stayed with me, supported me, taken care of me."

"I . . . heard he was rather a rude young man."

Ruby smiled. "A lot of people think that, and I guess he is, at least to some of the people anyway. He just has a chip on his shoulder. He's afraid to let people inside him or to learn to care for anyone. He's afraid of being hurt."

"You're telling me all this for a reason, aren't you? Why did you come back here? Did it have anything to do with me?"

Ruby was serious. "You must know that I'm dying. I can't imagine that Montero has changed much in the last years so I'm sure everyone must know about me."

He gave a curt nod. He didn't want to talk about her illness any more than she did.

"I told Ryan it was because I had a house here but the truth is, I wanted him to meet you."

"Me! You'd think you'd want just the opposite. If he's a good boy, I'd think he should stay away from the likes of me."

Ruby stretched her hand out to him again. "You always did hate yourself. Even when you were young, you thought you had to latch onto someone else to give you what you needed. You wanted Laura Taylor because of what she could give you. You never believed you could be anything on your own."

Garrick could feel himself getting angry. It was the first time he'd felt anything in years. "And do you think you're any better?"

Ruby laughed. "You look like Ryan right now. He inherited your temper. Ryan is always getting angry."

Garrick calmed himself. "Why did you want him to meet me?"

"I want you to help him, see if you can get him to stay here in Montero."

"Good God! I wouldn't ask a rat to stay in this town."

"He has roots here and he doesn't anywhere else. When I die, he might just wander. Every time anyone gets close to him, he pulls away. I want him to stay still and face people for once. You know, that sailor came back a year later and Ryan was so cold to him the man left and never came back. Ryan was afraid to get close to him."

"Ruby, this is a dream. I couldn't help him. Do you think he's going to *want* a father like me?"

Before she could answer, a car pulled into the driveway just outside the bedroom wall. "You'd better go. I'll introduce you to Ryan, but he won't like for you to stay. It's going to take some time for him to get used to you."

Garrick shook his head at her. He couldn't believe that she could be so naive as to believe Ryan could ever forgive him. Young people were such harsh judges.

Ryan glared at the big black Cadillac parked in front of his mother's house. God! he thought, she's started again. Soon there'd be one man after another, using her, taking from her. He braced himself for the man who waited in the living room.

What he saw was an old, rundown, thin man with sad-looking eyes. Ryan thought how his mother could always pick the losers. Ruby stood in the doorway, an old chenille robe on.

"Ryan," she said quietly, "this is your father, Garrick Eastman."

Ryan gave one quick, hostile look at Garrick and turned to his mother. "You shouldn't be out of bed."

"Ryan, please," she pleaded as he put his arm around her. "Talk to him. Don't send him away."

He was silent as she slipped under the covers, then he left, closing the bedroom door behind him.

Garrick stood still, watching his son. He could see the anger that ran through the young man.

"Am I supposed to welcome you with open arms?" Ryan asked. "Perhaps I should offer you tea, or is it bourbon you want?"

Garrick's voice was quiet. "I want to see your mother again," he said, turning toward the door.

"I've never been able to stop her, no matter what type of man she wanted."

Garrick's back stiffened but he didn't look back as he left the house.

Chapter 25

Clarry and Laura were eating lunch in the Greenery at the Mission. Clarry decided to do some probing.

"Laura, what's wrong with you? You've been acting very strangely for the last few days."

"Have I?" Laura asked. "I've just had a lot on my mind, that's all."

"Such as? It couldn't be the Mission. Julia's been working herself into the ground over the last week. You two haven't quarreled lately, have you?"

"Not at all." Laura thought that Julia was too busy trying to impress Brad to have much time for anything else. She saw them swimming together, playing tennis, horseback riding together. And every time she saw them together, she remembered the last time she had been alone with Brad. She had taken him the plans she worked on all night. He was astonished at them, absolutely in awe. They were good, a little crude, and there were a few structural problems, but the basic designs were very, very good. They spent three hours in the sunny little private courtyard, poring over the plans. It was the best time Laura had spent in years. Brad talked to her about how to make a three-dimensional drawing since she didn't know how.

It was all wonderful until Brad kissed her. It had been a long time since she had felt a man's arms around her and even longer since she had reacted. She practically ran from his room and later she didn't know what she had run from. She told herself she had run because Brad belonged to Julia but she knew it was her own aroused feelings that frightened her.

"Laura! You haven't heard a word I've said."

"I'm sorry. What were you saying?"

"I was just telling the latest Montero gossip."

"I'm glad I wasn't listening. Why in the world do you listen to those people?"

"Because I live here!" Clarry said with emphasis. "And so do you even if you pretend you don't."

"All right. You've made your point. What were you telling me?"

"I want you to swear you'll listen," Clarry warned. She continued only when Laura agreed. "I've been hearing about this for several days but I didn't want to tell you until I was sure."

"Whatever could any Montero gossip have to do with me?"

"A couple of weeks ago, or I guess it's longer now, an old Montero resident returned with her son. The boy's about twenty and he looks just like Garrick." Clarry grabbed her sister's hand when Laura started to rise. "You promised to listen."

"Clarry, you of all people should know how I feel about...him." She sighed, then sat back down. She didn't want another of Clarry's lectures about how hatred only hurt the one who hated. "All right. You have two minutes."

"It's taken the people quite a while to fit the pieces together. Someone wrote a letter to a man in California who used to own a little roadhouse called the Red Rooster, back in the thirties. The man said Garrick practically lived with a waitress named Ruby Lowery."

"So?" Laura asked coldly.

"Ruby has lung cancer and she's come back here to die and she's brought her son—Garrick's son."

"Clarry, I fail to see what this has to do with me or you for that matter. I'm sure Garrick is glad to have a little carbon copy to follow in his footsteps."

Clarry leaned back against her chair. "I just thought it would interest you, that's all. The whole town is buzzing about the boy. Some say he's just like Garrick and others say he's a dutiful young man for staying with his mother when she needs him."

Laura stood, tossing her napkin onto her empty plate. "I'm sure Garrick's son is a paragon of virtue, but as for me, I'd just as soon not meet him. Now, if you'll excuse me, I have work to do."

Clarry stared after her sister, wondering again why Laura was so nervous the last few days. She kept burying herself in her office, coming out today only because Clarry had insisted. Then her thoughts returned to Garrick's son.

The boy had been conceived that summer when she found she was pregnant with Scott Stromberg's child. Maybe that was why this Ryan Lowery interested her so much. If she hadn't lost her child, he would have been the same age as Ryan; he, too, would be a young man now.

Julia checked her hair in the mirror before leaving her little cabin. She was going to meet Brad for an afternoon swim and this afternoon she especially wanted to look good. For the last couple of days he seemed worried about something and last night he even mentioned leaving the Mission.

She wanted him to stay. In fact she wanted him to stay permanently. The last weeks had been wonderful. She had been so busy with Brad that she had hardly seen her mother. She had not missed their daily arguments. And Brad showed so much interest in the Mission. He asked her hundreds of questions about everything from the structure to the management of the place. Yet he talked about leaving. Julia thought that maybe he didn't realize how much she wanted him to stay.

She didn't meet him at the pool but went to his room. When he opened the door, his face was alight but it seemed to fall when he saw her. She decided to ignore the reaction.

"Aren't you going to invite me in?" she asked.

"Of course. It'll only take me a minute to change."

Julia took a deep breath to give herself courage. She caught his arm.

He turned, smiling at her. "Did you have something to say to me?"

She thought that she wasn't very good at seduction and wished he would help her, but then if he had, she wouldn't be in this situation. He had never made any kind of advance toward her. She moved closer to him, slid her arms around his neck, and lifted her lips to his.

Brad pulled his head away from her after touching her lips briefly, chastely. "I think we'd better go." He took her arms from around his neck.

Julia tried not to cry, but tears gathered in her eyes. "What's wrong with me?" she whispered. "We spend days and hours together but you never come close to me. And now when I touch you, you act as if I have leprosy."

Brad stared at her in surprise. "Julia, you're like a

daughter to me. I've never thought of you any other way. I never meant—"

"Daughter!" Julia cried. "You've thought of me as a child?" She didn't wait for his answer before she left slamming the door.

Brad looked at the door for a moment, then sat down heavily on the bed. He had refused to acknowledge that Julia thought of him in any way except perhaps as a father figure. He had spent a lot of time with her so he could get closer to Laura. He had thought maybe the mother's heart could be reached through the daughter.

He wiped his hand across his eyes. God! had he been using Julia? He didn't like to think he had. She was a sweet thing, eager to please, and he could sense her loneliness, but she didn't have the depth he felt in Laura. In a few years perhaps Julia could grow and mature but as of yet she was still a child.

He walked outside to the table set under the cottonwood tree. He looked again at the sketches Laura had made for the new resort. He couldn't get over what she was able to do with so little training. Her innate sense of design was astonishing. But Laura thwarted him at every opportunity.

Suddenly, an idea came to him. "No," he whispered aloud; it was too farfetched. But the more he thought of the idea, the more determined he was.

He left his room and marched into Laura's office without knocking. "I want to talk to you."

"Of course," she said calmly, putting down her pen. "I'm always available to my guests."

"Don't give me that, Laura," he said, leaning over her. "I want to know why you've refused my every invitation. I want to know why you're running from me."

She tried to remain calm. "I turn down passes made by my guests constantly, but this is the first time I've had such an ungracious loser."

"Don't give me that!" he said angrily. "I was attracted to you the first time I saw you and I felt it in you, too, yet you've refused me in every way."

She started to speak but he cut her off. "Does this have anything to do with Julia?"

Laura stood, walked away from him. "You are my guest
279

and I owe you cordiality, but I do not share my private life with my paying guests."

He was across the room in one stride and grabbed her by the shoulders. "Cut the guest crap, Laura. I want to know the truth. A few minutes ago Julia practically threw herself at me, and when I pushed her away she got very upset. She seemed to think we were having an affair."

"Please release me," Laura said coolly.

"Not until I get some answers. Julia seems to think there's something between her and me, so how many other people feel the same way? Is that why you've turned me down, because you considered me as belonging to your daughter?"

He watched her eyes and they were enough to answer him. "Damn!" he said and pushed her away from him. He could feel anger boiling through him. "The two of you were cut out of the same mold," he said quietly, through his teeth. "Julia decides she wants me, no doubt because I happen to love her damn Mission and because I'm not as demanding as a younger man. And you! You make the great sacrifice of giving me to your daughter to show her your love."

He took a moment to take a few deep breaths. "Did it ever occur to either of you women that I'm not something you can pass around like a piece of property? I like Julia, sure, she's a sweet kid, but she's so infatuated with this place there's not much room for anything else. And as for you, all you can do is sacrifice yourself. You live in this shrine," he waved his hand at all the photographs of Ross. "It's been my experience that when someone keeps playing the martyr, it's for a reason. Are you afraid Julia's going to hate you? You keep the Mission from her, so to make up for it you'll give her the man you want. Is that what you're thinking?"

Laura could only stare at him, unable to say anything.

Brad calmed himself. "What happened to the woman who built this place? When did you stop creating and become a holy martyr?" His eyes blazed. "And when did you assume that I was yours to give or keep?"

He couldn't say any more. There was too much he wanted to say. She and her damn daughter made him feel like something in a game of chess. And worse, he didn't know if he was a pawn or a more valuable player.

He turned and left the office. The sooner he got out of the Mission, the better off he'd be.

Laura sat down heavily on the couch. His words had struck home. She looked up at one of Ross's photographs. Was she playing God again and trying to manipulate people? The last time, she had forced Clarry into marrying Garrick. Was she trying to force Julia into a union that would make her daughter just as unhappy?

She clenched her fists. She had already considered offering Brad a percentage of the Mission. Was she trying to buy him as she had Garrick?

She stood and went to look at the photographs. In the past, Ross had helped her make decisions. Since he was gone she had felt so alone that she tried to avoid any new confrontations. Was she afraid of Brad? He seemed so exciting, all his ideas were new and alive. She very much wanted to help him with his new resort plans but she was afraid to become involved, afraid of change.

Where was the woman who had built the Mission? Laura looked at the big dark office. It hadn't changed in years; she hadn't changed.

She took a deep breath and then went to Brad's door. Her knock was firm in spite of her pounding heart.

He jerked the door open. "What is it now?" he demanded harshly.

She could see his open suitcase behind him. "I had some more ideas about the resort in Arizona. I thought maybe we could discuss them."

He watched her for a moment. "I'm tired of playing games, Laura. You come in here and I get serious. No more trying to give me to your daughter, you understand?"

She nodded once. This time she was going to control only her own life and no one else's.

He took her in his arms before he had the door completely shut.

Chapter 26

Julia had no idea where she wanted to go but she knew she had to get away from the Mission and, if possible, from herself. She had thrown herself at Brad and been rejected. She had always been a child to him, while she had felt herself falling in love.

She drove over some of the gravel back roads of the National Forest, where there was no traffic and no people to interrupt her thoughts. Suddenly, coming out of nowhere was an old Ford, tearing down the hill at breakneck speed. Julia swerved to the right, one wheel slamming hard into the steep bank at the side of the road. Her head snapped forward, then back.

When the car motor abruptly died and she realized she was safe, she put her head down on the steering wheel and began to cry. As if she hadn't had enough today.

Ryan Lowery had to stop his speeding car with the foot brake and the emergency brake. He swerved to the right to miss the oncoming car and felt a big rock tear out the underside of his old car. Before it had stopped completely, he was out and running toward the other car.

"Are you hurt?" he asked, opening the door. The girl had her head on her arms on the steering wheel, crying as if her life were over. "I think my car's damaged. Maybe we can get yours out and I'll drive you to the hospital. Do you think anything's broken?"

He reached out to touch her thick dark hair, but she jerked away from him and turned a very pretty, tear-stained face up toward him.

"Nothing is broken, but no thanks to you!" She sniffed and swiped at her tears. "What were you doing, practicing for the Five-Hundred?"

She swung around and put her feet on the ground. When he reached out to help her, she jerked away from him. "Don't you know that we have laws around here? Just
282

because you're a stranger doesn't mean you can break them."

He stepped away from her. "What makes you think I'm a stranger?"

She put her hand on the steering wheel to brace herself. Her head was pounding and her whole body felt as if it were made of rubber. "I know everyone in Montero and you're not one of my guests."

Ryan was trying to figure that statement out when Julia lurched forward and he caught her. He held onto her arm as he pulled her to the side of the road. "I think you'd better sit down. Are you sure you're okay?"

"Perfectly. I just love getting slammed into the steering wheel of my car. It just makes my whole day."

Ryan stood over her. "Look, I'm sorry. It was completely my fault. I was driving too fast and not watching where I was going. I don't have any insurance but I'll personally pay you for any damages."

"With what?" she snapped. "Your good looks?"

Ryan stiffened. "I'll leave you now. It doesn't look like your car's hurt. You should be able to drive it out of here." He turned away and started walking down the road.

Julia shakily stood. "Wait!" she called. "I'm sorry," she said when he turned. "It's been a bad day and I'm taking it out on you."

He looked at her, swaying on her feet, then walked back to her. "It's not been one of my best, either. Mind if I try your car? I'd like to make sure it works before I leave you."

She sat down again, then watched as he started her car, then turned it around to head back to Montero. She saw his sorry-looking old Ford by the side of the road, a dark river of oil pouring from beneath it.

He came back to her. "It's not hurt. If you just rest a minute, you should be able to drive it back down, if you take it slowly."

"What about you? Your car doesn't look like it's going anywhere."

"I'll send a wrecker after it tomorrow, I guess. And if anything is wrong with your car, let me know so I can pay for it." He turned away.

"Wait a minute! You aren't just going to leave, are you? I don't even know your name. How could I contact you?

And besides, how are you going to get down the mountain?"

"Walk, and my name is Ryan Lowery."

She held out her hand to him. "I'm Julia Kenyon." She didn't feel him flinch as he took her hand nor was she aware of what the Kenyon name meant to him. "Maybe we should make a deal. If you'll drive my car and let me off at the Mission, I'll call a wrecker for you—and I won't press charges."

He took her hand in his. "You don't owe me anything," he said. So this was the little girl who had been involved in the Montero scandal. Maybe he should blurt out who his father was.

"You're looking at me strangely. I don't look my best after a car wreck."

He recovered himself. "You do look badly shaken."

Julia laughed as she stood. "This is definitely not my day. I get run off the road run by a handsome man and he tells me I look terrible." She was trying to regain her composure, to cover her original outburst, but she was immediately aware of the way he stiffened. He wasn't reacting to her sweetness like most men did. "Did I say something offensive?"

His manner didn't change. "My face has been causing me problems ever since I got to Montero."

Julia had no idea what he was talking about for a moment, then she saw the resemblance. It had been many years since she had seen her Uncle Garrick but she still wondered at times if he could be her father.

"Uncle Garrick," she whispered.

Ryan abruptly walked rapidly away from her. He could see in her eyes what he had seen in the whole town's face.

Julia stood in a daze for a moment, then began to run after him. The quick exercise at the high altitude after the accident made her dizzy. She caught Ryan's arm and clung to it to steady herself.

He looked at the top of her head and wanted to touch her hair. He put his hand on her shoulder, then led her back to her seat. "You've got to rest," he said quietly.

She caught her breath, still holding his arm. "I know what this town can do to a person," she said. "It judges you by your ancestors instead of yourself." She looked up at him. "Why do you look like him?"

284

"He's my father," Ryan said flatly.

Julia frowned. "I don't understand. Why haven't I met you before?" Her mind was beginning to work quickly. She was transported back to the day when Garrick had told her he could be her father. All these years, she had kept that knowledge a secret, even though it gnawed at her, especially when she saw her mother looking at Ross's pictures. She looked up at Ryan and it occurred to her that this young man could be her half brother.

Ryan wasn't sure whether he should talk to her or not, but it somehow felt right. They were alone on an isolated road, they had just shared a shattering experience, and it all seemed right. "I just recently found out he was my father. My mother and I returned to Montero a short while ago, and the people of the town..."

"Let me guess," Julia cut in. "They stared at you, even pointed at you. They stopped and gawked as they passed you on the street."

Ryan smiled as he sat down beside her. "You have lived here a long time. But how could you know how they treated me? I mean, you're the town princess."

"The princess, yes, the princess who lives in the shadow of the perfect queen. Believe me, I know what it's like to be a freak. I don't guess I've ever done or said anything that wasn't compared to my wondrous mother."

He watched her. She was really quite pretty. It was strange to hear the bitterness in her voice. He would have thought a girl like her had it made: looks, money, security, a home. "Why don't you leave?" he asked quietly. "Why don't you just take off and go wherever you want?"

"Now you're beginning to sound like my mother!" she snapped. "Why does everyone think I should be idle and lazy? I like working and I don't like being pawed by a bunch of men who are after my money."

"Wait a minute!" Ryan said angrily. "If you're trying to insinuate—" her look stopped him. He stared at the trees in front of him. "I guess you have your reasons as well as anyone else. I've never had any money so I can't guess how I'd be if I did have any. Are you ready to leave?"

"Sure."

He gave her his arm to help her up. Julia felt close to him. For the first time in her life she didn't feel the need to mask her true feelings. Perhaps this unusual rapport was proof of their blood ties.

He drove them down the mountain.

"Why do you stay here?" she asked. "Surely the townspeople haven't made you welcome."

He kept his eyes on the road. "My mother has a house here, and when she learned she was dying, she wanted to return."

"I'm sorry, about your mother, I mean."

"Don't be, because it doesn't seem to bother her. She says she'd rather die than grow old and ugly so no man will want her."

"Have you met Uncle Garrick?" she aked, not wanting to pursue the subject of his mother and men. She wondered if there were more children at home.

"Today. I guess that's why I was driving too fast. It's not exactly pleasant to find out your father is a true-to-life villain."

"Or a living paragon of virtue," Julia said bitterly.

He turned and looked at her for a moment. He had never had much time for women in his life. There was always too much work to do. "Could I buy you lunch?" he asked quietly, preparing himself for her refusal.

Maybe getting to know a brother would help make up for Brad's rejection of her this morning. "I would love lunch, if you don't mind some extra stares. The people of Montero would love to see us together."

He was watching her closely. The last time he'd been interested in a girl, in high school, she'd been frightened away as soon as she saw Ryan's mother and their sleazy apartment. "I make a mean baloney sandwich and there's always beer."

She smiled at him. "With the way I feel, a beer just might make me fall asleep. Which, when I think of it, might not be a bad idea." She leaned back against the seat. "I haven't had a day off from work in a long time."

Ryan had kidded her about the sandwiches. He stopped at a grocery on the way back. "We've set them off now," he said, putting the groceries in the back seat.

Julia lazily opened her eyes and saw a couple of townspeople gaping at them. She waved gaily.

Ryan got in and started the car. "You actually like

286

them, don't you?" he said, surprised. "After what they did
to your father, I'd think you'd hate them."

"They're not a *them*. Not really. Not when you get to
know all the people. It's a boring town with nothing else
to do and they like to sit around and speculate. By tomorrow everyone in town will know about us"—she hesitated—"...Garrick's relatives." She twisted to lean over
the seat to look in the groceries. "What did you get? You
couldn't have just gotten lunch."

He nearly ran off the road looking at her legs. "Get out
of there! And sit down before I put you through the wind-
shield."

He turned into his driveway. "This is it. Anything like
your house?" he asked sarcastically.

"Like my mother's. It's not much different. I live in a
tiny little house at the Mission."

Ryan was set back by her announcement. "I would have
thought you'd live in a mansion."

"And take money from the Mission!" she said in disbelief, then laughed. "Neither my mother nor I spend much
time in a house, so why spend the money? Next year we
want to completely remodel the mineral baths and we'd
like a new guest limousine. I want to add a couple of
garages and get our own mechanic but Mother—" She
stopped.

"Doesn't agree," he finished. "Do you two disagree very
often?"

"If we speak to each other five times, we have five
arguments."

He took the bag of groceries and led the way into the
little house.

Julia had no idea she was being tested. Ryan was very
sensitive to the least hint of a snub. He didn't trust her
because she was something he had learned not to trust—
a rich girl. But he saw nothing as he introduced her to his
mother and later led her into the kitchen.

He did stiffen once as Julia stared at the tidy kitchen.
"Who cleans this place?"

"I do," he said stiffly.

"That's what I thought. You do a great job! You should
see my place, it's a mess."

"Is that an invitation?"

"Why not?" she answered. "Right now I need a diversion. Why don't you come to the Mission tomorrow and I'll show you around? How about for breakfast?"

He took a large bowl of spaghetti sauce from the refrigerator. "Is there some other reason for inviting me so early?"

Julia gave a nervous little laugh. "You certainly do get to the point, don't you? Let's just say you can help me avoid making a bigger fool of myself than I've already done."

Ryan didn't question her as he set her to grating cheese and putting water on to boil lasagna noodles. Ruby refused to join them in the backyard for lunch. While the lasagna baked, Ryan and Julia drank beer under a big shade tree.

"Tell me about when you were a little boy," Julia said comfortably as she snuggled in the leather Mexican chair.

Ryan did tell her some but not a lot. He left out most of the pain he felt and his anger at a world in which everything seemed stacked against him.

But Julia felt a lot of what he didn't say. "So what are you going to do when your mother... when you can leave here?"

He shrugged. "I don't know. Maybe I'll get a job and go to night school, just as soon as I find something I want to study, that is."

"The old, what-do-you-want-to-be-when-you-grow-up syndrome, eh?" she teased. "No one ever asked me, I just started doing what I wanted when I was nine years old."

"Your Mission, I take it. Do you know you talk about that place as if it were a person?"

"She is," Julia laughed. "Wait until you see her. She's an elegant regal old lady."

A bell to a timer went off in the kitchen and Ryan rose. "Like your mother," he said as he turned away.

Not at all like my mother, Julia thought angrily. The Mission isn't a woman who would marry a man like Ross Kenyon and sleep with a man like Garrick Eastman. And possibly make her daughter a sister to Ryan.

They ate lasagna until they couldn't hold any more and finished off an entire six-pack of beer. Julia was giggling by the end of the afternoon. He told about some of his childhood pranks and she gossiped about the guests at the Mission. Together they made up suitable punishments for the demands of some of the more obnoxious guests.

In spite of his intentions, Ryan asked questions about Garrick. Julia knew very little, was too young to remember much, but she told him the truth, how he had always repulsed her.

Ryan was also interested in her family life. The idea of two parents, an aunt and cousins fascinated him. He asked her questions about Christmas, and Julia told him about the many escapades of Clarry's lively little boys. She talked about her father and how he took her on overnight camping trips.

Julia was just finishing her third beer. "Maybe you and I can go camping together sometime," she said wistfully.

Ryan laughed, then took the empty bottle away from her. "I think you've had enough and I ought to get you home."

She jerked the bottle away from him. "Don't treat me like a child!" she said angrily. "I'm not a little girl, no matter what you and Brad think."

He moved back from her. "The last thing I'd consider would be that you were a little girl, and if this Brad does, he's a fool."

Julia smiled and handed him the bottle. She stood. "I guess I should go home." She began to weave about and Ryan caught her.

She looked up at him, feeling warm and sleepy and knew she wanted him to kiss her, even knew he was about to do so. She pushed away sharply. "I have to go now."

Ryan dropped his arms immediately. The rich girl wasn't too snobby to eat with her inferiors, just so long as they observed certain boundaries, he thought angrily.

Julia had her own thoughts as Ryan drove her back to the Mission. Her head was beginning to ache from the beer. Right now she wished she had never met Ryan Lowery or Mr. High-and-Mighty Bradley Northrup. Two men, one possibly her brother and one who thought he was her father, were too much for one day.

She gave Ryan directions to her little guest house. As she got out, she said, "You'll come tomorrow, won't you, when you return the car?"

It was on the tip of his tongue to refuse her but he didn't want to. He wanted to spend some time with her, even wanted to see her damned Mission. What did it matter anyway, he'd be leaving Montero soon enough.

"Sure," he said. "What time?"

"Eight o'clock too early?"

He couldn't help laughing. "No, it's not too early. Why don't you go in and sleep? You sure are a cheap drunk."

She stood back from the car and saluted him. "Aye, aye, sir."

He pulled the door shut and drove away. There had been only that one moment when she pulled away from him. Otherwise it had been a remarkable day, a day unlike any other in his life. As he drove, he thought that she had every right to pull away from him. After all, it was their first date and Julia was a nice girl, yes, a very, very nice girl.

He didn't realize that he was humming as he got home and started cleaning the kitchen. But Ruby was very aware of her son. All afternoon she had listened, in a haze of delight, to the laughter of the two young people. When Ryan brought her supper on a tray, she was thrilled to find out he was also going to spend tomorrow with Julia.

Chapter 27

It was Laura who suggested she and Brad go somewhere besides the Mission. She didn't say so but she wasn't sure she could handle leaving his room and running into Julia. They made several suggestions, but in the end they took sleeping bags and went into the forest.

After Laura got over her initial feelings of betraying Ross, she found herself responding passionately. Brad laughed and called her his tigress as she became the aggressor in their lovemaking.

After an afternoon of love, when they were both spent, he snuggled her on his shoulder. "Now I know where you got the energy to build the Mission. How in the world did you keep that under control all these years?"

She laughed and stretched lazily. "I just try to keep myself busy, at every moment of the day."

He took a firm grip on her shoulders. "I want you to talk to me. I want you to tell me what happened in Montero."

She couldn't pull away from him. "What is this?" she demanded. "Are you just another one of those sensation-seekers? You want to hear all the lowdown about a rotten town?"

His voice was soft. "You know I don't, but I see something eating you and I think it might help if you talked about it."

She pulled away from him, sat up, and began pulling on her clothes. "No, not yet, I can't talk about it yet."

He gave her a hard little shake. "And when will you be able to talk about it? In *another* ten years?"

She stared at him, blinking back tears, then she put her arms around his neck. "I don't want to lose you. It's been so long since I had anyone. Please, please don't be angry with me."

"Then talk," he said into her neck. "Tell me what hap-

291

pened here that's hurt you so much. What makes you so angry?"

Once Laura started, she could hardly stop. Brad listened to her but he heard more than her words. Hatred was eating through her. Not only was she angry at the past but at the present. When Ross died, he seemed to have taken away her love for anything. She told freely her feelings about the people of Montero. She spoke of their greed, and how she worked to keep them out of the Mission. She spoke of Julia, how they battled because Julia didn't mind that the town profited from the resort. Laura said she was afraid Julia would be hurt as she had been when the pack turned against her.

"You talk about them as if they were animals," Brad said.

"They are! They killed my husband! They turned against me when I needed them!"

He was quiet for a while, digesting what she had told him. "Laura," he said quietly, "why don't you leave Montero?"

"Leave?" she asked, incredulous. "But the Mission is here. How in the world could I leave that? It's part of me."

"Are you sure? Is it still part of you or do you just tell yourself that?"

"What are you saying? Are you telling me that at forty-three years of age I don't know my own mind?" She started to rise.

Brad caught her arm. "Sometimes an outsider can see things that others can't. When you talk of Montero, you speak with hatred. You're a young, vital woman, much too alive to feel so much hate. It's already changing you. You're afraid of new things, afraid even of changing your own resort. I know you weren't always like that so I know it's the hate that's done it."

"You don't know anything about me or how I feel. Just because I spent an afternoon with you doesn't mean you own me." She jerked away from him and stood.

Brad looked at her with great patience. "Look at yourself, Laura, take a good long look. Are you so happy here? Is that great mud palace of yours fulfilling your every need? I'm not trying to rule you. Of course I'd like you to leave here with me. I'd like to work with you, marry you

292

if you'd have me, but even if you won't consider what I want, think about yourself and what you want."

Laura grabbed her sleeping bag. He couldn't understand what the Mission meant to her, that there was blood in the mortar of those adobes.

They didn't talk as they drove back to the Mission. Laura was insulated by her anger and Brad was bewildered because he had so misjudged her. He had come to the resort with a preconceived idea of Laura Kenyon, but he found her to be timid, closed-minded, not the woman he was seeking. Yet even as he thought these things, he didn't want to leave her. Neither of them mentioned his leaving the Mission.

Julia was hardly out of bed before Ryan was knocking at her door. He smiled at her sleepy-eyed look. "Hung over this morning?" he asked.

"From a few beers?" she retorted and she went to the bathroom to finish dressing. "Make yourself at home, if you can find a place."

He cleared a chair of clothing tossed across the back and arms. "I figured you'd have been at work hours ago or maybe your guests don't get up until afternoon."

"Heavens, no! They like to get up at all hours. We always have hiking and hunting trips arranged and a couple of longer trail rides. One left this morning at four."

"I don't think that would be my idea of a vacation."

She came out of the bathroom, looking cool and elegant in a seersucker dress. "And what would be your idea of a vacation?"

He took one look at her and decided not to tell her his first thought. "A tropical island with hula girls to wait on me." To his utter disbelief, Julia put one hand under her elbow and hulaed to the door.

"You ready for breakfast, sailor?" she laughed as he stared at her.

Ryan knew better than to make any comment on her impromptu performance, but he found her more intriguing by the minute.

She led him around the outside of the Mission to the big greenhouse dining room. For the first time, he saw a bit of snobbish pride in her. She seemed to assume he knew nothing of the finer things in life, so she was quite sur-

293

prised when he ordered eggs Benedict, cautioning the waiter against too much lemon in the hollandaise, and chose an excellent bottle of champagne.

"I worked as a waiter in New York for a while in a little French restaurant," he smiled. During the meal he commented on the plants around them, telling her that some of them needed a good dose of iron and others were getting too much water. He suggested a couple of plants that would grow well in the cool greenhouse. In answer to her unasked question, he told her he had worked two summers in a nursery.

"Where else have you worked?" she asked. The eggs Benedict were perfect, and she realized they usually did have too much lemon in the sauce.

"You name it, and if you didn't have to have any training, then I've done it. We never stayed anywhere very long because Mom always had itchy feet, but I always managed to get a job. I've done everything from being a janitor to a vegetable boy in an elegant restaurant."

"That must have been very hard," Julia said seriously. "I don't think I'd like never having a permanent place to live."

He smiled at her, glad she didn't think his life was "exciting" as some less mature girls did. He put his napkin on the table. "Were you planning to show me more of this place?"

Julia's showing Ryan the Mission turned out differently from what she had expected. It almost came to be a mutual presentation. In the lounge he inspected the whiskey and informed Julia her bartender was watering the bottles, therefore getting more drinks per bottle and more than likely pocketing the extra money.

In the guest rooms, he pulled back the spreads and showed Julia a different way to tuck the sheets at the corners. One of the cottonwoods in the courtyard was infested with bugs and he told her how to drill holes and insert insecticide.

"Ryan! I feel like you're showing me the place."

He stood even taller because he knew she was complimenting him. She was eager to hear anything he had to say. When he saw the mineral baths, he groaned aloud.

"See what I mean? It's really dreary in here. Everything

is always so damp that we can't seem to keep it clean and it smells like a locker room."

"Have you had an architect look at it?"

Julia was immediately reminded of Brad. "No, no one. My mother says the baths are fine. Or at least they won't need the remodeling I have in mind."

"Who's more likely to win?" he asked seriously.

"Her," Julia said, looking away. "She thinks I'm too young to make up my mind about anything more serious than a boyfriend."

He moved to stand in front of her. "And what do you think of boyfriends? Have any?"

She laughed. "Sure, a long line of applicants but no one I'll accept."

He was quite serious as he spoke. "Could I apply for the position?"

Julia knew she wanted to tell him yes, wished she could. It wasn't easy to treat a man like Ryan as her brother. All day she felt herself being drawn closer to him. She loved the way he took an interest in the Mission, liked the way he was protective but not too much so.

She backed away from him. "I have to go," she whispered before she turned and fled.

The rest of the day she tried not to think. Two men in two days, she thought. She had lost two men in two days.

For four days she did her best to try to work until she could no longer move. She cleaned and inventoried the wine cellar. She got a nurseryman from Albuquerque to come and work on all the plants. She started relandscaping the courtyard and the swimming pool area. She started plans for new dressing areas around the pool.

And in back of everything was anger at her mother for making it possible that Ryan Lowery could be her brother. A couple of times she caught herself wanting to ask Ryan a question but she didn't dare call him or see him. It was better for everyone concerned if she never saw him again.

By the end of the fourth day she was extremely tired yet she still thought of Ryan, could still remember the hurt in his eyes when she ran away from him.

She decided that the only way to exorcise one man was with another one. She dressed carefully and knocked on Brad's door. She hadn't seen him in days, although she knew he had called her room several times.

"Julia," he said with a tone almost of relief. "Please come in."

She was glad to hear his welcoming tone. Perhaps there was a chance for them. She looked at him and he seemed older than she remembered but she knew she could love him. "I wanted to ask if you'd have dinner with me tonight."

Brad frowned. He wasn't sure Julia still thought of him as a lover but he wanted to set the record straight. "Julia, I think it's time we talked—as adults. Please sit down."

"I think I'd rather stand. That way, if you start telling me I'm a child again, I can leave."

He winced at her remark. "I guess I deserved that. I never meant to hurt you and I guess I was too blunt, but you took me by surprise. No, Julia, I don't want to talk about us, I want to talk about your mother."

Julia decided to take a seat after all. She had been working so hard over the last few days that she had hardly been aware of anything, but now she seemed to remember seeing her mother and Brad together.

Brad sat across from her, took her hands in his. "I've fallen in love with your mother," he said quietly. "I think I came here half in love with her already. I didn't need much of a push."

"And I'm sure she shares your adoration," Julia said bitterly. "And, of course, this new passion will lead to marriage."

"I hope so," he said.

"Will you build a honeymoon wing onto the Mission?"

"Why are you so angry?"

She pulled her hands away from him. "Angry? Why should I be angry? My mother is perfect, didn't you just say you loved her before you even met her? But have you ever considered what it's like to live with an angel?" She stood up, almost overturning her chair. "Let me tell you. It's seeing everything you want given to her. She has the Mission, she has you, she has Ryan, she has everyone and everything."

"Julia, I don't know what you're talking about. And who is Ryan?"

She waved her hand. "Excuse me, I have no right to burden you with my problems. Congratulations on your forthcoming marriage."

She turned to leave, but Brad caught her. "You're being awfully selfish, aren't you? All you've considered is how you'll be affected by what happens to your mother. Don't you care what she thinks and feels?"

"She should feel she's the winner, I assume," Julia said calmly. "She has everything she ever wanted. She'll have the Mission by day and a strong healthy man by night; what more could she want? Tell me, Brad, are you man enough to fill Ross Kenyon's shoes? Are you man enough to be second to the Mission?"

It was all Brad could do to keep from striking her. "I am sick of this place," he said. "I am sick of this war between you and your mother to control it. I wonder if either one of you can love a man or if you're only capable of loving adobe and sand."

"I wouldn't put it to a test," Julia said harshly as she left the room. She tried to keep her head straight as she walked down the gallery and toward the parking lot. So Brad and Laura were to be married! A few days ago she had imagined herself marrying Brad. He seemed so ideal. She had imagined the two of them, Brad at home working on his designs, she at the Mission. At night she'd go home to him and he'd fix her a drink, like her father used to do for her mother.

She stopped outside by her car. *Had* she thought of Brad as her father? Had she just wanted what her mother once had?

She had no idea where she was going but she wasn't surprised when she ended up in front of Ryan's house. The last thing she should do was go to him, but she wanted to talk to someone and she knew he'd listen.

Ruby's voice called, "Come in. Are you looking for Ryan, dear? He drove to Taos today to look for work." She leaned forward and peered toward where Julia was standing, just inside the door. She could see something was upsetting her, just as Ryan was upset. "Come talk to me, Julia."

"No, I can't. I shouldn't have come."

"You can't deny a dying woman any request, didn't you know that?"

With a pang of guilt, Julia went to sit in the chair by Ruby's bed, her head bent, looking down at her hands.

"Now tell me what sort of lovers' quarrel you and Ryan have had."

"We aren't lovers!" Julia said fiercely.

Ruby laughed. "Of course you aren't, but anyone can see you're falling in love. I've never seen Ryan so happy. You know that he never talks to anyone. It did my heart so much good to see the two of you talking like old friends that day in the backyard."

"Stop it!" Julia cried. "Please, please stop it."

Ruby was surprised. "Has something happened? Ryan's all right, isn't he? He hasn't been hurt?"

Julia recovered herself. "No, it's not Ryan, it's me. No! It's what my mother's done."

Ruby was quiet for a moment. "I want you to start at the beginning and tell me everything. You'll find I'm an awfully good listener."

Julia stood, walked to the tall dresser to stare at Ryan's photograph. "Do we look alike?" she asked softly. "Ryan looks so much like him, but I can't see that I inherited anything from him."

It took Ruby several moments before she understood what Julia was saying. "You can't mean that Garrick..."

Julia whirled on her. "That my father and Ryan's father could be the same man. That's exactly what I mean. I think Ryan and I were conceived in the same summer, the summer my mother married my...married Ross Kenyon. She must have been pregnant when they were married."

"Must have been?" Ruby said. "Are you just guessing about this then? Do you have any proof?"

"I don't need proof. I just know that my mother and Ryan's father—"

"Julia," Ruby interrupted, "why don't you ask your mother? Somehow, I can't see it. He wanted her so badly then. If he did take her, I'm sure it was by force."

"What does that matter? Even if she were chained to the bed, which I sincerely doubt, Ryan is still my brother."

Julia recovered herself. "I'm really sorry about this. I didn't mean to pour out my troubles to you." She picked up her purse. "I shouldn't have come here. Please tell Ryan—no, don't tell him anything. And please forget what I've told you. I wouldn't especially like for it to get around about whose child I am."

"You don't know for sure Garrick is your father," Ruby said, exasperated. "Please talk to Laura."

"Do you think my holy mother would even admit to the

possibility that I could be someone else's child? No, she wouldn't. She'd laugh at me and say of course Ross Kenyon is my father. She'd do anything to get Brad for herself and me out of the way."

"I don't know Laura but I know enough to know she's not like that. Talk to her."

Julia shook her head. "I have to go. I shouldn't have come." She gave Ruby a half smile and left the house.

Ruby looked at the photo of Ryan for a moment, thinking how her son never seemed to have a break in life. He'd get over Julia all right, but next time he'd be even more cautious when it came to women. She didn't want to see him hurt again and again.

A pain in her chest reminded her that she wouldn't be here too much longer to see anything. She grabbed the telephone book, found Garrick's number and dialed it. A woman told her quite firmly that Mr. Eastman did not accept calls from women.

Ruby dropped the phone onto its cradle and started writing a letter. She begged Garrick to see her as soon as possible. He held the key to Julia's and Ryan's problems. Perhaps through him she could learn the truth.

Chapter 28

Brad paced his room for hours. Julia's words had struck home and opened his eyes to a lot of things. Over the past few days he had been making a concentrated effort to court Laura. He was quiet, undemanding, and they talked for many, many hours. She told him of her fears during the Depression, what had driven her to build the Mission, how she had always had someone to lean on, first her father, then Ross, of how the two men supported her and loved her, made her feel independent yet were always there when she needed them. She spoke of her fears after Ross died, how alone she'd been since then.

In return, Brad told her of his life, of the wife he had left years ago. She had been strong, and independent before they were married, but she gladly gave up all claim to her own life to become his wife. After a few years, Brad felt he was living alone with a child to raise. He tried to force her to stop depending on him, but she wouldn't listen, wouldn't try. In the end all he could do was leave her.

She sued him for every penny he had. All her old independence returned in the form of hatred directed at him. Brad began to take any job he could get, anywhere in the world. He needed the money and he wanted to be too busy to think. In his travels he met many women who interested him, strong women, but for one reason or another, they weren't suited for each other. Then he learned of Laura, from reading her story in an old book, and he became fascinated.

Laura laughed when he said he hadn't yet lost his fascination, even after getting to know her.

They spent a great deal of time together, talking, laughing, planning imaginary houses. They drove to Albuquerque to see her paintings hanging in the bank, where they had been for twenty years. They went to a building site of an "experimental house," then spent hours agreeing how absolutely horrible it was.

Once, Brad suggested that Laura get her architect's license, but she balked at the 4-hour commute to the University of New Mexico in Albuquerque, claiming she couldn't run the Mission and go to school, too. He decided against saying there were other places to live besides Montero. He wanted so badly not to argue. He wanted her trust in him to continue, their friendship to deepen.

Now, as he thought of Julia's words, he wondered if he had done the right thing. Perhaps his silence was giving Laura some wrong ideas.

He found Laura in the open courtyard talking to some guests. He drew her away, outside, to a secluded area.

"Couldn't wait to see me, huh?" she teased, putting her arms around his neck.

He returned her kiss. "You know I want to marry you, don't you?"

She smiled, kissed the corner of his mouth. "You've mentioned the idea."

He pulled her arms down. "I want to talk about something serious. If we married, where would we live?"

"Why, here at the Mission, of course. I'll build a whole wing for us." She was so happy at the idea that she didn't see his look.

"And if we lived here, what would I do?" His voice was calm, patient.

"You could design the new wing. It would be just for us, anything we wanted."

"A honeymoon wing!" he responded angrily.

"Brad, what's wrong? I thought you just asked me to marry you." She lost her smile. "Or was I just imagining that?"

"I do want to marry you. I want to marry you more than anything else in the world. But what I want to marry is a woman, a strong, beautiful, passionate woman, not a pile of adobes."

She turned away. "I think you've said enough."

"I haven't said half enough," he said as he pulled her back. "You take it for granted that I'll live here, tucked away nicely in your new wing. And what do I do when I finish building a wing for your precious resort? Will you give me something else to do just so I'll go away and play?

Is that what you expect—a token husband who is there when you need him but stays out of sight when you don't want him?"

"You're twisting my words! What else am I supposed to do, walk away from everything I've worked for all my life?"

"Yes," he said quietly.

She glared at him. "You ask me to leave what I have, you seem to think I should. To do what? To follow you like some little pet? You want me to give up everything I *am?*"

He gestured toward the adobe wall. "This isn't you. What you are is inside you and no one can take it away from you. You're not a shopkeeper, you're a talented woman. You were alive when you created this place and even later when you had to fight the town. Even then you were *doing* something."

She could only stand stiffly and stare at him. "You don't understand what the Mission means to me," she began.

"I'm beginning to understand," he said quietly. "I thought you were afraid to leave, but it isn't fear that keeps you here, is it? You like being the wonder woman who created this place at twenty-two. It must be great for your ego. And you say you hate this town. At least, here you're still the queen. Queen of the hill, is that what you *have* to be?"

"Are you quite finished?"

"No, not at all. I believe in you, Laura. I know that inside you is that magnificent creature who built a *casa grande* from a pile of mud. I want to see her live again. You have so much talent, so much life in you. I want the world to see it. So what if you fall on your face? Isn't that better than staying here and being a monument to yourself?"

She pulled away from him because she couldn't bear to hear any more.

He grabbed her arm again. "Don't leave for me. I'm not asking you to do that. Leave for yourself before it's too late and you no longer *can* leave." He suddenly felt tired, seeing in her eyes that he had lost her. "I'm going to leave now. I'll stay in Albuquerque at that hotel where we had lunch. I'll be there for a week. Please come."

She gave him a cold look. "Just shut down all I've worked for all my life, what my husband died for, and
302

walk away into the sunset with you. Is that it? Ask yourself who is suffering from delusions of grandeur."

"Ross did not die for this place," he said angrily, "no more than an accident victim dies *for* an automobile. Ross was killed by a man who was only interested in profit. And what about Julia? She loves this place as much as you've come to detest it."

"Julia is a child!"

"Julia is a woman and you're as afraid to see the change in her as you are to see it in yourself. Don't worry. That's all I have to say. I'm leaving now, so the rest is up to you."

"I wouldn't count on seeing me again," she said flatly, her eyes hard.

He stopped and caressed her cheek. "I love you, Laura. I love what you are. Please come to me." He turned and walked away.

Laura couldn't watch him leave. Her anger vanished and she felt herself begin to shiver. She sat down on the ground and held her hands out before her to watch their trembling.

After a moment she felt in her pocket for her car keys. What she needed was a few days alone, isolated, away from everyone, a place where she could think. There was only one place like that: Ross's cabin.

She drove home, packed a few clothes, called Betty to tell her that she'd be gone for a while, then she stopped at the grocery and bought several bags of food.

No one had been in the cabin in years, though Laura often sent one of the gardeners up to see to it. Squirrel damage and spiderwebs had been kept to a minimum.

For the first day, she didn't think about anything. She walked about the cabin, lovingly cleaning everything Ross had touched. She thought how it had been so perfect when he was alive. The running of the Mission had still been a challenge to her then, every problem new and in its way exciting. She had still been trying to attract guests and each new name felt like a small victory.

At night she used to go home to Ross and he held her and loved her, never demanding anything from her. And Julia was small then and caused no problems. When she was upset, Ross looked after her. The people of Montero had respected her, loved her, and she had felt the same about them.

It was so pleasant to think of those times. She could almost imagine they still existed, that Ross and a pigtailed Julia were going to walk through the cabin door.

She cleaned, cooked a big dinner, then didn't eat a bite. When she went to bed, she cried herself to sleep.

In the morning, with her eyes swollen and her head aching, the old cabin didn't look so good. The furniture needed reupholstering, the roof leaked; a bathroom was needed.

She sat down in a chair, a cloud of dust rising about her, and looked—really looked—at the cabin. Was her life like this place—falling apart, drying up, in need of modernizing? What did she really want? What was she going to do with the second half of her life? Where was she going to be when she hit sixty? Was she still going to be sitting in this derelict cabin waiting for Ross and Julia to appear? Was she still going to be fighting the people of Montero, and worst of all, fighting her own daughter?

When she thought of the future and saw herself behind her big desk at the Mission, it looked boring but safe. She knew what was required of her, knew she could handle it. But what if she left that desk? What was waiting for her then? Would she end up old and alone somewhere without friends, no Mission to protect her?

She paced the floor, tried to busy herself in more cleaning, but it didn't seem to work. She kept asking herself what she planned to do with her life. Brad had said she was afraid to leave. Perhaps she was. He seemed to believe she could do anything, build other places like the Mission.

She paced faster and told herself that she had been driven to build the resort out of necessity. She stopped as she remembered Ross laughing and saying she could do anything she wanted, that her strength sometimes amazed him.

"Ross," she whispered and looked about for a photograph of him, but there were none.

She sat down heavily in a chair, her head in her hands. Why did he have to die and leave her alone to make her own decisions?

After a few minutes, she realized she wasn't seeing

Ross's face but Brad's. How long had she been putting Brad's face on Ross's personality?

She stood suddenly, refusing to think about the question. She scoured the kitchen, made herself something to eat, then tried to read one of Ross's books on trout fishing. After an hour she gave up and stretched out on the couch.

What if she did leave Montero? she wondered. What would she do? Where would she go? Perhaps to Spain to study Gaudi's work, then to see some of the great cathedrals. She'd like to see some of the old spas in Europe, too, perhaps study some of their buildings for ideas for her own resorts.

Night came and she was still thinking of things she'd like to do and see. She went to bed and for the first time in years she thought of something besides Ross.

She spent a week in the cabin, thinking, daydreaming, walking about the woods. Somewhere during that time she made her decision to leave the town, to turn the Mission over to Julia. She didn't think about Brad because she knew he was right, that she had to leave for herself, and not for him. Even if she never saw him again, she had to be sure she was doing what was right for her. She couldn't keep on hating the world.

At the end of the week she walked around the cabin, looked at it with love, knowing it was now part of the past. She felt as if Ross were smiling at her, pleased that she was ready to let him rest.

She got in her car and drove to the hill behind the Mission. She looked down at it in all its magnificent splendor. What was it Brad had called it? A *casa grande*, a grand house. She knew she was making the right decision when she realized the Mission was no longer a house to her but a place of business, only a place to work. Yes, it was definitely time to move on.

She was over her sadness by the time she reached the front parking lot. In a way she felt as if a great burden had been lifted from her shoulders. She never expected to create anything in her life as majestic as the Mission but at least she'd keep creating.

She walked past the reception desk, heard the girl patiently arguing with a guest about when the Caballero Suite would be available. No one ran to her with a thousand questions and she knew it was because Julia had been running the resort.

When she opened the door to her office, Julia was sitting behind her desk, her hair a mess, circles under her eyes, looking years older than just twenty.

"Where have you been?" Julia asked, her jaw set.

Laura smiled sweetly. "Away for a few days."

"Did it ever occur to you that someone might care where you went?"

"Why, Julia..." Laura began, then laughed when Julia said Laura's signature was needed on some checks. "That's all? No major crises that only I could solve?"

Julia refused to respond to her mother's joking mood. She wasn't going to tell anyone of the hell she'd been through for the last week. The extra work of being completely responsible for the Mission had given her little time for sleep. One of the guests had set his room on fire while trying to light the fireplace. Another guest had gone to play tennis and left the faucet in the tub running. Three rooms had sprung leaks during a rainstorm two nights ago. The nurseryman had had to spray the greenhouse to kill the red spider mites and the smell had permeated the overcrowded dining room, causing several guests to complain.

Besides these problems, Ryan had confronted her and demanded she tell him what she'd told Ruby. Julia, tired, overworked, had blurted the truth. She had never seen a person get so angry. He said she had used him just like everyone else had. Sarcastically, he called her his little sister and stormed out of the Mission.

For nearly a week Julia had had to cope with the pain she felt about Ryan in addition to her deep anger at her mother. Laura had caused all the problems and now she could hardly bear to be in the same room with her. She grabbed a handful of papers and left the office.

Laura had never seen before the depth of hostility in Julia's eyes. If she had any leftover doubts, they were gone now. She wasn't sure that the Mission was even one of the causes of hostility between Julia and herself but her daughter was more important than any business. She'd give up anything to gain her daughter's love.

There were several messages on her desk. She shuffled through them, hoping for one from Brad but there was none. There were several from Clarry, dated from two days after Laura had left, each marked urgent. She called Clarry's office and Clarry seemed calm, welcomed Laura back, saying they were all worried about her. Laura didn't spend time pondering why Clarry's notes had seemed so urgent but her voice hadn't.

She called her lawyer next and asked him to drive to Montero. He paused for a moment, but made no comment when she said she wanted to sign the Mission over to Julia.

For the next few hours she started to tie up loose ends. She attacked her filing cabinets, discarding boxes of useless material. When someone knocked on the door, she absently yelled, "Come in."

She turned but at first she didn't recognize the man standing just inside the door. When she did recognize him, she was too surprised to speak. Garrick had changed so much over the years. His handsomeness was gone and so was his look of aliveness.

"Laura," he said, "I know I'm not welcome and I wouldn't have come if it weren't something quite important."

For a moment Laura didn't know what to do. A week ago she would have screamed at this man. "Sit down, Garrick," she said coolly but politely.

He took a seat, moving like an old man. "You're still as lovely as ever, Laura," he said quietly. "I always knew you would be a beautiful woman."

She couldn't be angry with him; it would have been like being angry with a corpse. "What did you want to see me about?"

"My son, Ryan," he said, the pride in his voice unmistakable.

Laura vaguely remembered Clarry telling her about the young man. "If you want me to give him a job, you'll have to talk to Julia. Maybe it's fitting that you should be the first to know. I'm leaving Montero and turning the Mission over to Julia."

Garrick nodded solemnly. "I think that's a good idea. I've always felt you were too big for this town. I'm sure that whatever you do, you'll do well." He paused. "But Julia is part of the problem."

Laura stiffened. "I believe Julia can handle any problems or I wouldn't leave the Mission in her hands."

"Please, Laura, let's not argue. Not today. Let me explain everything."

He told Laura first of his son, of Ryan's life, of the hardships he had, then he told her about Julia, of her being a lonely child. Laura started to protest but he stopped her, saying he had a reason for speaking out. He said he could understand why Julia and Ryan were drawn to each other.

"Are you trying to tell me that my daughter is in love with your son?"

For the first time, Garrick smiled a little, and she could see some of his former handsomeness. "I'm not sure if they even know that they like each other, but Ruby, his mother, and I would like to see him settle somewhere. I think he could work well here at the Mission."

Laura frowned. "I still don't see any problem. I'm sure Julia could find him a job."

Garrick took a breath. "But she won't give him one, and if she did, Ryan wouldn't accept it." He stared at her. "Julia thinks there's a possibility Ryan is her brother."

Laura took a moment to understand, then she stood up. "You mean, she thinks they have the same father?" She felt her cheeks flushing as she remembered that night so long ago when she and Garrick had made love on the living room floor. "How did she know about...?"

He knew he had to tell her the truth. "I told her. God, Laura! I have a lot of things to be sorry for but this is one of the worst. I guess I was drunk. I don't really remember it, but she was just a little girl when I told her."

Laura sat back down, bewildered. All these years, Julia had thought that maybe Garrick was her father, that Laura—no wonder the child had pulled away from her.

"It's not true, is it?" Garrick asked quietly.

She hardly heard him. "Of course it's not true." It was a wonder Julia didn't hate her completely. "How did you find out about this?"

"I think Ryan made a pass at Julia and she got so upset she ended up telling Ruby about their possible kinship."

Laura winced that Julia would go to a stranger before she confided in her own mother. "What does Julia feel about Ryan?"

"I don't know but I do know Ryan feels he's being used in some game between the two of you. He's not a man who
308

has ever been given a reason to trust anyone. Ruby's afraid this new rejection may be too much for him."

"So, your concern is for Ryan."

He seemed to age in seconds. "My concern is for both of them. Julia has always been a loner and so is Ryan. Julia used to have Ross, then he died, and she found out it was possible he wasn't even her father. It must have seemed like the betrayal of all time. She needed someone to blame and I guess you were elected."

Laura sat and studied him for quite some time. "You've changed, haven't you?"

"I had to," he said curtly, then leaned forward. "I've not done much to be proud of in my life and Lord only knows how I could create something as good as Ryan, but he is a good boy, hard on the outside but warm and generous inside. I want him to have every chance in life. I don't mean I think he'll fall in love with Julia but I want the two of them to have a chance. I don't want them to pay for our past sins. And Julia doesn't deserve to carry such a burden any longer."

Laura stood. Her first idea was to forget her decision to leave the Mission, to stay until this thing worked itself out. But she immediately knew that would be wrong. "I'll tell Julia the truth," she said after a moment.

Garrick stood. "You know, I was half wishing you'd say she was mine. I'd be proud to have two such fine children, but I guess I'll have to make do with Ryan." He held out his hand to her. "Thank you, Laura."

She hesitated before she touched him, but as she took his hand, she knew she had forgiven him and with him, Montero. She was finally free. "Thank you for telling me," she said quietly.

As he turned toward the door she asked him to come back sometime. He didn't turn around. "No, I don't think I should." He opened the door and left.

Laura felt a pang of sadness at his words, almost as if she had lost someone. But the next minute she was on the telephone to Betty, asking where Julia was. "Find her immediately and send her to me!"

Laura knew the privacy of her office would be the best place for them to talk, and also, she needed to make a call—to Ruby. She paced and thought in bewilderment how Julia had kept her awful secret for so many years.

A tired, hostile Julia greeted her a half hour later. "I have an awful lot of work to do, so if you don't mind, I'd like to get back to it. What did you have to tell me that was so important?"

Laura, for the first time, understood Julia's hostility toward her. "I had a visitor this morning—Garrick Eastman."

Julia narrowed her eyes. "That must have been pleasant for you."

Laura ignored her tone. She knew no other way than to go directly to the truth. "Garrick said you believe he is your father and that Ryan is your brother."

Julia gasped. She started for the door.

"Oh, no, you don't!" Laura snapped, grabbing her daughter's arm. "You and I are going to talk. For once in our lives we're going to really talk!" She tightened her grip. "First of all, your father is Ross Kenyon."

Julia pulled away angrily, "Can you be so sure?" she said nastily. "From what I gather, you were balling both men at the same time."

Laura didn't slap her. It took a supreme effort on her part but she controlled herself. She spoke quietly. "Perhaps when you're twenty you can make such deadly judgments, but from where I stand it's not so easy. I was in love with Ross but he left me." She went on, louder, when Julia started to protest against anyone saying anything bad about Ross Kenyon. "Hey! I don't know what happened that night, but yes, Garrick and I made love, a few days before Ross and I were married."

Julia curled her lip. "Then you *don't* know who is really my father."

"Yes, I do!" She saw Julia wasn't going to believe her. She knew she was old-fashioned in not wanting to mention such facts to her daughter but she realized the urgency of the moment. "I started my period on our wedding night." She almost smiled at the things Ross had said about the blood all over the sheets. She looked up at Julia, saw she still didn't believe her. "Good God! Maybe we could find the hotel staff. I'm sure someone would remember that night. Ross had to buy the damn place a new mattress."

Maybe it was this last that convinced Julia. She sat down heavily in a chair and looked up at her mother in disbelief. "Then Ryan isn't my brother?"

310

Laura took a seat across from her. "Unfortunately, you are an only child. We wanted more but there never seemed to be time."

Julia buried her face in her hands.

Laura caught her daughter's hands. "Why did you keep this to yourself? Why didn't you just ask me? I would have told you the truth."

Julia's throat was swollen shut. Ross was her father! She had doubted for so many years but now she knew the truth.

"Julia," Laura said quietly. "What's Ryan like?"

The image of Ryan made her feel better. He wasn't her brother! "He's quiet, strong but very vulnerable inside. He was very upset when I told him about..."

"Do you think he could work here at the Mission?"

Julia smiled and Laura watched her tear-sparkling eyes gleam. "He's worked everywhere and he's helped me so much already."

"Why don't you give him a job?"

"Me! But you hire people." Some of her bitterness returned.

"Listen to me, Julia. I'm leaving the Mission." She laughed when Julia's mouth dropped open.

"Is it Brad? Are you leaving for him?"

"No," Laura answered honestly. "He made me see that it was time for me to go, but I'm not leaving because of him. I'm leaving because I'm drying up here. There's nothing for me here anymore, except you, and I finally realized that you'd be better off without my interference."

"But who will run the Mission?"

"That, dear daughter, is your problem. I am giving it to you with its leaky roof, contrary guests and every other problem."

"But...I can't...I don't know how to keep the books. I don't know..."

Laura cut her off as she stood up. "If I can leave my safe little nest and go out into the cold, cruel world, you can run the Mission. All I ask is for an allowance for one year. If I'm not earning my living in a year, I deserve to starve."

"But what about Brad?" Julia was incredulous, scared yet excited. To own the Mission! To make her own decisions and have them stand!

"He was waiting for me in a hotel in Albuquerque, but I imagine he left a couple of days ago."

"You don't know!"

Laura laughed. "Men aren't the only thing in the world." She lifted a box from the floor to her desk. "Julia, you weren't really in love with Brad, were you?"

"No, I think he reminded me of...Dad," she smiled at the meaning of the word. "I guess I wanted what you once had."

"Me, too. I wanted it all over again." She handed Julia a box. "Now, what are you going to do about your Ryan?"

"I'm afraid he's far from being mine. He hates me. He thinks I was using him."

"What do you feel about him? Do you love him?"

"I...don't know. He's so unlike anyone I've ever met. He's so smart and wise and thoughtful and he's not one of those men who thinks women should stay at home and cook."

"Julia, I've never heard you speak of anyone like this before. Are you sure you don't know your feelings for him?"

Julia clenched her jaw. "Of course I love him! Why else would it upset me so badly when he hates me? I've never met anyone like him."

Laura kept packing boxes for a moment. "Have you ever slept with Ryan?"

Julia gasped. "I thought he was my brother!"

"Of course," Laura said. "Something I learned a long time ago was that the best place to talk to a man was in bed." She laughed at Julia's violently red face. Why did all children think their mothers were pure and chaste? "I was just thinking that you should crawl into bed with Ryan, then talk to him."

"Mother!" Julia gasped, and furiously began to pack books. "Besides, he lives with his mother."

Laura kept herself from laughing. There was some of her in her daughter after all. "I talked to Ruby after I spoke with Garrick. She swore she'd somehow get Ryan up to Ross's cabin."

It took Julia a moment to absorb this information. "You mean that you, my mother, and Ryan's mother planned that I should...that we should..."

This time Laura did laugh. "You're making me feel like a procuress. We just agreed that the two of you needed some time alone and the cabin was the best place for it. If Ruby got him to leave right away, he should be there by now."

The two women stared at each other for several moments.

"What are you waiting for?" Laura said. "I need to clean out *your* office and the man you love is waiting for you in a lonely mountain cabin."

Julia suddenly grabbed her mother and hugged her fiercely. "I love you."

Laura didn't tell her what those words meant to her. "Go on, he's waiting."

Julia pulled away. "But what if he won't stay? What if he wants me to give up the Mission?"

Laura smiled. Brad had said that everything always came down to the Mission. "Make your own decision, Julia, but I have a feeling that what Ryan needs is an anchor, someplace he can call home."

"Yes," Julia whispered. "I think you're right." She left the office.

Laura smiled at the closed door for a few minutes, then began to remove Ross's pictures from the wall. She paused for a second, suddenly envious of Julia's youth, of the newness of the world to her, of the thrill of first love. Then she slipped the photo into the box. A whole new world awaited her, too. There were houses to design and build, places to see, people to meet and love. And there was one special man, who would never replace Ross, but who would add new things to her life.

She picked up the box and carried it to her car. She looked up at the great looming shape of the Mission and she could swear the elegant old lady was smiling at her. They were friends, close, deep friends and they would always be so, but now was the time for changes.

She closed the trunk lid, put her shoulders back, and breathed deeply of the pure, cool New Mexico air. Suddenly she felt as if she were twenty years old again and she was going to meet her lover, only her lover was the whole world. No, she wasn't envious of anyone on earth.